★ OXFORD

MONT SAINT MICHEL

COUTANCES

LE CHATEAU
DE PIROU

Vieste

★ Barletta
★ ★ Bari
Castel
del Monte

★ OXFORD

MONT SAINT MICHEL

★ ★ COUTANCES

LE CHATEAU
DE PIROU

Vieste

★ Barletta
★ ★ Bari
Castel
del Monte

THE BLOOD REMEMBERS

THE
BLOOD
remembers

A Novel by
Terry Stanfill

ELTON-WOLF PUBLISHING

02 03 04 05   2 3 4 5

ISBN: 1-58619-033-4
Library of Congress
Card Catalogue Number: 2001093529

First Printing: September 2001
Second Printing: April 2002

Published by Elton-Wolf Publishing
www.elton-wolf.com • 206.748.0345 • Seattle, Washington

Thanks to the following:

For permission to use text on pages 93–94.
Edward Ullendorff and C.F. Beckingham.
The Hebrew Letters of Prester John. University of London,
School of Oriental and African Studies.
Published: Oxford University Press, 1982.

For permission to use an image from *La Tapisserie de Pirou*,
Château de Pirou, Lessay, Fondation Abbaye de la Lucerne,
La Lucerne d'Outremer, Normandy

The Book of Runes by Ralph H. Blum

Carmina Burana, Carl Orff Lyrics from *O Fortuna*, *In Trutina*.

Poem on page 214, *The Coral Branch*,
dedicated to Tony Duquette, in memoriam.

Cover and text design by Gopa Design

For Dennis

A branch of the apple-tree . . . I bring
Twigs of white silver are on it,
Crystal boughs with blossoms.

The Voyage of Bran

Bassano del Grappa, Veneto, Italy.
Fresco with a court scene.
The young Frederick II contemplating a rose.

*No chapter of history more resembles
a romance than that which records
the sudden rise and brief fall of the house of
Hauteville. In one generation the sons
of Tancred passed from the condition of
squires in the Norman vale of Cotentin,
to kinghood in the richest island of the
southern sea. The Norse adventurers became
Sultans of an Oriental capital. The sea
robbers assumed together with the sceptre,
the culture of an Arabian Court.*

John Addington Symonds
Sketches in Italy and Greece

With special thanks to my friend
John Julius Norwich, in whose
inspirational book, *The Other Conquest*,
I first read this passage.

PROLOGUE
LUCERA OF THE SARACENS,
APULIA, ITALY, 1234 AD
THE END OF CHRISTMAS DAY

SAND TRICKLES THROUGH THE HOURGLASS. A bronze oil lamp, suspended by chains from the tower's vaulted ceiling, hazes the room with the scent of burnt oranges. On the Syrian-carpeted table, the Wizard Michael Scot brews potions for the dream incubation: vials filled with fluids bought from Greek and Arab chemists, bundles of dried herbs, unguents from Outremer in alabaster pyxides, mosses smeared with insect froth, packets of powdered gemstones, a heap of rune stones on a whalebone saucer.

He lifts the lid of an iron chest that will take the strength of four mighty men to carry. In it he finds a dark blue fustian cloak embroidered with zodiac signs. Taking off his Oxford scholar's robe, he wraps the cloak around his shoulders and fastens it with a diamond crescent.

Now the Wizard sits at his table. He chooses a sheet of parchment, dips a quill into the inkpot and writes. The letters thicken. With a paring knife he shaves the quill. Turning, scraping, turning.

Although the iron hat makes his head ache, he does not take it off. He puts down his pen and takes a deep breath of the perfumed vapor. He rises and begins to pace the room, hands clasped behind his back, eyes fixed on tongues of light licking the ceiling. From time to time he stops to survey the sky from the tower's small window. A rock crystal moon spreads silver on the olive and carob trees.

The Wizard Michael Scot hopes the Emperor has not changed his mind. The spheres are in harmony for the dream incubation to mark Frederick's fortieth birthday.

Scot has corrected the degrees and parallels. Venus, Mars, and Saturn are in alignment under Mercury with Capricorn, the Emperor's sign. He stirs the runes in the saucer, chooses one at random, and reads the symbol etched into the stone. *Dagaz*. He is pleased. A favorable moment for prophecy.

He hears footsteps on the staircase. Scot, who makes the Imperial Court tremble, falls to his knees, eyes cast down, awaiting the presence of the Emperor.

"Rise from the floor, Magus Michael. We have no time for ceremony. I have questions to pose before we begin the dream incubation. You have measured the distance from earth to heaven. Now consider the origins of the earth's foundations. Tell me how this earth is established over the abyss, how many heavens lie beyond ours. Who are their inhabitants? Who are their rulers?"

The Wizard sighs. With his fist he taps his iron hat. "His Majesty's questions are always profound. May I remind the Emperor of the letter I sent to him a few years ago when he was in Naples?"

"You have written much wisdom in these past twelve years. What was it that you told me in that letter? Repeat it."

"I wrote that if ever a man of this world could escape death by his knowledge, you would be the one."

The Emperor laughs. "You flatter me, Scot. Like any other mortal, even so-called Stupor Mundi cannot escape death. But I cannot deny that I seek immortality, power beyond the grave, a monument to my empire and to my name. Before we begin the incubation, show me the plan for my newest castle so that I may honor your design or dispose of it at once. For as soon as I give my signal, a thousand men will begin to quarry stone."

Scot unrolls a pergamon chart upon the table and weighs down each corner with lumps of fool's gold.

The Emperor studies the plan.

"You have given me an orgy of octagons, Magus. The core of your plan is not unlike that temple built upon the ancient temple of Solomon we once admired in Jerusalem. Or does it resemble that fabled eight-sided castle in the desert of Arabia Felix?" He smiles. "My Saracens tell tales of an eight-sided walled city buried in the desert sands."

"I commend His Majesty. He is a better student than I am. My design is indeed based on the logic of numbers, recounted by caravanserai folklore. First I drew a circle, symbol of heaven. I then imposed a square centered within its realm representing The Four Elements: Earth, Fire, Air and Water. A second identical square was placed upon the first. I rotated the second square forty-five degrees, keeping its center constant thus forming an octagon. I drew a smaller octagon within the interior, its lines parallel to the first to form the courtyard. On the exterior octagon I placed eight-sided towers on each angle completing ten octagons in all encompassed by the circle."

"Well done, Magus. Ten—symbolizing imperial unity, royal balance and perfection. Your design bespeaks a fruitful cosmic union between earth and the forces of the solar system."

Scot is pleased. "I have gone beyond the mystic number ten squared times eight to mark the year of Our Lord 1994, eight hundred years from the Emperor's birth date in 1194."

The Emperor seems puzzled. "But why should my castle mark eight-hundred years from my birth date?"

"To enter an edifice built of such geometric proportions is to enter an abode of eternal truth. Only Time Future defines the truth of Time Past."

The Emperor Frederick glowers at Scot and raises his voice. "Of what truth do you speak, Magus?"

Scot stutters. "I have had a vision, My Lord."

The Emperor is silent as he twists the carved emerald seal ring around his finger. At last he says, "A vision! Is that why you chose a barren hill above the Murge for my castle? There are many more pleasing sites in my beloved Apulia."

"I have good reason. In Britain, standing stones are esteemed as holy markers. At Corato, I have found such tall stones set by a sacred stream and a waterfall. These stones send energy to the proposed site. Scattered on that windswept hilltop are ancient ruins of the temple of Mercurius. The castle's sole portal will gather energy from those standing stones. Permit me to show you on this map."

The Emperor's finger traces the equal-sided triangle formed by the three points between Andria, Corato, and the hilltop site.

"You have convinced me, Magus," he says. "Your plan seems wedded to it."

Scot is pleased. "To prove it was the chosen place, I stood naked beneath the roar of white water. Through the rainbow of droplets I divined the future—as my grandfather taught me, as did his father before him, so back to the wisdom of Merlin."

"You are sure of what you saw, Magus?"

"As sure as the falcon soars in its pride of place toward dappled dawn."

"Good." The Emperor smiles at Scot's eloquence.

Scot knows Frederick loves his falcons even more than his women and understands them better.

From the iron chest, the Wizard takes a leather pouch and

shakes a giant ruby into the Emperor's palm. Frederick holds the gemstone to a glowing candle. "How it throbs like a heart in my hand. Redder than a cuckoo's eye. Redder than the ruby in my mother's crown. How came you by this gem?"

"Since those long ago days at Oxford, I have garnered knowledge like the Magi of old, traveling among other wise men and wandering scholars, listening to their lore, learning their wisdom. The Magus Umberto, Bologna's famed storyteller, gave the stone to me. He told me that Empress Constance, as she lay dying, entrusted Prester John's ruby to your father's tutor, Godfrey of Viterbo. It was Godfrey who passed it on with instructions to deliver it to her son, Frederick, to mark the fortieth year from his birth on the 26th of December in the year of Our Lord 1194. Tonight, as that day draws near, I give it to you as I promised."

"Michael Scot, you who have looked under falling water, through ice and crystal to the future—help me to look through darkness in that timeless night of dreams, far beyond to my own distant future. Now cloak me with invisibility that I may be transported to the year of Our Lord 1994. To the year of my eight-hundredth birthday."

Droplets of sweat begin to trickle from Scot's hat. From his great chest, the Wizard takes the fleece of a black ram and spreads it over the Emperor, who has stretched out on a pallet.

"As I prepare your philter, ponder the stone, meditate on the heart of the octagon." The Wizard empties vials into the chalice. From an alembic he pours fermented honey. "*Solve et coagula*," he chants three times as he stirs.

"Scot, I trust you more than I trust my poet or my cook. With my life, even. I take the risk that your potion might poison me."

"The master who poisons the student poisons himself, My Lord."

The Emperor swallows the brew in one quaff. He shudders, his tongue seared by the bitter vetch beneath the sweetness.

"Have you the question to pose to your dreams? What is it that you must know?"

Frederick's forehead glistens. He covers his eyes with his hands. Moments pass. "Magus, I want that truth you speak of. The truth of Time Past learned from Time Future," he says. "The Abbot Joachim hinted that my mother was made pregnant by a demon, an incubus who came to her in the night. Now I ask you, Magus, and I ask this stone: from whose blood, whose bones, whose nature am I born? Is my being from my mother's Viking forebears, or . . . " He lowers his voice. "Or am I shaped from my father's side? Who was my father? I must know what no man truly knows. Let me learn why my mother gave me birth in the public square of Jesi. How came Queen Constance by this stone? What powers does it possess?" The Emperor's eyelids are heavy and begin to close. "Magus, are not all oracles and omens related to wishes and dreams?"

"Dreams are but a link in the golden chain of reality, as past, present, and future form one continuum," Scot replies.

Frederick extends his clenched fist to the Magus.

"Let us begin then."

"Do not leave me, Magus. Stay by my side until the muezzin calls out the hour of dawn."

"I shall stay. My quill will record your sacred night." Scot takes the gem from the Emperor's hand. Then he anoints the flesh between Frederick's closed eyes with sticky unguent from the pyx and places the red stone upon it. Frederick's temples he bathes with pungent oil of lavender.

Now he pours water from a silver jug into a golden basin, then back again. "*Anima mundi, aqua nostra—anima mundi, aqua vitae libera est.* For the knowledge you seek, you must confront the anima, that part of your soul that is feminine. *Sublimatio, sublimatio*—travel swiftly. Sleep, Stupor Mundi, Wonder of the World."

Although his eyes are closed, the Emperor sees the ruby gleaming through his forehead like the shadow of a living heart, red as blood coursing through his veins, as red as the sun rising in the East. As he focuses on the blood-warmth between his eyes, the ruby grows larger and larger until it becomes a rose, a rose of a hundred petals unfolding, enlarging. Exploding roses, a million roses.

"*Rosa Mundi*," Frederick whispers. "*Gloria Mundi*." As he speaks these words, the roses turn as dark as aged Sicilian wine. Darker and darker until they meld into the black void of the Emperor's night.

That night, there was no moon to light the sky.

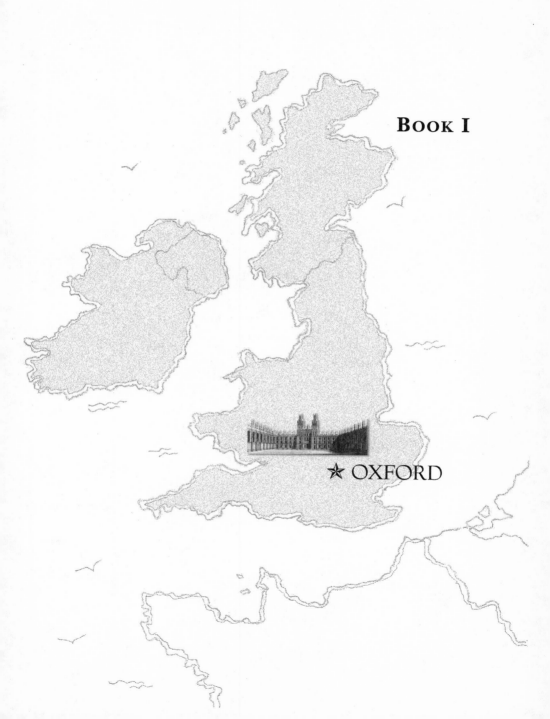

BOOK I

★ OXFORD

CHAPTER ONE
APRIL 1994

 **T**HE CAB TURNED into the High Street from the Turl. As I looked out from the window, nothing seemed to have changed in Oxford: warm amber stone, graceful oriel windows, bow-fronted haberdasheries displaying Scottish tweeds and emblazoned college ties. It all looked the same. I tipped the cab driver for lugging two heavy bags into the Lily and Crown Hotel around the corner on Merton Street.

Inside at the front desk, the eyes of the frazzled clerk worked me over like a wire brush scraping lint from a coat. I could almost *feel* it. No doubt she had a mindset about finding my reservation.

"What may I do for you, madam?"

"I've booked a room. My name is Kirkland . . . Rose Kirkland."

"Kirkland, Kirkland. Let's see." She clamped two large front teeth over her lower lip and searched the computer. "I'm afraid there's nothing under Kirkland. Nothing at all."

I gave her my tight, crisp smile. "Perhaps the reservation was made under my maiden name. Orlando."

"Orlando? Now that's a different story. Aha, here we are—Orlando-Kirkland, it's been double-barreled. Sounds rather nice." She slapped a bell with the palm of her hand. "Simon will take your bags and show you our nicest room."

I followed the porter up the staircase through narrow corridors made narrower by countless coats of thick écru enamel.

When Simon opened the door, lo and behold a room swathed in shades of porridge and puce. Floral chintz, draped, swagged, festooned from pelmet to bedpost. One yard would have been too much, but the decorator was clearly of the "when-in-doubt-use-more school."

"This is our loveliest room, and you do have a nice view," Simon said, drawing closed the heavy portières past lead-mullioned windows overlooking the High. "You've got an electric kettle and all the makins' for tea right here." He opened the oak cupboard to a flash of aluminum and brown stoneware. "There's an iron, too, but you'll have to ring the front desk for the board. The fireplace has a gas fire to give a bit o'cheer. Oxford can be quite damp, you know."

I smiled to myself, thinking of the time I'd lived in Oxford with Matthew. I'd worn my fleece-lined boots from the beginning of Michaelmas term to the beginning of Easter "vac."

"And if you should need your hair done, there's Mahogany just off the Turl, by the covered market." He handed me a card. "I help out there on Saturdays."

"I may just need something done with my hair before I leave." It would soon need some straightening in this damp weather. I fished around in my purse for a tip.

When the door closed, I flicked on the light in the bathroom—content to find it outfitted with brand-new, sleek Italian fixtures and a brightly lit glass mirror with no shadows.

I kicked off my shoes, flopped down on the duvet while I gazed at the shirred, ruched, and pleated walls. What was that funny smell? Mouse turds and boiled cabbage mingled with old-fashioned Lysol disinfectant. Too bad I'd left my joss sticks at home.

"What the hell are you doing here, Rose?" I asked myself out loud. "Why have you left your husband, your home, your jewelry business for this smelly stifling coffin?" In the same breath I answered, "Don't kid yourself, you know exactly why you're here."

It was just one week ago that I'd awakened during the night, not remembering my dream, only that I'd dreamed it. I remember burying my face in the pillow, focusing on the shadow feeling lingering in my bones. An instant passed before it surfaced. I captured it. The Viking dream. I grabbed the tape recorder on the night table and fumbled my way to the bathroom, tugging off my sweaty nightgown. Matthew was fast asleep and wouldn't hear me close the door or flip down the toilet seat cover.

I'd begun taping my dreams when I first sensed that I would die before my fortieth birthday.

Then I sat down and whispered the dream into the recorder.

That night, there was no moon to light the sky.

Long boats glide up the river. I hear oars slicing through water. The Vikings at the helm are red-bearded, skins of animals flung across bare shoulders. Their agate eyes are fixed beyond prows carved like fire-breathing dragons. I huddle behind tall marsh reeds, frightened that they might have seen me hiding there.

When I finished recording, I found the bottle of lavender oil and rubbed my temples and wrists. Then I retraced my steps into the bedroom and crept into bed naked, hoping not to disturb Matt. But he was wide-awake, waiting for me.

He reached over. "What's the matter, darling?"

"Vikings sailing up the river. I was hiding from them."

"Rose, Rose—what am I going to do with you? Come on, over here. Closer to me."

"I got my period this morning."

I felt his body tense, heard his controlled voice. "I'm sorry— why didn't you tell me when I came home?"

"I didn't have the heart. You seemed so exhausted after the flight."

"You should have told me. The least I can do is share your pain."

Same old kind, compassionate Matthew. But that night I heard the lump in his throat.

I broke down and cried when he pressed me against him. The warmth of his body calmed me a little. I wiped away the tears with the edge of the sheet and nestled my back against his chest, heaving a great sigh, releasing my anger. My body began to harden his, but I was still hiding in the reeds. I could still hear the swish of the oars. My head was too full for my body to respond.

I remember how it used to be, before we began to try so hard, before this fear came upon me. The blood-surging, skin-tingling, lightning-bolt hunger as my husband's hands caressed my breasts, stroked my thighs. He ran his hands over my belly, over my breasts. He pushed my hair aside and buried his face at the nape of my neck. But now I drew away.

"I'm too tired," I said, tugging the sheets around my nakedness.

"I've been gone for ten days, Rose." He pressed me back.

I wondered how much longer he would tolerate my moods, how much longer before I'd have to confide in him about my death-fear. His arm still around me, I pushed my face into the pillow, breathing in the lavender scent.

Forming a circle with the thumb, index finger, and middle finger of my right hand, I began to count gemstones instead of sheep. Suddenly, it was as though someone had spread a weight-less blanket of calm over me.

Garnet, lapis lazuli, coral, sapphire, amber, carnelian, chal-cedony, topaz, emerald, beryl, ruby, moonstones. As I made my way down the sparkling list, visualizing the color, the brilliance, the cut, the polish of each stone, I nearly always fell asleep. But not that night. My treasure chest was empty and I was still wide-awake, thinking of the first time I heard her voice.

❧

The phone rang. It was Matthew calling from California.

"I was just about to call you!" I told him. "I was feeling alone and blue here all by myself."

"You're jet lagged, remember. Have a good night's rest. Drink a glass of college port or two before you turn in. The hotel must have a supply. Has Oxford changed very much?"

"It looks the same—even smells the same—that fusty-musty smell in the Oxford train station."

He laughed. "My Rose of the sensitive nose."

"The High hasn't changed—but I haven't roamed around St. Aldate's yet or the Cornmarket, or walked up to Magdalen Bridge. Part of me is happy to be back. Only part, though. I miss you."

"As it turns out, I'll be flying to Osaka in a few days—the Japan-ese are in the deal now so I'll stay there for a few weeks. That should make you feel better about being away."

"*Much* better," I said, feeling the weights slide off my shoul-ders. "I hated the thought of you being home alone. What hap-pened at the board meeting?"

"The project is still on track. When's your meeting with Brian Lambeth?"

"I have an appointment on Wednesday morning. I'm a bit

anxious about meeting him. He's probably become a stuffy, book-ish don with one of those high-pitched, whiny drawls. '*Oh reahlly, my deah gel.*' "

He laughed. "You're sounding more like your old self already. Maybe this change was just what you needed. You might even want to go on to Italy sooner."

"Depends on Professor Lambeth . . . "

"Try to be assertive with him, Rose. Don't pull that self-effac-ing act of yours."

I laughed. "My shyness isn't an act! By the way, I went by Spink this morning. Mr. Yardley sends regards to you and Uncle Ray-mond. I left a list with him—can you believe he's shocked that I'm still using *their* coins for jewelry?"

"Did you draw in your new sketchbook?"

"I started to but didn't get very far."

"Have you eaten dinner?"

"Not yet—and it's past nine-thirty already. I'd better go down-stairs before they close the kitchen."

"I'll call you in a few days. Hang in there, darling. For God's sake, now that you're in Oxford make something of the visit. Don't moon around in your room. Get out! Enjoy yourself. Too bad I couldn't have been there with you."

After our extended goodbyes, I shook out my wrinkled rain-coat and set Matt's picture on the dresser. I tucked a velvet herbal cushion behind the bed pillows. My blouse was rumpled, so I plugged in the iron, spread a towel out on the bathroom floor, and began to press. At least I'd look neat for my first dinner in Oxford.

As I buttoned the blouse, my eyes met shiny mirror. When I was a teenager my mother used to scold me when I looked into the mirror too much. But it wasn't as though I admired what I saw. Quite the contrary. The image reflected in the glass was a relief, a reassurance, a glimpse of the persona I'd invented for an elusive self. "I see Rose Kirkland, therefore she exists."

I raked the brush through my hair. I saw her face. For the first time. *A blaze of red hair, hair redder than mine. A younger face. Not my face. Three drops of fresh blood ooze through her white shift—just where the heart beats.* My knees buckled. I grabbed the sink to steady myself as I listened.

❧

A moment passed. She faded away. I pulled myself together and walked down to the lobby. The snooty woman at the reception desk—"Just call me Mavis"—was now eager to dish out advice.

"Our restaurant is Arthur's Round Table. You can have a proper meal there, or there's The Lamb and the Flag, our downstairs pub. They serve simple lunches and dinners."

The Lamb and the Flag. The Sign of the Templars. A pub would be less formal, but I felt conspicuous walking into the noisy, jostling pub on my own.

"Good evening," said the hostess. "Table for one? Or are you expecting anyone else?"

"I'm alone."

I followed her all the way to the back, my eyes fixed on the embroidered border of her ankle-length skirt.

What a relief to be put in the far corner, as out of the way as possible. I could read *The Anglo-Norman Journal* I'd bought at Hatchard on my way to Spink. As I'd flipped through its pages, I saw an article on a certain Seigneur de Pirou, a Norman knight mentioned in the epic poem, *Le Roman de Rou*. The name had sounded a distant gong in my head. Pirou. Where had I heard of Pirou? Most likely in one of my Medieval Romance Literature classes.

A waiter appeared with a blackboard menu.

I scanned the menu. "How's the navarin of lamb?"

"Very good. Just a fancy name for Irish stew. Lamb is our specialty. I can recommend it," he said.

"I'd like to have it, please, with a cider. And a little of that ripe Stilton on the bar." Greedy, I knew, ordering the cheese before I'd eaten the stew, but the blue mood had given way to euphoria.

I looked across the table at a woman's back. Sleek blonde hair fanned out over her shoulders and, when she turned, her young profile seemed chiseled like a Neapolitan cameo. Sitting across from her was a dark-haired man with graying temples, very handsome. Black Irish looks, I decided. They seemed to be arguing, although his eyes never left her face. His face had a past written all over it.

I scanned the Pirou story, but my eyes kept wandering back to the young woman and her handsome older lover. The waiter brought another bottle of wine to their table.

I took small, slow bites. I hated hearing myself chew. So I wouldn't look lonely and frantic, I picked up the journal to read. Words marched along the page, not one sinking in.

I nodded to the waiter, who took away my plate, the stew only half-eaten.

"Some coffee, madam? Irish coffee is our specialty."

"No, thank you very much, but do you have any college port?"

"We've a very nice old port from Exeter College."

"Good, may I have a glass, please?" I could hear the changed tone, the English pitch to my voice. And after only a few hours in Oxford! I didn't try to sound English. It's just that I've always been a mimic. I drank two glasses of port, paid my bill and made my way out. The pub was almost empty except for the man and the woman, still engrossed, their foreheads almost touching across the table.

❧

Back in the room, I took a hot shower and got into my pajamas. I yanked the rubber band from my hair, gave my head a vehement shake and ran my fingers through the springy waves. I yawned, and feeling almost normal, crawled into the strange, clammy bed.

In our bedroom in Santa Monica, a Plains Indian "dream catcher" hangs over us as we sleep. It dangles from the ceiling on a blue satin ribbon, a circlet of bent willow and webbed gut, a falcon's feather woven into its center.

Our apartment overlooks patchwork gardens and small wood houses built in the twenties and thirties, now transformed from sea shack to "Palladian-Regency." When Matthew and I moved to California, I'd urged him to consider remodeling one of those little houses.

"We can't waste time, money, and energy on one of those shacks," he'd finally said. "We should use our energies developing our businesses. We're our own principal assets." So we'd settled for an apartment at Sea Village, one of the rental complexes on Nielssen Way in Santa Monica.

I'd grown up in Rhode Island so I looked forward to our move to California, a return to the Mediterranean climate of my Southern Italian heritage. California would be my Garden of the Hesperides. A place where I'd grow oranges and lemons, olives and oleanders, prickly pears, pomegranates. On clear days, if I stood on our concrete balcony and leaned forward, I had an oblique view of the Pacific, a sliver of silver and splintered pearls.

In one corner grows a potted orange tree with green-veined yellow leaves. Blossomless. The basil seedlings I'd planted in February keeled over and died. Geraniums were shriveled-up brown, nasty borers drilling inside their buds. My Wasteland. More than once I'd taken a nail file and stabbed the earth around the two stunted rose bushes.

That morning, after waking up with the Viking dream, I'd reached for the pouch of runestones on my night table. I remember how hard I'd shaken it, listening to tiles grating, clicking, a sound I looked forward to hearing. I chose one at random and read the scratched-in symbol. *Dagaz*, the rune of breakthrough and transformation. *Dagaz*. The only rune I'd never—ever—drawn before. I read from *The Book of Runes*.

Dagaz. 180-degree turn. Transition so radical that you no longer continue to live the ordinary life in the ordinary way.

Whatever that meant, I decided to allow myself to be late for work. Not exactly a breakthrough, but for me, at least a change. I heard the telephone ring and for once I didn't leap to answer it. Let the damned machine take the message, I thought. I ran hot water into the tub, then added a few drops of Sicilian neroli oil.

Stretched out in the aromatic liquid, I let her float to the surface. Who was she, where inside me was she coming from?

The first day I'd heard her voice was in November. On our wedding anniversary. I stayed home from work that day—something I rarely ever did. I remember having a terrible case of cramps, followed by my period. Another try, Rose, another failure. Still, Matthew sent me, as he always did on our anniversary, a big bouquet of red roses. As I buried my nose in their pale, greenhouse fragrance, her voice rose above the crackling cellophane.

Tomorrow I must leave my home forever.

I was baffled. Were my failed pregnancies driving me crazy? Or was it those stressful deadlines designing jewelry for other women's birthdays and anniversaries?

One morning in December I had the first clue to her identity. Before I even opened my eyes.

That morning I had no dreams to record. I woke up with a

name. Only a name. Hauteville. A name I heard echoing in my head. Why Hauteville? I didn't know a soul by that name. I looked it up in the Encyclopedia Britannica index. Hauteville. *See Roger of Sicily.* I read.

Roger was the youngest son of the second marriage of Tancred of Hauteville. He was thus the youngest brother of Robert Guiscard, whom he went to join and then conquer Southern Italy in 1057.

Hauteville-la-Guichard, a town in Normandy, was associated with a petty seigneur of the eleventh century, Tancred de Hauteville. The Hautevilles were descended from Viking raiders who had sailed up the Seine in dragon-prowed draakars, pillaging villages along riverbanks, raping the women. Before long, these plunderers had settled in the Valley of the Seine, plowed fertile soil and planted apple trees.

I learned the Norsemen became Normans as they abandoned Thor and Freya, as they accepted Christ's cross in place of Odin's pine tree. These descendants of Viking marauders began, over the next century, to build power in kinship, on the strength and speed of horseflesh and the stirrup.

I began to read everything I could find about Tancred de Hauteville, the petty Norman squire whose sons conquered the south of Italy and Sicily about twenty years before Duke William, their distant relative, conquered England in 1066. I harbored a repeated, haunting image of Tancred's restless sons making their way on horseback through the salt marshes of the Norman Cotentin as they set out to conquer Southern Italy from the Byzantine Greeks and Arabs. Their Norman Kingdom in the sun. Before long, the Norman reign in South Italy and Sicily became my Hauteville Underworld. But how did *she* fit into this world?

So there I was thousands of miles from Santa Monica alone in a strange bed, unable to sleep, curled up on my side, knees tucked under my chest like the baby I longed to have inside me. Now that I'd seen her face, I wondered if I'd ever hear her voice again. I squashed my nose into the velvet cushion, inhaling the mingled scents of lemon verbena and crushed rose geranium leaves. I closed my eyes and listened.

CHAPTER TWO

O N WEDNESDAY MORNING, exactly one minute before eleven o'clock, I stepped into the quad at All Souls College. I found the porter's lodge and asked for directions to Professor Lambeth's office.

"Take the first staircase to the third floor, madam."

I stood, out of breath, before Lambeth's door and tapped with a timid touch.

"Enter," a deep theatrical voice boomed out.

I turned the knob and saw last night's Anglo-Irishman sitting behind the desk in a room stacked floor to ceiling with books. The spaces not jammed with books were crammed with Tanagra figures, Egyptian bas reliefs, and incised clay tablets.

"Good morning, Professor Lambeth—I'm Rose Kirkland." I had to clutch my shoulder bag to keep my hands from trembling. I didn't mention that I'd seen him in the pub last night. But neither did he mention having noticed me. When he stood he extended his arm across the desk for a firm shake. He was tall and wore a sage green heather tweed jacket and a Balliol tie.

"Please sit down, Mrs. Kirkland. Just push the books over on the chair. Better yet, hand them to me, please."

His voice was mellow and rich, what used to be called a BBC Third Programme voice. How could I be fearful of anyone with a voice like that, I wondered. I handed two old leather-bound volumes across the desk. As he wedged them onto a shelf I noticed a gold signet ring on his long, tapered fingers. That morning I'd worn my dark blue tights and a skirt. I always feel a bit vulnerable when I'm not wearing my usual trousers so I crossed my legs and folded my arms.

Looking intently at me, he sat back in his chair. His thick dark eyebrows grew close together and the blueness of his beard showed through at eleven o'clock in the morning. In my nervousness I remember wondering how many times a day he ran a razor over his face.

As we discussed Matthew and Balliol, I wasn't sure if it was amusement I was reading in Lambeth's black-flecked green eyes. I think the most compelling thing about him was their intensity.

Sometimes blatant curiosity overcomes my lack of my confidence, so I asked, "And you stayed on in Oxford after you went down from Balliol?"

"Yes, after a few years in Venice, at the Marciana Library, where I worked on my thesis on Michael Scot."

"Michael Scot? That's a familiar name."

"One of the great minds of the early thirteenth century—the greatest mind after Alexander of Neckam. Scot was astrologer and wizard to Emperor Frederick II."

"I've read Kantorowicz's biography of Frederick. I bought it when we lived here in Oxford. I still have it at home."

"Was Kantor-o-vitz how you got started on the Hautevilles?"

I'd mispronounced the name and felt my face warming from the flush.

"Not exactly." I couldn't very well tell him that my recent encounter with the Hautevilles had come from a mysterious voice in my head.

"How can I be of help to you, Mrs. Kirkland? Your husband tells me you'd like to do some research at the Bodleian."

"Perhaps if you'd steer me in the right direction. If you could point me toward material on the Hautevilles of Normandy and Apulia, maybe some primary sources. There's so little written about them that when I read you were an expert on the Norman reign in Apulia and Sicily, I knew you were the man I had to see."

He smiled and went on. "Small modesty—you have, I think, managed to find the right person. My work began with the Hautevilles and their conquests in Calabria, Apulia and Sicily, but now I'm devoting all my time to their descendant, Frederick II. Did you know that this year is the 800th anniversary of his birth in 1194?"

"No—but eight hundred years *is* a momentous anniversary," I said.

"I'm writing a book to commemorate it. On Frederick's friendship with Michael Scot. What do you remember from your Kantorowicz?"

"Very little, I'm afraid." Was he mocking me or was he genuinely curious about my research?

I uncrossed my legs and scraped the callus on my finger with my thumbnail. "My interest is . . . serious."

"I would assume so—otherwise why would you have come all this way? Of course I'll try to be of help."

"That's very kind of you, Professor Lambeth."

We talked about mutual friends, Matthew's work, the Oxford of fourteen years ago until Lambeth looked at his watch.

"Unfortunately, they've called a meeting for us dons at noon. Look, why don't we have lunch sometime this weekend? We can continue our talk then."

I accepted with pleasure.

"I'll ring you up when I get back from Bristol. I'm lecturing there tomorrow night on Michael Scot and his magic."

An All Souls scholar lecturing on magic?

As I stood up to leave, the bells of Saint Mary's began to toll. Across the city other college bells chimed in. "Bells, bells, everywhere the sounds of bells," I mused aloud, "just as it must have been in the Middle Ages."

He gave me a reproachful look. "In the Middle Ages one was never very far from the sound of a scream. Screams of bodily anguish, of childbirth, of torture. Think about it, Mrs. Kirkland."

I was chilled by Lambeth's chiding words. He most likely saw me as a hopeless, incurable romantic. I extended my hand. He held it a bit longer, a bit tighter than I expected. The heavy gold ring hurt my fingers.

"Until the weekend, then," he said.

"Thank you very much, Professor Lambeth. Until then."

"I'll be looking forward to it. And please call me Brian."

❧

After the meeting with Brian, I took a long walk. From Balliol I walked past St. Giles's, up the Banbury Road toward Summertown, North Oxford, where Matthew and I used to live. I was disappointed to find the block of brick Edwardian row houses replaced by a slick mini-mall. I stopped to look in the sari-swathed windows of Rajahstan Specialties.

My thoughts flew to Rajput Baryani, a gem dealer who has a shop in the Jeweler's Mart in Los Angeles. Baryani of Jaipur is well known for stones old and new, cut with primitive tools by craftsmen from his homeland. Here was my cavern of Ali Baba; a cache of diamonds from Golconda's extinct mines, emeralds carved like little melons from maharanees' coffers, amethysts and topaz faceted *en briolette*, like chandelier prisms. Gems large and small, common or rare, of fine color and character, all cut with style. It wasn't from the course I'd taken at the Gemological Institute in Santa Monica, but from Rajput Baryani that I had learned the romance, the magic, the mysticism of gemstones.

The very morning I'd chosen Dagaz from the runes, I found Mr. Baryani's message on the answering machine.

"Good morning, Mrs. Kirkland," I heard him say in his lilting voice. "This is Rajput Baryani. I have just received a splendid stone. I am anxious to show it to you. You must come by to have a look. I will be here until noon."

"No way I can drive to L.A. today, Mr. Baryani. I'm already late for work," I remember thinking as I ran down four flights from the apartment to the garage. I tossed my lunch bag on top of everything else on the Volvo's back seat. A gypsy on caravan, Matthew calls me. A few Beverly Hills parking tickets, yet to be paid, were scattered among the Taco Bell wrappers and tapes that littered the floor.

I unwrapped my newest cassette of *Carmina Burana* and slid it into the tape deck. I thought about strapping myself into the seatbelt, but the thought was so fleeting that, as usual, I forgot it right after I remembered it.

The Dagaz symbol flashed through my mind.

Instead of driving toward my studio in Santa Monica, I found myself making a 180-degree turn. It was fifteen miles down Olympic Boulevard to the jewelry mart in downtown L.A. The Santa Monica Freeway would be faster, but I was still afraid of the freeways, afraid I'd get off at the wrong exit, afraid I would find no exit.

❧

Mr. Baryani turned the knob of his safe, twisting it clockwise and counterclockwise in what seemed to be an endless number of turns.

He opened the lid of a small ivory box, crazed and yellowed with age. Nestled inside was a cabochon gemstone of an intense shade of crimson, about the size of a pullet's egg. Huge. "Here—take it in your hand—clasp it tight," he said.

I picked up the lustrous stone and held it between my fingers. "What a strange oblique cut—flat on the back, rounded on one end, narrower on the other. As though it might be half of a larger stone," I said, leaning against the counter, holding it up to the light. "What depth—so red, yet so clear—like fresh blood over ice." I turned it over. "I've never seen an unfaceted gem as glorious."

"Nor have I, in my much longer lifetime." Mr. Baryani's kindly eyes were serious. "This was found in Naples by one of my cousins who has a shop there. Brought in by an old woman in desperate need of money. She swore it had been handed down in the family for generations. Munu paid her handsomely for it. You see, he had the same strong reaction. The old woman told him that there was a legend about the stone. That it was handed down from Prester John's treasure. I have no idea who Prester John was, do you?"

"Prester John? Come on, Mr. Baryani. Give me a break!" I grinned and shook my head in total disbelief.

He laughed. "What do you know about him?"

"Not much. I've always thought the fabled kingdom of Prester John was just a medieval legend. I'm not sure he ever really existed."

"A tall story then . . . but who knows?"

"But your stone is to die for, really."

"*'To die for,'* Mrs. Kirkland? "

"Just an expression, Mr. Baryani—an expression I loathe. I don't even know why I used it."

Just as I was about to find my loupe to study the stone, the light fixture above our heads began to sway. I held the stone tightly in one hand and grabbed hold of the counter with the other.

Screeching alarms went off throughout the building.

In a few long moments the shaking stopped.

I took a long deep breath. "It is a powerful gem, isn't it? That after-shock must have been at least 4.5 on the Richter scale, wouldn't you say?" My heart hammered in time with the stone's beat as I clasped it tightly.

I closed my eyes. *I see red. Redder than fresh blood on new-fallen snow.*

She is wearing a white shift. Blood oozes through the place where the heart beats.

I can't see her face. But I hear her voice.

Tomorrow I must leave my home forever.

The name Hauteville crossed my mind.

Then, in one of those mystifying, spine-chilling, quicksilver instants, it came to me. Hauteville and Altavilla were the same name! Yet Altavilla was an Italian name, a name I seemed always to have known. A name I must have heard years ago in Providence—most likely at my father's knee as I listened to his stories. A name like Galileo, Dante, Garibaldi, Marconi. Giannini of the Bank of America.

I gave the stone to Mr. Baryani, thanked him and turned to leave. I knew at that moment I had to find the source of that voice. The voice invading my reality, filling my head, compelling me, urging me back eight hundred years to the twelfth century. Convincing me that I had to leave my home, my husband, my work to follow it. So that I could go on living.

❦

My studio in Venice stands behind our small retail showroom. I pushed my way through a jungle of tangled vines and Australian tree ferns and banged on the studio door. An eye peered from the peephole. Linda pushed the electric buzzer and let me in.

"Hi, Rose. Mrs. Cartwright left on a quick trip to Washington. She can't see the necklace design today. She only phoned a few minutes ago."

Linda was everything I was not. Always cheerful. Organized and explicit. I have a very hard time being exact. I'd long ago convinced myself that organization stifled me, blocked my imagination. On my desk I keep a framed paragraph I read every day before I begin to work.

The mystic would transcend the limitations of conceptual thoughts. She prizes intimate insight and lyrical expression, but sets no value on precision and refuses to be caught in formal definition.

"Thanks. I'll go check on the boys and be right back. Then I promise to sit down at my desk and tackle that miserable pile of papers."

Until then I hadn't been a commercial success. Our accountant insisted that my markup wasn't high enough to pay my rent, to meet my payroll and my expenses. And make a profit. He kept telling me that I was "giving away the store." Maybe I should sell my business. Since my only sense of achievement came from seeing my jewelry being worn by other women, I dismissed the thought.

I followed the progress of every piece as it evolved from my sketchbook page. We use no molds for our jewelry. Instead skilled craftsmen hammered, chiseled, beat twenty-two carat gold: they scraped and filed and polished by hand. I wanted our jewels to look as though they were treasures dug from the earth—like treasure from Priam's hoard.

In the small workroom, Arturo huddled under intense spotlights. He looked up when I entered, as eager for my daily praise as I was to bestow it. He was tapping the shank of a ring into shape, preparing its bezel to receive a carnelian intaglio of the goddess Demeter.

Serge had been trained by his Russian grandfather, a master craftsman for the House of Fabergé. That morning he was soldering microscopic droplets of molten gold from a crucible onto the smooth surface of a golden disc soon to become an earring. To me, this ancient technique was like the harmonious, geometric sprinkling of seeds. Two artisans worked outside in the little yard, firing enamels in the kiln. They were experimenting with plique à jour, transparent glass enamel.

When I'd finished inspecting the workroom, I went to Linda's desk. "I'd like to talk to you. Let's sit down for a moment."

An anxious look crossed her face. "No thanks, I'll stand. Give it to me straight, Rose."

I put my arm around her. "Please don't worry, Linda. Your job is secure. I'm not going to let everybody down by folding up this business. I wonder who started that rumor."

She sighed. "That's a relief! I can't afford to miss any payments on my car or house."

"You won't have to. In fact, I'd like you to take on even more responsibilities. First I'm going to spend some time in Oxford—then I'll go on to Italy. Do you think you'd be able to manage without me for a while? Six weeks, maybe two months?"

She hesitated. "I'm not sure. You know you don't have to worry about the boys and the workroom. But we'll have to hold off on the enamel experiments until you get back."

I sensed her reluctance. "Is anything wrong?"

"I'll give you the bad news first."

I took a swallow of coffee to brace myself. "Go ahead. I'm ready."

"Your accountant called this morning. *Again.* He seemed eager to talk about the balance sheet. But he told me that you bounced another check from your personal account."

I'd been waiting for that dreaded call.

"You also had an inquiry from a ladies group in Santa Barbara. They'd like you to give a short talk on your jewelry designs at one of their charity luncheons."

"I hope you made a good excuse for me."

"I told them you couldn't commit to a precise date with your busy agenda."

"That's exactly right." But what she didn't tell them was that I was terrified of facing an audience. "Now what about the good news?"

"You had a big order from La Bijouterie in Dallas—along with a nice fat deposit. So you'll have some money in the bank as of tomorrow. Where are you going?"

"I have to make an urgent trip. First I'm going back to Oxford—to do some research—then on to Italy to visit my relatives." I didn't offer any more details. "Do you really think you can handle things for me?"

"I'll do my best. You could use a vacation."

"I don't consider it a vacation."

"I'd never have the gumption to take a trip like that on my own."

I laughed. "But I'm still not driving the freeways!"

"We all have our own little hangups, Rose. Don't worry! I'll manage—and the fax helps. When do you want to leave?"

"I'd leave tomorrow if I could."

"Tomorrow? Not if you intend to use your Frequent Flyer

coupons—you should have enough for a free round-trip ticket by now. The airlines need a few days notice."

"As soon as you can make the booking, then. I'll need a reservation in London for one night, and then if you could get me a hotel reservation in Oxford. A small hotel, nothing fancy. Try the Lily and Crown first. Our friends used to stay there when they visited us."

I went straight to my office-sanctuary and turned on another tape of *Carmina Burana*, this time the Rafael Kubelik recording chosen from at least five other versions.

I lay my head down to listen; I had learned the Latin lyrics by heart.

O Fortuna
Velut Luna
statu variabilis
semper crescis
aut decrescis.

Now I was beginning to understand why these commanding, pulsing words inspired me in this medieval tribute to Fortuna, the Roman goddess of chance. Now that I'd made up my mind to follow her voice, I knew that the road I might follow, the risks I might take, would imply chance, enhance chance. I knew that Fortuna would guide me as I stood at the crossroads, wondering which way to turn.

By the time I'd played the tape through once, I felt better able to face the paper mountain. I wiped away tears that lately flowed with only the slightest provocation, gave my nose a good blow and leafed through the pile. Linda was right. There were enough commissions for a few months' work. The orders were variations on the same old boring classical themes—the ones clients still wanted but which no longer interested me. I pushed them aside. Instead, I opened my sketchbook and turned to a blank page. I stared down at the paper for a moment before I reached for my colored pens and began to draw.

I was startled when a mermaid appeared before my eyes, double tails curling in opposite directions around the rock she sat upon. Her rock would be a gray baroque pearl, her tails green enameled scales. The design was different from anything I'd done before, a design from the depths of the sea. A Melusina. She would hang from a heavy gold chain—a chain that I would forge myself. I remembered floating in the morning's fragrant water. I could still feel the thrumming of Mr. Baryani's ruby in my hand. I would never forget that stone. What kind of setting could I design for it? Oh no, I decided, and I wasn't sure why, but that ruby should never ever be set into metal.

Linda knocked and stuck her head through the door. "All done!"

I looked up from my drawing board. "All done?" I checked the time on my watch. Four o'clock! How had two hours gone by so fast!

"You had enough coupons for British Airways flight 268—L.A. to London direct—this coming Saturday. And you have your reservations at the Lily and Crown in Oxford. Okay?"

"Thanks. One more thing. I have to find Professor Brian Lambeth's telephone number. He's a don at All Souls College at Oxford. Will you please call overseas information for it?"

❧

Matthew's office/laboratory takes up the first floor of a boxy fifties-style building on Pico, near Bushnell. The Rand Corporation is nearby, as well as various conservation organizations and architectural firms. I walked to the lab from my studio. At Market Street and Nielssen Way the morning storm clouds finally

burst. Bad for me, without an umbrella, but good for Matthew.
He'd been hoping for rain to make his seeds sprout. In October
he'd ordered a hundred-pound sack of California wildflower seed
from Smith and Hawken catalog and had broadcast it along freeway shoulders and vacant lots. A side of my tough husband known
to no one in the world but me. Last year we shared his secret
pleasure in the stand of black-eyed Susans along the Pasadena
Freeway and the orange blanket of California poppies covering a
vacant lot on Pacific Coast Highway.

I sometimes felt that I was cut out of cloth less sturdy. Matthew
was a man of reason, of balance, of judgment based on facts.
Because I lived by instinct, because I couldn't conceive his child,
I often felt diminished next to him, although I never let him
know this. Nor was it Matthew who consciously made me feel
this way. It was I who had chosen to live in perpetual concern
over his opinion of me. Yet I love him so much I pray I die before
he does.

I tried to sneak past his door, heading for the rest room to mop
myself up, but he caught me. "My God, you're shivering and soak-
ing wet, darling." He took out his handkerchief, blotted my hair,
and wiped my nose.

I brushed one of his prematurely gray hairs from the dark blue
blazer. "Can we go in to your office?"

"Come on in."

Scale models and dioramas displayed on low tables made the
room look like a miniature city.

"How about something to warm you up?"

"I'm fine, thanks . . . just cold. I'll wait until I get home for a
drink."

Around the walls of his office were giant blow-ups of the scale
models on the tables. "Those photographs are new, aren't they?" I
asked. "They make your city look as though it's all been completed.

Even the trees look mature. I'll bet we never see them that way in our lifetime."

"Come on, Rose—don't be such a pessimist! That's just about what the city should look like in five years—if we ever get started."

Matthew had patented a reduction-conversion process that used genetically altered bacteria to turn organic matter, refuse, and even some non-organic plastics into a material that could be used to fill in desert canyons. Mountains of Los Angeles trash would provide a solid base upon which affordable housing could be safely built. Since shallow-rooted trees could survive on the stratum of earth that would be hauled in to cover the substratum of simulated rock, the houses would be surrounded by gardens and ponds. He had been working with scientists, botanists, and engineers to create an oasis near Palmdale.

Matthew thought of himself as a biologist-cum-businessman, but I saw him as a visionary alchemist changing trash into viable earth. As a graduate student at Oxford, he'd been influenced by the work of the biologist James Lovelock, who believed that "the Earth exhibits the properties of one gigantic, self-containing, self-creative living organism—a live Earth, in contrast to an Earth with life upon it." Lovelock calls his theory the Gaia Hypothesis after Gaia, Greek goddess of the earth. The small plants in his terrarium were thriving in a black-brown substance that looked like soil but was actually a sample of the matter created by breaking down trash of all sorts. It had occurred to me that Matthew and I worked at opposite ends of a circular process. He transformed waste to replenish the earth, and I used materials dug from the earth—silver, gold, gemstones.

"That reminds me, Mr. Baryani showed me the most incredible stone today—a ruby."

"How much did it cost?"

" I didn't ask. Why do *you* always ask how much things cost?

Besides, it was the kind of stone he'd never sell. When I was finished at the mart, I went back to have another look because I hadn't really examined it with my loupe. But Mr. Baryani was gone. The jeweler in the shop next door told me he was leaving for India tonight."

"What made the stone so incredible?"

"Color, for one thing. And when I held it . . ."

"And when you held it?"

"I felt as if the source of all life was in my hand. The earth shook under my feet—it was that powerful."

"This morning's after-shock was sheer coincidence, I'm sure— but I'm amazed you didn't try to buy the stone."

"I told you I never even bothered to ask the price."

"Why not?"

I laughed. "Are you kidding? A ruby that size would be beyond my means. Besides, I was sure he'd never sell it."

"If you really want it, you know, we could use some of our savings or borrow from the bank, or you could sell your . . ."

"What savings? We've used most of our savings on the *in vitro*. And please don't start on my business again! We should talk about yours, now that I'm here. Any news today from the backers?" I knew that was a sensitive subject.

"Not yet."

I got to the point of my visit. "I made a big decision today. Matt. Now I know what I must do."

"What is it?" His eyes were intent, eager.

"I'm going back to Oxford—this coming Saturday. That's where I'll begin, then on to Italy to visit my father's family."

At first he seemed to think I was joking.

He laughed. "Oh, really? Just like that? Oxford and Italy?" he said with more than a trace of sarcasm in his voice.

"Yes. I decided this morning. On my own." Without consulting you, my accountant or anyone else, I thought.

"I was sure you were going to tell me you'd made up your mind about finding a surrogate." He looked at me plaintively. "Time's running out for us, darling."

After fourteen years of marriage without pregnancy, I was still convinced I could bear a child. Air had been blown into my tubes, my uterus flooded with sinagraphin. Matthew's sperm gathered, sorted, and counted. Everything seemed to be in working order for both of us—yet nothing happened when we finally tried the *in vitro*. We'd waited until we were financially secure before starting a family. Perhaps too long. I had my first period very late, at sixteen, like my father's mother and my Aunt Caterina, who was childless. They both had early menopause—in their thirties, which they say is usual for women who begin to menstruate so late. I didn't have to be reminded, then, that my productive years might soon be over—even with estrogen replacement. Matt wanted us to find a young woman surrogate to bear our child. If possible, an Italian American woman. Preferably one who looked like me.

He grasped my shoulders and shook me. "Can't you see that you're fleeing from your body and its inability to conceive? You've exchanged reality for a fantasyland, complete with flag-flying turrets! Anything to keep from making a decision. That's what you're doing— retreating to an imaginary world!"

"I'm not running away. I have to follow this voice. The idea came to me just this morning. After I read my runes."

I heard the exasperation. "Voice! Runes! You keep telling me that you've never felt at home in California, yet you come home loaded with New Age junk and books from the Bodhi Tree. And all those tapes stashed under the bed. One of these restless nights I'm going to reach up and yank down that goddamn dream catcher that's ruining your sleep—and mine. Let's face it! While our lives are on hold you're living in a complete state of denial— a funked up New Age Californian in spite of yourself!"

I began picking at my index finger with my thumbnail. A callus had formed on the side of the finger.

I could see parenthood only in terms of bearing a child, Matthew's and mine. He was eager to raise a child, preferably a child who was half ours. I knew I was irrational on the subject. Why was I so repelled by the idea of his sperm fertilizing another woman's egg in a laboratory beaker? Why was my body so resistant to conception, my womb as unyielding as a gemstone?

"Please listen to me. I *have* to make this trip. Let me go with your permission—with your blessing, even. If not—I'm still going."

He muttered under his breath, then raised his voice. "Don't you think you ought to look for some tough body and soul-searching therapist other than that little old lady from Pasadena you visit at the clinic? You must be dragging around a lot of baggage that should be trashed. Admit it to yourself, Rose. Something inside you must be locking you up—keeping you from surrendering to mother nature. How can I believe you want a baby?"

"I do want one, you know I do! It's just that these past few months my mind has been on other things. I've got to get at the bottom of all this, can't you understand?"

"I'm glad you admit that much, at least. That's a high wall you've built around yourself these past two years and you're hiding behind it. You're closing me out—and all our friends as well." He pounded his palm with his fist. "I'm running out of patience."

"You're not hearing me, darling. Please listen. Can't you see how urgent it is for me to take this trip? I'm desperate! Something—someone—inside me is trying to tell me something." I bit my lip to keep from crying.

"I'm hearing you, all right, but what the hell do you expect to find in Oxford? The Holy Grail?"

An image of a rock crystal, gem-studded chalice flashed across my mind. "I don't know—yet," I said. "I'll try to make an appointment with a don at All Souls, an expert on the Hautevilles. I keep reading his name in the bibliographies. His name is Brian Lambeth."

"Lambeth? The fellow I knew at Balliol? He was in medieval history . . . used to like a drink or two, I recall."

"Do you think you could call him for me, ask him if there's any way I can do some research at the Bodleian?"

"Why not call him yourself? You're a big girl."

"I don't know him. You know how the British are. You're English. I'm not."

He sighed. "Okay. If it'll make you feel better, of course I'll call him." He put his arms around me as if to heat my shivering body with his own. "Now go home, change into some dry clothes. You need a stiff drink to warm you up. My office is no place for a conversation like this—light a fire and we'll talk later. I'm glad my squash game was canceled, but I've still got a conference call to make."

I gave my husband a grateful kiss and walked to the car under his big black umbrella, listening to the raindrops drumming the tightly stretched silk.

CHAPTER THREE

I REMEMBER that the first thing I did when I got home was to phone my mother. She answered after the sixth ring instead of the usual second.

"Rosie—what a surprise! It's not even Sunday . . . "

"When you didn't answer right away I thought you might be at Novena," I said.

"We were all in the parlor watching 'Golden Girls.' I invited Comare Nicolina and some other lady friends from the Sodality over for coffee 'and.' "

"What are you serving for 'and?' "

"I made a nice *torta di ricotta*. I wish you could enjoy a piece with us."

I couldn't hurt my mother's feelings by confessing that I'd never cared for Italian cheesecake. Lemon meringue or plain old apple pie was more to my taste.

"And I also made a nice pot of stewed tripe the way your father liked it, the way they make it in France."

"Ugh—*mi fa schifo.*"

She laughed. "I remember how you used to leave the house when I boiled it first to take the smell away."

"The smell *still* disgusts me," I said.

Her voice turned sober. "*Figlia mia*, when are you going for your blood-work again?"

She'd asked me that same question last Sunday.

"I told you I went to the doctor two weeks ago. All's well, so please don't worry about me, Mom. I called tonight because I've got a real surprise for you."

"Don't tell me at last you're expecting!" I heard the wariness in her voice.

"I should have known you'd ask that."

"What kind of a surprise could it be it then?"

"I'm going to Vieste."

"Well, you have surprised me, all right. *Finalmente!* Are they going to be thrilled! Especially your Aunt Caterina. She never fails to ask about you in her letters. I've been wondering when you'd decide to pay your respects to your father's family."

I asked her if she had any associations with the name Altavilla.

"Of course I've heard the name. I've seen the advertisements for that ritzy new development near Pawtucket. Altavilla Heights. You've heard about it even in California?"

"No—but did you ever hear Papa mention a family called Altavilla? Think hard, Mom. It's something I *have* to know."

"Rose, Rose, you never change—always so full of questions. You know how bad my memory is these days. Maybe when you get to Italy Zia Caterina can help you out."

We ended our conversation chatting about the usual things— the price of lettuce in California as compared to the price of lettuce in Providence. I crossed my heart and promised to send her postcards from Vieste.

❦

That night I set our dinner tray tables side by side in front of the sofa. Our living room is a hodge-podge of old and new. Mostly old. My favorite object is a painted wood sculpture of Adam and Eve. A snake winds around the tree and glares at Eve as she offers the apple to Adam.

That winter I'd tried forcing narcissus bulbs in water and pebbles but I kept them in a dark closet too long. Their roots were like skeins of tangled string, their leaves pallid, bowed over reaching for the light. I buried my face in the exploded white stars and took a deep breath. Usually I love their fragrance, but that night I smelled the grave beneath their sweetness.

I turned on the gas jet in the fireplace. When the fire was blazing away I touched an Agraria joss stick to a glowing ember. I settled down on the sofa with an old fringed shawl over my legs.

The front door opened and closed. Matthew would wash up and change before he came in. I lay my head against a cushion. Sparks popped from the unseasoned wood. I inhaled bittersweet orange incense fuming from the spiraling curl. I closed my eyes and listened.

❦

"Earth calling Rose—wherever she is up there." I heard Matthew's laugh, felt his chin, rough from late-day stubble, brush my cheek as he kissed my parted lips. I rubbed my eyes and swung my legs off the sofa. His "earth to Rose" routine always cheered me up.

"I was centuries away," I said.

"Do you want to tell me about it?"

I shook my head, wrapped the shawl around me and fell back against the pillow.

He had changed into a crisp plaid shirt and a pair of his favorite faded blue jeans from Oxford. His still fit. Mine didn't. He poured cream sherry for me, Dry Sack for himself, the kind that tasted of Spanish earth.

I took a sip.

He sat down, put his arm around me, and drew me close. "Rose, I don't like harping at you all the time—but don't you have anything better to wear than that spotted, beat up bathrobe? Where's the one your mother sent you for your birthday?"

I bit my lip. "I'll put it on right now."

I changed into the periwinkle robe and sat down by his side.

"That's better." He kissed me. "That shade of blue makes your eyes look more blue than green. Now—let's talk about this so-called quest you intend to make."

"I'm going. That's all there is to it," I said defiantly.

"Calm down! Don't be so goddamned defensive."

As I looked down at the glimmering watermark pools in the blue moiré, the mermaid surfaced. "I'm sorry," I said, "but this voice—these words I hear over and over again—like a siren song beckoning me . . ."

"Siren song?" His brows knit together. "Then maybe I should lash you to the mast like Odysseus—so you can't be lured away from me."

Suddenly I was three years old, roped to a cement column in the basement, as punishment for straying from home. That day I'd nearly been run over by a passing car.

"Or better yet, maybe a straitjacket might do the job!"

"What a rotten thing to say. You know I'm not crazy." I started to cry.

He sighed and put his arm around me. "I apologize. Please forgive me."

I kissed his cheek.

"Now *you* listen to me," he said. "I admit I've been totally immersed in this deal so I'll take a good part of the blame for what's going on between us. I leave you alone at home a lot. And even when we're together my mind is on my work and you accuse me of closing you out of my world. I thought about all this walking home. Being apart for a while might not be a bad thing. It may, in fact, be a very good idea to clear the air. But you've got to promise me that when you come back . . . by the time your birthday rolls around—."

"I promise you by then I will have made up my mind about the surrogate. Or adoption." Or divorce, I thought, but didn't say. I put my arms around him and kissed him.

"Is that a deal?" He drew away. "Promise me again, please."

"It's a deal. If you want, put it in writing and I'll sign the document," I said.

He laughed. "Not necessary. I take your word for it."

"I know you'll hold me to it."

"I don't want you to leave me, but I do sense that you've got to work out things for yourself. This time, without me. You know how often I've urged you to visit your family. So, if that's what you want to do, go ahead. But please don't come back and tell me that you still haven't made up your mind. Face it— you'll soon be forty years old . . ."

"I'm only too well aware of it."

"You know you're everything to me, Rose. But lately it's a little more than I can handle. I know that I risk losing you by letting you go."

"Risk losing me?"

Matthew hesitated. His muscles went rigid, his back stiffened. I knew him well enough to know he had already changed his mind about what he wanted to say. "Maybe you should consider selling the business. Your accountant called me today. After all these years you're making a real profit. Now's the time to sell," he said.

We were aware that a surrogate baby would take all our savings.

"Just think, Rose. At last you're on the verge of being a commercial success. Maybe you should be staying right here, working extra hard to make sure profits stay this way. I don't think it's a good time for you to be waltzing out of here on a self-realization tour."

"I thought we just made a deal. Why don't *you* make up your mind?"

He shook his head. "You seem bent on sacrificing yourself, your business—even your relationship with me. And by the way, he also told me that you bounced another check on your personal account."

My anger flared. "I'm willing to take those risks! This morning Linda told me there was money in my personal account." I knew I was heading for trouble but I couldn't stop myself from goading him. "I'm worried about you and your project. You're far too trusting. I'm afraid those supposed backers of yours will do you in. I get so frustrated when I hear you talk about them."

He began pacing the floor. "Don't start that again. I don't discuss landfill at home any more because it upsets you."

"But it doesn't," I said. "The landfill idea is brilliant, like everything else you come up with. Those backers are something else. They're not worthy of you and they're not on your side." I heard my voice growing shrill. "I may be insecure about who I am and what I want to be, but I'm not insecure about my instincts or my feelings about people."

Matthew sighed out of exasperation. "This isn't constructive, Rose."

"I feel it every time we're with them at those boring dinners. It kills me to be nice to those . . . ."

"That's always clear enough. They can't look you in the eye, you make them so nervous. Don't think it hasn't come back to me more than once." He hurled a log in the fire. Sparks flew.

"They don't look me in the eye because they know I don't trust them." I tried to control my voice. "I hate to leave you to those hyenas. Please believe me—they're out to get control of your business. They'll sabotage the project and you along with it. Listen to my intuition!"

He jabbed the logs with the fire tongs. "Your intuition again! Don't you think I watch everything? For God's sake, let me run my business."

"Then don't tell me to give up mine!"

I stalked into the kitchen. Cooking might calm me. There was no way that I could eat, but at least I'd cook some pasta for him. I opened the refrigerator for the marinara sauce I'd made on Sunday. There, propped between the plastic container and the milk, was the shopping list I'd misplaced that morning. I slammed the door shut, gave it a good swift kick, tore the list to bits, tossed them into the garbage pail.

Matthew had his dinner alone. I fell into bed without washing the dishes or my face, and cried into the pillow. I thought of the tenderness with which he'd wiped the rain from my cheek. Where was his handkerchief now? I tasted my tears. They tasted of the sea. Mermaid tears.

❧

My suitcases were packed by Saturday noon. At two o'clock Matthew found me standing in the living room, taking a last look at all I was leaving behind. I should have sent the slipcovers to the dry cleaner. The broken leg of the front hall commode needed mending. Everything would just have to wait until I came home.

My home. Why should I leave this place? Those words again. *I see blood on her white shift.* I felt myself grow cold.

"Well, darling, are you all set?" Matthew said.

I plopped myself down on the sofa. "I'm not going."

"What do you mean you're not going?"

"I've changed my mind."

He put his arm around me. "You have to go. If you don't, you might never forgive yourself. Stick by your instincts, Rose."

"That's potent advice coming from you."

"I'll put your bags in the car."

Resignedly, I plumped the sofa cushions. The fireplace grate was banked with ashes and needed sweeping out. The wall above the mantle was still bare. I had wanted to hang the Broome coat of arms, an azure field with a dove with a sprig of yellow broom in its beak, but Matt found the idea silly and pretentious so I hadn't insisted. My Italian immigrant descent was so vastly different from his elegant English ancestry. I liked to compensate for this by trying to "connect" us in my fantasies. To while away time on long car trips I'd entertain him, making up whimsical stories about how our ancestors might have met and fallen in love centuries ago.

"Suppose," I'd imagine out loud, "that one of my Italian ancestors was a soldier in the Roman Legions, and suppose that he wed one of your ancestors—some flaxen-haired damsel from East Anglia— or suppose he carried off a Druid priestess from a sacred oak grove near Stonehenge. Or what if . . ." I'd fill in outrageous details for each story and then transpose this scenario to other times, other places, other "connections."

Matthew appeared and took my hand in his. "Come on—time to leave. You can daydream all you want on the plane." He kissed my cheek.

"I'm feeling very nervous about leaving with no one to take care of you and cook your meals."

"I can take care of myself." He pulled me to his shoulder. "But it's not going to be easy—being without you, sleeping alone every night."

"Don't make me feel any more guilty than I already do."

"I wish you'd throw 'guilt' out of your vocabulary. I can still say I'll miss you, can't I?"

"Sometimes I almost wish you wouldn't miss me. But if I thought you were the least bit angry about my going . . ."

"Don't get me wrong, but right now I've got so goddamned much on my mind. At least I can be preoccupied in peace."

It occurred to me that Matt, in his characteristically dignified way, might be trying to reject me. And it also dawned on me that my leaving him might be my way of rejecting him before he could reject me.

He handed me a package wrapped in marbleized Italian paper. "For you, darling."

I opened it, trying not to tear the thick, handmade paper.

"It's a sketchbook," he said.

But the pages were blue-lined, more like a journal. He knew I hated to write. I was scared stiff by his computer. And I'd never learned to type. I sketched easily, spontaneously, but I was petrified of writing. *Horror scrivendi.* I was consoled that there was a name for my affliction. I did as little writing as possible, the absolute social minimum, and Linda transcribed my business letters from a dictating machine.

Yet I was somehow pleased to have the journal, and I thanked him. I tucked it in my travel bag along with the small red velvet, herb-scented "dream pillow" I never travel without.

We arrived at LAX in good time for the British Airways Saturday evening flight.

"Are you sure you have your passport?"

I checked my purse. "Yes, darling."

"Your wallet?"

I grinned. I'd gone off without my wallet and my passport more than once so I really didn't mind his checklist.

"Your checkbook?"

"I have it."

"All set, then." He handed me the boarding pass and walked me to the departure gate.

I threw my arms around him and buried my face in the familiar curve of his shoulder. "Thank you, darling—for letting me go. I have to make this trip. It may be the only way to find out what's happening to me. My last chance . . . otherwise I worry about . . . what might . . ."

"What last chance? Don't ever say that again! I feel threatened when you talk that way." He kissed my hands and tears welled up again.

"I love you too much," I said.

"I love you, too— and always will."

I found a tissue and wiped my eyes, thinking of her words as she left home, knowing that I, too, must go. Alone.

Tomorrow I must leave my home forever.

Words I'd been hearing over and over again. Not my words, her words. Forever. *Forever?* The dreadful finality of forever. Panic stabbed me. I looked into Matt's tearful eyes. Supposing that I *were* leaving my home forever. Supposing this was the last time. I pushed the frightening thoughts away.

Matthew must have sensed my anguish because he held me tighter—as though he might have suddenly changed his mind about letting me go. Then he brushed back a wisp of hair from my forehead and kissed me again. "Good luck, darling. Remember to call me as soon as you arrive in Oxford."

❧

After my long walk it was twilight by the time I got back to the Lily and Crown. Simon, today in his gardening guise, was clipping the boxed green bays flanking the entrance. The air around them smelled so delicious, I asked if I could have some leaves.

"Aye—help yourself! Mavis says these aren't the *laurus noblesse* [sic] variety. I don't know if they're any good for soup or stews— but I sure wouldn't let her catch you cookin' on the hot plate if I was you."

"I wouldn't dream of it," I said.

CHAPTER FOUR

THE NEXT MORNING my first sensation was a vague awareness of soft April rains on the High. This awakening had been a dream in which I'd gone to the window and parted the curtains to see if the real world of Oxford was still there. In the dream I returned to bed.

I gazed at the ceiling for a long time, until cracks began to take shapes, to form words. A hand began to write, a ringless hand holding a golden pen. I couldn't read the words, but I saw magenta vines like eglantine tumbling over palace terraces and the lush yellow-green tangle of honeysuckle. The image stayed with me all day.

At half past three that afternoon, I turned on the gas fire in the grate, lit one of the Sri Lanka sandalwood joss sticks I'd bought at Oxfam, and plugged in the electric kettle to begin the tea ritual I'd learned when I first lived in Oxford. I scalded and rinsed the pot with boiling water, added two spoonfuls of tea—one of Earl Grey, one of Darjeeling—and poured more boiling water over the leaves. In three minutes, a perfect cup.

While I daydreamed I picked up a bay leaf from the pile on the mantel and began to nibble away. Come on, why not toss a few on the gas fire while you're at it, Rose, I thought. I'd read that priest-esses of ancient Greece burned laurel leaves in braziers filled with smoldering olive pits, then inhaled the dense, stupefying fumes before proclaiming their oracles. I'd never tried chomping on a fresh bay leaf before and I was disappointed that it didn't have the same flavor as a dried leaf, but I still managed to get it all down.

Soon the room turned hazy with exotic sandalwood mingled with singed laurel. Outside, the sun was casting long, oblique shadows against the golden stone of Queen's College. Strange. There was hardly any traffic on the High—just a few undergrad-uates cycling home for tea, black gowns flapping behind them. A man astride a glossy black stallion was riding down past the old Mitre Hotel at a slow trot. Stranger yet, I couldn't remember *ever* having seen horses and riders on the High.

As he drew closer, I could see the rider was in costume. His hair was reddish, his face ruddy, square-chinned. He was wearing a dark green tunic. An ivory horn hung from one shoulder, a shield was thrust against the other. I couldn't make out the emblem on the shield. An eagle? I wondered if he'd ride all the way down the High toward Magdalen. Was there a pageant going on? Maybe it was the anniversary of one of the colleges. Most of them had been founded in the early Middle Ages and they were forever commemorating something or other.

Some undergraduates stood chatting at the corner of Merton Street and the High. As the horse and rider passed beneath my window they didn't give the horseman a glance. Maybe they were all used to this sort of thing. I was still trying to make out the emblem on the rider's shield when he, turning the corner, disap-peared from view.

I grabbed my room key, raced down the stairs, out the lobby onto Merton Street. I rounded the corner onto the High and looked toward Magdalen Bridge. No sign of him.

"Could you tell me, please, which way the horse and rider went?"

The students looked up, then at each other.

"What horse and rider?" one of them asked.

"Surely you had to have noticed him."

When I turned back toward the hotel, I heard someone snicker, "crazy American."

My heart was racing but I tried my best to look nonchalant as I crossed the lobby. Otherwise Mavis, the desk clerk, might catch on that there was something amiss. Back in my room I poured myself a cup of what had become very strong, bitter tea.

My forehead was damp, my hands clammy. Something *was* wrong with me, even more wrong than in California. And it was happening in Oxford, this place I loved more than any other.

The telephone rang. It was Blackwell's bookshop. "We were able to find you an old copy of Kantorowicz's *Frederick II*, Mrs. Kirkland. We'll be open until five-thirty this evening if you'd like to pick it up."

I threw my raincoat over my shoulders and hurried to Blackwell's. I would stay there until the shop closed. Among people and books, I wouldn't be alone. Glancing over titles, picking them up, reading bits of them, I might almost be sane.

❦

The closing bell rang. I paid for my book at the reserve desk and was the last customer to leave Blackwell's.

From the Broad, I cut through the Turl. I glanced at the window of Past Times. Propped against the *Aquae Sulis* Bathsalts were Eileen Powers' *Medieval Women*, Amy Kelly's *Eleanor and the Four*

Kings, and an assortment of audiocassettes and CDs. *Sounds of the Vikings*, *Sounds of the Normans*, and rolls of brilliantly whorled and spiral-patterned papers derived from Celtic designs and the Lindisfarne Gospel.

As I raised my eyes from the window display, I saw him inside the shop. The horseman. A gold object gleamed in his hand. A pen? I stood transfixed. The man in green turned and gazed out through the window—at me.

He held out his hands. In one palm lay the glowing red stone. An enormous ruby? In the other he held the golden pen and seemed to be reaching through the glass. How could I resist? As I thrust out my hand to accept it, he stared at me with commanding eyes the color of water emeralds.

Then he disappeared.

I pressed my nose to the glass, looked down again at the display. A gold pen was nestled in a dark green velvet box.

Bound by the spell, I entered the shop, hearing myself ask in a steady, measured voice. "May I please see the pen in the window? Like the one the horseman just bought."

"The horseman?" said the sales clerk.

"May I see it please?"

The clerk seemed puzzled but she took the box from the window. "We've not sold any of these yet—they've just arrived. You're the first to ask for one."

"I'll take it," I heard myself saying without examining the pen, without asking the price.

"You'll need ink for it, you know—this is a fountain pen. We have *La Perla Noire* from France, a good black ink."

I paid the saleswoman, raced back to the Lily and Crown and bolted up the staircase to my room, my heart drumming so hard my chest ached.

The room still smelled ratty and moldy. I lighted the gas fire and set a joss stick to the flame. My head seemed to clear as I inhaled the fragrant smoke curls. Was the horseman a phantom? Or a mirage? Crazy or sane, I was convinced of one thing. He was pointing the way.

I ripped the paper and lifted the golden pen from its box. A Greek key pattern was engraved around the cap.

I unscrewed the bottle and heard gurgling and slurping as the ink was sucked into the barrel. A welcome, nostalgic sound I hadn't heard in years. I took Matthew's sketchbook from my suitcase, sat down at the desk and, with a steady hand, began to draw on the lined paper. A rose. I paused, took a deep breath, and reflected on what I'd drawn.

A rose. Then with a shaking hand, I began to write.

Rose Kirkland, née Orlando—The Name of The Rose. Rose's name.

A rose by any other name. Rosamonde. Who are you? Where inside me do you come from?

I lay my head on my arms and cried. It was so painful I wasn't sure how I could go on. Tears plopped onto the water-marked paper. I began to force the golden pen across the page. Word by word by word. At last the thoughts began to flow.

❧

When I heard early-morning sounds, lorries delivering produce and groceries to the colleges, I was still at the desk. Writing. I put down my pen and stood by the window to watch men unloading crates of cauliflower, cabbages and yellow-fatted haunches of beef. Yes, I was still in Oxford.

I fell into bed without undressing and was asleep in an instant.

At ten o'clock the telephone rang. It was Brian Lambeth.

"Good morning, Brian." I tried to disguise the sleep in my voice. "How did it go in Bristol?"

"Very well—a good audience—asked lots of questions. You'd be surprised how receptive academics and undergraduates are to arcana."

"Arcana?"

"Well, yes. Michael Scot was involved with the arcane, the hermetic, and the occult. Most people don't realize that magic played a large part in the everyday life of the Middle Ages. Among the uninstructed folk and the learned as well."

"I found a copy of Kantorowicz but haven't had time to read about Scot." This time I pronounced the author's name correctly.

"Don't worry, I'll fill you in tomorrow. Is there a place you'd like to have lunch for old times sake?"

I thought for a moment. "Yes, there used to be an inn—by a river. Maybe the place doesn't exist anymore. The Rose Reborn."

"Yes. In the Chilterns—I know it. I'll ring them up straightaway to book a table. I'll pick you up around noon tomorrow."

"I'll be looking forward to it."

"So will I.

"See you tomorrow then."

I drew the curtain and looked up the High—another sunny day. Although I was weary, I felt a physical relief, an unburdening, as though I'd just climbed a mountain and, through a path in the billowing clouds, could look down upon a green valley below. Had the hours of writing done this for me—the pouring out of ancient voices buried like the hoards of coins I found for my jewelry?

I opened my journal and began to read what I had written. Rosamonde's words.

 Tomorrow I must leave my home forever. This land, this castle, my friends, the day-to-day pattern of my life.

Already loneliness claims me. My heart was once light, but now it is a stone, and tears fill my eyes. Minstrels may stroll with ribboned lutes into the great hall to sing of love and gallantries in foreign lands, of far off amours and betrayals and majesties, tempting me to look away from here.

They fail.

Tonight the elder sings his song, but not with strumming lyres or harps picked with ivory-tipped fingers. His eyes are closed. In thick and solemn voice, he chants the words of our old homeland—of who we were and how we came to be in Normandy.

That night, there was no moon to light the sky.
The darkness had been planned.
The fog rolled in from the deep green sea
blanketing the land.
At the helm stood Harald Wolf-tooth
Son of Thor Wordmaster
Son of Ivan Ringscatterer
Son of Gunnar Creeknose
Son of Erik Sigridson.

He sings of how our Viking kinsmen sailed to Normandy across the vast dark sea, rowing up rivers in their great boats carved like dragons breathing fire. He sings of how they seized the struggling Frankish maidens as their own.

Shivers of remembrance chill my spine, for I relive those frightful nights in the visions of my dreams, as did my mother and the mothers before her.

The minstrel's words begin to soothe as he sings of how our Viking kinsmen plowed this earth and planted apple trees. Is this the last time I shall hear him chant these words?

Tonight the great hall is full. My cousins and uncles and friends come to bid me godspeed. They bring gifts, small things to pack in my saddlebags—amulets of bone and coral, relics of saints in precious packets to keep me from the dangers of the long journey across rivers and mountains and gorges to the bluer sea they say is calm. Far from the black-green ocean that pounds the coast of Mont St. Michel.

I am cold again. Fear makes me cold. Why should I leave this place? My home. The trees have shed their leaves. Frost has blighted kitchen gardens and the eglantine clinging to the old stone wall. When April comes, I know where the first violets will push their way through clumps of heart-shaped leaves; the thicket where bramble berries ripen; where nests of quails' eggs are cradled in apple branches; the dark swamp where the moss lies green and smooth like the cloth the Flemings sell in the markets of Coutances.

Already I am homesick, and the journey has not yet begun. Would not have begun had my father not summoned me from Sicily after all these years. It is time, he says, that I marry. Eighteen years "too long unwed" I've been. And too old to want to change, to want to share my life with a stranger chosen by others. My mother's family—the Hautevilles, who once owned this castle—has asked for me, threatened to deprive my father of other lands if I fail to obey their call.

I want to run and hide.

And what if, during our journey, we are victims of marauding bands . . . or our boat sinks . . . or Arab pirates capture us and sell us into slavery? They've frightened me with such stories.

I have thought these past few weeks of fleeing to the

convent in Jumièges, where the nuns might take me into their cloistered walls and protect me from this marriage. But I am too much of the world, and although I know the King of Kings would come to me in spirit, this would not be enough to keep me in a wretched cell. So I shall go and serve these faraway people, however much I want to run and hide.

The horses have been made ready, the bags prepared, my trunks of clothing packed. No dowry comes with me from Normandy. My father will arrange my dowry in Palermo, where they say merchants sell golden cloth, well-tooled leathers, and furs to offer my betrothed. So our load is light. Blaise de Hauteville, who knows the route of pilgrims, will lead us, and his wife, Editha, will be my companion.

The children are asleep. Not barking dogs nor laughter nor singing minstrels—nor my tears—will keep them from their dreams. Tomorrow begins now, for I shall not sleep this night.

I must have fallen fast asleep on the hard pallet by the hearth. A coarse blanket keeps me warm, spread on my sleeping body by someone who knew better than to shake me out of fragile sleep to lead me to my bed. Others lie snoring soundly on the rushes. Just before dawn I awake and move sleepily to my own room. I shudder to think that it will be the last time I shall awaken here. The blanket is so warm, its familiar coarseness against my face so comforting. It is hard to move my limbs, but I must ready myself for the journey ahead. My clothes are laid out on the bed, fresh linen to start the journey. I know not where my head will lie at night. Be it in cleanliness or filth, weariness makes us less squeamish.

The relics I place around my neck—how I wish I might believe they would protect me! Somehow I cannot trust the vendors of bones and hair, these supposed chips and splints of saints and martyrs probably taken from the heaps of bones in charnel houses. But I shall wear them anyway, to please the rest. My aunt, Lady Hauteville, journeyed from Coutances to wish me well and give me an amethyst talisman to bring me good fortune. My father sent a coral amulet from Sicily to ward off evil.

Editha tells me it is time to leave. The sun will be rising soon and we have far to go today. The moment has come. Who will bid me goodbye first? Who dares to?

They all gather outside the castle, beyond the moat. My little cousin runs to embrace me, tears filling the wells of her pitted face—the pox left her as ugly as she is good. I weep with her. One by one we all say goodbye and make promises to remember one another for however long we are alive. My anguish is here for all of them to see. I cannot hide it, and why should I try?

Blaise de Hauteville helps me mount my horse. The horns sound, blaring to clear the way.

My journey begins.

What shall I think of as we ride? I will let my mind wander, close the door of my home behind me and think no more of it today. My dreams must be of Palermo now.

The rain pelts us. I smell rancid wet wool. I hear howling wolves, geese honking as they fly across the autumn sky.

Editha has been curious to know about the man I am to marry. I tell her no one has revealed his name, but she is convinced that he has been chosen. "Otherwise, why would your father call for you so urgently?" Perhaps she is right. She must know that I would not hold the name back from her.

The leafless trees seem like phantoms against the dusky sky. A hawk circles for prey. We pass village after village. The sun never pierces through clouds on this dark twilight day. My body aches from the saddle. Hungry and chilled to the marrow, I struggle to keep my head up. I want to sleep. To sleep.

Night falls and we can no longer see the color of our horses' ears.

At last we come to an open meadow where fires burn. In an old manor with a thatched roof we are given a room. I share it with four people from our entourage. The vermin straw has been cleared, and fresh straw is thrown down.

Editha kneels and prays to God to keep us in His safe hands so that we may reach Sicily in peace.

I unclasp the silver buckle around my waist and am relieved that its weight is taken from me. I wear it because it was my mother's. I trust it to keep us safe—more than the sacred relics, as though my mother's arms somehow thus encircled me in safety.

My mother—dead of madness when I was eleven. I was her only child; she was a loving mother. We took pleasure in each other's company until the day her nature changed. She spent her hours gazing from the tower, barely speaking except to tell me that she was waiting for a valiant knight to ride across the meadow. When I called to her she would turn to me, her eyes vacant and staring, as though she hardly knew me.

She was beautiful, I remember, with long red hair she stopped taking care of long before she died. Her carved ivory combs lay unused; she would allow no one to touch her head or wash her tangled hair. When my father came home from Rouen and saw her, he wept. She had become thin and wan, her eyes hollowed, her gown grease-spotted. Lice nested in her hair.

She told me once she was Agatha, the martyred saint whose breasts had been sliced off. My heart pained me when I heard this. I wanted to embrace her, but she would push me away and say, "You mustn't come near me unless you're a leper. A leper's bride I'll be. I am worthy only of lepers."

What can a child do when she hears her mother speak that way? My father tried to reason with her, gently, although he was not given to gentleness. I saw him more patient than I had ever seen him, this man who would curse and shout if he had no bite on his hook when he fished in the stream.

Then, one day, my mother seemed suddenly much better. It was in November, on my birthday, the feast day of Saint Odo. She washed her tangled hair and changed her clothes for a dress of deep rose fustian with a cowl of white embroidered linen. She came down to dine with the household in the hall. And when the songs were sung and the toasts drunk she drank one, too. But into her wine she dropped a deadly poison.

She told us all what she had done. As her eyes closed and her breath came in gasps, I screamed and beat at her with my fists for leaving me this way—on my birthday.

Why did she leave me? Why did she want to leave me?

I threw up all that I had eaten. I felt angry, helpless to see her dying, dressed up and dying right before my eyes. She had spited me as well as my father. Why? Why?

And then she was gone. I don't remember what happened

next. I think I hit my head against the wall when I tugged away from my father, who tried to hold me calm in all my rage.

I do recall the cortege to the burial ground behind the castle, the priests in black with no vestments. No Mass could be said for one who died in mortal sin by her own hand. Nor could she be buried in the hallowed ground of the chapel, in a crypt with an effigy of stone where she could look up to heaven as my ancestors do. She had not quite a pauper's grave, but almost.

I left offerings to her over the years, violets from the woods, or lady slippers, or the first unfolded roses of summer. I even planted tiny daisies there, the ones that grow in meadow grass. Pulled them up and wrapped the tangled roots in chestnut leaves to keep them moist, then poked them into the earth that blanketed her grave.

I missed her sorely, though as time went by I felt a certain freedom from my loss. But then my father went off to wage campaigns against the Greeks in Thessalonica, having told me that when he returned he would take another to wife. I was jealous. At thirteen I should have been thinking about a husband for myself.

CHAPTER FIVE

ON SATURDAY MORNING the sun shone California-bright in a cloudless English sky. England in April and girls were wearing their floral print dresses, their August-in-Spain frocks, rushing the season in what was to the British a hot day. I too changed from my serviceable wool cardigan to a flowered skirt and white cotton shirt, my Italy clothes.

Brian Lambeth called for me at noon. In an open-necked shirt without coat and tie, he looked less intimidating. More like a Celtic poet than an All Souls scholar.

His mini was parked on Merton Street. As the motor started, the tape player turned on, blaring the love duet from Tristan and Isolde. "My all-time favorite . . . next to Parsifal, of course." He lowered the volume and we drove off.

"Tell me about yourself, Rose. You told me that you're a jewelry designer. How did you arrive at it?"

"It runs in the family. My father was a jewelry designer.

Costume jewelry. Providence, where I grew up, is called 'the costume jewelry capital of the U.S.' I started designing after our marriage in England. Matthew's English Uncle Raymond Broome wanted to buy me an antique Victorian necklace as a wedding present. Then, sensing my interest in medieval history and Greek mythology, he took us to Spink in Saint Jame's. The clerk showed us trays filled with bronze, silver and copper coins. I chose some silver coins for a bracelet—ancient Greek coins from Apulia impressed with the wheat of Metapontum, a silver denarius that Julius Caesar had struck to pay his army, a thirteenth century Venetian ducat. Matthew was surprised at how little all this history cost, but the clerk was horrified that Madam would buy history to dangle from a bracelet."

Brian chuckled. "Spink is a very serious place. Fourteen years ago coins were still a bargain. What sort of jewelry do you design?"

"Nothing the least bit modern. My designs look as though they're very old because we use only ancient techniques. Intaglios, seals, gemstones, not necessarily the most expensive. Stones that speak to me. Lots of rock crystal. I guess you'd say that rock crystal is very California. I prefer it to diamonds.

"Before long, I was in business. I began transforming Assyrian cylinder seals, carved intaglios, amulets, and Minoan seals into jewelry. I like creating jewelry from found objects and talismans." I laughed. "I often wonder how many miles I've walked around the Pasadena Rose Bowl Flea Market on the second Sunday of every month searching through junk for coins, seals, orders, and decorations to transform."

"You must feel a great sense of accomplishment."

"Especially when I see my jewelry being worn by other women."

"Do you recall that the Emperor Frederick collected ancient intaglios and gemstones?"

I shook my head. "As I told you, I did get hold of the Kantorowicz. Blackwell's found a copy for me. Do you know, the only part I've never *ever* forgotten is Frederick's public birth, how his mother, the Empress Constance, wanted to prove that she bore her own child. I guess she didn't want any rumor that he was a changeling. Every now and then that story pops into my head."

"Do you have children, Rose?"

"No, I don't. We want children, but so far—well, no luck in that department."

"Luck doesn't usually do the trick," he said wryly, with an odd sideways glance at me. He rolled down the car window. "Pretty countryside, isn't it? Trees are leafing out in this warm weather. We should be there by one."

"I've never seen The Rose Reborn in daylight. I drove by there only once on my way home from London one late afternoon in January. It was dark and foggy. I was scared, but I kept on driving until I saw a pinpoint of light in the distance. I followed it until I came upon the brightly lighted inn sign. The Rose Reborn. I've never forgotten how it loomed up before me. I think of it often."

"I wonder why it meant so much to you. Do you know?"

"Maybe the memory has become larger over the years. I remember a ringless hand with a pen writing The Rose Reborn in swirling Spencerian. But instead of the word 'rose,' a full-blown rose, almost entirely unfolded, was painted in. Like a Fantin-Latour rose, or one out of a Flemish still-life."

We turned off the main road onto a country lane. On either side of the road stood tall trees in full spring leaf.

When Brian nodded for me to go on, I told him I'd adopted that rose as a trademark for my jewelry. "Since my name is Rose, it seemed fitting."

"I can't imagine a better logo," he said. "Now we're driving through the forest game preserve of Lord Cherwell. This is where you were lost, no doubt."

The landscape gradually changed as we passed the high stone wall that marked the end of the Lord's demesne. In the distance, I could see the towering inn sign. Almost, but not quite, as I'd remembered it in my mind's eye: A many-petaled red rose—cupped like a chalice, nestling a baby lying on a cushion of yellow stamens. I had forgotten the baby. "The Rose Reborn" was written in black ink by a ringless hand.

I stepped out of the car to take a look. The pen on the sign was gold with a Greek key design around the cap.

My pen. The horseman's pen.

❧

The host led us to a table in a private garden behind the inn. On the main axis of the garden, surrounded by a high clipped yew hedge, stood a weather-beaten stone statue.

"Do you know which goddess she represents?" Brian asked me in a testing way.

"She seems to be an eighteenth-century copy of a Roman sculpture—nicely carved—not one of those cast composite stone sculptures. And since she's standing by a wheel she must be Fortuna."

"You're right. The goddess of fate. As the moon changes from day to day, as it controls the tides, so does Fortuna change."

I started to speak, remembering the hymn to Fortuna in *Carmina Burana*, but Brian, plainly born to teach, didn't give me a chance.

"Fortuna remained important in the Middle Ages—the survival of a pagan goddess in an outwardly Christian world."

I stared at Fortuna surrounded by greenness so cool to the eyes on this out of season day. At the pediment's base grew mounds of lavender, not yet waving long purple wands. I took a deep breath trying to imagine the lavender's nose-thrilling aroma.

Brian ordered a bottle of Pouilly Fumé.

I barely sipped my wine.

He seemed to be drinking his quickly.

"How did you become interested in Frederick II? Did you read history at college?"

"I have a B.A. from Brown. In art history and Medieval French Literature."

"*Le Roman de la Rose?* Chrétien de Troyes? " he asked.

"I wrote my senior thesis on Chrétien's *Le Chevalier au Lion*."

"Ah yes! *Yvain and the Lion*. Then how did you discover Frederick II?"

"Right here at Oxford. Pinned to the bulletin board in the porter's lodge at Balliol." I laughed. "You know, advertisements for bicycles and digs in Summertown—that sort of thing. Among the notices was a purple-bordered card that read: '*Stupor Mundi, Puer Apuliae*. If you are interested please call . . . ' I was intrigued. 'Wonder of the world, boy of Apulia.' My deceased father was born in Apulia. But who was Stupor Mundi, I remember thinking. And what did Apulia have to do with it?

"Anyway, I copied the number and rang it up when I reached home. Some young undergraduate answered and told me that he and some other students had organized a club around Frederick II, Holy Roman Emperor. They didn't have any women members but would be delighted to have one. He was charming, I remember. He recommended that I read the Kantorowicz. I rushed over to Blackwell's and it was right there on the shelf. It was still in print then, I guess."

"I remember the incident very clearly, Rose."

"What do you mean?" Shivers traveled up the back of my arms, anticipating his response.

"Your voice on the other end of the phone. The story about your father. I waited for you to turn up at one of our meetings.

Why didn't you come?"

"Incredible! It was *you*. After all these years. *You* were the one who told me to buy the book and read it."

"You haven't answered my question, Rose. Why didn't you come?"

"I guess I was shy. I wanted to, but I guess I didn't feel qualified."

"But you're here now."

"Maybe I sensed unfinished business. There's still so much I need to know. Fourteen years have gone by, and, as I told you, the only image that's stuck with me all these years is one of Constance setting up her tent. To give birth right in the middle of the market square."

"It's an astonishing bit of non-causal synchronicity, as Jung calls it. Your finding me this way." He touched his glass to mine.

"Tell me, Brian, what does synchronicity mean—exactly?"

He took a long swallow of wine. "Sychronicity is a seemingly accidental occurrence of a coincidental event which appears both highly improbable and yet highly significant—if I may paraphrase Arthur Koestler."

"That kind of coincidence is always happening to me. Especially lately. I can be thinking of a person and the phone will ring almost instantly with that person on the line. I've always called it mental telepathy."

He laughed. "Not the same thing. But you must be a very intuitive woman."

"I am. My intuition gets me into trouble sometimes."

"Thomas Aquinas said what the heart knows first the mind knows later."

He went on. "Dr. Jung was convinced that the deeper one goes into the unconscious by way of one's dreams, or through meditation, the more one becomes in touch with special powers."

THE BLOOD REMEMBERS ❧ 73

"What kind of powers?"

"The powers that connect one with similar happenings on many levels. Sychronicity is all about connectedness."

"Matthew's always talking about the Gaia Principle, the connectedness of every living organism on a seething, live earth. As far as dreams go, I've been recording mine for a few years."

"You're obviously in therapy, then?"

I wasn't about to tell him about the psychologist at the fertility clinic. "My former therapist in New York was Freudian, not Jungian. I know very little about Jung. But I do record my dreams."

His mischievous eyes turned serious. "Dr. Jung would have thought there might be a possibility of great danger to make the descent into the deep, dark pools of the unconscious alone. Exploring the realm of the shadow can be a frightening experience. You never know what horrors might linger there. Even Dante had Virgil's guidance as moral support." He smiled provocatively, as if to offer his services.

"I'm not afraid to go it alone," I said impatiently. "You were explaining synchronicity to me."

"Have you ever heard about Jung's Golden Beetle?"

A vision flashed—a gold scarab pinned to the collar of Mrs. Cartwright's Saint Laurent jacket. "No—please tell me," I said.

He took another long sip of wine, leaned way back in his chair and spoke. "A woman patient of Dr. Jung's was describing a dream she'd had about an ancient Egyptian beetle. As she was speaking, Dr. Jung heard a tap-tap on the windowpane. He opened the window and caught a beetle as it flew in. The woman was so stunned by the arrival of a live beetle that her psychological blocks were broken—and she could open herself to her analysis."

"What a bizarre coincidence!"

"Some of us believe that there's no such thing as coincidence. This case history was amazing because the beetle was a scarab type that hadn't been seen in that part of Europe, one that was virtually extinct. This is a good example of the link between dream image and external reality."

I felt his mesmerizing gaze, his intense, greenflecked eyes, as though he were aiming to make a believer out of me.

The bottle of wine was almost finished, though I'd barely touched my glass.

"Now tell me about yourself, Brian, are you married?"

"I was. Divorced now. One daughter. My former wife is married to a German count. Petra spends the summer holidays with her mother in a schloss near Salzburg. She's an undergraduate at St. Hilda's. She was sitting with her back to you that night in the pub."

"I thought you hadn't noticed me."

"Of course I noticed you!"

I felt my face warming. "Your daughter is lovely."

"That she is—and a bit headstrong, as well."

"Do you stay in Oxford over the summer vacation?"

"No, I have a house in the south of France, near Aigues Mortes—in the marshes of the Camargue. Rustic, to say the least. I do a great deal of riding and writing. And Petra comes for a weekend now and then. You and Matthew should come to visit one day."

"You haven't remarried, then?"

"No, I haven't." He looked at me soulfully.

A question I wished I hadn't asked.

Brian ordered dressed crab and salad followed by grilled Dover sole and the tiniest new potatoes I'd ever seen.

"Garden infanticide," he said as he speared a potato the size of a marble. "Pulling up these baby potatoes from the ground— uprooting them from Mother Earth when they're so tiny. 'Lest Flora angry at thy crime, to kill her infants in their prime.' "

Silly, I know, but I left the potatoes on my plate.

I was eager to get on to the Hautevilles. "May I ask you a question about the Normans? Just one?"

"You may."

"After the Hautevilles conquered the south of Italy and Sicily, did they continue to keep in touch with their relatives in Normandy? For instance, were marriages still arranged between Norman families in Italy and Sicily with those who had stayed on in France or settled in England after the Conquest?"

"Yes. It was taken for granted that any English Norman or French Norman family might have a relative settled in the Sicilian kingdom, just as someone today might speak casually of an uncle in India or a sister in Capetown. You should read Miss Evelyn Jamieson's paper on the subject, *Proceedings of the British Academy, 1936*."

"So a woman in Normandy could be sent to Sicily for an arranged marriage?"

He gave me a quizzical look. "Of course—it must have happened all the time. Do you have someone special in mind?"

"Oh, no," I said. "No one at all."

We talked about the Oxford of fourteen years ago and old mutual friends until we were the last people in the dining room.

"The waiter seems to be giving us the eye," I said.

He signaled for the check. While he was paying the bill, I dove into my purse for a compact. I started to flip it open but then I quickly shoved it back in my purse.

"Why did you change your mind about looking in your mirror?"

I made up a silly excuse about the British thinking it rude to powder one's nose at table.

He chuckled. "Nonsense. Come on now, Rose, don't be such a Puritan. If you knew that the Goddess Fortuna is shown with her attribute the wheel, then you must know that Aphrodite sometimes holds her mirror. Why not take a look at your lovely face? Consider Aphrodite. You're obviously dedicating all your energies to Athena. You must be your father's daughter."

"Hardly. My father died years ago when I was only twelve years old. I hardly knew him." I didn't want to pursue the subject. Besides, I was annoyed by this familiar, un-English remark uttered by a man who'd had too much wine to drink.

"Aphrodite's other attributes are the dove and the seashell," I said hoping to have the last word on the goddess's iconography even though I'd never felt very much kinship with her.

But Brian had the last word. He smiled. "And don't forget the obvious one. The rose. Aphrodite's flower."

I folded my napkin to its original creases, something I don't normally do. We stood to leave.

It seemed as though we were back at the Banbury Road roundabout in no time at all.

"Come by the house with me to have a look at my garden. I live just across the corner from Blackwell's on Holywell Street."

I hesitated a moment before I replied. "I'd like very much to see it, thank you."

❧

A bronze knocker cast as a clenched fist reached out from the cypress black door of Brian's rowhouse. Was there anything in that hand? As Brian unlocked the door, a coal-black Doberman barked and nuzzled against his master's side.

Brian stroked the growling dog. "Good boy, Luci—be nice to our lady."

I'd already backed down the steps to the curb.

Brian laughed at my cowardice. "Come on in, please. Don't be afraid of my dog. Lucifer isn't nearly as fierce as he looks."

The sitting room was stark, the few pieces of furniture uphol-
stered in a scratchy gray-brown fabric I imagined to be the color,
the texture, of a medieval hair shirt. The fitted carpet was cream-
flecked black tweed, the room's only color provided by book-
bindings in tall, glassed cases. Over the mantel hung an old
wrought iron cross, square in shape, enclosed by a circle. Not typical Georgian house decor.

Brian went to the kitchen to let out the dog.

I had a good look. Blue hyacinths, the only sign of life in the
room, stretched and curved powerful, pale jade stems toward window light. That afternoon when I bent to sniff the sybaritic scent
my stomach didn't turn.

The effect of the room was curious, weird, unlike the jumbled
rooms of dons we'd visited when we lived in Oxford.

Brian's library was eclectic—books on botany and science, phi-
losophy. An entire shelf given to poetry by T.S. Eliot and Yeats.
There were books in French and Latin, books on the Grail. On
psychiatry and dreams. Shelves of works by and about Carl Jung.

"Why don't you have a look at my collections, as well?" he said
as he returned and saw me reading titles. "Then I'll show you my
little gallery."

My eyes scanned the old oak cabinets crammed with oddities.
A small ivory-carved skeleton reclined in a miniature coffin. "German, seventeenth century," he said; a human skull, silver-mounted
and inlaid with corals and turquoise; dust-filmed hourglasses. On
a tabletop a curious snake, woven of hundreds of pieces of artic-
ulated tortoise shell, curled around until it swallowed its own tail.
I ran my finger over its simulated scales. Why I didn't flee from
that morbid setting is still beyond me. But something inside me
urged me, forced me to stay. As though this were a trial I had to
endure.

A large photograph of his daughter was on the sofa table. It was signed, "To Daddy with love-1992, Petra." She looked just like her father.

The image of a faceless surrogate mother suddenly loomed before me. I pushed it away.

The walls on either side of the gallery beyond were hung with paintings—all pertaining to death. A still life of a skull resting on a pile of books among parchment letters. A hideous scene of cannibals: one disemboweling a victim on a table, another with the bloody head of a European in his hand and, in the background, bits of his flesh being barbecued on a spit.

"By Van Kessel, a Flemish painter," Brian informed me. "My savages from the land of Gog and Magog," he said. "The land beyond Prester John's."

"Prester John?"

"Yes—his name has been bandied about ever since that film. What was it? *Raiders of the Lost Ark and The Last Crusade? Or was it Romancing the Stone?*"

He didn't give me a chance to mention the ridiculous story of Mr. Baryani's so-called Prester John ruby.

"Let me quote from Prester John's letter. 'And on the other side of the desert there is a people who live on living flesh only, be it of animal or man—and they are not afraid of death . . . and the name of this people is Gog and Magog.' "

I wondered how this attractive, brilliant man had come to be obsessed with art and objects relating to death.

"Most women who come here won't come back," he said matter-of-factly. "I'm not apologizing for my taste, but I did want you to see all of this before you get to know me better."

I thought for a moment. "It isn't everyman's taste—or every woman's, as you say. But at least you have a point of view."

"Preoccupation with death?" he laughed.

"You may, in fact, be preoccupied with life."

"You're right, I do love life, but I don't fear the end of it—because I'm sure it doesn't end. Are you a Catholic?"

"Sort of. Are *you* a Catholic?"

"No, though, like you, I was. Now I call myself a Cathar."

Somewhere I'd read that the medieval Cathars believed that a war was being waged throughout the whole of creation. A war between two equal and irreconcilable principles. Darkness and light. Spirit and matter. Good and Evil. A Manichaean religion.

He picked up the sherry decanter from a tantalus on the sideboard and poured us both a glass of dry Amontillado, the kind Matthew liked.

"Here's to eternal happiness." And then he raised his glass and exclaimed, "*Floreat* Rosa!"

I wanted to ask him how he got started on this sinister collection, but I'd already asked enough questions. I sank into the deep sofa.

As did he, right next to me.

"Matthew has been lucky," he said. "To have had you all these years since Oxford."

"I'm the lucky one," I said. "But he's not been completely lucky with me." The instant the words came out of my mouth I regretted them.

"How do you mean?"

"I mentioned earlier that we don't have children although we've always wanted them. You at least have a daughter—a beautiful one."

"For that I'm grateful, Rose. But I still say he's a lucky bloke." He stood up, jingling the coins in his pocket nervously. "Now, would you like to see the rest of the house?"

I followed him up the narrow stairwell and into Petra's bedroom. The walls were papered in the same bright, posy-sprigged print as the curtains and bedspread, making a cocoon out of the garret-ceilinged room. I was relieved by its Laura Ashley normality.

Downstairs he showed me his small library, lined floor to ceiling with more books. In the center of the room was his desk—a table covered with an old Turkish carpet. A single quilled pen lay across an ink stand. Above the desk, suspended from the ceiling, hung a conical green glass lampshade that threw a light disc upon the writing surface.

He opened a door to a small garden enclosed by high brick walls edged with jagged broken glass. Chiseled on a stone marker under the trees were the words: *Et in Arcadia Ego*. Under an elm tree, ferns and hellebore grew and clumps of bleeding heart and Solomon's Seal, with its long fronds dangling waxy pearls. "I haven't seen that growing since Providence," I told him.

"I look for unusual things to grow in this shady garden, but my garden in Aigues-Mortes is sunny. Plenty of lavender, thyme, buzzing bees, oranges and lemons. All that Provençal flora. Roses, too. Old roses, especially."

"I've always dreamed of having a garden like that—a sunny walled garden with a fountain splashing in the middle, climbing white roses all around."

"Your little *hortus conclusus*, Rose. Your earthly paradise. Since you live in California, a garden like that shouldn't be too far out of your reach."

No need to disillusion him by describing my balcony wasteland, I thought.

We talked about our favorite gardens until it was time to leave. I was expecting a call from Matthew.

When I walked into my room, I was surprised to find a vase of pale apricot-pink roses on my bedside table. Gigantic garden roses with ruffled petals, blowsy and wide open, like the one in The Rose Reborn sign. I buried my nose in their nectar, then sat at my desk and began to write.

Strange as it seems, I don't have many thoughts of wedlock. Oh, marriage seized my mind a time or two when I was eleven or twelve. But as I saw my friends marry and bear child after child—or die a screaming death while delivering—I began to dread leaving my freedom, my green meadows, my peaceful garden for a husband to whom I must devote my life.

After my mother's death, I would cry if I suddenly thought of her bent over the embroidery I have always hated. My mother had great patience when I tried to master a stitch, but my mind would wander. I was not given to planning out what went where, for I didn't really care.

Then came that day my mother's nature changed, and her eyes gazed at me without seeing. She ceased to pick up her embroidery, a coverlet of wool for my bed—golden flowers entwined in leaves of cinquefoil, with deer and squirrels and foxes and rabbits—in tawny colors that were ripe and warm and comforting. She never finished it. When last I saw it, it was half eaten by mice.

That night I dreamed about a woman who sat beneath an apple tree with a child who looked like me. Strumming her lute, she sang sweetly about travels and mountains and rainbows. She told me, "I'll sing you a song now about a woman who searched for the end of the rainbow."

The melody was pleasing to my ears and soothed me, but it was the words that pleased me most. "Don't you know? You should know, my Rosamonde, that the beginning of the rainbow, the end of the rainbow are one and the same. It depends upon where you stand, then you shall see for yourself that beginning and end are one and the same." The riddle startled me. I have yet to understand it.

It was the first dream I had remembered in a long time.

So clear to me, in its embroidery of the night. My dreams have been fragments of late, mostly of hiding in the reeds, watching longboats sail up the river under a moonless sky. Full dreams have been rare, and I do miss them. In the past, when I dreamt, I tried to remember my dreams during the day and even wrote them down on the unused pages of my Latin Psalter from St. Wandrille. I have it with me still, wrapped in linen at the bottom of my trunk. If someone were to find it, I might be accused of madness or witch-craft. Few women I know have been taught to read and write. I owe my learning to Emma, my distant cousin who left the convent at Jumièges before taking her final vows so that she might stay with us after my mother's death. She must have been nearly thirty when she came to us, with a smile that showed every one of her perfect, tiny teeth.

Perhaps she looked upon me as a challenge. She could win me over, replace my mother and, in the meantime, teach me how to read. Day after day I would study her bre-viary, then her missal and her Psalter from Jumièges. It did not take me long to learn to read. The pages—the color of clotted cream, with precisely copied letters that I never learned to do as well—were treasures that Emma kept locked in an iron box.

When my father returned from Thessalonica, he was pleased that we had spent the time this way and yet seemed to care little for her. I knew she loved him by the sadness in her eyes that followed him whenever he left the room.

Sunday morning. When I woke up, a steady rain was snapping whips against the windows. I drew the curtains and looked up and down the High. Not a soul in sight seemed to be heeding the bells of St. Mary the Virgin as they pealed for High Mass.

The phone rang. Matt, home from San Diego, where he'd had a meeting with Japanese bankers. It was one-thirty in the morning and he was tired but anxious to talk to me. He would be leaving for Japan in a few days to continue the meetings.

"How was your lunch with Brian Lambeth?" he asked me. "Did he remember me?"

"Yes, he said you were the tall, handsome blond from Brown."

He laughed.

I could just see his face turning red. "He's a strange man, though."

"What do you mean?"

"I went by his house after lunch yesterday. He's so eccentric. He collects, of all things—hold on—*memento mori*."

"*Memento mori!*"

"Anything to do with death. Macabre, isn't it? Perfectly legitimate things, you know, little carved ivory skeletons, *vanitas* paintings with skulls in them. You've seen objects like his in auction catalogs."

"One more English eccentric!"

"I was put off at first but then I forced myself to stay. He's got a daughter, an undergraduate. Beautiful."

"He's married, then."

"No longer—and no wonder, considering that collection of his. He said women are horrified by it. I tried not to be! But he does like to garden, so that's a relief. We talked about gardens and the good old days at Oxford. We have some mutual friends. Remember Jimmy Waddell?"

"Sure—Rhodes Scholar. Alabama and Braesnose."

"Anyway—Brian took me to lunch yesterday. At The Rose Reborn."

"Is the place still the same?"

"The inn sign was almost as I'd remembered it all these years."

"What have you planned for today?"

"I'm going to stay right here in my room. It's pouring rain and I've got a good book . . . and I may do some writing."

"Writing?"

"Yes—in the notebook you gave me." I reminded him. "It wasn't a sketchbook."

"I'm glad you're using it for a trip journal, then. I hope you'll let me read it when you come home."

When I hung up I got up to turn on the gas fire, went through my joss stick ritual, then climbed right into bed to read about Frederick II. The rain was beating down in slanted gray sheets. I kneaded the red velvet cushion to restore its fragrance, tucked it behind my head, and listened.

 As we journey toward Palermo, I remember the evening before Christ's Mass. All during last year's season of Michaelmas, the hall was strewn with fresh rushes from the marsh, dried lavender, hyssop and germander, costmary and rosemary from my garden. We cut them to make our rooms smell fresh and clean during the feasting days. New tallow candles were skivered to pricket sticks around the hall to burn during the vigil. Grouse and quail and lardy pies were baking, and rabbit stew simmered in cider and cream.

But for me it was not a happy season.

My father dined with me on that night before the vigil. He told me, as we watched chestnuts crackling in the cinders, that he planned to marry Emma. I was enraged but dared not show it. How could he do this to me? Why? I was so sure that he had not noticed her in the way she noticed him.

"Rosamonde," he said, "I am lonely for a wife. Emma is a good and patient woman. I have made up my mind."

And so they wed in a quiet ceremony, and I did force myself to accept Emma as a mother after those hateful feelings passed.

Then I began to think that perhaps she would bear him children. The thought of my father in his bed with her made me sick. I prayed—selfishly—that there would be no children by their marriage.

A few months after their wedding, my father and his new wife left for Sicily to be in service to King William in Palermo. My aunt, Lady de Hauteville, came from Coutances to mind the household. And when I came of age I would manage the castle that for many years had belonged to my mother's family. I was young but the castle was my home and so I learned to care for it. And I learned to live without parents and to rely upon myself.

From time to time, word sent by father comes to me from a pilgrim who has journeyed to Apulia. King William had given my father, as an award for his fealty, a small castle in Apulia just three days sea journey from Palermo. I sometimes try to imagine what life is like there, but I have never wished to journey to such a distant place. Perhaps I am too content, too busy running the castle and tending my little garden.

A few years after they were wed, my father lost Emma to a high fever that took many lives during the scorch of summer. We learned that he survived his own fever and buried Emma by the cathedral in Trani in a grave facing the sea.

And now he has called for me, having decided to join me and his lands to another. He has not told me who is to be my husband, though he surely has already made his choice. I hope that my betrothed will be kind to me and even love me.

At two o'clock that afternoon when Brian Lambeth called, I tried not to sound as though he'd just awakened me.

"I was just sitting down to write you a note thanking you for lunch yesterday—and for the beautiful roses."

"What roses?"

What a relief he couldn't see my face flush. "When I went up to my room last night I found some gorgeous roses in a vase. Old-fashioned roses. Like the one in The Rose Reborn sign. I really . . . ."

"Matthew must be a very thoughtful husband."

"Well—yes, he is," I said, trying to cover up my embarrassment. Strange that Matthew hadn't mentioned the roses when we spoke this morning.

"Why don't you come by later for a light supper. Do you like baked beans on toast?" He chuckled. "Or would you rather have a 'toad in the hole'?"

Neither sounded appealing. "That's very kind of you," I said, "but I think I'll just stay in and read all about Frederick."

"I can tell you more about what you've come to Oxford to learn," he said. "I've gone far beyond old Kantorowicz."

"Will you tell me more about your Michael Scot?"

"Of course. Come by however you are, whenever—"

"I'm in jeans."

"Don't change. But wear a warm sweater. I'll come fetch you in the car."

"It's not raining now and I really could use some exercise," I said.

By the time I reached Holywell Street it was dusk. A thin mist had fallen over Oxford. I lifted the clenched hand and let it swing back hard against the door. I heard Lucifer's barks.

Brian, wearing corduroys and an old Aran Island cardigan, opened it.

"Please come in. Don't worry. Luci's in the garden," he said with a bow and sweep of his hand. He looked as if he'd just shaved. I had a whiff of vetiver and musk—and something else I didn't recognize.

Light shone from one lamp. The room was dim. Smoke from the smoldering fire and the sound of a melancholy Gregorian chant made me feel as though I should genuflect.

"How would you like a White Lady? I just mixed a pitcher."

"What's in it?"

"Gin, Cointreau, egg white. Tastes of oranges. Someone told me the drink is named after The White Lady of Avenel, a character in a novel by Sir Walter Scott."

"I'd better stick to sherry."

Brian had a stony glitter in his eye. I was sure he'd already had more than one drink. But his voice was steady.

"I don't want to bore you with my taste in music." He removed the Gregorian CD and replaced it with another. "This is a bit less somber—the *Carmina Burana*. Do you know it?"

I closed my eyes and listened. "That's the Rafael Kubelik recording, isn't it?"

"How in the devil's name did you know that?"

"I have all the recent recordings—and some old ones. I'd been playing them a lot before I left home. Where's Petra?"

"She's gone off to Prague to visit an aunt. Don't worry."

"I'm not the least bit worried," I said, wishing it were true. "May I help you in the kitchen?"

"Thanks, but I've already cooked our dinner. Come, have a look."

He checked the roasting meat in the Aga cooker. Simmering on a burner was an earthenware pot of spring vegetables, on the counter, a glass bowl of young lettuces and mustard cress and my favorite deep-dish apple pie. A bottle of uncorked claret sat on a silver wine coaster.

"I thought you were serving 'toad in the hole'."

He smiled and looked at me wickedly. "I misled you. I can transform Sunday's joint into bubble and squeak for Monday's dinner. Come back tomorrow night for some. It's my specialty."

"Thanks—but I don't want to wear out my welcome."

"You couldn't do that, Rose."

He poured sherry the color of liquid carnelians into a crystal glass.

"To your research." He raised his glass of frothy White Lady.

"Thanks for all your help," I said.

"Now what would you like to know about Michael Scot?"

"Anything you want to tell me. I'm curious to know what he had to do with my Hautevilles."

"Why your Hautevilles?"

"I . . . seem to know one of them very well."

"Which one?"

"One you probably haven't heard of."

"I doubt that," he said. "What makes you think so?"

"Because . . . well . . ." I stammered. "Tell me about Michael Scot."

"All right. Here goes," he said. "Michael Scot attended

Oxford, wherever Oxford was in the late twelfth century. Probably right up the street near Merton. He came from Fifeshire—in northwest Scotland—probably a mixture of Celtic and Viking blood. For many years that coast was raided by Vikings from the Orkney Islands.

"Legend has it that Scot was supposed to have worn an iron hat at all times because he prophesied that he would be killed by a falling stone, and alas, so he was. One day while attending Mass, he took off his hat at the Elevation of the Host, and a loose stone fell from the ceiling—right on his noggin—and killed him."

I leaned forward in my chair, held in thrall by story and storyteller.

"Frederick II most likely met him in Bologna when Scot was in his fifties. Scot admired Frederick's brilliance, his Renaissance mind, two hundred years before the Renaissance. And surely Frederick admired Scot for his scholarship.

"You see, I've always suspected that Scot had a great influence over Frederick. Probably inspired him to build Castel del Monte in Apulia, that mystical perfection of geometry in architecture."

"I plan to see it when I go on to Apulia. My relatives live in Vieste, which isn't too far away."

"Let me take the roast from the oven before I say anymore. I'll be right back."

While he rattled around in the kitchen, I settled back on the sofa. The fire was blazing, crackling, the smoke had subsided. Tall shadows leaped around the room.

Brian walked in and poured another White Lady. "I've been researching documents from the Ben Sira collection in the old Bodleian, as well as other manuscripts tucked away, still untranslated. Not so long ago a letter addressed to the Emperor Frederick was discovered, in Hebrew—another of the many legendary Prester John letters. At first we thought it was addressed to

Frederick's grandfather, Barbarossa, but we've now decided that this letter was written to Frederick II."

"What would a letter in Hebrew from Prester John have to do with Michael Scot? Or Frederick—or the Altavilla, for that matter? Who exactly was Prester John? Not too long ago I came across a ruby in Los Angeles, supposedly handed down from his treasure."

Brian slapped his knee, threw back his head and laughed. "Just as I told you, Rose. Ever since those Indiana Jones films . . ."

I was serious. "I've always thought that Prester John was a legend."

"Yes—he has become exactly that, but someone had to have written that first letter. Who was that person? That's what I'm trying to find out in my research. There's a missing link somewhere. Maybe you'll discover some clue for me."

"Hardly. I can read a little Latin, some French. But—"

"No Greek?" His malicious little smile let me know he was teasing me.

"Sorry, no Greek," I laughed.

"Never mind," he said. "There are letters from Prester John in just about every other language, but none has ever been found in Greek. Which is odd, because the original letter was supposedly sent to Manuel Comnenus, the Byzantine Emperor whose language was of course Greek. Manuel had promised his daughter Maria's hand to the king of Sicily, William Altavilla. Have you come across him in your reading?"

I nodded. "William was the last Hauteville king. He had no heirs, so he relinquished the Norman throne to his aunt, Constance de Hauteville."

"And Frederick II was her son," Brian said. This time his gaze was penetrating. "Tell me, why has Frederick become such a hero for you, Rose?"

I felt the blood in my face. "Are you joking? My hero?"

"Maybe he's the hero animus at work within you. The tough, adventuresome, questing side of Rose Kirkland that even she may not be aware of, although I am," he said with a grin. "And your fascination with Tancred de Hautville and all his sons!"

"You're starting to sound like my old therapist," I said, alarmed by my defensiveness. "Let's talk about your missing link. Have you found any clues?"

"A few, but intuition tells me you're going to uncover another for me."

"Are you kidding? Here in Oxford? I'm flattered that you think so, but I'm no scholar, Brian."

"I saw your slender ankles in those blue stockings the day you came to my office."

"Worn only for warmth," I laughed. "Well—you may be right. Maybe it was wishful thinking on my part. I've always wanted to be a bluestocking."

He stood up and offered his arm. "Shall we go in to dinner? We'll start with our salad first. California style."

When Brian had eaten half the apple pie and finished all the claret, he said, "Tell me, now—you're a jewelry designer, have you any interest in gemstones and their magical properties?"

"Now and then Mr. Baryani, a gem merchant from Jaipur, shows me unusual stones. I've learned a lot about the mystical properties of gemstones from him. Strange that only a few weeks ago he showed me this fabulous, so-called 'Prester John' ruby—I still get gooseflesh whenever I think about it. The stone had a powerful, almost mystical effect on me."

This time he looked serious. "Then let me read something to you. Stay right here while I go to turn on the coffee—and find a book."

He had replayed the *Carmina Burana*. I curled up on the sofa, staring into the fire, listening to the Courts of Love from side B.

Lucia Popp's haunting high soprano voice filled the room.
I translated the Latin words in my head.

In the balance of my feelings
set against each other
lascivious love and modesty.
But I choose what I see,
and submit my neck to the sweet yoke;
I yield to the sweet yoke.

I looked up through misty eyes to see Brian standing beside me, book in hand.

"*In Trutina Mentis Dubia. In the wavering balance,* that's what she's singing," he said. "Do you have Streisand's old recording?"

"I do. I love it. I once told Matthew it was the sort of thing I'd want to have sung at my funeral."

"Do you think about death a lot?"

"Especially when I hear something as beautiful as this." I then admitted to him that these past two years death was never very far from my mind. "My father died of heart failure when he was forty. I have this haunting fear that I will never live beyond forty . . . ."

"You of all people! An obviously healthy woman so vibrant, so full of life. You're going through a passage we must all go through in middle years. It's change we fear. And, too, as we get older we must begin to face death. Look at it squarely. My dear Rose, you mustn't be afraid." He took my hands in his and murmured, " 'so the darkness shall be the light, and the stillness the dancing'." Then he put his arm around me as the soprano's voice floated on the last poignant note of *In trutina*. "Don't you know what those words mean?"

I lied. "I've forgotten. I just remember some of the lyrics from side A."

"These words aren't about courtly love, or worshipping a lady from afar. This song is about a woman who must make the choice between libidinous love and modesty. There's nothing sad about that, Rose."

Again, those intense eyes.

"Did you find your book?"

He sank down on the sofa close by me. He held up a wine-red volume. *The Hebrew Letters of Prester John.*[1]

"It's been translated into English. May I read to you?" he asked in his melodious voice. "Since you're intrigued with gemstones, this should appeal."

I sat back to listen.

"This is the text of the letter which Prester John sent to Frederick, Emperor of Rome. By the will of God I send you peace and friendship to the exalted Frederick of Rome."

He turned to another page of the text,

"And you may know that there are in our country some who take fishes similar to those from which one dyes the purple.

"And you may know that our palace is made like the palace which Godfrey of India had built. And the entry of the palace is made of wood called ebony which cannot burn; and at the top of the palaces are two capitals of gold . . . and upon each of them are two stones called carbuncles, because the gold shines by day and the carbuncles by night.

"And our big stones are of sardonyx, surrounded by jewels . . . All the windows are of bdellium—and the table at which we eat is amethyst, and the stones on which the tables rest are of ivory . . . and the room in which we are resting is made of gold and pearls, and a candlestick of gold burns inside it, and in it are scents, and another candlestick of gold burns in the palace in which we hold our court and feasts, and there are in it the best smells in the world and of the best spices in order to create in it a good smell."

I laughed. "I burn my joss sticks for a similar effect."

He read on. *"And the bed on which we lie is sapphire . . . and also we possess a table at which we eat made of emerald, and it has the faculty that no one can get drunk during the meal."*

"Could I use an emerald table like that!" Brian added.

When he finished, I applauded. "Do you have any idea when the first letter was written?"

"The first real mention we have of a letter received from Prester John is the one addressed to Pope Alexander III in 1177. The Pope was staying near the Rialto in Venice after his famous meeting with the Emperor Barbarossa at San Marco.

"You see, Rose, medieval minds yearned to hear of a world far beyond their own—far richer, far more exotic than Byzantium. A world enormously wealthy and powerful—yet led by a good and Christian prince. Why don't you take the book with you tonight and give it a good read? Unless . . ." He moved closer, putting his arm around me.

I disengaged myself. "Let's go to the kitchen. I'll help you with the washing up."

I started to get up from the sofa, but he drew me back.

"The cleaning woman comes tomorrow morning—she'll straighten up." He grasped me to him, his hands cinching my waist. "The moment I saw you in my office, Rose, I . . . Well, I haven't felt this way about a woman in a very long time. You don't know how lovely you are—how sensual. So sincere—and vulnerable. But I sense your distance. I wish I could find a way of snapping the band that holds you away from me." He reached up and deftly unclipped the barrette holding the hair back from my face. He ran his long fingers through its length. "See how the firelight burnishes it to copper," he whispered.

My eyes closed. I was hypnotized, under the spell of his voice that seemed to echo from far away.

"When you close your eyes that way, I feel that you're mine. Do you hear me, Rose? Mine." His hand clasped my arm tight. It hurt.

My body remained motionless, immobilized.

"Rose, Rose—you're beautiful with your lovely skin, as though you've been dusted with gold from an alchemist's mortar. Everything about you gives me pleasure."

He moved closer, his late-day stubble grazing my cheek.

The spell was broken. I wrenched away.

"I'm flattered that you find me attractive—and I won't deny that you are to me, but I didn't come to Oxford for romance. I'm still in love with my husband, even though I haven't had much of myself to give to him—or anyone else—these past few years." I put my hand on his arm. "Can we just be friends?"

He grasped my wrist. "Of course I'll be your friend. 'Rose of all roses, Rose of the world,' Rosamonde—"

"Why on earth did you call me Rosamonde?" I said abruptly.

"It's a line from Yeats." He shook his head. "You're a perfect rose, but far too serious, you know."

I laughed. "Just look around at this room. You can't say you're not serious."

"I am. But at least I know when to let go, relax, and enjoy life a bit."

By drinking, I thought.

"Come on," he said, the next moment, "I'll take your offer to help with the washing up." He stood, jingling his coins again.

We went into his brightly lit kitchen that looked like a wizard's laboratory, with rows of Pyrex glass beakers, bowls and alembic-like bottles along the shelves of an old Welsh cupboard. He had already scraped and rinsed the dishes.

He took an apron from a peg and looped it over my head, wrapped it around my waist and tied it.

I washed. He dried.

"Come on—I'd like to show you something else," he said when

we were finished. "Maybe it will make you feel better about being with me."

He led me down the corridor to another room, opened the door and flicked on the light.

His bedroom was dead white. Unpigmented white. On one wall hung a long narrow scroll, almost as tall as I. The symbols painted on it gave me pleasurable shivers.

"It's an alchemical chart. By Sir George Ripley. Yorkshire," Brian said.

I moved closer. "When was it painted?"

"Around 1570. This is a facsimile of one in the Bodleian."

"Those strange signs—what are they all about?"

"The quest for the rubedo—the ruby. In one of his seminars, Dr. Jung referred to the rubedo as the heart of Cybele, the great goddess of the Mediterranean. In the Middle Ages it was called the philosopher's stone. Can you find the rubedo at the very top—exploding from the alchemist's beaker?"

I moved even closer. Reading from the very bottom I saw a crouched, curled dragon carrying a silver-black crescent moon on its back. Above the moon shone a golden sun-in-splendor. In its center were what looked like three coins connected by a triangle of silver threads.

Above these was a peculiar bird perched upon a globe. The bird had a human face, a bearded man's face.

"What's he supposed to represent?" I asked pointing to the strange symbol.

"The bird of Hermes is my name, eating my wings to make me tame." He smiled. "At least that's the way I read it."

Above the bird a pair of lions guarded the portal, then a double-tailed melusina like the one I'd sketched. And above the melusina what seemed to be an eight-sided castle with Adam and Eve in its center, the snake seductively spiraling the tree trunk between.

Down each side of this puzzling chart, I saw feathers floating past four flasks of the elements, clearly marked Earth, Air, Fire, Water.

"What strange symbols! Mysterious. Do you know what they mean?" I asked.

"They're alchemical images. Images experienced in dreams and visions. Symbols that connect the individual with the rest of mankind."

I turned to Brian. "I've always thought that alchemy was about turning base metals into gold."

"There are many goals in alchemy. The quest for the wholeness of spirit and discovery of the self is one. In this chart the rubedo, the ruby, is a symbol for wholeness of the self through feeling."

"Wholeness of the self through feeling? I've always believed that I would feel whole by conceiving and bearing a child."

He shook his head. "I can assure you, Rose, a woman can bear children and still not feel whole. My former wife, for one. Being whole has to do with facing the shadow in one's self—the part of the self that most people never get to know. The uncivilized, unacceptable, aboriginal part of themselves that they reject."

"Is the discovery of the ruby—the philosopher's stone—at the end of the journey like the birth of a child, then? An alchemical child?"

"You've got the idea."

I stood on tiptoe to study the ruby, the philosopher's stone, the culmination of this quest for wholeness of the self.

I wondered if I should remind him yet again of Mr. Baryani's mysterious ruby—the ruby the horseman held in his hand, but I restrained myself. It was getting late and, besides, I didn't want to court disaster any longer than I had to.

As we walked through the dim hallway, he stopped to point out a polychromed wood sculpture of the Virgin, placed on a stone plinth. A spotlight beamed on her metal mandorla decorated with carved and silvered wood roses. The double Madonna, carved on both sides, was standing on a crescent moon. On one side she held the infant in her arms. On the other side her arms were empty. An ominous black bird spread its wings over her head.

"She's lovely, isn't she?" said Brian, noticing my gaze. "Years ago I bought her in Toulouse. She's a processional figure, meant to be affixed to a long pole and carried aloft so she can be seen on both sides by the crowd. Walk around her, have a look."

"She is lovely," I said. "But disturbing. Why?"

"Because there are two sides to her. Like me. You see, Rose, within me the line between the sacred and profane is as thin as the proverbial razor's edge." He smiled. "I am not yet prepared to take the Cathar *Consolamentum,* to reject the world of the Prince of Darkness for the Light of God."

I smiled. "Saint Augustine said, 'Make me chaste, Lord—but not yet.'"

"You're right, darling Rose—but not yet!"

We laughed together.

"Pax," he said.

"Pax," I answered, taking both his hands in mine.

He put his arm around me—this time without fervor, but with loving kindness.

"Come on—let me walk you home, then. It's late—I'll get your coat."

When we reached the Lily and Crown, he grasped my arm and led me up the steps to my room.

"Please, Brian, I can let myself in."

"No, I'm only curious to see what your room is like—and the roses Matthew sent you. Don't worry. We're friends, remember?"

He opened the door. My slight disorder had been tidied, the bed turned down. I was embarrassed that a sheer nightgown, my best, one I'd never worn—had been swirled and puffed enticingly around the turned-back bedcovers. The maid must have taken it from the drawer. The nightgown was a wedding gift, and I'd kept it for some special occasion that had yet to arrive.

The roses weren't in the room. I looked in the bathroom. Not there, either.

"Perhaps the maid took them out for the night," I concluded. "They sometimes do that, you know." I rang the front desk. "Mavis, may I have my bouquet of roses, please? The maid must have taken them out for the night."

"Roses? I don't think so. We never take flowers from a room unless they're dead."

"But they were delivered yesterday. I found them when I returned last night."

"We had no flower deliveries yesterday."

"How could that be? Roses in a crystal vase were on my bed table when I returned from . . . how strange. Well, thanks anyway." I turned to look him straight in the eye. "I know there were roses here this morning."

"Not to worry, Rose. Tomorrow's almost here. We'll spend it together at the Bodleian—I'll be your guide through the library system."

He kissed the top of my head. "You're very tired. You won't need 'poppy nor mandragora' to make you sleep tonight." He kissed my cheek and held my hand tight for a moment before leaving.

❧

I stood by the door he had closed behind him. Was I going all the way around the bend? Flowers beside my bed when there had been none?

My body was weary. I kicked off my shoes. Off came the gold bracelets. I yanked off my jeans and sweater and underwear. I slipped on the silk nightgown. It felt cool on my skin as it slid down my body.

And there on the carpet, no longer hidden by the nightgown, I saw a petal—a pink rose petal. I picked it up, rubbed it between my fingers and felt its velvety smoothness.

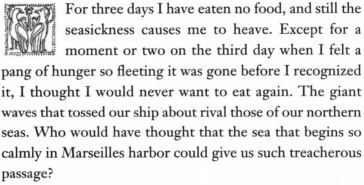 For three days I have eaten no food, and still the seasickness causes me to heave. Except for a moment or two on the third day when I felt a pang of hunger so fleeting it was gone before I recognized it, I thought I would never want to eat again. The giant waves that tossed our ship about rival those of our northern seas. Who would have thought that the sea that begins so calmly in Marseilles harbor could give us such treacherous passage?

I do not remember much else about the remainder of the voyage between Genoa and Palermo. Blaise de Hauteville says that I burned with fever and that my skin jaundiced yellow as Sicilian lemons. Editha forced all kinds of potions through my lips and lay herbal poultices across my forehead. A woman they call a *strega*, who frightens away the evil eye, sat with me for hours, pressing cold, flat steel blades against my forehead to draw away the fever's heat. They say that I called out for my dead mother and for my father, and that I raved. They do not tell me what I raved about.

When the fever lessened and I could recognize the faces around me, we seemed to be sailing along a coast so beautiful that when I saw it my body began slowly to heal itself. Surely I found myself in paradise. Gnarled olive trees grew silver-smoke green to salt-white beaches and clear blue sea. Almond trees stretched bud-swollen branches against a cloudless sky. The sun seemed warm for March, the air balmy to my skin. When they carried me to the deck to breathe in clean dry air, Editha was happy to see me smiling.

At last we drop anchor in the harbor of the Golden Shell, as they call the Sicilian city of Panormus, a port crowded with ships and galleys from all Christian nations and from Outremer as well.

I know now that I have come to a country more wondrous than my own. In a few moments I will at last see my father. I am strong enough to be the first to run ashore to embrace him. The wide oak planks stretch down across the face of our ship. I hope that I will never have to sail again, except perhaps to sail home— not even in a halcyon sea.

Crowds throng about as we make our way down the dock. I stare ahead at all the waving folk, looking for my tall father in his shiny mail. I cannot hold back my tears when I do not find him there to greet me.

An old crusader stooped with age and grizzled comes limping forward. "Welcome to Norman soil, Rosamonde de Roland. I bring greetings from your father, Seigneur Robert. Two months past he was called to arms in Thessalonica by King William."

I weep that I will not see him now. Editha puts her arms around me to console, "come now, Rosamonde—you must understand your father's fealty to King William. His heart must surely be as sore as yours."

Then Editha falls upon the ground to kiss it. "Rosamonde," she says, "I vow to the good Lord to one day make a pilgrimage to the Monte Sant'Angelo, as holy a place as our own shrine to St. Michael in Normandy. We will journey there to give thanks for our safe voyage."

"But where," I ask, "is the knight I am to marry?"

CHAPTER SIX

IN THE MIDDLE OF THE NIGHT I woke up damp with sweat, kicked off all the bed-covers, slipped off my nightgown and tossed it clear across the room. What did Rosamonde want from me? I lay in bed, dazed, listening to night sounds. The bed made creaking noises I'd never heard before, the radiator clanged, wind whistled around corners. I was sure I heard rats scratching, gnawing behind the baseboards. I must have fallen asleep toward dawn.

Mavis woke me. "Good-morning call, Mrs. O.K. Seven o'clock. Quite cold outside, we had frost this morning."

I leaped out of bed shivering and grabbed my robe. Something glistened on the swath of ivory silk on the floor.

I picked it up.

The silken petal had turned to fragile, beaten gold, quivering as though it were alive in the palm of my hand. Simon and Mavis were playing tricks on me. I smiled and carefully laid the petal on the night table.

As I stood under the shower I began to sing Mimi's aria from *La Boheme*. "*Germoglia in un vaso una rosa . . . foglia a foglia la spiro*—I gaze at each petal, one by one."

While I applied some lip gloss I took a good look in my travel mirror.

The freckles across my nose were "like gold dust sprinkled from an alchemist's mortar." Brian's words. Not bad, I thought. For the first time in a long while I liked what I saw in the glass. I was feeling alive again. The Rose Revived. It was time to begin my research.

As I set the mirror on the sink, it fell flat on its face to the floor. Apprehensively I picked it up. The glass was shattered yet intact, a web of splinters bound by a rigid metal ring.

"Come on, Rose, pull yourself together—it's only a mirror, after all."

The phone rang. It was Brian. "Can you meet me for coffee, around the corner at the Mitre? Afterward I'll show you the ropes, introduce you to the librarians at the Bodleian."

"Thanks, I'll be there as soon as I finish getting dressed."

I left my room and turned the key, then remembered the rose petal. Just one more look at it before I left for the day. I unlocked the door and went back inside, but the golden petal was no longer on the table.

 Editha tries to calm me, as does kind Blaise de Hauteville. He tells me "you will be taken to a castle beyond the city. Your knight will greet you there."

Then I am helped onto a mare—not so clumsy a horse as I was used to riding at home but supple and graceful and saddled with decorated leather. Bells pealed. Children run to greet us as we make our way through narrow streets. I ride as the bride of the knight my father had chosen, the knight for whom I'd journeyed so far from home in Normandy. Here in Sicily at last, this strange, new world: Genoese and Amalfitans dressed in bright tunics of soft wool, Greek sailors, black men from Africa—the first I have ever seen.

We enter city walls. Inside are stalls with merchants hawking wares—piles of rabbit skins, bales of bombex haggled over by Genoese merchants, baskets of wheat spilling golden tassels on the ground, piles of precious pepper, wizened old women sitting cross-legged beside mounds of red and yellow spices, stalks of tall sugar cane they said was sweeter than honey—all these things I see for the first time.

The streets are not as filthy as at home. But when we pass the fish market by the docks, the putrid offal of tunny makes me retch. The horse path is smeared with blood and silvery fish-scale slime. Salted cod hangs board-stiff drying in the sun. Cuttlefish and spiny sea creatures and red gold mullet are heaped in wicker baskets.

Blaise points out rich Lombards and elegant Saracen ladies carried in litters, and bearded Jews, who are much respected for their knowledge. I hear the cries of the muezzin from the minarets. An old Greek priest passes, bearing a long board over his shoulder, calling his people to worship by tapping it with a small hammer.

Women wear layers of cloudy fabric spun, they tell me, from the cocoons of worms, colored stuffs so sheer I see the light shine through. Hawkers sell golden fruit that I have never seen before, balls the color of gillyflowers or egg yolks—oranges, Editha calls them. As I ride to meet my betrothed, my disappointment and homesickness turn to excitement.

After passing through the city gates, we stop. I am bid to come down from my horse. There, for as far as my eye can see, are trees of greenest green laden with yellow lemons I have heard of but not seen before. The air wafts a fresh, sweet smell. We walk a few steps to a way station, where a tall man meets us. His head is wrapped in white linen, his eyes are paler blue than mine, his pink cheeks soft and downy, his lips pouty, full. "Hold still, for I must wrap your wrists." His voice is shrill, like a nagging woman's. He does not greet me or tell me who he is. Instead he grasps my hands and quickly knots my wrists together with long white cords while two other men hold my shoulders.

"Please," I shout, "please let me go! What have I done to merit this?"

"Not to worry, Rosamonde. You shall not be harmed. 'Tis for your own good."

Editha screams for me. "Let her go! Let her go!"

Then they hood my eyes tight with black cloth, like a falcon, and lift me to sit upon a chair. As I fall against deep, soft cushions of a litter, I smell a scent like sweet herbs. Then, rocking to and fro, I am carried to meet my groom in this outlandish way. I can hear people shouting as we pass. At last we halt, and then it is strangely quiet. In the distance I hear dogs barking, bells tolling—and, louder than either of these, my heart pounding in my chest. I am lifted from the perfumed chair and led up steps, then more steps to a place where I hear running water, jingling bells, and the sounds of plucked strings. I catch the familiar smell of the eglantine that grows on the stone wall by the castle at home—but here it is much stronger, as if hundreds of blossoms are growing together, bloom on bloom. I hear a door open and close, soft footsteps padding on the floor.

The music stops. Now I hear only water flowing. Though my eyes are tightly bound, I can feel eyes all upon me.

I hear a man's voice say, in my own language, "I have seen her now. Take her to her chamber."

Door latches open. Doors are closed. I am led some distance.

The black scarf is unknotted from my head.

I am not prepared for what I see before me.

The room is not large but far grander than any I have ever seen. The floor is inlaid with colored stone; the wood ceilings patterned like a honeycomb, gilded and painted; the walls hung with silvered silk the color of powdered ripe plums, windows enclosed with panels of pierced wood. Ribbons of smoke curl from a copper brazier. Piled about on divans are cushions gleaming with golden threads. I see pearly glass bowls heaped with strange fruit.

A slender, black-haired woman enters the room. "Don't be frightened, Rosamonde." She begins to unfasten my cloak. "You will remove your clothes now. My name is Irene. I will help you."

"Where am I?" My voice sounds hollow and far away.

"You are at Favara, one of the King's palaces. They are strung around the hills that encircle Palermo, like pearls around the throat of a woman."

"How can I be at the palace of the King?"

"You are here because of the King."

"But I do not know him."

"You will."

Where is Blaise de Hauteville? Where is Editha? Why have they abandoned me? And most of all, where is my betrothed?

Night falls. I press my hands against the cushions to push myself up from the divan, but I fall back too weak and dizzy to sit as yet.

Irene bends to help me. "Rest, My Lady. The dizziness will pass. You will see. Tomorrow you will stroll in the garden with me."

I have no strength to argue with her. Bells toll in the distance.

When I open my eyes, the room is dark but warm from the glowing stones of the brazier. Strange spices thicken the air.

A soft coverlet lies smooth and weightless on my body. Irene sits close by, cross-legged, sniffing vapor from a silver bowl.

"Breathe in, My Lady. 'Tis the oil of neroli."

I take a long, deep breath and my head seems suddenly to clear.

"What is neroli?" I ask.

"Oil pressed from orange and lemon blossoms of Trinacria."

"Trinacria?"

"Another name for Sicily."

In the center of the room is a tub into which water seems to flow from nowhere. Irene pours from an ewer. Oil makes a shimmering green film upon the water. I shudder as I step in, thinking it might be cold, but it is tepid and feels refreshing to my skin, which has not known water in many weeks.

Irene sponges my back and rinses my hair and body with a scented liquid, then scrubs and scrubs until I protest.

When she is content that I am clean enough, she rinses me with clear water from copper buckets, then rubs my body with a great, coarse linen towel until I am red and dry.

She pares my toenails and fingernails close with a small silver knife, then takes a swansdown feather and flicks me all over with what looks like the flour we grind from barley corn. Through all this strangeness, I am compliant.

"You have lovely breasts," she says lifting them in her hands, almost as if to weigh them. I push her hands away.

She unfolds a robe of pale rose-colored sheer silk, places it over my head and draws my arms through its sleeves.

"Now you are like a Damascus rose," she tells me. She slips a sash of plaited golden thread around my waist and ties it loosely.

Then I feel such wretched shame for she bids me to lie upon the cushioned pallet and begins to pluck all my body's hair except that hair which grows upon my head. When I cry out, she slaps me gently and gives me something sweet to chew. She claims that it will ease my pain. I fall asleep while she is finishing her task.

When I awake, Irene lights the glass oil lamps and hoists them to the ceiling. I gaze at the shadows wondering how long it will be before day breaks.

At last she says, "you may look out the window now."

What a sight I see below! A lake with a pavilion set in its center, flaring torches, figures garbed in golden, glowing robes. Tall, pointed trees ring the lake. A crescent moon hangs low in the sky.

The door opens and a honey-skinned girl bows her way in. She carries a tray of quinces and medlars and blushing apples made of almond paste.

She kneels before me then backs her way out.

Three black-skinned girls follow with more trays. They pour blood-red orange juice and pomegranate syrups from ewers. I taste sweetmeats, nougats of almond, flaky pastry filled with honey and studded with pine nuts. Roasted birds, quail and pigeon, perch daintily on white linen napkins, and bits of skewered lamb. Platters are piled with dried figs, melons.

Before long I am feasting. My eyes feast, too, on the beauty of the food before me. At home, livestock and fowl were served in chunks or slabs that recalled too easily their careless butchery.

I eat all I can and sip tisane poured from a golden ewer. Then I fall asleep.

This is how I spend my first day in Palermo. No one has yet come to claim me as a bride.

CHAPTER SEVEN

BRIAN WAS WAITING for me at a corner table of the Elizabethan oak-paneled coffee shop at the Mitre Hotel.

He stood as I walked in and gallantly offered a chair. "How do you feel this morning? After the way I behaved last night, I got very little sleep. I hope you did."

"Not much. I had a terrible night, too."

"Frightening dreams?"

"May I have a double coffee?" I replied.

He explained the morning's plan to me. "And tonight you can tell me all about it over the bubble and squeak. You'll like it. I cook it up myself."

Bubble and squeak again: it had always had a witchy sound for me. "No, thanks, Brian." I smiled and gave his arm a gentle pat. "I don't think so—and not because I wouldn't like your bubble and squeak."

"You're wary of me—I sense it."

"I'm not the least bit wary of you. I'll be reading tonight—and every night from now on. I've been here for almost a week, and it's time to begin what I came here to do."

We walked to the Bodleian, where I chose a table that would be mine for the stay. Brian guided me through the maze of stacks, then opened his battered briefcase and handed me a bibliography he'd prepared.

"You can start with these sources—they should have all of them right here. If not, we'll go over to Merton or Corpus Christi. One day when you have the time, I'll take you to the vault here at the Bodleian, show you our Prester John letter to Frederick II—and the manuscript of Frederick's great Sicilian Questions . . . Remember, Rose, you know where I am if you need me. Ring me up any time."

"I can't thank you enough—it's good to know I have a friend close by."

"You have no idea how it feels to me to have you nearby—so near and yet so far," he said with a wickedly suggestive glance. "Good luck!"

He left me there happily flipping through card files and taking notes. Later that same afternoon, I came across an eighteenth-century history of William II Altavilla written by Francesco Testa, in Latin and Italian. I had a hard time translating the Italian, with all those *S*'s that look like *F*'s, but I was overjoyed because I'd found a real connection between William II and Vieste. I learned that King William the Good had given the counties of Monte Sant'Angelo and Vieste to Joanna, his wife and Queen, as a wedding present. Joanna was the daughter of Henry II of England and Eleanor of Aquitaine.

Il Re Concedette	The king conceded
Il fuedo contea	the feudal counties
Il Monte Sant'Angelo	of Monte Sant'Angelo
e di Vieste	and of Vieste
alla sposa regina	to his bride and Queen

❧

I spent most of the next week researching in Duke Humphrey's library. From my desk, I could look out to the lofty oaks and the shady garden of Exeter College. I kept my books overnight so I could continue work each morning without re-calling them. I was cozy in my little carrel, working among students and scholars, the hum of conversation all around—none of that sacrosanct library silence here.

One day I made still another discovery. In a hundred-year-old philological journal I came across a theory written by a German scholar. He believed that William Altavilla might have been a troubadour and poet, rewriting the poetry of a Norman poet and subject, Grandor of Brie, to suit his Sicilian Norman subjects. An offbeat theory, maybe preposterous to other scholars, but I was pleased with myself for finding it.

The Tower in Lucera

T HE EMPEROR still sleeps. A cricket chirps behind the arras. Michael Scot puts down his pen, rises from his writing table and shakes the heavy cloth. Blessed silence. From a pierced coconut shell he sprinkles powder on the pergamon sheets to hasten drying, then fans them with a gilded leather fan from Cordoba. Or is it from Salamanca? Or Toledo? Alas—so many years now since Toledo. Thirty, to be exact. And fifteen since his old colleague from Oxford, the Magus Umberto, summoned him to Bologna and gave him the giant ruby now affixed to the sleeping Emperor's forehead.

"Prester John's ruby will be yours, Magus Michael, for some years of your life, then it must be passed on to Frederick Hohenstaufen when he reaches his fortieth birthday. And with it, this letter from his mother, the Empress Constance."

Only a few moons later, he'd been summoned from Bologna to the Emperor's camp in Padua. "I have called for you, Michael Scot, because they say that you are the most learned man in Western Christendom, that your mind is in harmony with the wisdom of the ancients and the heavens. Henceforth you will be my advisor and astrologer."

Not a word of the stone. The Emperor Frederick seemed unaware of its existence. Scot sighs. He reaches for a pot filled with fat lupin seeds soaked in vinegar, pops one in his mouth and presses the salty liquid from his tongue. He spits the lupin skin into his hand and reaches for another—and another.

Scot knows that the gemstone has the power to stir the imagination, to transport its possessor to other worlds, to plumb the deep, jeweled ponds of memory that lie beneath the mind's glassy surface. After all, was it not soon after the Magus Umberto of Bologna had given him charge of the ruby, that he, Scot, had written his most original work, the *Liber Introductorious*? And the ruby had inspired the Magus Umberto to write, as well.

True, the Emperor had urged him to write the book; but Scot is convinced that it was the philosopher's stone that empowered him to fathom the depths of his mind. Now with the stone in the Emperor's possession, Frederick, too, might be inspired to write his long-deferred treatise on falconry.

The philosopher's stone had been delivered with a letter from the Empress Constance, sealed with a blob of porphyry-pigmented wax and impressed with her regal cipher. Would that letter reveal the identity of Prester John? And if it did, would His Majesty, the Emperor Frederick, share that revelation with Michael Scot?

But who was this Prester John? Where was that sumptuous palace with its walls and floors of lucid crystal, its ceilings glittering with diamonds in an obsidian sky? Who had traveled to such a place? Or imagined it?

❧

A few days passed and the weather turned wintry again. I found myself daydreaming about Apulia, about the Altavilla. Maybe the time had come to move on to Italy. Wasn't it Browning who had described Italy as "that gaudy melon flower?" I imagined the melon sliced open, revealing golden-seeded orange flesh, green tendrils curled around a yellow blossom hidden among its downy vine leaves.

One bitterly cold and sunless afternoon around tea time, I left the Bodleian for Merton College Library, just beyond the Lily and Crown.

"I'm Rose Orlando-Kirkland," I said to the librarian. "I believe Professor Lambeth has sent a letter of introduction for me?"

"Yes, of course," she said.

"I'm looking for some information on Constance de Hauteville —or Costanza d'Altavilla—perhaps a monograph."

The librarian handed me a call slip. "Please fill this out. If we have anything on the subject you'll find it here in the morning."

"Thanks. And while I'm here, would it be all right to visit the college gardens?"

"Of course—stroll along the terrace walk—the old city walls. You'll have a splendid view of the city and Merton Meadows. Too bad we haven't produced a nice sunny day for you."

I climbed up to the walls of Bellesitum—the Fair Place, the old Roman name for Oxford, and walked along the lime avenue, the trees in fresh full leaf the tender green of peridots. The tall spire of the cathedral soared above Christ Church, and across, the sharp gray gables of Merton College were crenelated against a smoky topaz sky.

It was quiet. Only sounds of doves pecking and cooing. How lucky I was to be by myself in this serene garden looking down on Merton Meadows. A perfect setting for meditation, something I hadn't done lately. I sat on the garden bench, knotted a scarf tight under my chin, and tugged the coat collar up around my ears.

I closed my eyes. I took a breath of cold damp April air and whiffed the odor of bergamot and burnt laurel still clinging to my coat.

With my thumb, index, and third finger of my right hand pinched together, I took another deep breath and let it out. "Five, four, three, two, one," I counted then took another.

On the blank screen inside my head, a red oriental poppy bursts its green calyx, unfurling huge crimped petals. I look into its onyx center. I feel its fuzzy green-gray leaves, its wiry stem, its grooved, jade-hard nubbin.

Scarlet poppies swaying in a field . . . pink Canterbury bells tolling, tolling, the scent of lavender—I imagine its pungent odor as it's drawn up through my nostrils and into my eyes. Shivers run through me.

In this secret garden the sky is lapis blue, a blazing sun warms dark, rich earth below. I enter the walled garden. A fountain gurgles and splashes in a roseraie looped like garlands thick with crimson roses. I have arrived at my mind's enclosed garden, the place where I meet my inner guide. I extend my hand.

The crunch of gravel broke my peace. I looked up. An old don, wearing a long black academic robe, walked toward me. Not wanting to stare, I opened a book as I listened to his tread coming closer and closer. He paused beside my bench.

"Good afternoon." I looked up and smiled. "Not a very nice day, is it?" I said.

The don had gray hair, almost touching his shoulders, and a gray beard. A bald head. In one hand he held a metal object shaped like an old barber's basin. He stared at me with kindly eyes that sparkled like cornflower-blue sapphires, but he did not speak. Or move.

I grabbed my purse, stood, and backed away from the bench.

His lips moved without a sound. "Pax, Pax, Rosa . . ."

He opened his right hand. Mr. Baryani's immense ruby lay in his palm.

I was frozen in place by the stone's heat. My heart was beating in time with its throb. *To die for, Mr. Baryani.*

And then the old don took the metal basin and put it on his head.

I fled down the lime walk, through the college garden and along Merton Street, into the lobby of the Lily and Crown.

"Afternoon, Mrs. Orlando-Kirkland. Good heavens—you're as white as a ghost! And shaking all over, just look at your hands. Let's get you some water—or would you prefer a nice cup of tea?"

"Water, please, Mavis. I was in the garden at Merton, up on the Terrace Walk. I saw a man—he tried to show me . . ." I stopped.

"Somebody bother you? Shocking! My dear, Oxford isn't what it used to be! Flashers and sex fiends . . ."

She filled a paper cup with Malvern water and put it to my lips.

"No one bothered me. I saw someone I thought I recognized." I gulped the water down. "I have to make a phone call—please excuse me, Mavis."

I raced up to my room, fell on the bed, and dialed Brian at All Souls.

"Rose, I'm so pleased to hear your voice. It's been too long since we . . . what's the matter?"

"I saw him."

"Who?"

"Michael Scot."

"Good Lord, Rose—"

"I took a walk along the old city walls, sat down on a bench to meditate, and he came right up to me and I didn't realize what was in his hand until he put it on his head. In his palm was—oh, Brian, it was the ruby Mr. Baryani showed me. I'd recognize that stone anywhere."

"I'm sure you would. Now calm down, I'll be right over."

There was a knock at the door. Mavis.

"Here you are, dear, a nice cup of tea. I brought a cup for myself as well—mind if I join you?"

"My friend Professor Lambeth is coming by in a few minutes, but please stay until he arrives. I don't want to be alone."

Mavis took my wrist and listened to my pulse.

"A little faster than normal but not racing. The color has come back in your face."

"Are you a nurse?"

"Years ago I was a midwife. Gave it up when I bought some shares in this hotel. You'll be all right, my dear."

Brian walked in without knocking.

"I'll leave you two now," Mavis said. "So glad you're better, Mrs. O.K." She closed the door.

"Tell me what happened."

"I told you. I saw Michael Scot. He wore an iron hat. I remembered that you said he always wore one on his head." I looked at his intent face. "And the ruby—"

"You're sure it was a ruby?"

"It looked exactly like the ruby Mr. Baryani showed me. And like the ruby the horseman held in his hand."

"What horseman?"

"The horseman I saw riding up the High soon after I arrived in Oxford. He was wearing a green tunic and an ivory horn slung over one shoulder. He was riding a black horse. Then I saw him again in Past Times on the Turl. He had a ruby clutched in his hand—bigger, almost twice the size of the ruby the old don showed me—but it was the same color." I wiped my forehead with a wad of Kleenex.

"I think it's a good stiff drink you need—not a cup of tea. Let's go downstairs."

❧

He ordered a whisky and some sherry on the rocks for me.

"I promise you I'll only drink one, Rose."

"I think I'm going crazy, Brian."

He put his hands on mine.

"Why did you ask me if I was sure—about the ruby?"

"There's a legend about a ruby," he said, "in an old Italian tale about Frederick and Prester John. The ruby is the zodiacal stone of the ancient Romans, the stone of December and Capricorn. Frederick II was born under Capricorn—the day after Christmas. You just told me you saw Frederick II on the High Street."

"But I'm not sure it was Frederick . . . it was just a man on a black horse wearing a green tunic." My spine felt as though an army of ants was marching along it.

"I say you saw Frederick. Riding Dragon, his black horse. Frederick liked to wear his hunting-green tunic, even in court procession."

"You must think I'm falling apart. Hallucinating."

"I doubt it, Rose. What you're telling me makes too much sense to be a hallucination. I told you that night over dinner that I thought you were going to unearth something for me. I hadn't expected . . . a ruby."

"I haven't really found anything for you in my research. I've learned some interesting new insights on the Hautevilles, yes, but—"

"Somehow you're tied up in all this, Rose. I don't think you're mad. Possessed, maybe, but not mad. Not the same in my book. It may be time for you to leave Oxford. Go on to Italy, visit your family. Take some books with you. I can have copies made of anything you'd need. You need some healing, warm spring sunshine. Besides, I have ulterior motives. I had a call from Italy today."

I remember that he gave me a strange stare, as though he were trying to read something in my eyes. "I may be called on to help decipher some almost deteriorated manuscripts in Bari. That's not too far from where you'll be—in Vieste del Gargano. Perhaps we can meet."

"These past two weeks have been so sunless and damp, I've found myself daydreaming about Italy," I said. "But you might be right. I may have learned all that I can here, and after today—well, I'm convinced it's time to leave. I'm afraid to stay any longer."

"Don't be frightened. You're part of a grand design—I'm sure of that. Revel in it."

"Do you believe in magic?"

"How could I not?" He grinned. "I'm involved with Michael Scot, after all."

He escorted me up to my room and kissed my cheek.

"Now get into bed. Watch telly. Call Matthew—and don't forget, ring me up if you need me."

"Thanks for everything, Brian. How would I have done without you?"

"Very well, I suspect. You've got a lot more strength than you give yourself credit for. You're not going to fall apart so easily."

"I'm glad you think so. Left to myself, I might just have packed up and flown right back to Los Angeles."

"I doubt it. You still have, as you once said, 'some unfinished business.' We both do." He kissed my forehead. "Goodnight, dear Rose."

As soon as he left I unknotted the scarf from under my chin and ran my fingers through my damp hair. I went into the bathroom and splashed my face with cold water. I looked into the mirror.

A white streak ran through my hair from temple to tip.

My knees buckled. I clutched the faucet taps. The Malvern water sloshed around in my stomach, whipping up a tidal wave. I knelt over the toilet and threw up. I wasn't dying. I was going mad. Why not just accept it? Go home, Rose. Go home. Be honest with yourself. You're crazy. Possessed. Brian's word.

I staggered to the telephone. I should try to reach Matthew. But how could I tell him? If he knew what had happened today, he'd insist I take the next plane for Los Angeles. Then he'd press me to make the decision I wasn't yet ready to make. No—there was no turning back. All I could do was burn a joss stick, crawl into bed, tug the covers up over my head and try to sleep it off.

 The days go by. I stopped counting. I stare with wonder at the bustling scene below my window. Long black boats with silver prows float on the lake. Ladies in bright gauze garments—like the ones I wear now—step in and out of covered pleasure boats and decorated barges. I marvel, still, at the flocks of pink flamingos and blue herons. Tall papyrus grow in clumps, lilies float on green pads. Sometimes Irene bids me walk with her in the garden beyond the palace, past the avenue of date palms, through aviaries where parrots, larks, and nightingales squawk and sing. Peacocks fan their tales when we pass. In the royal menageries, lions and tigers and panthers stalk, apes hop and scratch themselves and make me laugh.

Beyond the palace are groves of myrtle and laurel and orchards of orange and lemon trees, their waxy white blossoms giving forth a powerful perfume, as though it had wafted down from heaven. *Zagara*, they say the Saracens call it.

I am taken to the Tiraz, the weavers' workshop. Women and men bend over their looms; bobbins unwind precious filaments of silk thread spun by fat worms fed on tender mulberry leaves. I watch designs and patterns grow on the cloth as the loom moves to and fro—stretching leopards, back to back; baskets overflowing with fruit; tendrilled vines and flowers, all in colors such as I have never seen before. Rich shades of red, red the color of rowan berries; the green of feathery tops of fennel, green the color of bronze.

I find the women beautiful—slim and almond-eyed, with long black hair like Irene's. Captive Greek slaves from Byzantium. Irene tells me that King William used the women for his pleasure, which made me blush to look at them. They take such pride in their work, embroidering silk in tiny stitches that strain their eyes and will eventually make them blind. I, who have always struggled with needle and thread, is this to be my destiny as well?

CHAPTER EIGHT

O N THURSDAY NIGHT I was back at the Lily and Crown by eleven o'clock. "Evenin,' Mrs. O.K." Simon the porter had the night shift. "Here's your key. You have one message. Mr. Kirkland called from Osaka."

"Thanks, Simon." I remembered that Simon moonlighted on weekends. "Since I'll be leaving for Italy next week could you please get me a Saturday appointment at Mahogany? My hair needs straightening and some color." I pointed to the streak. "About eleven o'clock?"

He was only too happy to comply. I trudged up the steps, exhausted. I might as well have stayed in my room. I'd gone to see *As You Like It* at the Oxford Playhouse, but my mind kept wandering from Rosalind to Rosamonde. What a waste of time and Shakespeare—not to mention missing Matthew's call from Osaka. It was late. Even though I was feeling morose I would send him a cheerful fax.

Hotel Osaka
April 20, 1994
Osaka, Japan

Darling—I'm sorry I missed your call. I went to see The Royal Shakespeare's *As You Like It*. I didn't mind going by myself, but having you next to me would have made it heaven on earth, or at least The Forest of Arden!

I'm anxious to get to Italy, so I'm cutting short my stay in Oxford. Remember Atalanta Travel on St. Gilles'? They've booked me London-Bologna direct on Alitalia. (I remember you advised me to avoid Rome airport *at all costs!*) From Bologna, I take the night train (I have a couchette). My cousins will meet me at San Severo, an inland town not too far from Vieste. I arrive very early in the morning (about 5:30), but they insisted on coming—wouldn't hear of a taxi. They want me to stay with them, but I explained that I wanted to write, so they understood my need for solitude. I'll be staying at the Hotel Vesta in the historical part of town.

Hope you're making headway on your negotiations. Take lots of pictures in Kyoto. I spoke to Linda again this morning. They're doing very well with orders for the same old stuff. I'll be waiting to hear from you.

I love you—XXX and more love—Rose.

I've actually found an Altavilla connection with Vieste!! Things are looking up!

I gave the fax to Simon and went straight to bed.

❧

Weeks pass and still no knight to claim me. Long dark days of rain make me dream of Normandy and my home. It must be springtime there, the violets blooming down by the marsh.

Tonight, when thunder cracks across the sky, Irene comes to my room with the man who had bound me on my first day in Palermo. He holds white cords in his hand and a black scarf. I begin to shake the moment I see him.

He binds my hands and my feet as Irene muffles my screams. The two of them lift me onto the divan against the wall, where he ties the scarf over my eyes. I lie there a long time trying to escape my bonds, but the knots are too tight.

Outside, I can hear rain pelting the lake. The brazier in my room smolders with yet another sweet scent I have never smelled before, this one like burning herbs.

The door opens and closes. I feel a presence. I hear breathing—someone leaning over me—then a whispered, gentle voice.

"Rosamonde, don't be afraid. I am your lover. It is for me that you have been brought to Sicily. Remember this, I will not harm you ever."

At last, my knight has come. And now to hear his voice, so lilting in tone.

"Please unbind me, sir. Let me be free to look upon you, to touch your hand. Please, I beg you—"

"Hush, hush. Not yet. For now, simply lie and let me love you as you are."

I hear the slash of silk and feel the robe slip from my shoulders and through my bonds. I feel his hands on my skin. Not rough hands, weathered and scarred like the hands of our men in Normandy, but soft hands. The hands of a nobleman.

He tells me to stand, and I struggle to obey him. He kisses the berries of my breasts, which are fuller now than when I came here. He kisses me over and over again, sucking my skin into his mouth, starting with the spot where I was cut loose from my mother's womb. I feel his bearded face against my belly.

I do not want to scream, even when he begins to take tiny, gentle bites of my flesh. Tasting, not wounding me. I feel my body tremble as his lips move to the part of me that Irene had bared of my body's hair. His tongue finds the hidden plum in what had been my most secret place. He begins, again, with tiny, gentle bites; I feel as if I might faint with fear that he would harm me there.

Suddenly, I feel a switch strike my body, as though a hundred silk cords are hitting my skin. He does not strike hard. There is no sharp pain, only a light stinging. I hear his moans, feel his quick breath, his excitement.

He pulls me down upon him. My face is buried in his beard, then I feel my mouth pushed open by throbbing flesh. I gag. For a moment he leaves me.

Then he must have cut the cords at my ankles because I feel my legs stretched open. Pain cuts through my body, and the black night comes down. I swoon away.

He is gone now. I lie still for a long while. There is nothing to do but cry.

What could I have done? Who would have listened to my cries?

The rain has stopped. I hear the sound of high pipes, a tune I have never heard before—a melody that gives my heart a hollow ache. I feel empty and alone. The bandage on my eyes is soaked with tears.

Irene comes to remove the bandage, untie the cords and take them from my chafed wrists. I sit here, dazed in the harsh light. At first all is a blur, and then I see set before me a platter heaped with delicate twists of thin fried dough, aglaze with sugar. Atop this lies a fragile rose of beaten gold, its petals trembling and shimmering in the brazier's unsteady light. Irene lifts the rose as if it is spun spider webs, places it in my hand, and bows out of the room.

When I arise, I see my blood spotted on a silken pillow.

Unsteadily I climb the steps to the latticed window to look down upon the lake below. The heavens flicker tiny crystal lights. The pale topaz moon sits high above. A flock of cranes moves across the sky.

One by one, I pull the petals from the golden rose and push each one through the grille. I watch them float to the ground.

The next day I dare ask to see King William to protest this wicked treatment by my knight.

"The King is in meetings with his ministers of state," Irene tells me, "and with Walter of the Mill, the Archbishop of Palermo."

Then I beg to see Queen Joanna.

"You must wait until the Queen returns from Bari. You see, Rosamonde, Queen Joanna goes to pray for a child at the Cathedral of St. Nicholas—the patron saint of children."

I have never believed that women gave birth through

divine power, but I know better than to share such godless thoughts, even with Irene.

"King William and Queen Joanna are very close," she tells me, "but alas, she is barren as the desert sands beyond the holy city of Jerusalem."

Some weeks pass. One afternoon an early lion sun beats down. Even the parrots in their cages are mute. No breeze bends the cypresses, no palm fronds rustle. I am half asleep when suddenly Irene began to chatter in the Saracen language. I hear fuss and much ado outside my room. She unlatches the door and falls to her knees, hands stretched out before her, head touching the floor.

The dazzling vision that appears before us I know at once to be Queen Joanna. She is dressed in a white cendal cloak. The hem of her gown is thick with gold embroidery inset with sky blue gems. Her hair, not covered by a veil, ripples down her shoulders like a field of ripe felled wheat. She is small of stature, slender and poised. The palace major domo, the eunuch Caid Gregory, stands by her side.

I fall upon my knees, as Irene had done.

Queen Joanna stares at me hard—in a way approving, yet in those eyes I see a hint of anger and sadness that I do not understand. "Stand, Rosamonde de Roland," she says in a dulcet voice with the accent of *langue d'oc.* "You have come a long way from Coutances. And you have been here in Palermo for a month and a fortnight. Have you wondered why you have come here?"

"I have indeed, My Lady. I was told by my family that I would marry in Palermo, yet no one has come to claim me for a bride. I have sent word to Lady de Hauteville in Coutances that I would sooner return to Normandy than marry a stranger who has taken so long to come forth to be my husband." I long to tell her of my outrage and disgrace, but how can I speak of such matters to the Queen?

She smiles, her face losing in that instant any sadness I might have glimpsed. She claps her hands for a servant to unfasten her cloak, then she sits, with two eunuchs behind her, stirring the air with fans of peacock feathers on ivory poles.

Irene comes forth to serve us cool mint tea.

Queen Joanna begins to question me about my father and my mother. She asks me how my mother had died and at what age. I am loathe to answer but she draws the truth from me. She seems alarmed to learn that my mother died from her own hand.

She knows we are the same age, that I, too, can read and write. We speak of what gives me joy and what gives me sorrow. The questions seem strange for a Queen to ask with servants standing by. I answer her questions in truth, even one that seemed most outrageous.

"Is your moment of the moon regular?" she asks.

"Yes, Your Majesty." I tell her.

"When I first married King William," she says, "we had no doubt that there would be children. We did not worry then, because we were still young and hopeful. But ten years have passed and I have not yet conceived a child. Walter of the Mill has convinced my husband to concede his throne to his aunt, Constance. She is the same age as King William, and since they were brought up as brother and sister, they have great affection for one another. Now Queen Constance has wed the German Prince Henry, and we are uneasy with the alliance. Henry is known to be cruel, and we fear his power.

"You, Rosamonde, are a healthy woman of good stock

from a family akin to my husband's own forebears in Normandy. That is why I am choosing you to bear for me, as in the Holy Bible, when Sarah and Abraham chose Hagar to bear for Sarah."

That is how she tells me. For this I had come to Sicily—to be harlot to a king. In horror and shame, I find the courage to ask, "And what if no child is conceived in me?"

"You will be given one year. If by that time, you are not with child, you will weave silk in the Tiraz for the rest of your life."

I feel the blood rush to my face and then I faint dead away.

We soon grow to know each other well, Queen Joanna and I. It is as though she offers me her past so that I might become part of her future.

On these long, soft afternoons in late spring, we stroll the gardens or recline in hooded pleasure boats on the lake. The season of jasmine begins to warm the blood.

One day the Queen trails her jeweled fingers in the lake as the boatmen pole us to a little island where stands a cool stone kiosk.

Joanna speaks of her childhood in England—how she was taken from her mother, Queen Eleanor, and sent away to Sicily. "One day when I was playing with my doll—I had embroidered a new dress for her of scraps of russet linen—my mother came with red eyes to tell me that I was to wed the Sicilian king, William. She had pleaded with my father, Henry, not to send me so far away so soon. I was their youngest daughter and I had been taken to live with her at

Salisbury tower. And there and then began a closeness between us we had never known before.

"My father would not listen to my mother. He had made up his mind that I should marry King William."

I think of my own sad parting from Normandy, not so different from Queen Joanna's.

"Within a few months, my dowry and wardrobe were made ready. It took seven ships to carry all the gold and silver cups, clothes, furs, tapestries, and fine horses to be presented to the Sicilian ambassadors as my dowry.

"I cried in my bed every night, afraid to leave my mother for this unknown man. I was frightened of my father. As for my mother, she was not the sort of woman to keep a child by her side. But when it came time for me to leave, she was sadder than I had ever seen her.

"When I think back on it, I wonder if on my departure she felt the loss of her own childhood—leaving her father and her beloved Aquitaine for Paris, that stinking wretched city she never learned to love. She was weeping more for her own childhood than for mine. So I kissed her goodbye and left her crying in her tower."

"When I left Normandy," I say, "my heart was filled with much the same sadness as you have known, My Lady."

"I know that, Rosamonde. Blaise de Hauteville told me how you wept to leave your home. We must share our joys and sorrows, you and I."

I beg to hear more.

"We arrived in Palermo in January. As we rode into the city, King William waited at the gates to bid me welcome on the palfrey he had sent for me to ride."

I make no mention of the abuse I had suffered upon my arrival in Palermo.

"Torches were lighted all along the way," she tells me, "and great bonfires burned so that Palermo seemed a blaze of light. We could hardly see the stars it was so bright. I was so shy, so frightened."

"Please tell me of more of your wedding."

"King William was so fair and handsome, with a short reddish beard that made him look older and more kingly. I liked him right away. His blue eyes seemed to approve of me."

How hard it must be for her to know that I have been in King William's arms, I think.

"William was so different from my father, Rosamonde. You see, I had always feared my father's anger. How he would shout at my mother, how he ranted after Thomas à Becket. I was just a small child, but I still remember how my mother sobbed when my father had Thomas murdered by his knights." She heaves a deep sigh. "But all of that I put aside for I was to be King William's wife."

"My Lady, Irene told me how she marveled at the splendor of the court on your wedding day."

The Queen seems pleased. "We were married in the chapel of the palace in Palermo. Bells pealed for miles around. The bishops, arrayed in vestments from Byzantium, waited for us at the altar. William wore the scarlet mantle of King Roger—embroidered with fierce lions attacking camels. I wore my blue and silver dress. Around the hem the English nuns had worked little white doves with sprigs of yellow broom in their beaks.

"The chapel, with its golden walls and a ceiling painted with Saracen musicians, was packed with ambassadors and prelates from foreign lands. During the ceremony I felt faint, for I could not eat that day. The Archbishop stood at the altar. His eyes bore into me. Although he looked like an austere saint, I have never liked him. The priests chanted the liturgy, Benedictine monks sang the plain song.

"A chalice was held aloft—a chalice studded with more gems than you have ever seen. Then the archbishop anointed me and proclaimed me Queen of Sicily."

I listen to Joanna, enthralled by her story, amazed that she would tell me all of this. It is as though she is giving me part of herself.

"Eunuchs offered tasty morsels on golden platters. Tiny plover eggs, legs of pigeon simmered in honey, sugared almonds, St. John's bread, sticky delights of dates and almonds. Troubadours from Occitan sang love songs in my mother's tongue, Trouvères from France recited *chansons de gestes,* and verses from Chrétien de Troyes, court poet to my sister, Marie of Champagne.

"Then my husband William sang verses he composed, and the court storyteller read King William's letter from Prester John in the faraway Eastern kingdom."

Her eyes, the color of larkspur, gleam with tears. "On that day, the eve of the fourteenth of February, my husband, William Hauteville, was twenty-four years old. I, Joanna Plantagenet, was eleven."

Were she not the Queen, I would put my arms around her.

CHAPTER NINE

O N SATURDAY AFTERNOON I stepped out of Mahogany and into the Turl for one last look in Past Times' window. I saw Brian chatting with some undergraduates just as they were leaving the Taj Mahal Restaurant.

I waved to him and he crossed over to greet me.

"You look ravishing, Rose. You've changed your hair. It's very becoming."

I thanked him, relieved that he would never see the white streak the hairdresser had colored when she shaped my hair.

"Now I insist that you come along to the covered market," he said. "We're going to find some lunch for tomorrow's picnic. Sunday's supposed to be glorious and this time I won't let you say no. I'll reserve a punt for us down at Magdalen Bridge."

"Thank you—I'd like that. Tomorrow's my last Sunday here. I'll be leaving on Tuesday."

"So soon?" He gripped my arm as we walked into the market.

"The place has hardly changed," I said, "as damp and cold as ever. Even the same greengrocer stalls."

"Still the place *has* been tarted up a bit during these past few years."

While Brian was at the poulterer's choosing tomorrow's lunch, I waited by my favorite seed and flower shop. I found myself staring at a Victorian wire rack terraced with pots of daffodils. A miniature orange tree in a moss-clad clay pot sat on the top shelf.

The pathetic orange tree on my balcony, pale, without blossoms—the scented orange groves of Favara where Rosamonde strolled. It was as though I had two sets of memories. One of this world, one from another distant world, back and forth, each slipping into the other. Rose here, Rosamonde there, two souls melded, turned in two directions like Brian's processional statue of the Virgin of the Roses.

"You're admiring that little orange tree." Brian had materialized by my side.

"It's charming. I felt a little homesick for a moment," I said. Homesick for where? For California? Or for the scented groves of Palermo? I was glad to be leaving Oxford on Tuesday.

"The tree will be your present from me," he said.

"No, please, that's thoughtful and generous of you, Brian, but I'm only here for a few more days and I won't be able to take it on to Italy."

"Then you'll leave it for me to pick up at the hotel. I shall smuggle it into France and plant it in my garden at Aigues Mortes. And cherish it, knowing that it was once yours. It will flourish there, I promise you. No other orange tree will have more love lavished upon it than this one."

"I didn't think romantics like you existed anymore."

He laughed. "Death, my darling Rose, lies at the heart of all romanticism."

There was no way I could argue that.

I soon lagged behind as he kept talking, striding with the orange tree tucked securely in the crook of his arm. He turned back to find me standing by the portal to St. Aldate's.

"Have you seen something familiar?"

"I'm sorry, I thought I saw a fishmonger's stall here." *Heaps of silver cod, mackerel, like the glossy blue enamel of Byzantium—slabs of dark-fleshed tuna oozing blood.* Wasn't the stall in this corner? *Or was it in Palermo?*

"*Oublier Palerme,*" I said out loud. Those words had been lodged in my head this whole week.

"What did you say?"

"The title of a French novel I read a long time ago. It stuck in my head, don't ask me why."

"What was it again?"

"*Oublier Palerme.* To forget Palermo."

"I *do* remember the book—won the Goncourt, but what could it possibly mean to you? Have you ever been to Palermo?"

"Now you really sound like my New York psychiatrist. He always asked me what I thought things *meant.* I don't know what to think any more. I'd leave here tomorrow if it weren't for my cousins having made plans to meet me on Wednesday. To answer your question—I didn't mean to evade you—no, I've never been to Palermo." Not in this world, anyway, I thought.

"What's happening, Rose? Maybe you ought to tell me. Or at least tell Matthew."

"I can't talk about it now and I'm not going home. Matthew is in Osaka for ten more days—maybe longer. Besides, I need to see my family in Apulia. I have questions I have to ask them. I know things will be better there."

We passed the English bakeshop. What was left in the window didn't look appetizing or fresh—banbury tarts, mince meat tarts, cream horns and other teatime angloexotica. "Come on, let's go to the corner shop for some of those American cookies," he said.

He chose the darkest double chocolate filled with walnuts. "They're the best. Crispy on the outside, soft and warm inside. Like you, Rose."

I laughed. "Something you'll never ever know, Brian."

"I'm sure of that," he said with a grin.

He broke a cookie in two and gave me half. "Try it. You've never tasted anything as delicious as this."

"No thanks." I didn't know why but I just couldn't take that bite.

His green eyes riveted my own. "You don't know what you're missing."

I looked away, unable to sustain his gaze.

He guided me through St. Aldate's portal into the throngs of County shoppers. Again he insisted upon walking me to my room.

"I'm going to put this orange tree on your bed table. By the way, did you ever solve the case of the missing roses?"

I didn't like his arch tone. But I couldn't tell him the truth about the roses any more than I could tell him about the voice.

"As a matter of fact, I did. Mavis found them in the restaurant larder the next morning. The maid must have put them there."

"You're sure?" He asked skeptically, searching my eyes.

I turned away. "Yes—I meant to tell you but I forgot."

He set the tree on the night table by my bed.

"Thank you, Brian. I'm happy to have your orange tree to keep me company until I leave."

"Not to overwater. Orange trees don't like wet feet."

"I'll be careful."

"And if you take good care of it, its fruit will turn to gold, like the golden apples of the Hesperides." He smiled broadly.

He couldn't possibly have known about the rose petal turning to gold.

"Tomorrow at noon, then. I'll come by for you and we'll walk down to Magdalen Bridge together."

He kissed me on the cheek—a brother's kiss. He smelled of dusty, unrecognizable spices. A strange, archaic scent.

I locked the door after him and picked up the potted orange tree to move as far from my bedside as I could. I set it on top of the television and stood back to stare at it.

 From my window at Ziza Palace, I watch the arrival of Empress Constance, who has returned from Germany to visit King William, her nephew. A long veil of sheer silver silk falls upon her shoulders and floats around her white palfrey. The sheer veil cannot conceal her beauty, and the light of goodness shines from her face and form as if she has been bathed in sunshine. William welcomes her as though she is his sister and not his aunt. I hear her tell him her first wish is to visit his Monreale, to admire his tribute to Our Lady.

A palanquin is made ready for King William and the two Queens, horses and mules for the others. We all set forth together to see the new mosaics that have been set in place by a Greek from Byzantium. I have not seen Monreale so I am pleased to be invited. We arrive there in five hours.

When we enter the holy place, I see the giant face of Christ staring down from above the altar. All who have seen King Roger's Church in Cefalù say the Christ there is more awe-inspiring, but I tell you that even I, who do not pray to God as often as I might, am moved. I like the Bible stories of Noah and the Ark, of Rebecca at the well, and Jacob and his ladder.

King William claims that two hectares of glass squares

have been fixed to its walls. The Greek tile-setter begs the King's permission to show him the mosaic picture he has just completed for Queen Joanna. In the left curve of the apse, we are shown the image of Thomas à Becket, the martyr of Canterbury.

When Queen Joanna sees Becket's tribute in the small squares of stone and glass, she falls on her knees and weeps. I wonder why she so reveres the man her father's knights had murdered in Canterbury Cathedral.

I hand the Queen her silken scarf. King William helps her stand, then puts his arm around her slender shoulders.

I stay for a long while, praying that the King will soon treat me like the woman who is to bear his child.

We spend a week at Monreale, the King as proud as though he'd built it with his own hands. For all that Archbishop Walter of the Mill strove to make his cathedral in Palermo the jewel of the city, it can never rival King William's Monreale.

Each evening we sup while the King studies the tile designs. He seems a different man to me then, and when he sees my interest he begins to talk and look at me in a different way.

Tonight I am so weary that I beg to have dinner in my room, a cell but not so rude as most I have seen. I am brought a tray of soup with morsels of fowl and celery. When I have supped, I wash my face and unplait my hair. My travel dress is heavy on my tired body, so I take it off and lie on the bed, still in my shift,

Within the cloisters, no one stirs. It is the hour of the night when even the abbots, tired from travail, fasting, and prayer, lie upon their hard pallets, some in their own small cells, while others lie across the doors of their masters.

Some, I have heard said, in their masters' beds. I creep between the soft rabbit skin coverlet and doze off.

I awake when I hear the creaking door open and close. The candle has burned out. I lie there, frozen in my bed, until I realize that I am safe in a Benedictine abbey.

I sit bolt upright, eyes wide open. It is the King who has come to visit me. He stays for just a moment. He does not touch me. When he bids me goodnight he takes my hands in his. He gazes at me with loving kindness in his eyes. At this moment I know things will change between us.

One afternoon during the week, I sit daydreaming in the cloister of Monreale, that enclosed square of fragrant herbs, of lavender, of crimson roses looped like growing chains.

I see the Empress Constance enter, a tall man by her side. She is almost as tall as he. Her pale gold hair brushed back from her face is caught in a fillet of gold and pearls. The gown she wears is of soft silver green, the color of velvet almond shells. The man wears the dark robes of a scholar. His gray hair is clipped short in the style of the ancient people who had once lived here in Sicily. I know him to be Godfrey of Viterbo, tutor to Constance's husband, Prince Henry Hohenstaufen.

They sit together on a marble bench, her hands resting upon a breviary in her lap. They seem to have eyes only for each other and are unsuspecting of my presence behind the zigzagged column. She leans forward to stroke his arm—a lover's touch, I have no doubt. Then he leans forward to kiss her lips. They do not know that I have shared their private moment.

That night, King William proclaims a feast and celebration
in honor of the Queen Joanna's birthday. The throngs outside cheer and shout for the Empress Constance, always a
favorite of her people. There are thunderous cheers from
Saracens, Lombards, Franks, and Jews alike. King William,
Queen Joanna, and Constance review the parade of enter-
tainers.

I do not tell Queen Joanna of the tender scene between
Queen Constance and Godfrey of Viterbo. I am, instead,
wont to treasure their precious moment as though it has
been my own.

Poor Constance. They tell me she never knew King
Roger, her father— dead before she was born. No wonder
Constance could love a man so much older. She must
always have yearned for a father.

"What is Prince Henry, her husband, like?" I ask Queen
Joanna.

"He is ten years younger than the Empress Constance.
She was thirty years old when she was forced to leave the
convent of San Salvatore and made to marry that cruel German, Henry Hohenstaufen. So far, like me, she has not
given him an heir."

We hear the trumpet fanfares. The celebration has
begun. We are led to the great dining hall. William raises
his golden goblet: "I bid welcome my aunt, the Empress
Constance, on her return to Palermo."

The guests cheer and clap their hands.

Tonight the Empress Constance wears her royal crown,
a cap embroidered with thick gold threads, a huge carved

ruby centered above her brow. Tiers of golden triangles, affixed to the cap, hang to her shoulders.

King William raises his goblet once again. "And I drink to the precious pearl of the Golden Shell, my Queen, Joanna."

I feel a twinge of envy when he proclaims these women thus but I am soon distracted by sights such as I have never dreamed.

Dancers from Cadiz stamp their feet and click henna-stained fingers to the music of lutes. Other dancers snap small wooden discs looped on their hands. Greek weavers from the Tiraz begin their stately dance, clasping one another's shoulders in a circle, their white gauze trousers wrapped with sashes of colored silk. Old embroiderers from the Tiraz, blinded by years of stitching, sit cross-legged in the far corner of the room clapping in rhythm to the music. Eunuchs with shaved heads swathed in turbans snap their fingers, ordering the servants about in high-pitched voices.

I recline on a damask cushion, enjoying all the fuss.

The shiver of tambourines shushes the guests. Black-haired houris start their dance. They are dressed in gossamer silk, spun of worms' threads and tinted purple with dye made from the rotten flesh of seashell creatures that cling to rocks along the coast of Mons Garganus.

Next the Carthaginian dancers bow in, each with a solid glass ball held high above her head. One's ball is amethyst glass, another's emerald green, another's ruby, another's sapphire. The leader's ball is crystal, clear and sparkling like a white-hot diamond. When the music sounds, each dancer stretches her ball before her, then places it on the floor, standing upon it. The musicians play faster, faster, faster. The dancers curl their toes around the spheres, their bodies moving to and fro, waists twisting and turning.

What a sight to behold! These slim, lithe maidens make the men's blood boil up as they posture their limbs in the most brazen ways. Twirling, bending—forward, backward, sideways, never still. Cries of pleasure rise from the guests, then roaring applause. Cymbals clash as the dancers jump over the balls and hold them high. Their bodies glistening wet, they bow to us, never raising their eyes. The eunuchs clap their hands: King William offers Muscat wine and almond paste puddings for their endeavors.

And then we listen as King William reads his famous letter from Prester John.

When we return to Palermo, things do change between us. I no longer fear the King's nightly visits, for I have seen this man's gentle side. It pleases him to sit on his throne by the trickling rill in the music room at Ziza. A frieze of deer, leopards, peacocks, archers, and date palms works its legend around the walls. William tells me these were ancient symbols for the sounds of music. He sings a song he's written just for me in the style of the Saracen poets, a *gahzal* he calls it.

> O painful yearning I do feel
> Whenever I before you kneel
> Heart's worship eager to conceal
> Lest you disdain my love
> With this blade of burnished steel
> I cut the red and waxen seal
> Then beg you never to reveal
> How I expressed my love.

King William comes to me one night, weary and tired from meetings all day with his battered knights. He has received news of the losing battle waged at Thessalonica. His army is warring against the Byzantine Emperor Comnenus. I worry about my father, in battle, at the head of his men, but the King assures me that no harm has come to Seigneur Robert de Roland.

For the first time I bend forward to place my hand on his arm. In the past I would not have dreamt of being so bold. But now I am not bound at the wrists.

When I touch him he pulls me to him in a rough and angry embrace. Has my touch, then, insulted him? He pushes me into the cushions and falls upon me, tearing off my gown, unwinding the sash of his dalmatic. He slaps my face.

"You should never have come from Normandy to bear my child for her," he says. And then he weeps in my arms.

This is a man, not a king. A man who has not had what any commoner would expect from a wife. His love for Joanna has turned to anger, and that anger into love for me.

"I am ashamed that I have succumbed to the flesh in the way I have with you," he says. "I want to be guided by the light, not by the darkness of my spirit, Rosamonde. Queen Joanna and I have great love for each other, but my love for her is akin to the love of a man for the Madonna. I worship her from afar, as though she were the Holy Virgin. It is in her honor that I build Monreale."

"I have begun to perceive that, My Lord."

"You must have heard the palace story, Rosamonde, of

how the Virgin came to me in a dream—to tell me where to find King Roger's buried treasure. It was here at Favara that I unearthed it. In my dream I saw myself walking through the groves beyond the palace, where the oranges grow, and at the foot of an old orange tree I found my father's treasure. In it was a gem such as I had never seen before—a ruby the color of blood. When I held it in my hand, it sent a message rushing through me. I knew it to be a holy stone and have guarded it with my life."

"May I see the ruby? May I hold it in my hand as well?"

He seems surprised at my request. From a leather pouch that hangs from his waist, he takes the stone.

"Only to you, Rosamonde, do I show this gem."

The stone is of a red such as I have never seen. In color it is like the ruby in the crown that Constance had worn at the banquet. But this stone is huge, and it is not engraved.

He places the ruby in my palm.

And when I clasp it, I feel the source of all life is in my hand.

"I call this the ruby of the Altavilla," the King says, "a present to my beloved Queen as a gift for our first born. Our child would have been the offspring of the greatest Norman families, the Altavilla and the Plantagenet. Now I know that this may never come to pass. I have not yet decided who shall have this gem."

He speaks to me for the first time as a man to a beloved woman, and from that moment on we share his secret.

Before long I know that I carry William's child within me. The telltale signs of my monthly courses have not appeared since March. When she hears my glad tidings, Joanna is sad and happy, her tears and laughter mingle as we embrace. I weep for her joy.

We will depart in May for the Queen chooses to leave Palermo before the sun-scorched months of summer. She will at first feign squeamishness and spewing up and weariness, and then when three months have passed she will feast on rich foods to swell her girth.

Then we shall set out together for Mons Garganus.

"You will come to my Apulian counties with me," she tells me, "and you will forget my husband. You will never return here, Rosamonde. You must forget Palermo!"

On Sunday, when we had settled in the flat-bottomed boat, Brian grasped the long pole and pushed the punt off from the mooring.

Glorious weather, just as he had predicted. Convivial punters were already into their wine cups.

"We'll have our picnic under a weeping willow," he said. "In my favorite little cove."

Hawthorn petals had flecked the Cherwell white. Clumps of fuzzy-leaved borage with pale blue star eyes grew along the banks.

I picked the fragile petals from my shoulders, feeling the silent thumps of the long pole as it hit river bottom. I was far away, gazing into the river, listening to spring birdsong. *Rosamonde in the barge, floating on the lake at Favara.* I dipped my hand into the water, trailing my fingers as Joanna had done.

"Penny for whatever you're thinking."

"A penny doesn't buy much these days."

"Come on, Rose. Candor is what I want from you."

"Do you really want to know what was on my mind? I was thinking that you reminded me of Charon on the River Styx— ferrying me to the Underworld."

"You're seeing my shadow side again, Rose. You're as much as a romantic as I am, I've decided. You have that pagan outlook on life. For you, danger and death lurk everywhere."

"You may be right, though I've never thought of danger as being particularly pagan," I said. "But since I should be candid I do have a confession to make." I felt the blood rush.

"You do?" He nodded and waved, "hello, lovely day," to three undergraduates in a passing punt.

"Yes, I lied last night. There were never any roses. They must have bloomed in my overly-fertile imagination. I didn't want you to think I was crazy, so I fibbed."

"You're sure?"

"What else am I to think?"

"Come on, let's have a drink. There's a bottle of cold cider inside the hamper."

I opened the fancy hamper all strapped up with cutlery, plates, and cups—the kind of basket I'd always wanted for our beach picnics in Santa Monica. For some reason I had never allowed myself the luxury. I handed the cider to Brian, who took a long quaff.

"We're almost at Lambeth Cove." He guided the punt expertly to the sandy bank and spread out the lunch he had prepared.

As we ate our chicken sandwiches, we talked about my research in the Bodleian. I told him of the Altavilla connection, of William's wedding gift of Vieste to Joanna Plantagenet, and of my other discovery, that William might have been a poet-troubadour.

He put his sandwich down on the plate. "Sorry, I should have thought to tell you about William's wedding gift of those counties to Joanna. You can read about it in the *Annals of Roger of Hovenden*. But where did you find that other bit, Rose—about William's being a poet?"

"In a German nineteenth-century philological journal. I can

give you the call slip."

"Amazing. I had a feeling you were going to find something for me."

"You have more faith in my scholarship than I do. How does William's being a poet tie in with your missing link?"

"It's too complex to explain now. I haven't yet sorted it all out. As soon as I finish my paper I'll send it on to you. Better still, I may be able to tell you more by the time I fly to Bari. Vieste is just up the coast. We could have lunch in either place, or better yet at Castel del Monte. I'd love to be your guide there; I know it well. More cider?"

"No thanks." I wasn't sure I wanted to see Brian in Italy.

He poured only half a glass this time and raised it to me.

"So much for L*e Roman de la Rose*." He grinned. "On second thought make that Le Roman de L.A. Rose. Get it?"

I shook my head and laughed at his bad joke.

"For my *Princesse Lointaine*, it will only be *l'amour courtois* between us, then. Only from afar shall I worship you, Rose of the World, Fair Rosamonde."

I felt a tremor flash up my spine. "Why do you insist on calling me Rosamonde?"

"Why should that bother you so much, my dear girl? You know, I've become very concerned about you."

Maybe the time had come to tell him about Rosamonde's voice, but I lost my nerve. I bit my lip hard and kept quiet. Although I couldn't wait to leave Oxford, I was beginning to feel that Italy might give me the answers I was seeking. There was no way I could go home now, however frightened, however mad. I had to steel myself and see this venture through.

At last I said, "it bothers me because I am not *Rose* of the World." I smiled. "I'm just plain, unworldly Rose."

He threw back his head and laughed. "Oh really? You expect me to believe that? I suppose that makes me just a country bumpkin from Cornwall."

⚭

We walked straight up the High, back to the Lily and Crown.

"I'll run up for the call slip. It's on my night table."

I found the slip and glanced at the orange tree sitting on top of the telly. Maybe I should give it to Brian today.

I stared at the tree, now gleaming with little golden oranges. I touched them. The gold was hammer marked so it looked like real orange skin. Each leaf was glassy-green enamel, its blossoms turned to creamy pearls.

Should I have Brian look at my enchanted orange tree? But if he didn't see its transformation, he would think that I had become insane. No, I didn't dare say a word.

I ran downstairs to the lobby, waving the slip to disguise my shaky hand.

"Here you are," I heard my chirpy voice say, "I hope it's as important as you seem to think." I kissed his abrasive cheek, palely fragrant with that same curious scent. "Thanks for all your help. I'll be forever grateful to you." Oh, how I hoped he wouldn't linger!

"Until Italy, my dear Rose. Castel del Monte, I hope. In any case I know we'll meet again. Soon." He clasped my hands in his and kissed my cheek.

I looked down at his hand still clasping mine, his ring pressing against my fingers.

"I've always meant to ask you, Brian. What is that crest on your signet ring?"

He took the ring from his finger. "Here, have a look for yourself."

I studied the engraved figure. "It's Mercury—or Hermes wearing his winged helmet."

"What good eyes, Rose."

"And those initials on the shank. M.M.S. What do they stand for?"

"They're my mother's initials. She wore this ring until the day she died. My mother was known all over Devon and Cornwall for her supernatural powers."

"What was her name?"

"Margaret Michaela. Scot was her maiden name."

Three months later, we set forth for Apulia together with our loyal servants, ones we trust above all others. We journey by land and sea. When we arrive in Vieste, Joanna's county, we will spend our time secluded.

"When we married I was too young to understand King William's wedding gift to me," Joanna tells me. "Yes, I deemed my lands worthy to behold, but what did land mean, really, to a twelve-year-old?

"The first time I set foot on my properties was soon after we were wed. We had accompanied Pope Alexander as far as Vieste. The Pope was on his way to Venice to make peace with the Emperor Barbarossa, but the sea was so rough, the weather so dreadful, that he could not set sail for weeks. William amused himself by writing—gazing out across the sea and writing, always writing, I remember."

As the Queen's galley drops anchor at Siponto, in the distance we see the tall church tower beyond the marshes. We hear bells tolling thanks for our safe landing. Sumpter mules carry us up the steep hill that winds around to Mons

Garganus, where we will visit the shrine of Saint Michael the Archangel. We are to rest at the castle of a knight whose family came here from Coutances.

We are offered cool milk of almonds to quench our thirst and fine biscuits made from honey and almonds spread between pastries as thin as the Holy Wafer. As we savor these rich comfits, a knight on a white stallion gallops down from the Mount to give us greetings. His tunic bears an emblem of a crouching lion.

"I am Serlon—cousin thrice removed of your aunt, Lady de Hauteville," he tells me. "My forebears came to Sicily with Tancred's sons. I was born in Apulia. I have never set foot in Normandy."

The Knight Serlon is handsome, tall and strong, with wavy reddish hair not unlike my own and clear blue-green eyes, deep set. His right temple bears a small red mark, as though a drop of blood had fallen there.

I dare not look upon his face too long, because something strange happens inside me when I do. But when I risk a glance, I find him staring back.

Joanna senses our interest in each other.

Tonight she speaks with sternness in her voice that I have never heard before. "All your thoughts must go now to this child you bear. My child. William's child. You must not have flights of fancy, Rosamonde." And again she warns me. "Now, you *must* forget Palermo. Put it out of your mind. Forever!"

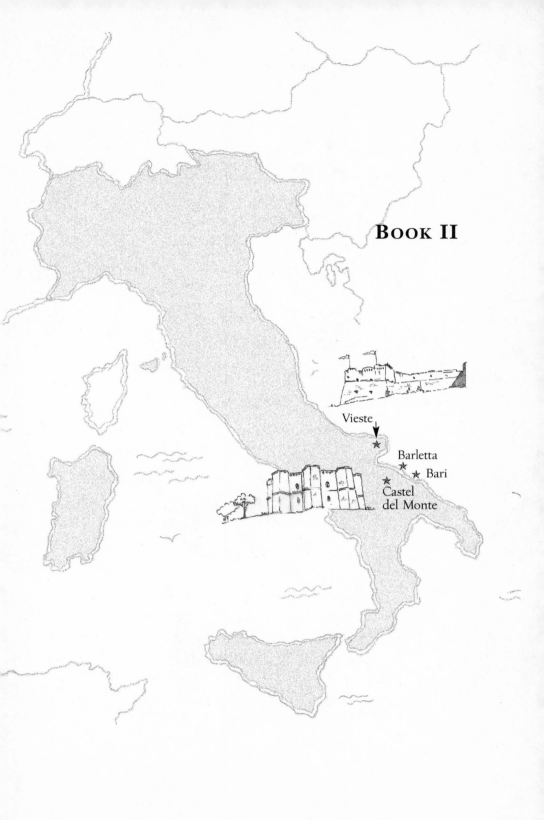

BOOK II

Vieste

Barletta

Bari

Castel
del Monte

ANDRIA, PROVINCE OF BARI, PUGLIA, ITALY
APRIL 20, 1994

IT WAS ALREADY PAST NOON. All around the piazza, shopkeepers rolled down iron shutters with a clatter and clang. In a Norman church, the thunderous organ and choir voices masked the sounds of restorers repairing the 12th century Cosmati work floor in the nave. Each colored marble lozenge, roundel, and octagon was gently pried up then stacked with great care onto a canvas drop cloth.

Just as a restorer was lifting an octagonal tile, his tool struck metal. The others paused, looked at each other in surprise and, without a word, began to lift the surrounding tiles.

What they uncovered seemed to be a bronze chest.

The master craftsman, the oldest of the four, made the sign of the Cross. "We had better call the *architetto. Subito.*" He tried not to betray his excitement.

Outside, the architect, Giovanni di Serlo, patted the smooth rump of one of two white marble lions crouching on either side of the entrance. Time, weather, and now air pollution had transformed their once fierce bared teeth into benign, toothless smiles. He wondered how much longer the pair could remain guarding their ancient charge.

As the architect aimed his camera to record the lion's deterioration, the master restorer appeared, beckoning him to come back into the church.

"What happened, Marco?" he asked.

The restorer only gestured for him to hurry. The architect followed the restorer into the church. The choir was just leaving for lunch. By the time he reached the side chapel, the architect's eyes had readjusted from the brilliant Apulian sunlight to the soft gray haze inside. He saw what the men had discovered in the excavated pavement. He blinked again to make sure he was seeing, not imagining.

"Go find the sacristan and bring him here," the architect ordered, then motioned the others to close all doors.

Then, in a hushed voice, he ordered that the chest be lifted out and opened.

CHAPTER TEN

A FEW DAYS after saying goodbye to Brian, I boarded the night train from Bologna, heading due south along the Adriatic coast toward Vieste.

"What time would the signora like her morning call?" the porter asked me in the formal Italian way. "I can bring her coffee and a croissant, if she'd like. We arrive in San Severo at five-thirty in the morning."

He opened the cabinet door that concealed the automatic chamber pot. "You see, one has every comfort. Be sure to bolt the door, signora."

"*Grazie mille*." I spoke to him in clear if not always correct Italian. "Please wake me at four forty-five." That would give me enough time to get ready.

I signed the breakfast order, slid the door shut, flipped the steel bolt. Linda once told me a horror story about an opera singer who'd chatted with a fellow traveler on a night train to Vienna and drunk a Coca-Cola with him. The next morning she woke up with a deep burn on her hand where the thief tested her consciousness before taking off with her jewelry, her wallet, and passport. I shuddered, rechecked the bolt and punched the mattress; a bit thin, but the sheets were fresh, the blanket clean. I flopped down on the cot, my body swaying with every twist and turn as the train headed toward Apulia. But I was too excited to sleep.

Matthew and I had spent our honeymoon in Italy, and in recent years we'd taken business trips to the Veneto to buy findings and glass intaglios for my jewelry designs. But I'd never visited my father's birthplace in Vieste, the spur on the heel of Italy's boot. Three years ago, on our last trip, Matthew insisted that we drive south along the Adriatic Coast from Venice to Vieste. But I put him off. As I'd put him off the last trip, the trip before that. "Maybe on our next visit," I had insisted. "This time we have to see Mantua and Ferrara."

Last time Ravenna had been my excuse. I could never admit to Matthew that growing up in New England had made me reject my Italian roots. Nor could I admit the startling relief after we married, of sharing his Anglo name, Kirkland. I was ashamed of my feelings of shame about being Italian. Southern Italian, no less. Now, without knowing why, I felt pent-up longings—longings for what I wasn't quite sure. For silvery light on hillsides of olive trees? What was so special about that light? After all, Mediterranean light is hardly different from Pacific light.

I tried to imagine what my cousins would look like. Their mother, my father's younger sister, had died when they were in their teens. So many years had passed since I'd looked through the photo album at my mother's house. I remembered Marta as a skinny, old-fashioned looking girl, knock kneed and pigeon toed, and Lorenzo with his shock of high, dark hair, all buttoned-up in a hand-tailored jacket. Aunt Caterina, my father's older sister, the red-haired beauty of the family must be late seventy-something by now. I was determined not to bombard them with questions about the Altavilla. Or tell them about Rosamonde's voice. Or about the surrogate plan Matthew was pushing for. What would they think of their American relatives!

In my travel bag I found the newspaper bought at Heathrow and turned to page three to read the article one last time before turning off the light.

Imperial Artifacts Stolen

April 20–Andria, Province of Bari, Italy (Reuters News Service)–The contents of a metal chest discovered by workmen restoring the ancient marble pavement in a church in Andria were stolen last week from the office of the Superintendent of Monuments at Bari. Among the items taken were a mysterious map on vellum and various gold medieval coins. Scotland Yard and the International Police suspect Mafia involvement. The documents are believed to have been the possession of Frederick II, Holy Roman Emperor (1194–1250). One document, impressed with a magenta wax seal, is thought to be a letter from Empress Costanza d'Altavilla, mother of Frederick II. This letter remains with the Superintendent of Monuments, Bari.

A group of international scholars had been scheduled to convene in June to decipher the document, damaged by temperature changes over the centuries.

Each time I read the article, a shudder crept along my spine. An instance of Brian's synchronicity, perhaps? Strange that this discovery and theft should happen just as I was on my way to Apulia. On my own quest. A quest for what I wasn't yet sure, but I was sure that I had to visit that church in Andria to see for myself the very floor where the chest had been excavated. I snapped off the reading light and listened to the hypnotic train sounds.

Before setting off for The Shrine of Saint Michael the Archangel, we rest at the castle of the Knight Serlon. Joanna has taken St. Michael as her patron saint because his ancient shrine stands on her wedding property.

In the afternoons, Joanna bends over her embroidery, working Saint Michael's story on linen woven for her by Norman nuns in Aversa.

I watch as she sits beneath the awning on the parapet, stitching the legend with fine wool strands. She embroiders the table where Tancred de Hauteville sits with his wife and his sons. The Knight Serlon is pleased that his great grandfather Serlon has been drawn upon the cloth—and scenes of Outremer as well. Duke Robert on his palanquin and the palm of the holy city of Jerusalem on his left.

I struggle to work the palm tree in the cloth.

This morning as Caid Gregory and I stroll along the beach, we glimpse the Knight upon his white horse, half hidden by the tall grasses in the dunes. I wave to him. He edges his horse down to the flat beach where I stand, the basket by my feet full of seashells I have gathered. Although I have missed five months, my body does not yet reveal the child I carry. Caid stands by, not wanting to leave the two of us alone. It matters not to the Knight Serlon that Caid watches over us, listening to the Knight's sweet words to me. But I hope Caid will not tell Queen Joanna.

That afternoon, as we embroider side by side, the Queen confides in me. "You should know, Rosamonde, that King William stayed at this very castle with the Knight Serlon, long before our wedding was arranged. The Emperor Comnenus had promised the hand of his daughter Maria to William, to form a strong alliance between Byzantium and Sicily."

"I have heard the story, My Lady. The eunuchs say Maria left King William waiting at the altar and that he smarted from the slight until you were brought from England to be his bride."

"Yes, poor William journeyed to Taranto, but Maria never came. He waited two weeks, then journeyed here to Monte Sant' Angelo—to pray and give homage to the saint. Still Maria never came."

"I can imagine his disgrace. The King of Sicily betrayed by a Byzantine Princess."

"Disgraced and outraged, he was. William confessed to me that in his wrath he vowed to wreak vengeance on Manuel Comnenus for this dishonor and shame."

Now I understand William's anger when he first made love to me. He is angry with all women except his wife, for she is as the Virgin and for him she will remain that way.

Joanna must be reading my thoughts, for she says, "not long after we were wed, my husband began to dream about building a monument to Our Lady. He even pondered taking holy vows. His mother saw his reserve with women, and begged him to spend more time with the Greek silk weavers in the Tiraz, for they are skilled in many ways. Soon our marriage was arranged—the union of the two great Norman families. The Plantagenet and the Altavilla."

My eyes were wide open before the wake-up call. As the sun rose, all I could see from the train window was a pale sapphire sky above a vast green plain. The *Tavoliere*, as it was called, was as flat and green as Prester John's emerald table. Demeter's wheat land. Green wheat turned golden making Apulia rich over the centuries. I twisted my bracelets so I could admire the ancient Greek coins I'd forged into the hammered gold. On one cuff, the goddess Demeter's portrait with her symbol, an ear of wheat; on the other Persephone, her daughter's portrait with her symbol, the pomegranate.

❧

"*Carissima cugina!*" Lorenzo embraced me as I stepped off the train. I stood back, hands resting on his shoulders, to look at him.

"At last—I can't believe I'm really here, Renzo." Even in my elation, I felt a tinge of sadness that Renzo bore no resemblance to my father.

He pressed a bouquet of garden roses in my hand. I kissed him on both cheeks and turned to hug my cousin Marta, in whose features I could see something of my own.

I felt the tears well up.

Marta's eyes were shiny, too.

"We speak of you so often, Rosa. We've always kept your wedding picture on the piano."

I was surprised that Marta was so American looking. She was wearing tight Levi's, a red and white striped shirt, a white cardigan knotted over her shoulders; her blonde hair was short-clipped chic.

Marta kept quiet while her brother did all the talking. Everything was quick about Renzo, his movements, his speech, his mind.

"You've chosen the right time to visit us. Just in time for the feast of Santa Maria di Merino"

I smiled. "I knew something was urging me here." Santa Maria di Merino was part of my childhood lore. Her picture always sat on my parents' dresser. I'd forgotten that her Feast Day was on the ninth of May.

"How's Matthew? And his project? I'm sorry he couldn't be with you," Renzo said as we drove off in his Lancia.

"He's still in Osaka. The Japanese are really interested in his patent." I explained as best I could the process by which inert material was transformed.

"We ought to start thinking about recycling in this country— even the Gargano is beginning to change. *Caspite!* They just built a pasta factory on the *promontorio*—in a pine forest. I couldn't believe it! The world is going crazy."

He drove southeast toward the coast road of the Gargano peninsula. Soon the landscape changed to pines, ancient olives and small villages perched like white doves on cliffs high above the ultramarine Adriatic. The Gargano had become a major resort area, mostly for northern Italians and Germans. Olive groves turned into campsites and fancy hotels dotted the coast.

"Stop! Let's buy some fruit," Marta ordered her brother, as we were about to pass a truck farmer unloading produce at a roadside stand. "I'm hungry, and I'm sure Rosa must be, as well."

The vendor was selling baskets of *nespole*, loquats the color of old rose gold.

"Taste, taste," the old man called out to us. "The last of the season and sweeter than the teat of a virgin." He gave them a tweak.

I had been too excited to eat on the train, and my mouth watered from the ripe, apricot-like fragrance of *nespole* that wafted in when Renzo opened the car door. "Fruit isn't nearly so per-fumed in California," I said.

"All your imagination, Rosa. Here, we think everything in the

States is bigger and better." Renzo paid for the *nespole* and we sat down to feast before driving on.

"I've never eaten one before—it's delicious." I bit into another.

Marta said, "These are juicier than the first-of-the-season—don't you think, Renzo?"

"In my opinion, last year's crop was better." Renzo replied. "Remember how sweet they were? I thought this year's early spring crop was too acid."

Long and detailed conversations about the food at hand were part of the Italian eating ritual, I remembered.

"What's that tower overlooking the beach?" I pointed to what looked like a tiny castle built on the side of a hill facing the sea.

"Once a tumbledown Saracen watchtower," Renzo said. "Now turned into a summer castello by some director from Munich."

"Come on—let me get a picture of the two of you enjoying the *nespole*," Renzo said, "so I can send one on to Matthew to show him what he's missing."

When we were back on the coast road, he pointed out Rodi. Then Peschici, terraced to the sea, so blinding white in the sun that I had to squint to see it.

"The roads seem less dangerous than the way my father used to describe them," I said.

"They are. But don't forget that Vieste was always accessible by sea. The Venetians traded here. If there's time, we'll visit the harbor lighthouse built over a grotto where you can see for yourself the records of ships passings scratched into the walls. A Venetian doge—Pietro Orseolo—left his marks in 1002. One day when you come to Italy again, you must visit Venice as well."

I nodded without saying a word, hoping he wouldn't notice the blood rushing to my face. I didn't have the heart to admit to Renzo and Marta that I'd already been to Venice. Many times. I'd sailed to all the islands in the lagoon, I'd roamed its *calle*, visited its museums, its churches, dealt with goldsmiths in Padua and Verona and ordered glass intaglios in Vicenza.

We drove toward new Vieste built around the port, past the avenue of palms and the park, then into the very heart of medieval Vieste. Lorenzo seemed to find his way easily through winding streets just wide enough for his Lancia.

"Here we are!" He pulled into the parcheggio, near the Hotel Vesta.

Needing solitude and quiet to write, I'd asked Renzo to make a reservation in a small, simple hotel in the old town, close by my Aunt Caterina. More family awaited me in the lobby of the hotel. More kissing and crying as I tried to match my cousins' faces with the ones from the old photographs.

Some things hadn't changed with the times.

But my cousins had. They were much more modern and up to date than I ever could have imagined. Ironically some of my relatives in Providence still tried to preserve old world customs, some of them still speaking the dialect of seventy years past.

We drank cappuccinos and Coca-Colas in the T.V. lounge bar that overlooked the orange and green striped umbrellas on the small coved beach of the hotel.

"*Andiamo*," Renzo clapped his hands in the air, announcing to our noisy group. "Rosa should have a rest."

"Caterina expects you for lunch at her house. Just the two of you," Marta said. "I'll be cooking with the ladies. Preparing this evening's dinner."

"Caterina has become somewhat of a recluse, you know, but I insisted that she come to the party. Do you think you can find your way to her house? It's just up by the Duomo. You can't miss it."

"Of course I can find my way."

"*Brava!*" We all embraced and kissed again.

"*Buon riposo*. Until this evening."

⚘

The view from my third-story room was worth the steep climb. I stepped out to the terracotta tiled terrace that overlooked the lichened red-tiled roofs of the *Centro Storico*. Maybe I could find some pots of geraniums to blossom on this balcony. When I turned my back to the sea, I looked up to a huddle of whitewashed medieval houses clustered around the Duomo's cupola, the highest point in old town. If I turned east, the sea lay before me like a length of shimmering aquamarine silk.

I scanned the complimentary guide to the Gargano and made a mental list of all the places I had to explore—places I remembered from my father's stories. The mysterious Foresta Umbra, a secret grotto where he used to swim and where he'd found his gold coin, the ancient necropolis, the medieval sanctuary of Monte Sant'Angelo. And of course Frederick II's Castel del Monte.

By the time I unpacked and put Matthew's framed photo on the dresser, it was almost noon. My Aunt Caterina would be waiting for me.

⚘

I took a deep breath, lifted the knocker on the ironclad door and let it drop. I knocked again. I heard her footsteps on the staircase. Caterina opened the door slowly, peering out from a darkened room.

I wrapped my arms around my aunt's spindly body. "*Zia, Zia,* I'm Rosa, your brother Tommaso's daughter."

"I know," she said. "I could not come to greet you with the family—I hardly ever leave the house these days. And they were right, you were a beautiful child and now you are a beautiful woman. You look just like your father. He was so handsome."

I stepped back, my hands still clasping my aunt's.

"None of us were given your beauty, Caterina." My aunt's fine skin was embroidered with tiny lines. Her famous red hair had turned white, but her perfect, classic features were as lovely as ever, her smile still dazzling despite a missing tooth I noticed only when she smiled wide. Her eyes were the same gray-blue as my father's.

I stepped into the *salone*. The blinds were closed against the afternoon sun, the sofas and chairs covered with white sheets, I assumed to keep them free of dust.

My aunt asked about my mother, Matthew, my life in California, my jewelry business. I searched the bottom of my purse for the red felt bag holding the pin I had designed, an ancient silver Greek coin of Apulia surrounded by amethysts, her birthstone.

"Such a beautiful remembrance from California," she said as I helped her pin it to her pale gray suit jacket. "I will always treasure this. And since I have no children myself, I will leave it for you, Rosa, and for your daughter. You must never give up, Rosa. Never."

"Give up?"

"Never retreat, as I have done. You must visit the Madonna. Perhaps she will hear you pray for a child. *Make* her hear you."

I put my arms around Caterina's frail shoulders. She seemed so much smaller than the robust looking woman I remembered from photographs.

"But now we must take an *aperitivo* before lunch."

While Caterina busied about in the kitchen, I picked up an old snapshot framed in carved olivewood.

Memorial Day. Four-year-old Rose and her parents all smiling and happy under an umbrella at Narragansett Beach; the coin still hanging from the chain around my father's neck—an ancient Greek gold coin he'd found as a boy. He had mounted the coin as a good luck charm. According to family lore, I'd torn away that chain and tossed it into the Sound during the dreaded swimming lesson later that afternoon. My father, convinced that I was ready to swim, had let go of me. "Swim! Swim, Rosa!" he'd shouted. But I sank. Right to the bottom. Flailing limbs, mouthfuls of salty water, a blur of tangled seaweed and broken Quahog shells, all I remember of that Memorial Day. Often I'd wondered if Atlantic tides have worn away the coin's portrait or swept it to another shore. Or if it still lies buried beneath tamped sand, submerged forever.

I'd finally trusted Matthew enough to teach me to swim across the shallow end in the pool downstairs, but to this day I'm still too scared to swim in water over my head. Yet I was grateful that I lived with a view of the sea I love. And hate.

Caterina returned with a tray holding a cut-glass decanter. She poured an opaque white liquid into two fragile Venetian glasses, diluting it with clear water from a pitcher. "This is made from the milk of bitter almonds. I hope you like it, Rosa. It has always been my favorite drink. Or perhaps you'd prefer a Coca-Cola?"

"Thank you. I'd rather try your drink." I sipped the *orzata*, which tasted like sweet almond extract in milk. I didn't like it, but I finished it.

After lunch, as we were having coffee, I brought up the subject of the Orlandi.

"Caterina, how long have the Orlandi lived in Vieste?"

She thought for a moment. "As far as I know, for hundreds of years. The Orlandi and the Ruggieri as well, my husband's family. Our roots are so deep in this place. Forever."

"How would I go about researching our family's ancestry?"

She gave me a curious look. "I suppose you'd start at the *municipio*. My friend's daughter, Valeria, works there. You should call on her."

"Have you ever heard of the Altavilla? Is that a name one hears around here?"

"A name, yes—but one we read in history books. I don't *know* anyone by that name. Why do you ask?"

"I've come here to learn about the Altavilla. King Roger, William the Good of Sicily, and Federico Secondo . . ."

"You must know that Sicily and the South of Italy were one country in those days. Come to think of it, my husband's mother used to boast that the Ruggieri descended from the famous Count Roger Altavilla. I never took her seriously—but, you know, there *are* families in this town who *can* trace their roots back for centuries. You are like your father, Rosa. He was always full of such questions to his parents." She sighed deeply. "*Le buone anime*—good souls in heaven, may they all rest in peace."

Caterina had just told me exactly what I had come to hear. My father was as curious about the past as I. We went on and on for at least an hour after lunch. When I saw her nod I felt it was time to leave. I put my arms around my aunt again. Caterina had probably not been held so close in a long time.

"Thank you, Caterina. I've had a lovely time with you. I hope you'll come to Uncle Carlo's tonight."

"How could I not?" She kissed my cheek.

As I prepared to leave, Caterina began to smooth and straighten the sheets on the chairs where we'd sat. I wondered if— and when—she ever removed them.

CHAPTER ELEVEN

IT WAS SIESTA, and the old town was quiet. I still had time to roam the stone-slabbed streets of the Centro Storico before dressing for the family's welcome dinner. I climbed the steps to the Via Judeca, once the medieval Jewish quarter of Vieste, and walked along the ramparts through an ancient passage. Tufts of henbane sprang out from cracks in the limestone walls.

On the other side of the passage I found a shop, the door sign read *Antichità*. In the window was a carved wood sculpture of the Flight into Egypt, the Virgin and Child astride a donkey being led by Joseph. Over them swayed a palm tree carved to look as if it were blowing in the wind.

I studied the sculpture. Early eighteenth century, I was certain. I pulled the highly polished doorbell. A young woman opened the door.

"Good evening signora. May I help you?" she asked in English.

"I'd like to have a look around," I said in my so-so Italian.

The shop wasn't large, nor was it crammed full like some California shops. A tall vitrine displayed ancient Roman glass, coins, a Deruta majolica charger, and jewelry. Hanging on a Lucite stand was a pair of earrings, stylized gold rosettes studded with garnets, from which were suspended hollow gold crescents. Even without my jeweler's loupe, I could see the faint hammer marks in the gold.

"What beautiful earrings. Are they Greek? Or Roman?" I asked.

"*L'architetto* Di Serlo will have to tell you, signora. I'll go find him."

I remember smiling to myself. So many titles in Italy! A*vvocato, Ingeniere, Maestro, Architetto. Dottore* for anyone with a university degree.

Architect Di Serlo appeared a moment later—a tallish man with sandy hair, a deeply cleft chin, and eyes like blue topaz. He looked as though he spent a lot of time in the sun. A small red birthmark, like a drop of congealed blood, marked his right temple.

"*Buona sera, signora.* My name is Di Serlo, Giovanni. How may I help you?"

"I'm Rose Kirkland—from California," I said. "I was curious about those earrings. May I have a look?"

He took the earrings out of the case and handed them to me. "Please, try them."

I moved to the ornate Venetian mirror, threading the fine gold wires in my ears, searching the dark, mottled glass for my reflection. I turned my head from side to side, wondering who might have worn these earrings centuries ago. Maiden or matron? Persephone or Demeter?

"Where are they from?" I asked.

"Taranto, Magna Grecia," he said. "About the fifth century B.C. But I must tell you that only one is authentic—from an old collection. The other is a copy."

At least he was honest. I asked the price and found it not unreasonable for such quality.

"I'd like to have them," I said.

He smiled. "Because you didn't bargain with me, I would like to offer you this antique Neapolitan box in which to keep them. I hope you will enjoy wearing the earrings—or looking at them, as I have done these past few weeks."

Matthew would have called me a pushover American, but I've always hated bargaining, even for gemstones at the Mart—where, especially with Indian and Chinese dealers, it was part of the expected formality.

"Thank you," I said. "It's a charming box." I ran my fingertips over the inlay of nacre and tiny gold stars finely worked in the tortoise shell.

"Where are you staying, signora?"

"At the Hotel Vesta. It's very convenient—some of my relatives live nearby. Perhaps you know them? My maiden name was Orlando."

"Yes, of course! But you're obviously American or English, with a name like Kirkland."

"My husband's name."

He looked down at my left hand and my wide, old-fashioned wedding band.

"I'm visiting my family, but I also plan to do some research."

"Here in Puglia?" he said. "Interesting to hear that for a change. Most foreigners spend their time in the north of Italy. It shows how little they know—but then, you're not a foreigner."

I felt a flush. Little did *he* know.

"You must know that Puglia—or Apulia—was part of ancient Greek culture. Until the Normans conquered it to give you your blue eyes," he said, looking at me intently with his own.

I turned my eyes away from his. He was flirting with me. "In a way, I'm here because of the Normans," I said. "The Altavilla."

"Altavilla! Why the Altavilla?" His eyes seemed to narrow slightly.

I shrugged my shoulders. "Oh—just an interest of mine. Are the Normans an interest of yours?"

"I work with the *Soprintendenza* in Bari. On the restoration of Norman monuments in Puglia. In the summer months I'm here in Vieste to mind my shop. Do you collect? Perhaps I can help you find what you're looking for. I've computerized a vast inventory of paintings and objects available in shops all over Italy—and Europe. Networking, as you call it in the States."

I thought for a moment, then said, "I like old fabrics. Supposing I were interested in finding textiles from the Norman *Regno*. Where would I find something like that, some small samples of early silk from the Tiraz workshop in Palermo, for instance?"

Again that oddly penetrating look. "I can answer that without a computer," he said. "The Swiss are ardent collectors of textiles. I know of a shop in Bern where you might find some."

He went to a bookcase behind the counter and pulled out a thick volume. "I've just begun a new project with a Swiss colleague. If you're interested, permit me to show you a book she recently sent to me.

"These are remarkable discoveries. Most of the book is technical, but the pictures speak for themselves." He set the book on the table and turned to a color photograph. A fragment of ancient cloth in close detail.

"This was found at Vergina—in Macedonia—in the grave of Phillip II, the father of Alexander the Great. It was the shroud that wrapped his bones. You see, it is purple woven with gold threads, and from Taranto, the experts believe, where your earrings were found. They are of the same period."

I tried to make out the design. It seemed to be a vase filled with climbing morning glories, with flowers that looked like fuchsia and periwinkle.

"That's only the beginning." He turned to a picture of a red cloak, intact except for one missing corner. "The mantle of St. Anthony of Padova, patron saint of people who lose things."

"People who lose objects or their heads? I've tried praying to him on occasion." I laughed at my joke but he didn't seem to notice.

"St. Anthony's body was exhumed not many years ago, but by the time the cape found its way to the conservation laboratory, a corner was already gone, stolen by relic seekers. The Vatican was outraged. The cape has been under guard ever since."

"This happens a lot in Italy, doesn't it?" I said. "You must have heard about the recent discovery in Andria, and the theft of that strange map. I just read about it in an English newspaper . . ."

"A terrible crime—unspeakable," he said almost vehemently. "Here, let me show you this picture, the cloak of Saint Francis of Assisi. "

That was odd. I wondered why he'd dismissed the theft so abruptly.

I examined the inset of the patched-up cloak. The photograph and diagram were documentations, textile conservation at its most scientific.

He turned the page to a similar study. "This cloak comes from the convent of Saint Claire in Assisi. The conservator had long suspected that Saint Francis' cloak might have been patched with pieces from Saint Claire's cloak. She wrote to the Mother Superior, and at last, a few years ago she was allowed to examine Saint Claire's cloak. Sure enough, those patches on Saint Francis' cape were exact matches of pieces cut from Saint Claire's lovingly sewn in by her own hand. From these diagrams you can see exactly where the patches were cut from her cloak and sewn onto his."

I hoped he hadn't seen my eyes well up with tears. "What a remarkable book—I'd like to have a copy. May I take the publisher's name?"

I wrote it on one of his cards and slipped it into my passport case.

"How long do you stay in Vieste, signora?"

"Perhaps three or four weeks. I am very anxious to visit Monte Sant'Angelo and Castel del Monte, then I'd like to go south to Trani, Barletta, Bari."

"You intend to see the south in depth, then. Please do not hesitate to call upon me if I may be of assistance."

His tone was formal, but I sensed that he meant what he said. I thanked him, paid for the earrings with a credit card, and climbed the stone paved streets back to the Vesta, still under the spell of his tender story.

❧

The *passeggiata*, the evening walk, the Viestani called *lo struscio*, which means the swish of skirts. It was a ritual for the Viestani, as it is in virtually every other Southern Italian town. Everyone turns out for it. My cousins and I strolled through the crowded park. Old men huddled on benches philosophizing under the plane trees. Others played *La Legge*, The Law, with Tarot cards, or gossiped over glasses of *grappa* at the Sports Café.

I was introduced to my father's childhood friends, hugged and kissed and exclaimed over by strangers who told me I looked just like him. "Same coloring, same eyes, same high cheekbones," they said.

Renzo nudged me as groups of German tourists, some way too hefty to be wearing shorts, sauntered by, licking gelati cones, ogling the locals. "We see lots of Germans here. Fewer Americans," he said.

Teen-age girls strolled arm in arm, aware of their powers as the boys' eyes tracked them as they passed. They were all dressed just like teenagers in California, in jeans and t-shirts, some emblazoned with Berkeley and Yale logos, most likely sent by American cousins.

Mothers pushed prams with dolled-up babies. Others carried toddlers sucking candy pacifiers. Well-to-do couples dressed in simple taupe or pale gray Armani looked smart in that throw-away-chic Milanese way.

"*La bella figura,*" I said to Lorenzo. "Still as important to Italians as ever, isn't it?"

"Oh yes, we're still preoccupied with how we appear to others—but the Viestani do have taste. They've had a long time to learn. It's in their blood. Centuries before Christ Vieste was a seaport, most likely the ancient Greek Uria, city of Aphrodite, goddess of love—still a very revered goddess in this town." He winked and laughed. "*Andiamo*, let's have an *aperitivo* at the Bar del Corso—then we'll be off to Uncle Carlo's."

We passed a newspaper kiosk where I bought the promised postcard for my mother. A view of Old Vieste from the sea. We all signed it while we had our drinks, then we piled in Renzo's Lancia and drove north of Vieste.

Because it was so warm for May, Marta and Renzo decided we should have the family gathering in my great-uncle Carlo's olive groves that edged the sea north of Vieste. The night was cloudless, the sky diamond-studded ebony, and in the distance the lighthouse beacon flashed its red wand across the Adriatic.

Renzo hung lanterns in the olive trees and lighted a fire to boil the *orecchiette*, "little ears" of pasta cooked with wild broccoli and drizzled with garlicky olive oil. We sat at tables draped with whiter-than-white linen and feasted on grilled sea bass, baked eggplant, crisp vegetables *sott'olio*, wine from my uncle's press.

Marta's two pretty teenage daughters seemed awestruck that their American cousin lived near Hollywood! They were curious about my bracelets, and twisted them round and round my wrists.

I pulled them off. "Here, try them on. The coins are ancient Greek—from Metaponto, a city near where Taranto is today. Matthew's uncle gave me the coins as a wedding present. I set them into the cuffs myself."

Caterina was pleased that I had followed in my father's footsteps and become a jeweler. She told stories that revealed a side of my father I'd never known: the dashing young adventurer who had left Italy to seek his fortune in America.

Renzo jumped from the table when a car door slammed in the shadows beyond the olive trees. "Excuse me—it's my old school chum, Giovanni di Serlo, a well-known restoration architect. I've invited him to come by. He promised to entertain us with his guitar."

I felt a little leap inside.

In a moment Renzo appeared with the architect and introduced us. We shook hands but Giovanni di Serlo didn't acknowledge our previous meeting. He allowed me to do so.

"We've already met." I said. "I found the architect's shop on my way back from Caterina's. If there's an antique shop to be found, I'll surely find it." I laughed, a bit too girlishly.

Renzo poured a glass of wine and pulled up a chair for him. As Giovanni di Serlo strummed his guitar, everyone shouted favorites.

His voice was untrained. A manly voice, a bit coarse, yet perfectly pitched.

He sang their old favorites, as well as some newer popular ballads.

"Signora, is there a song in particular that you would like to hear?"

"I used to hear a song at Italian weddings. Sometimes my father would sing it after a few glasses of wine. *Oi lì Oi là*. Do you know it?"

"Of course. It's an old Neapolitan song." He strummed the first few measures.

I laughed. "I may even remember a verse or two."

"Come on, come on, Rosa, sing it for us, then," Marta called out.

Now I've never sung except in the bath or shower. Hardly ever lately. Certainly never before an audience. But after a stanza or two I joined in.

Comm' acqua la fontana
Ca non si secca
L'amore e n'a catena
che non si spezza

Water in the fountain
Never dries up
Love is like a chain
that never breaks

"*Brava, che brava!*" As they applauded, I found myself wondering why I'd never sung as a child. It was as though tonight, with my father's family, I'd lost my inhibitions and found my singing voice. Both at once.

After dinner Caterina unwrapped the linen cloth from a huge block of almond nougat and chipped away at the rock hard candy with a small silver chisel. I hadn't eaten *torrone* since I left Providence. Making up for lost time I must have eaten at least five pieces.

Marta asked, "how would you like to spend your time in Vieste? Besides visit with all of us. Renzo and I play a lot of tennis. You're a Californian—so you must play, as well. Or do museums interest you more. Or the beach?"

"I enjoy museums—and a little bit of sun, but I don't play tennis. I've always been kind of a misfit in California."

They seemed surprised by my honesty.

"I told Architetto di Serlo that I need to see some of the sites of Frederick II, Andria, and Castel del Monte. And I must do some research in the church records." I began to talk non-stop about my interest in the Altavilla; of Federico Secondo; of Costanza, his mother, and of his public birth at Jesi, in the Marches near Ancona.

I felt Giovanni's eyes. My relatives put down their glasses. I was flustered to have had the floor so long. "I hope I'm not boring you with all this."

"You know so much more of our history than we do, Rosa," Marta said. "I know that Federico restored our Duomo, that he built our fortress, but I never knew that Vieste, Siponto, and Monte Sant'Angelo were wedding gifts to Joanna of England from King William the Good of Sicily. Where did you learn that?"

"At Oxford. I can give you the source if you like."

"Did you know that Frederick's tomb in Palermo Cathedral was just reopened?" Giovanni asked.

I shook my head. He went on. "1994 is the 800th anniversary of Frederick's birth. The tomb had been opened once before—a hundred years ago, but this time the scientists were looking for a bit of bone or hair—perhaps to determine Frederick's DNA."

Renzo said, "Not too long ago I read that scientists are trying to locate descendants of Utzi, the Neolithic man whose frozen body was found in the mountain pass between Austria and Italy. When I read about it, I felt the *pelle d'oca*."

"I have goosebumps right now just hearing about it." For the rest of the evening I was subdued, sensing that my imagination had been stirred up by all these gene-tracing DNA stories.

Giovanni spent the rest of the evening chatting with my cousins as I sat there, half-listening.

When Renzo and Marta drove me back to the hotel it was past midnight. I reached Matthew in Osaka and told him all about the dinner in the olive grove.

"You sound wonderful, darling," he said. "More like your old self. Being with your family seems to have done you a world of good."

"I do feel so much better here than at Oxford. Things seem to have calmed down. Sort of. I'm still writing in the notebook you gave me."

"What about that voice?" he said.

"Almost gone." Not quite the truth, but why worry him?

I was tired when we finished our long conversation. I washed up and fell into bed, turning off the light, tucking the velvet cushion beneath my head.

 Astride our mules, we curve our way along the steep path to St. Michael's mountain, pilgrims all. The lame, the blind, light-hearted crusaders on their way to Outremer, haggard, wasted crusaders on their return from Outremer; pilgrims with bleeding feet, penitents hobbling with pebbles in their shoes; some in evil-smelling haircloth, others clothed in softest wools from the markets of Ypres. Faces weathered amber and bronze, faces burned like bracken from the sun. Pilgrims from the gates of Paris, the plains of Spain, from English heaths, from

Sicily's ports, some holding crucifixes aloft or tall, waxen tapers. Vendors of relics proclaim their wares to be of the utmost verity.

"Here, here—a finger bone of Saint Radegonda!"

"Parings from the nails of the True Cross!"

"Three hairs from the head of Mary Magdalen!"

I put my hand to my throat. Lady de Hauteville's amulet still hangs around my neck. It has kept me safe all these months since I left my Normandy. Even more than safe-keeping, it has brought me love. We come at last to the pine grove at the entrance to the Archangel's church, built over his cave deep beneath the earth. Votive stones dangling from long red strings make the pine boughs hang heavy. Smoking torches light the night-dark tunnel. I peer into the deep passage. The Knight Serlon will lead us into the cave. We grasp the rope tight, and step by step, we make our way deeper and deeper into the earth's core.

Ex votos hanging on the wall shimmer in the torchlight. Thin silver shaped like arms and legs and ears and eyes, others like breasts and stomachs or bundled babies. All left by grateful palmers for favors received through the divine grace of Saint Michael. Welcome vapors of galbanum and frankincense mask the rancid animal smell of burning tal-low. Fumes and smoke clouds make us cough and our eyes tear.

At last we reach the great bronze and silver doors. Licks of flaming torchlight catch saints and Bible scenes. We rat-tle the door handles, as is the custom. Doors fling open, and we enter, tiptoeing on cloths spread out on the cavern's wet floor. Overhead, rocks glisten with crystal beads of water dripping down on us. The aged, wizened Bishop of Siponto, leaning on his jeweled crozier, welcomes the

Queen of Sicily. We fall to our knees following the reverence made by Joanna, who then crosses herself three times. The muttering of prayers and the splashing of the water in the holy well are the only sounds I hear.

We pray until the bishop begins to sing his Mass. Flambeaux flare and sputter. Puffs of sweet smoke thicken the air as censors swing. I breathe in incense and leave the liturgy of the Mass behind, letting my mind wander willy-nilly in this bosom of the earth.

All of a sudden I see something dart between a cleft in the oozing rocks, startling me from my faraway world. A fat snake slithers out and curls itself into a circle by my feet. I do not move nor have I fear of the serpent, for this cavern has been its home long before St. Michael came to claim it.

CHAPTER TWELVE

THE NEXT DAY was so hot it seemed like July. I read in the local newspaper that all of Europe, as far north as England, was gripped by an unseasonable heat wave. Most Viestani were cooling off at the beach, but I would walk down to the Municipio, the city hall, where the birth records were kept, where I would research the Orlandi as far back as I could.

Valeria, Marta's friend was friendly, helpful—and candid.

"Come back later today and I'll have everything from 1850, the time of the Risorgimento up to the present. If you want anything before these dates, you'll have to visit Don Gesualdo at the Duomo. All the early church records are filed away in the back of the sacristy. But he's so lazy it might take him years to get through those dusty books. I think you'll have a real problem unless you do it yourself, and that might take weeks."

Hot and dejected, I walked back to the hotel. Better to stay in my room to write. As I trudged up the steps I heard my phone buzzing. I ran.

"*Pronto*," I said, trying to catch my breath.

"Good morning, Signora Kirkland. Giovanni di Serlo at her service. I have someone to watch the shop today, so I am free to be her guide if she would like."

"I think it's all right. My family hasn't planned anything special. We're still recuperating from the family reunion last night. I'd like to see the town if you have the time."

"It would be a great pleasure to show her," he said, speaking still in the third person formal *Lei*.

He picked me up at noon. "They're decorating for the Festa of Santa Maria di Merino," he said as we walked down to the parcheggio at the edge of the old town.

Workmen were draping the bandstand with garlands of lights. Hoops of light bulbs, no bigger than 15 millimeter pearls, arcaded the Corso, white wire angels perching all along the top. Small canvas vending tents were set up under the piazza's palm trees. The old white grillwork fish market had been transformed into a Gargano information office dispensing slick brochures of Vieste's clear blue sky touching deep blue sea.

We drove off in Giovanni's old but well-maintained red Ferrari.

"I like your car," I said.

He laughed. "It drinks far more *benzina* than it should," he said, "but I still won't part with it."

Vespas and Lambrettas whined and darted in and out among the cars. I sensed his impatience with the noise, the traffic.

"Vieste isn't at all like my father's description of a sleepy little southern Italian town with all those fancy hotels along the *Lun-*

gomare. And so many cars with foreign license plates."

"Viestani return from all parts of Italy—and from all over the world for this *festa*. If you would like, I can show you the six kilometer procession route to Merinium."

"Where does it begin?"

"At the Duomo. The devout lift the Madonna from her altar and carry her on their shoulders through the old town. Then they proceed along the beach until they turn inland to Merinium, to a chapel built by the ruins of an ancient Greek city."

"Why do they carry her to Merinium?" I asked.

"For thousands of years she was worshipped in that place—under another aspect. Did you know there was once an ancient cult of Demeter here?"

I shook my head, although I wasn't at all surprised.

"Demeter's cult was later fused with Vesta's, the Roman goddess of sacred fire. I'm sure the Feast of the Madonna of Merino relates to the fertility myth of Demeter and her daughter Persephone's return from the Underworld. Do you know the story?"

I was glad I did. "While Persephone was in a meadow smelling narcissus, Hades snatched her away to the Underworld. Her mother, the Goddess of wheat and all growing things, wept for her and the crops died."

He seemed surprised that I knew the myth. He added, "Hades had given her pomegranate seeds to eat, and because she ate them she had to return to him every year."

"I guess old customs die hard in this part of Italy," I responded.

"Especially those involving pagan gods and goddesses—even in such an overtly Christian country." As he spoke, his intense blue eyes never left mine. His sunburned face made his eyes seem bluer, his cheekbones higher. I sensed the seriousness in his voice.

We were driving north along the coast. I was curious about the enormous contraption of poles and nets jutting out over the sea.

"Our famous landmark," he said when I asked him to stop. "The *trabucco*—those seven wooden poles support immense nets that the fishermen lower into the water. When the net is full, it is hoisted up. God knows how many centuries the Viestani have been fishing this way.

"This promontory has always had mysterious aura, signora—a feeling of the supernatural. We have a legend about our Gargano, and the Tremiti Islands beyond."

"Tell me more legends," I urged, enjoying his elegant speech, his old-fashioned turn of phrase.

"We like to think the legend is truth."

"Ancient legends often have a basis in truth," I said.

"After the Trojan War, Diomedes, a Greek hero, was angry when he returned to Argos and found his wife with a lover. He sailed off until he came to these shores and to the small islands. For centuries the Tremiti were called Islands of Diomedes.

"In those earliest times, this region's principal production was *porpora*, purple dye. The shroud of King Phillip of Macedon, which you saw in my book, was probably dyed from *porpora* produced on these shores."

"I thought only Phoenicians from Tyre traded purple dye."

"The *porpora murex* was once abundant here. I can show you some shell pits along the shore toward Merinium."

"Does the dye come from the shells?" I asked.

"Not from the shell, but from a small gland inside. To start the process, shells were tossed into a pit and left to rot. *Che puzza*, what an odor!"

I inhaled, trying to imagine the hideous stink drifting across the Adriatic to the plain of Argos.

He went on, "Pliny wrote that the mass turned many colors before the rotten mass transformed itself into its most precious shade, the reddish purple of congealed blood. When the dye was extracted—only a drop from millions and millions of mollusks. Imagine! One pound required more than five million shellfish."

"I can just imagine a gram of purple dye balanced on my jeweler's scales. Worth more than its weight in gold!"

He seemed amused that I was reacting like a child spellbound by a fairy tale. I wondered if he enjoyed enthralling me with his stories.

He pulled to the roadside to show me grottoes and coves along the coast toward the point of Pugnochiuso, the "clenched fist."

"The grottoes have romantic names—the Emerald, the Bell, the Doves. There are more along the coast here, extraordinary ones, Rosa—may I call you Rosa?"

I nodded.

"One grotto can be reached only from an underwater passage."

"I wonder if it's the grotto my father always talked about."

He laughed. "Who knows, it may be. I'll show you one day if you would care to swim from my boat. It's the only way you can enter it."

I felt a twist in my stomach. "I'm not sure. I don't swim very well."

He seemed disappointed.

"Where is the necropolis I've read about? Is it far from here, Giovanni?" I liked the feel of his name on my tongue.

"It's just up the road. A group from the University of Lecce is excavating the site. It's been closed to visitors—but I know the archaeologists. They'll surely let us through."

We drove north for a few miles, then turned towards the sea onto a dusty, unpaved road with a chain link fence stretched across it. "No entrance," the sign read. Giovanni called out in Viestano dialect. A workman wheeling a sand-heaped barrow recognized Giovanni and opened the gate.

We walked along the beach, the hard, damp sand crisscrossed

with seagulls' webbed tracks. I could make out horizontal slots carved into rock now blanketed with buttercups and scarlet field poppies, shelves where bodies had once lain. I picked some dried poppy pods and shoved them in my pocket.

Giovanni took my hand and we descended into the hollow, once a Bronze Age necropolis. We were surrounded on three sides by these walls of "shelves." Beyond, I could see the entrance to a dark cavern. Stalactites dropped from its ceiling. A shallow, muddy stream flowed through it. Tall reeds choked with white morning glory blocked our passage into the cave. I was disappointed.

I folded my arms; feeling shivers traveling all the way up my back. My ancestors of generations ago had been buried here. What is it like, I remember thinking, the feeling of obliteration, to be unaware of lying in such a setting? Instead of being depressed, I felt a strange elation, as though my ancestors were more alive in me than they'd ever been.

"You seem so far away in your thoughts. What are you thinking?" he said.

"About these people. Who were they?"

"Pre-Greek peoples. This was the territory of the Daunians, a Celto-Illyrian tribe here centuries before the Greeks built their colonies in Apulia. My friend Guido Lanciani from Otranto is an expert in this field—early deities and the cult of The Magna Mater, besides being a scholar of the Norman *Regno*, as well. He's here in Vieste for the Festa. I think you would enjoy meeting him—perhaps we should have lunch together."

"I'd like that."

We climbed back up an improvised stairway of wide wooden planks that led to a path to the sea.

Two young archaeologists were digging with small hoes, painstakingly recording the shards so that each stratum could be identified precisely. It was slow scientific work, one of them explained, but nothing was overlooked.

"Have you found anything important?" I asked.

The archaeologist seemed grateful for a break.

"Only last week we found a Phoenician agate seal carved with a chimera," he said.

"May I see it? I'm a jewelry designer—I've mounted many ancient seals for my jewelry."

"Unfortunately it's in Foggia being photographed. We've found more archaic fertility goddesses, too—broken up, but none as important as the Goddess of Uria we found last year."

"Was this an ancient Greek sanctuary?"

"Yes," he said, "and at an earlier epochs most likely dedicated to cthonic deities, the Great Earth Mother. The ancient town of Uria wasn't far from here. In the salt marshes on the coast. Now scholars say Uria was Vieste. Signora, you can forget about those Lombard cities up north. This is where Italian civilization began. And then, long before the Renaissance, we had Federico Secondo."

I laughed. "You see, Giovanni, he sounds just like you!"

We climbed back to the car and he took me to a simple trattoria by the sea where the owner assured us that the *triglie*, red mullet, we ate had been fished up a few hours ago by the *trabucco* down the road. After lunch we drove along the beach.

"Whose house is that we just passed?" I asked as I turned my head to look back at a villa sitting on a high hill overlooking the sea, its facade a series of Apulian arches.

"That house belonged to my Uncle Cesare. It's built on the remains of a castle owned by our family for centuries. He's been dead for at least fifteen years now. Since he was the biggest landowner around, he was called 'Don Cesare.' He was an old satyr, lived with a woman who'd been his mistress for years. Then, when she grew older, her daughters took their turns in his bed."

"What did the people around here think about that?"

"Uncle Cesare was a law unto himself. A vast landowner, almost feudal, with workers who depended upon him for everything—the roofs over their heads, their food, even the quinine tablets. When we were boys, it was rumored that he was still claiming the daughters of his workers when they were to be married. '*Jus prima noctis.*' You must have heard about that sort of thing."

"*Le droit du seigneur*—in France."

He nodded. "Uncle Cesare is buried behind his villa. He never married. He was afraid he'd make the wrong choice."

I wondered if Giovanni had also been afraid to make his choice.

"Everyone is liberated here now," he said. "We have good roads, television. And no more old satyrs like Don Cesare to claim the women, just an occasional Don Giovanni."

"Don Giovanni?" I laughed.

He looked at me and smiled. "Don Juan, I should have said."

Soon we were back at the portal of the *barbacane*, principal gateway to the old town.

"Thank you for a lovely day," I told him as he left me at the hotel.

"May I call you again, then?" he said.

"Yes," I heard myself saying with no hesitation whatsoever.

We were all invited to Marta's the following night. After dinner Renzo, suggested that we go to a disco in the old town. My cousins, it seemed, loved to dance. *Sapore di Mare*, the disco, was crowded, but Renzo had called ahead for a table and ordered wine. I stayed with San Pellegrino.

Renzo spun me around on the floor. He's a great dancer—and

I'm not too bad myself. Matthew and I used to dance a lot when we were first married, but now, when we go to a fancy party, he's always too deep in conversation to feel like cutting it up on the dance floor.

I sipped my water and listened to the music. "*Sapore di sale, sapore di mare,*" the restaurant's languid, romantic theme song popular in the Sixties, Marta said.

I heard a voice behind me ask, "May I have the honor of a dance?"

It was Giovanni, at his most courtly. I looked at Renzo, reading in his eyes that he expected me to accept the invitation.

I rose from my chair and walked to the dance floor with Giovanni. He put his arm around me and drew me to him. I heard myself heave a deep sigh as we began to move around the small, crowded dance floor.

"*Sapore di mare, sapore di te—taste of the sea, taste of you.*"

As he held me close, I thought I heard him whisper, "I wonder how you taste, Rosa." But a moment later I was sure I was mistaken.

 We remain at Siponto for seven nights. Joanna and Caid Gregory amuse themselves playing chess, with ivory pieces carved by a Saracen in William's court. In the balmy evenings I leave my chamber to gaze down the flat salt marsh, where fireflies sparkle in the waving grass like the sea trembling with the reflection of stars.

Tonight I stand on the parapet lost in my thoughts, trying to forget William, to forget Palermo, to forget my home in Normandy. Never have I thought I would miss the hoot of scritch-owls, the distant wail of wolves.

"What is in your mind, Lady Rosamonde?" The Knight Serlon's voice startles me. "Alone, in the pale light of the May moon?"

"Only a nameless fear that overtakes me now and then," I tell him. "The fear that grips my heart for no good reason." I bear my burden and my secret well, for in my flowing robe, my body still shows no signs that I have missed five months.

He puts his arm around me and draws me close.

"Have no fear, My Lady. The Queen has entrusted me with your secret. I know you are the bearer of King William's child, and I have sworn my fealty to the Queen as her protector on her return to Palermo with the newborn heir. She has given me consent to ask for your hand in marriage. If you will have me. But we must wait until the King's child is born before we repeat our marriage vows." I look in his eyes, so many tears in my own that his face is blurred.

"Do not weep, Rosamonde, when Joanna told me of the ruse I gave my oath to her, to the Black Virgin of Siponto and to God himself. Until Rosamonde bears the Altavilla child for a Plantagenet, I shall not touch her."

I turn my face from his so that he can not see the sorrow in my eyes. My heart is kindled by his words, by his care for me, by the fealty that he has sworn to Joanna. But William is still in my heart. How I will miss those hours in his arms, the poems he writes for me, the stories he reads aloud—his strange way of loving me. I must forget.

CHAPTER THIRTEEN

 I SAT AT THE DESK in my nightgown watching the sun come up red in the eastern sky. Not a hint of scirocco to stir up a breeze. Even within the thick walls of the old hotel, the *persiane* rolled down tight, Rosamonde was still with me as I wrote.

I heard a tap at the door. It was Filomena ready to change the sheets and towels. "Madonna! We could die from this heat."

I must have given her a vague nod. I wanted to tell her to come back later but I knew she'd have to help downstairs in the hotel kitchen, peeling vegetables and washing salad greens.

As she polished the mirror in the bathroom I heard her say, "I hear you danced with the *architetto* the other night at Sapore di Mare."

Now she had my full attention. "Who told you, Filomena? Come on, tell me."

She stepped into the room wiping her hands on her apron. "Nunzia's brother is a waiter there. I saw him on my way to work this morning." She chuckled. "'Maybe we were wrong about him being a *femminuccia*—the way he danced with you, the way he looked at you. Everybody's talking about it."

I put down my pen. "You're a gossip, Filomena. Giovanni di Serlo is a good dancer, and I like to dance."

"I may be wrong about him. He is away from Vieste so much. Or maybe he takes after his Uncle Cesare after all."

"Uncle Cesare!"

"*L'architetto* will tell you about him sometime, I'm sure. He was famous all over the province. A lecher, he was." She peered at me through her camel-lidded eyes.

"That's all you seem to think about. *Lasciami stare*. Leave me be!"

"I'm sorry, Signora Rosa. I didn't mean to upset you. I just want you to take care. Don Cesare made love to everyone—and everything! Budding virgins, boys. The herdsmen swore he did it to the goats! *Figurati!*" She rolled her eyes, then looked up to heaven.

I felt my temperature rising.

"Come on now, Signora Rosa, a few kisses and hugs from the *architetto* won't make a hole in you," she said in dialect, cackling at her own joke.

The phone rang. As I heard Giovanni's voice on the other end I looked up at Filomena, and, without saying a word, ordered her out of the room.

"Today we will explore the grottoes in my boat," Giovanni said, as though he didn't expect no for an answer. "It's so hot that you should bring a bathing suit so you can have a swim."

I paused. "I'm not sure I want to swim, but I'd like to visit the grottoes."

Yesterday, in Peschici with Marta, the sun had been blazing, the streets empty and scorched. People stayed indoors and complained of the unbearable, still, African heat.

"What time would you be leaving?"

"At noon. I'll pick you up at the hotel mooring."

I rummaged through the drawer for my bathing suit, the one I usually packed for hotel pools on business trips. A plain black maillot, not the least bit Malibu or *provocativa* like the suits of Italian women. I thought the swimsuit made my skin look too pallid, but it was the only one I had with me. Over it I wore an oversized t-shirt that almost reached my knees. "The Great Wall Hotel, Beijing" was stamped across the front. I'd bought the shirt in China when I'd gone with Matthew to buy freshwater seed pearls. I tied a cotton scarf over my unruly hair.

I wound my way down the staircase, spiraled like a chambered nautilus, to the private cove with its rocky beach already crowded with hotel guests. I recognized Giovanni in his motorboat racing toward the mooring. I waved. He turned off the motor, as he approached the rocky landing, then reached out to help me climb aboard.

A crinkled cotton Greek shirt splashed with seaspray clung to his chest. He was lithe and slim, with the broad shoulders and strong thighs of a kouros. At his waist was a knife in a leather sheath. I turned my eyes away from the knife and from his tight lycra swimsuit. A spear gun was lying on the floor of the boat.

He started the motor. As we pulled away from the moorings, I had a good view of Old Vieste—and the Hotel Vesta, built on the edge of the cliff over the sea. Opaline water swirled and splashed into the grottoes. A school of porpoises skimmed the calm waves in the distance.

The boat sped toward the beach of the Hotel Pizzomunno, named after Vieste's famous landmark on the nearby beach: an immense white rock, a monolith. "Piece of the world," or "navel of the world, if you will," he said in dialect. "The rock was most likely worshipped as the Great Goddess in the Neolithic period."

Once past the beaches, he slowed the motor and dropped anchor. The sea had carved deep, mysterious caverns in the limestone cliffs.

"We have arrived at the Baia di San Felice. The Viestani have a legend about these rocks."

"Tell me, please."

"*Una volta*—once upon a time, as you say in English—there lived in Vieste a young girl of such rare beauty even the mermaids were envious of her. One night, as she waited for her lover, the mermaids took her away and chained her in a prison under the sea. Her lover waits for her still and weeps for her.

"Once every hundred years the mermaids swim with her to the surface so that she may have one day with her lover. But she is attached to a golden chain, so fine it cannot be seen. All day long the two are so happy they forget they are not free, but when evening comes the mermaids pull on the chain until slowly she is drawn away from the arms of her lover, back into the depths of the sea.

"Her lover is overcome with grief. And if you listen, Rosa, you may be able to hear his voice here, by these caverns. Hear it?"

The sound was eerie, human, like someone wailing above the wind.

He unbuttoned his shirt. An ancient gold coin hung from a long chain around his neck.

"Follow me. I'll lead you to my secret cavern that can't be seen from the boat. You'll have to swim underwater—just for a few seconds."

"How deep is it? I'm not a good swimmer."

"Not very deep. Don't be afraid. Have faith—I am a very strong swimmer."

"I'm glad I won't have to practice my life-breathing techniques on you, then!" I laughed. I hadn't dared to call it "mouth-to mouth-resuscitation." A few years ago, I'd taken a CPR course at the local Red Cross—just in case.

He jumped overboard and beckoned to me as he tread water.

I looked down from the boat. I could see straight down into the limpid water. At least ten feet. No way I could jump into water that deep.

He called out to me again.

"I can't do it," I shouted back. I felt my heart hammering away, the fierce noonday sun burning my back. I stared down into my father's transparent, turquoise Mediterranean, then at Giovanni, his gold chain glinting in the sun's bright rays.

"*Coraggio!*" he shouted. "Come on! You can make it!"

It's now or never, Rose. I unknotted the scarf and yanked the Great Wall t-shirt over my head. I took a long, deep breath then placed the first three fingers of my right hand together.

Another deep breath. I blinked the tears away as I felt myself letting go. "I forgive you, Papa," I whispered. "I forgive you with all my heart for dropping me into the ocean when I wasn't ready for it."

Then I closed my eyes and jumped. The water felt biting cold to my warm skin, as I swam a few strokes underwater, following his kicking feet, between rocks where mussels clustered like silver-black butterflies. I held my breath for those few moments—until I surfaced to find Giovanni standing before me, silhouetted by a spectral light. We were in a small, dim cavern hidden between two large grottoes.

"Easy, wasn't it? You're a better swimmer than you think."

I was jubilant as I shook the water from my hair.

The floor of the cavern was strewn with tiny pebbles, like shiny grains of pearl barley. We laughed as a crab scuttled past on the damp sand, rocking back and forth on stilted legs.

"Have you told other people you know about this cave, or do you keep it a secret?"

"This grotto is my castle," he said. "I discovered it when I was a boy, swimming with my father. I've only shown it to a few friends from the university, none of them women. I've kept it as my private reserve for sea urchins and mussels. Here in Puglia the water is still clean, unpolluted, unlike the Northern Adriatic. We never have problems eating raw shellfish."

He sat on the hard sand floor of the cavern, stretching his long legs into the lapping water. I sat beside him wiggling my toes at the water's edge, aware of his tanned body next to my pale one. He picked up a piece of sandblasted green glass from a broken bottle polished by the waves, and handed it to me.

"*Ecco*, an emerald for you."

I held the glass to the light. "No inclusions," I said. "Very rare. This is the second present you've given me, and yet I hardly know you!"

"I hope you'll know me better soon."

I looked into his deep-set eyes. Suddenly I wanted to touch the red birthmark on his temple, to put my arms around his neck and kiss him with my open mouth still salty from the sea.

"Would you like some lunch?" Giovanni's hand brushed against my thigh. I felt lightning zigzag between my legs. Something I hadn't felt in a long time.

"I've brought bread and cheese and beer. It's in the cooler. You swim out first. I'll follow you and cut some of the mussels away from the rock. I may even find some *ricci di mare*."

It was easier the second time. I held my breath and dove under, eyes wide open, past the mussel clusters along the tunnel, out to the open sea. I managed to hoist myself into the boat and waited for him to come up with his catch. He surfaced waving a large clump.

"Toss me that plastic bag, Rosa. I'll get more."

I reached for the sack and tossed it to him. When he surfaced the second time, his head and shoulders were draped with sea-weed, the sack full of mussels and *ricci di mare*, spiny sea urchins.

I shouted, "You look like Poseidon!"

He swam back to the boat and climbed in. "Have you ever seen these before?" he asked brandishing a sea urchin as though it were a trophy.

"My father used to buy them at the Italian fishmarket in Providence, but I've never had the courage to taste one."

"You will try some, then, with me. I'll open one of these mussels first." He unsheathed his knife and split two shells, each with just one quick thrust.

Putting the mussel shell to my lips, I sipped the briny, sea-scented juice, savoring the chewy flesh. He did the same with his, his eyes not leaving mine as he sucked the salty liquid from its shell.

"*Sapore di mare*," he said. "Like the song, Rosa." He tossed the shell into the sea, then reached into the bag with his bare fingers for one sea urchin. As he pried it open, the knife slid, making an inch long slit on the side of his hand. Drops of blood oozed from the wound.

He cursed in the Viestani dialect. Ignoring the bleeding cut, he dipped a crust of bread into the "yolk" of the sea urchin and handed it to me. He dipped a crust for himself and ate it.

I couldn't bring myself to eat the yolky bread while his hand still bled. "Here—take my scarf to bind the cut," I said.

"I don't need it. Here's nature's best disinfectant," he said, plunging his hand in the sea.

When we had both had our fill, we tossed the shells back into the sea. He pulled a skein of seaweed from his bag and wrapped it around my head as if it were a crown.

"Now you look like *la sirena del mare*, the melusina who has come back to shore to have a day with her lover."

I laughed. "I've often wondered what a melusina looks like."

He reached in a compartment and pulled out a mirror. "Have a look."

I held it out. In the harsh sunlight I glimpsed a blaze of red hair. *Hair redder than mine. A face younger than mine. Rosamonde's face. Three drops of fresh blood oozed from the front of her white shift. Just where the heart beats.* I quickly handed the mirror back to Giovanni, and brushed away the seaweed from my hair, hoping that he hadn't noticed my fearful eyes, my trembling hands.

We spent the afternoon exploring the grottoes on the coast along the promontory of Pugnochiuso. When sooty clouds darkened the sky and changed the cobalt sea to blackened silver, Giovanni turned the boat and sped us back to the mooring just as the heavens unleashed sheets of rain on Vieste, old and new.

 On this summer day cicadas sing their coarse songs in the bracken beneath the olive trees. I have no patience with my needle and beg Joanna's consent for an outing with Caid Gregory.

"You may leave the fortress for the afternoon, Rosamonde. But take care that fatigue does not overtake you. Caid must never leave your side—not even for a moment."

To pass the time, I gather the washed-up shells of sea creatures. As I ride the painted tumbrel from Joanna's high fortress to the sandy beach below, Caid walks by my side, flicking the donkeys with a switch.

Grasses grow tall along the dunes. From afar I spot the Knight Serlon riding toward me, half hidden in tall reeds.

I wave. He gallops along the sandy beach to meet us.

"Greetings, Lady Rosamonde. Why do you gather shells? What pleasure can they give you, since there is no longer life in these sea creatures?"

"They give harbor to thoughts of beaches near Coutances. This shell we find in Normandy, as well." I hand him the cockleshell of Saint Jacques. "I will confess to you that I feel a dearth of home in my heart. I am so far from Coutances—and now I must forget Palermo, although I would as soon forget my Normandy."

"Forget Palermo? Will you not return to Palermo one day when you have borne the Altavilla child?"

"No, I shall never again return to Palermo," I said. "The Queen has told me this. Have you not had a wish to see Normandy some day?"

"One day I shall journey there with you," he said. "To leave tribute on the altar of the cathedral in Coutances— built by my forebears, the sons of Tancred de Hauteville."

"My forebears as well, for my mother was of the same Hauteville kin as yours."

Caid stands watching as we speak. I dare not ask him to leave us, though I would wish him away had I the power of magic to make it happen.

"Follow me, Caid Gregory," the Knight says, "and we will show the Lady Rosamonde the shore a few leagues beyond us, where she can find more sea shells than she could ever gather. It is an easy ride this day with breezes soft as the balsam of Outremer to cool us."

Caid nods. He sees no harm in that. The road is straight, the donkeys slow. We pass the rocky point where the road turns away from the sea.

The Knight Serlon reins in his horse.

"We shall pause for a moment's rest," he says to Caid, "for I have something to show the Lady Rosamonde." He leads us past some sandy dunes, where we find deep stone pits filled to overflowing with the bleached shells of sea creatures—shoals of seashells as far as we can see.

I begin to gather them, but soon I see they are all alike.

"Come, I'll show you more. We're still far from the hour of dusk. You will be safe at the fortress long before the evening star marks the sky."

We ride side by side past olive groves, past the mulberry plantations of the Olivieri, to a small chapel built in a meadow where broken blocks of stone and rubble lie about the dried grasses alive with the rasping racket of bees and crickets.

"Hundreds of years ago this was a city. So say the local folk. I do not know whose city it was. The Byzantines from whom we took Apulia said it was Greek many years before the birth of Christ, our Lord."

In the small chapel I see a statue carved from pale, cream-colored stone, not unlike the image of the Virgin, but no infant sits upon her lap. In one hand she holds a pomegranate. On her lap lies a stem of wheat.

"The farmers call her The Daughter," the Knight tells me.

"The Daughter?" I ask. "What can this mean? We pray to Mary, the Mother."

"Tis the old religion kept alive still by farmers' wives. They whisper secrets to one another and sing to her in strange high voices on her feast days. The farmers leave her offerings, wheat and olives, almonds and oil."

"They say The Daughter returns to The Mother in the spring, from the dark land where she ate the seeds of the pomegranate. Each year they celebrate her return and leave her jewelry and bits of silver."

"If that is so, then shall I offer a part of me to The Daughter? Leave my wish and prayer that one day I may return to my home in Normandy?"

I reach around my neck for the strand of floss that holds Lady de Hauteville's talisman. I tug at the silken cord. It does not break.

"I beg you, please unsheathe your knife and cut the cord for me."

With the tip of his dagger he slashes the red cord at the base of my neck. Caid leaps forward and knocks the dagger from his hand. The Knight Serlon steps back and silently picks it up.

I hold the pendant in my palm, put it to my lips, then place it upon the stony folds of The Daughter's robe. Mother and Daughter united in the springtime. Tears fill my eyes, so full of love and sorrow is my anguished heart— for I am daughter soon to be mother. I kneel before The Daughter, remembering my own mother, and the daisies I planted on her grave. Such a painful thing for me to do, to leave the talisman that had kept me safe on the long journey to Sicily from my home in Normandy.

The Knight Serlon sees my tears and gathers me in his arms.

Caid jumps forward to protect me, unsheathing his own dagger and thrusting it toward the Knight's heart.

"Leave him be, Caid Gregory!" I shout. "The Knight means me no harm." Caid steps back, uttering a Saracen curse or two, but he obeys my words.

The Knight holds me close and speaks into my hair. "Fear not, Rosamonde, I know not what fortune has in mind for you or me. But let us pray that one day, together, we may set forth for Normandy."

Before the sun rose I'd jumped out of bed, anxious to take part in the ceremony of Santa Maria di Merino, wondering if this ancient ritual might somehow lead me closer to my origins.

Dawn was breaking as I climbed the steps to the Duomo. Along the narrow streets women were hanging their best bedspreads over balcony railings as though they were heraldic banners; crocheted and embroidered cutwork coverlets, counterpanes of lace and damask, provincial symbols of fertility and fruitfulness. A giant peacock preened his tail and arched his crest on a gaudy American chenille spread.

The church was already packed with pilgrims, but Lorenzo had saved me a place up front, next to Caterina.

The night before, the life-size gilded and painted wood statue of the Virgin had been taken down from her high niche on a side altar. Now she sat in her golden sedan chair before the main altar curtained in crimson and white satin. Hundreds of gold chains were looped around the Madonna's neck, each of her fingers ringed in gold. One hand was raised, her eyes wide open, her lips parted, as though she were surprised by her new regalia.

The air was thick with incense fumes. I took a deep breath, put my arm around Zia Caterina, and knelt to pray. But prayer, I knew, did not come easily, so I began to meditate.

The scarlet poppies unfurled. I saw their black velvet center. Another deep breath and my hand went to the base of my throat. *The amulet from Lady de Hauteville was gone. Rosamonde had offered it to The Daughter in Merinium.*

The mass was sung. Soon bells tinkled, announcing the elevation of the Host. I stared as the priest raised it from its paten. Was it that I no longer believed, or was it that my belief was deepening, moving closer to the root? I'd read somewhere that the Host was a relic of a pagan symbol, the raising of a blade of Demeter's sacred wheat in the rites of the Great Mysteries at Eleusis. I tried to imagine what those initiates must have felt in that blazing moment, convinced that they had been given a glimpse of immortality. A reconciliation of life with the terror of death.

While my family filed from the pew to accept Communion, I sat there, only remembering the taste of sweet rice paper melting on my tongue.

Mass ended with a rush to the altar. The faithful thronged to the Madonna, pushing and shoving to touch her robe, then putting fingers to their lips as though to taste her holiness. I watched them thank their old goddess for the abundant crops of olives and almonds, for sweet grapes that hung heavy on the vine, for the plentiful catch of fish from the *trabucco*, for free-spending tourists who filled their town in summer. The people in Vieste might look modern and up-to-date, but today they were pagan.

My hand went to my throat again. *It was gone—the amulet.* I filed out of the pew, behind my family, then I turned toward the altar.

"*Permesso, permesso*," I heard myself murmur to the throngs pressing against me. I moved closer to the Santa Maria, pushing up my cardigan sleeve. I unclasped the gold bracelet from my wrist—the one with Persephone's image—and in one deft movement looped it on the upraised right arm of the Madonna. *It was a painful thing to do, to leave a part of me with her. The talisman that had kept me safe on my journey from Normandy to Sicily.*

I knelt before the Madonna. "*Make her hear you, Rosa. Make her hear you.*" Caterina's words rang in my ears. But how could I make her hear me?

I turned from the altar so that the Viestani could venerate their icon. They had waited a year for the Madonna to come down from her niche; now they would escort her to her ancient home, the sanctuary where she had lived since the beginning of time.

At dusk her jewelry would be stored in the treasury until next year, and then she would be carried back in candlelight procession to the Duomo while the high-pitched voices of the old women celebrants sang lauds to her.

Santa Maria di Merino, siamo tutti figli tuoi, prega per noi.

By midnight she would be back in Vieste, high over the side altar again, wearing only her painted robes.

CHAPTER FOURTEEN

THE FESTA came to a finale with a burst of fireworks at one o'clock in the morning. From the rooftop of Renzo's house we watched the panorama of fiery Catherine wheels spinning on the rocks beyond the Convent of San Francesco, and above us silver fountains overflowed with sprinkling showers of golden stars. We were all tired by the time we said goodnight at the Hotel Vesta.

The next morning, the old town was still quiet after the late night revelry. I walked to the Duomo to ask Don Gesualdo to find time to help me research my family records.

The church was empty. The Madonna di Merino looked out enigmatically from her altar. I felt my bare wrist and missed the familiar weight. Why had I done such an outrageous thing? To have left my gold cuff was madness. Even my family would think so. Rosa leaving a part of her husband's wedding present. Yet I wasn't exactly sorry that I'd left it, only amazed that I'd given in to such an impulse. One of the chancels in the adjacent sacristy was stacked with chunks of marble and carved limestone—fragments of the Duomo's earlier foundation. I stepped around them to read a wall plaque ; a *stemma*, or coat of arms, chiseled in the marble. Three coins or torteaux on a shield. Strangely like the symbol on Brian's Ripley chart, I thought. Below the shield was inscribed:

ANSELM. ORLANDUS

MDLXXXIV

I heard footsteps. "Good morning, signora. I'm Don Gesualdo, the sacristan," said the young priest. He looked as if he'd just come out of a seminary.

"Good morning, Don Gesualdo. I came here especially to talk to you. My name is Orlando, Rosa Orlando. I was caught by the name on the *stemma*. I couldn't figure out the date. I'm terrible at reading Roman numerals."

"1584. Anselmo Orlando was named Bishop of Vieste a few years after the sack of Vieste by Dragut Rais, the Turkish pirate. Of course you've seen the *Chianca Amer* where Dragut slaughtered some of your ancestors."

I passed the "bitter rock" whenever I walked to Caterina's. "What can you tell me about Bishop Orlando?"

"He was one of only two native sons ever to attain the office of bishop of Vieste. He came from a family long settled in Apulia. Most likely a Norman family from at least the twelfth century."

"My father, Tommaso Orlando, originally came from here," I said.

"Really? Well, you Orlandi are all related. This was a very small town back then."

"I'm surprised my father never mentioned that he had a bishop in his family or that an Orlando bishop had a plaque in the Cathedral."

"This coat-of-arms was just discovered a few years ago. The Belle Arti in Bari had ordered the church stripped of all paneling and later decorations." He tapped his knuckle against the stone. "Some historians say that Federico Secondo resided in the old Norman fortress while he had this church rebuilt. That's why the Belle Arti took it down to its original marble and limestone surfaces." He sighed. "Sometimes I miss that worm-eaten baroque paneling. But the authorities seem to think the older the better."

"I'd like to take a few photographs of the *stemma*. May I?"

"Of course."

When I'd snapped pictures from all angles, one with Don Gesualdo standing beside the coat-of-arms, I said, "Valeria at the Municipio told me you're the one to see about researching family records."

"Yes, they're here, but they require a lot of time, you know. It's a very slow procedure. How long do you stay?"

"A few weeks, perhaps. My husband is in California. That's where I live."

"You mean you left your husband all alone at home to come to Vieste?"

"To research the family records. He encouraged me."

He hesitated. "I'll try to get to it as soon as I can, but I'm not sure when that will be, signora. You see, I must first clear up all the paperwork from the Festa. Rome insists upon it. It might be weeks before I can help you."

I walked down to the hotel, thrilled to have discovered that an Orlando had lived here in the sixteenth century, yet thwarted because Don Gesualdo seemed not particularly interested in helping me

❦

The day after, Filomena and Gaetana were hanging sunbleached sheets on the adjacent terrace.

"Don't you two worry about the swallows making a mess on your beautiful clean sheets?" I asked.

"*Magari*, that they would make on them, signora. It only means good luck, you know."

Filomena had turned my terrace into a garden with pots of pink and red geraniums. A dragonfly beat its flimsy wings around the blossoms. Their buds weren't shriveled brown like my geraniums in Santa Monica. I crushed a leaf in my palm and inhaled its peppery scent.

Time to get ready for lunch. I capped my pen. Filomena and Gaetana were gone now. I read aloud what I had written.

My room with candlelight would shine
With walls that I myself had lined
In mother of pearl and purple shale
Like scales along a mermaid's tail.
I would spread out upon my bed
A cover sewn of seaweed thread
Pulled from a tattered siren's shawl
Lost in a sudden summer squall.
I'd pile stones around my fire
Stones made smooth by time's desire—
Translucent, wet, against hard sand,
To show true colors in my hand.
Rubies from broken goblet stems
Would be stars in my diadem.
A coral branch for the golden cuff
These jewels I'd dreamed would be enough . . .

I had some work to do on the rhythm and rhymes, but the idea was there. All those jewel images made me think of Prester John's letter, the one Brian had read to me.

I hadn't yet heard from Brian. He was supposed to have been in Bari around the second week in June. Never mind, I hadn't really wanted to see Castel del Monte with him. Besides, I'd begun to connect him with those strange happenings in Oxford.

I heard the campanile in the Duomo toll the noon hour. Giovanni had invited me to lunch with Professor Lanciani. I was to meet them at *Sapore di Mare* where we had danced that night. I would wash my hair, dry it in the warm sun, and find something light and summery to wear.

The trattoria faced the parapet on the rocky cliff overlooking the beach and the Pizzomunno. Wild capers with puffy white buds sprang from rubble between the rocks; cactus plants with spiny, oval leaves edged the parapet. *Fichi d' india*, or *figadini* in dialect. *Las tunas* in California. In Providence we used to eat prickly pears by cutting off each end, slitting one side, and peeling back the spiny skin with gloved hands. Nowadays, when I buy them at my California market, they're always rubbed clean of prickles that splinter under the skin.

Beyond the *barbacane*, by the entrance of the trattoria, a real fig tree grew from the hillside, shading the restaurant's entrance. I couldn't find any figs hidden among the leaves. I'd never seen a barren fig tree. Not even in Providence where my father used to burlap-bundle his tree to protect it from frostbite.

An old fisherman, dressed in black and smoking a pipe, leaned against the parapet. At the entrance to the restaurant, two little boys were picking small crabs and seaweed from a net stretched over long poles.

The dining room of Sapore di Mare had once been the first floor of a medieval *magazzino*, or storeroom. The vaulted limestone walls were painted and sprayed with an iridescent plastic fixative to keep dust and grit from falling over the diners. I felt as though I'd walked into a giant mother-of-pearl conch shell.

❧

Fragments of Romanesque and Renaissance sculpture hung on the walls. Sunlight streamed from one tall arched window overlooking the sea. Giovanni's table faced the panorama.

A hush came over the room as I made my way across the room. I was wearing a scoop-necked white cotton blouse and a soft dove-gray and white print skirt. And my single gold cuff.

The two men stood up as I approached. Lanciani was almost as tall as Giovanni, and because of his baldness and slightness, he reminded me of photographs I'd seen of Gabriele d'Annunzio. Dark hairs sprouted from one nostril, which only made matters worse. I felt Lanciani's heavy-lidded eyes sweep over me.

"You did not tell me, *architetto*, that *la Signora* Kirkland was also beautiful." Lanciani was nattily dressed to match his flowery, formal speech, as puffed up as the paisley handkerchief that poked from his pocket.

"Thank you, *professore*," I said, for once not turning away the compliment. Instead I reveled in it. "What may I offer you to drink?" Lanciani asked.

They were drinking Campari and soda.

"The bartender used to work at Harry's Bar in London, so he can mix anything. A Bellini, perhaps, with peach juice?" He waved for the bartender as if he were the host, but I knew Giovanni had offered the lunch.

"Then he can most likely mix a White Lady," I said. "I would like a White Lady, please."

"A White Lady," Lanciani repeated. His hooded eyes searched mine. My request had irritated him. I felt the flesh creeping beneath the long sleeves of my blouse.

The waiter came to take our order.

"A White Lady," Lanciani said.

"I'm sure the bartender can make one," said the waiter.

Lanciani turned to me. "I have just returned from a congress in Milan where I read a paper on the Cult of the Cybele in Apulia. It was well-received by my colleagues."

Although Giovanni had prepared me for his dogmatic style, I was still put off by this haughty professor.

"Giovanni tells me you are interested in the history of the region, signora. That's unusual for an American, especially an American woman."

"Yes, *professore*. My love of research, among other things, has brought me back to Vieste where my father was born. I guess I've come back to find my roots. I've been in England doing some historical research, now I intend to do some genealogical research at the Duomo."

"You should at least visit some of the historical sites until you can begin. That would be infinitely more interesting. Why shut yourself up in a dusty old sacristy and waste this marvelous summer-like sun?"

"I plan to drive *la Signora* Orlando to Monte Sant'Angelo and to Castel del Monte," Giovanni said. "She's already seen the dig at the sanctuary."

"What did you think of our project, signora? Did the archaeologists tell you about our discoveries?"

"Yes, they were forthcoming. I was disappointed, though, that

I couldn't see the stone goddess holding the wheat sheaf and the pomegranate."

"Yes, our little Demeter," Lanciani said.

"No—she's Persephone, The Daughter—I'm sure of that," I retorted.

The farmers come to leave her offerings, wheat and olives, almonds and oil. They call her The Daughter.

I had an urge to be argumentative, to confront and battle with this man—a contrariness I didn't usually feel in social conversation.

The drink arrived. Professor Lanciani raised his glass to me.

"*Buona Fortuna,*" he said with just a trace of sarcasm.

"To Fortuna," I replied in English. I smiled, raising the glass first to him, then to Giovanni for a silent toast with my eyes. The frothy white liquid tasted like a potent California Orange Julius. "Well, *architetto— la signora americana*—I bow to her and to her success in her research of the Altavilla."

I could feel his discomfort, his masculine hostility at my new-found confidence.

"Do you know, signora, that William Altavilla once came to Monte Sant'Angelo?"

"Yes. I do know that."

"You know your history well. *Complimenti!* What is your source for that information?"

"A woman told me."

"A woman? What woman?" He flashed a strange look to Giovanni.

I smiled.

He waited at Vieste, it seems, forever. William amused himself by writing—gazing out across the sea and writing—always writing.

The waiter served me a plate of *spaghetti alle vongole,* but I paid no attention to it, unusual for me, because I tend to dig right in.

"You see, *professore*, I do have some ideas about the Altavilla. For instance, do you remember how Costanza d'Altavilla gave birth to Frederick II? Why do you think she gave birth in a tent on the square in Jesi? Of course, she was forty years old and wanted to prove that Frederick was her son, but a normal birth with midwives in attendance would have been enough."

I heard my passion. "Instead, she allowed herself the indignity of public birth. She must have had reason to want such proof for the world. Perhaps it was rumored in high places that her nephew William had a child somewhere—an illegitimate child, not from a woman of the Tiraz but from a woman of Norman blood like William's own. A child who, although illegitimate, would be a rightful heir."

"However did you learn that?" Giovanni was looking at me curiously.

"Oh, call it feminine intuition," I said.

An uncomfortable silence. "Signora, why do you do this?" Lanciani said finally. "After all, you are *not* a scholar."

"Would you like me to apologize for my interest? Or feel humility in the face of *your* scholarship?"

Lanciani raised his left eyebrow. "Humility is a most repulsive virtue."

Giovanni lit a cigarette, fumbling the pack, and took a deep drag. I hadn't seen him smoke before.

I bit my lip hard. "I'm the first to admit I'm not a scholar, I'm here to research my family's roots—and to learn about the Altavilla. What do I need—special permission from the bureaucracy in Rome to do research on the subject?"

The room became quiet as heads turned to look.

"*Per carità*, of course we respect your rights. We're amazed that you want to do it in the first place," Lanciani said. "Most Americans who come here have no such interest."

"Rosa, you are, *senza dubbio, una puella Apuliae.* Don't you agree, Guido?" Giovanni said.

Lanciani responded with a thin, forced smile.

I couldn't help laughing at his defeated look. The tension broke. Giovanni and I laughed together. Then Lanciani joined in. He wasn't that bad after all, I decided.

"Let's make a *brindisi* to that. *Beviamo à Rosa, la nostra puella Apuliae,*" Lanciani raised his wine glass.

"We're all far too serious at this table! *Buon appetito*—I'm starving." I twirled the spaghetti around my fork as we began to talk about the piquancy of the sauce, the mellowness of the wine—more normal conversation for Italians *a tavola.*

Dinnertime. The day tourists had deserted Vieste. Umbrellas on the beach below were furled and, in the sea beyond, boats twinkled with lights. The Faro flashed its red beacon across the Adriatic.

The phone rang as I was washing up, trying to decide whether or not to turn in early. I wasn't used to such late nights.

I hoped the call was from Matthew.

I was surprised to hear Giovanni's voice. "Why don't you come here for supper? We can discuss the Altavilla. You seem to be so determined to learn about them—the way you spoke today."

I had just called Renzo to say that I was so tired that I'd be staying in tonight.

"I'd love to," I said.

Giovanni lived at the top of Via Federico Secondo, close by one of many fortresses Frederick had built in Apulia. *Il Castello*, as it is called, was built on the rim of a limestone cliff, facing the sea.

Giovanni's house was just across the esplanade. The arched portal over the door was capped with a baroque stone cartouche. I could just make out the words: *Le sang se souvient.*

"The blood remembers." I was troubled by the strange effect those words had on me.

I lifted the double-tailed bronze mermaid knocker and let it slam hard against the weathered walnut. I stroked the gray-green patina, thinking that the melusina was almost like the one I'd sketched in my studio.

The door clicked open. Lights flicked on. Inside, the ceiling was vaulted, the stairwell flanked by zigzagged columns. *Like columns in the Cloister of Monreale where Constance sat.*

I climbed two flights of stone steps scooped out, worn smooth by time. The door displayed his name. *"Di Serlo, Giovanni. Architteto, Belle Arti."* Seeing it written disconcerted me.

"Welcome to my home." He kissed my hand. "Please come in." He wore a double-breasted blazer, a blue and white striped shirt with no necktie.

The small, octagonal living room had white walls and in one corner a massive stone fireplace. Curtainless windows opened to a view like my own.

I commented on the shape of the room.

"This building was most likely part of the older Norman fortress. Because of the room's octagonal shape, I like to imagine that Frederick might have lived here while he visited Vieste."

I laughed. "You romanticize as much as I do."

"You may be right." He smiled.

I thought I saw a flush under his tan. "Please make yourself comfortable."

I sat on the edge of the deep, cushion-piled sofa and looked across the room at a large red-figured Greek krater placed on a stand between the windows.

"Apulian," he said, before I did. "Four centuries before Christ."

"I've seen vases like yours at the Getty. They're much fancier than the Greek vases from Athens."

"Uncle Cesare dug up this one from the salt marshes at Uria long before there were laws prohibiting excavations. Come, have a look. I'll give you my interpretation."

I leapt up.

"The krater was the traditional vessel used for mixing wine. This scene represents the *hieros gamos*. The Sacred Marriage." He pointed to the veiled votary priestess of Aphrodite seated on a ritual throne, a naked male figure standing before her. A small winged Eros perched on the priestess' shoulder. The top edge of the krater was bordered with a Greek key.

I studied the scene from all angles. He must have sensed that I was ready to hear more.

"In Greek mythology Zeus and Hera were joined in a Sacred Marriage. Eventually the ceremony came to mean the harmonious union of a couple. Or the meeting of opposites."

"What kind of a ritual was performed?" As soon as I heard myself ask the question I realized how naïve I sounded.

"The hierophant would invoke the goddess of love, and the male worshipper would then be invited to surrender himself to her, offering his masculinity to Aphrodite through the priestess."

I felt myself redden under his intense gaze. "Renzo told me that Aphrodite is still much revered in this town."

He nodded. "She's usually called by her local name, Venere Sosandra. Venus, Savior of Men."

Savior of men? I kept myself from asking how.

"May I offer you a nice chilled prosecco? A colleague of mine sends it to me from his vineyard in the Veneto."

"No, thanks. Do you have a San Pellegrino?"

A disappointed look on his face.

I laughed. "I've changed my mind already. I'd like to have a taste, thank you."

"I'll get it from the *frigo*."

I looked over his collection of local Daunian pots, decorated with spirals and meanders.

Against a wall stood a dark oak *cassone*. On it a large rustic basket was filled with sprays of yellow flowers like those I'd seen billowing along the hillsides like golden fleece.

He returned with the chilled prosecco in two tall glass flutes and handed me one.

"Isn't that gorse—or broom?" I asked. Like Matthew's Broome coat of arms over the fireplace mantel. *The little dove with a sprig of yellow broom in its beak.*

"We call it *pianta genista* here," he said. "Henry Plantagenet wore a sprig of it in his cap."

"You know your English history."

"I've spent many summers in London."

We drank the sparkling wine and he asked me about the sights I wanted to see.

"First of all, Monte Sant'Angelo," I said. "I'm anxious to visit this place that was part of my childhood lore."

"You must know it was one of the great pilgrimage destinations of the Middle Ages."

"My father often spoke of it—but it was only recently that I learned of its importance to the Normans. You're very kind to offer to drive me there. "

"I'm honored to accompany you. Rosa. I must say, I find you a fascinating woman."

He didn't give me a chance to protest.

"Come—the pasta is almost ready, and it can't wait. Let me seat you."

The table was placed in an alcove.

I watched as he tossed the *garganelli*, a local pasta, with chopped red-ripe tomato and handfuls of sweet-smelling basil leaves.

He handed me a plate. "I meant what I said."

"What was that?" As though I hadn't remembered. "Oh, yes. You Italians are always so full of *complimenti*. I never pay attention to them." I laughed.

He looked at me with critical, amused eyes. "You are a woman of varied interest and talents."

"I seem to know bits and pieces about a lot of things—probably because I read a lot. And I'll admit I've been a fair success as a jewelry designer, but I've yet to produce a child for my husband." The instant I uttered those words I regretted them as I had when I spoke them to Brian.

No response.

I wanted to tell him about the surrogate plan, but kept my mouth shut. "I'm sorry," I said, "but I do feel that way—especially here in Italy . . . with Italian women."

He reached for my hand. "Tell me the truth," he blurted out angrily. "What else are you searching for? Who are you? And why do you come here with this passion, this obsession with the Altavilla?"

I drew my hand away. "I'm here tonight because you promised to tell me what *you* know about them," I snapped back.

His tone softened. "Last night I ran into Don Gesualdo. He told me that you'd gone by to see him."

"News gets around fast in Vieste," I said. "Did he tell you that I asked about researching my family records?"

He nodded.

"He doesn't seem to want to help me."

"I expect he's just busy with the Festa paperwork."

"Festa paperwork! I can't imagine what that could be. That's *just* the way he said it, but I had the distinct feeling he was putting me off."

"Do you put a lot of credence in your feelings?"

"I do. It gets me into trouble with my husband, who's all reason and intellect. For me, the heart knows first."

He smiled. "Maybe it's that the blood remembers," he said.

"Isn't that what's inscribed on the *stemma*, over the door?"

"It's our family motto, a very old one. *Il professor* Lanciani tells me that . . ."

"I took an instant dislike to that man."

"Why?"

"Maybe it was his patronizing manner. He struck me as pretentious."

"Well, I can assure you he's not. He knows more about the Normans in Apulia—and Federico II—than anyone I know. He was to organize a team of scholars in Bari to read the contents of the bronze box from the church in Andria."

"Who found that bronze box?"

"My workmen and I. We hit a tile, one of the *pavimenti*. We found the box buried underneath."

I felt my stomach tighten. "Don't you remember how I brought up that discovery the very first day we met? And you quickly changed the subject!" I tried to stifle the anger I was hearing in the tone of my voice.

"I didn't think I should discuss all this with a woman who'd just walked into my shop from the street."

"I am *so* sorry," I said sarcastically.

"Can't you imagine how much of an embarrassment the whole episode was for me and my colleagues at the *Soprintendenza*? It was such an important discovery for our team. We had experts lined up to read the letters. From the Morgan Library, the Huntington, the Bodleian. Maybe now we'll never know."

"Who's coming from the Bodleian?" I asked, knowing, at that instant, exactly what his answer would be.

"Brian Lambeth, an old friend of mine. Do you know him?"

"I've just been with Lambeth in Oxford! I can't believe this coincidence!"

"I don't believe in coincidence."

I laughed. "Neither does Brian. He'd told me he was going to Bari—that he would take me to Castel del Monte. I've been waiting for a call from him."

"I would like the honor of showing it to you."

"And I would be happier with you as my guide. I'm not too thrilled about seeing Brian in Italy. I find something strange about him. How do you say it in Italian? What's the male for *strega*? Witch? But that's not quite what I mean . . . I had that feeling."

"It's *stregone*. Or Magus, in Latin."

"Magus—that's the word I was searching for. Anyway, I'm relieved not to have heard from him. How do you know Brian?"

"His father was a British Foreign Service officer in Rome. We went to the same preparatory school. We've followed each other's careers, so after the discovery of the chest, I reached him in Oxford."

We talked about Brian until I was bored. I glanced at my watch. Only ten-thirty. Early for Vieste. The locals would still be drinking espresso and sipping *digestivi* at the Bar Del Corso. I rolled up my napkin.

"Please—don't leave," he said, "I thought we were going to talk about our common interest, the Altavilla."

"What about them?" I said brusquely.

He reached for my hand once more. "Rosa, sometimes I feel as though I'm part of the distant past come to life again. I've often thought about reincarnation. But then I'm not looking for Nirvana. Nirvana, to me at least, is the absence of fear—the absence of desire." He smiled and looked straight into my eyes. "Desire is not absent in me. Do *you* believe in reincarnation?"

"I'm not sure. Although part of me longs to believe in resurrection," I said. "It might make facing death easier."

"Did you know that it was here in southern Italy that the belief in resurrection took hold?"

From the look on my face he must have known I was eager for more.

He went on. "Around the sixth century before Christ, many Greeks in southern Italy were fed up with the Olympian religion of the Here and Now. They yearned for something beyond this life. It was in Apulia that The Great Orphic Mysteries of rebirth came to be celebrated—where Pythagoras preached his doctrine of the soul's transmigration."

"Since I've come here, I've learned how ancient my roots are," I told him, "how far back into Italian civilization they reach, how diverse the peoples who made me what I am. I've never told anyone this but . . . ."

"Tell *me*, then."

"Sometimes, in my imagination, I invite all my ancestors to a reunion in a huge amphitheater. I stand in the center and look around, trying to envision all these women and men filing in, filling up the tiers. I try to picture what they might have looked like, what they might have worn—or might *not* have worn!" I laughed. "There are always some very shady characters in the bunch."

He smiled and said, "You realize, of course, that if you go back far enough, you might even find that you're related to every single person who ever lived on this peninsula."

"When I was growing up in Providence our Yankee neighbors used to think they were complimenting me when they said, 'Oh—

cute little Rose. She doesn't look the least bit Italian does she, with that auburn hair and all those freckles!' "

"But what *are* Italians supposed to look like? We're a nation of people descended from Illyrians, Greeks, Goths, Etruscans, Celts, Arabs, Jews, Normans—not to mention all the Latin tribes."

His face was a curious mixture of seriousness and excitement, like a child eager, at last, to part with a long-kept secret.

"There's a tradition in my family that the eldest son searches for the perfect woman. It comes from ancient family lore, and in truth, all it manages to do is put pressure on each generation. Invariably, the wrong woman is chosen. Uncle Cesare avoided making a choice altogether. And I haven't yet made mine."

"Why are you telling me this?"

He gazed into my eyes. "We have a riddle that has been handed down from generation to generation." He poured himself another glass of prosecco and took a swallow.

I was filled with such clashing feelings I couldn't find my tongue.

He pronounced the words deliberately watching their effect on me as he spoke.

Quando si stacca dal muro l'eglantina
Quando lascia la sala scura la donnina
Per sempre restaurata sarà il lineaggio,
Allora troverò la nostra sposa.

When the eglantine pulls from the wall
When the lady leaves the darkened hall
Our line is restored once and for all
And I will find our bride.

"I suppose you're still looking—waiting—for that lady to turn up one fine day," I said matter-of-factly.

His eyes probed mine. I looked away.

After a moment he said, "So you left a piece of jewelry for the Madonna?"

"Who told you that?"

"No one told me."

"You said you weren't there, how could you have known, then?" I said angrily.

"No. I wasn't there, but I saw you take the bracelet off your right arm and slip it on the Madonna's wrist. I could see you were very moved." He smiled. "We're in the new era. The ceremony was televised for the aged, the infirm—for those like me who must work."

"I felt compelled to do it—as though the choice had already been made for me, as though I'd been through this same ceremony before."

"Do you always follow your compulsions?"

"Lately that's all I've been doing." I looked at my watch again.

"I'll escort you home," he said.

"It's not necessary."

"I insist."

He was gloomy and silent as we walked down the polished stone slabs of the old town, through narrow streets past door stoops where black-dressed old women gossiped. The pizzeria was still open. The air smelled like woodfire and ashes, rising yeast and oregano. A radio was blasting out a popular ballad. "*La vita è adesso*" was all that I could make out.

Life right now? No—those lyrics were all wrong, I remember thinking. The life of a soul is mostly Time Past—with only a moment of Time Present. And a boundless Time Future.

We said goodnight under the great forged iron lantern of the Hotel Vesta.

"Signora," the night porter said, "you received a phone call from *Giappone*—Signor Kirkland."

"When did he call?"

"An hour ago. He was on his way to Tokyo for a few days. He didn't leave a number. He said he'd call tomorrow."

 Our summer days are peaceful—how quickly they pass for us. I do not want to leave this harbor. Even Normandy is out of mind. William's fortress perches on a rock high above the sea. It is a simple place, not rich in the comforts of Ziza, but at least I have no grief over Palermo.

Caid Gregory tells us that "if you turn your back to the sea and follow the path north over the hills, you come to a dark forest where there are dense woods of beech and oak, where wild boar sniff for acorns, deer roam, wolves prowl. Where hermits live in huts."

Caid guards me always, a dagger in his sash to protect me from a stranger who might do me harm. We make a strange pair, Caid and I. He is a good soul even if inclined to gossip. Here there is much talk of the evil eye—foolish talk, to my mind. The country folk say, "Beware of those who give it with a glance!" Joanna does not like it when I walk the parapet. But my child-heavy body feels better for the walk.

I am no longer sick to my stomach and weary as I was when we left Palermo. But I am heartsick over the day when Joanna takes my child and raises it as her own and William's. I will never hear it call me mother.

On clear days I gaze out to the wooded islands. I look beyond to the coast of the Slavs' Dalmatia, where the Venetians have a fortress. The sun is strong so close to the sea. I shade myself with a hat of leaves plaited from the dried stalks of sugar cane. Sometimes the sight of a black eagle wheeling against the sky chills my blood, and Caid leads me inside the fortress, afraid of an ill wind that might blow in from the mountains in the north.

That night it was too hot to close the shutters. I took a tepid shower and put on my coolest gauze nightgown. Lines from Giovanni's cryptic, romantic poem kept running through my head. I wanted to squelch them once and for all. Instead of writing, I searched my book bag for the copy of John Julius Norwich's *The Other Conquest*. Brian had recommended it as having a colorful chapter on the Normans arriving at Monte Sant'Angelo in the eleventh century. I was excited about seeing the Mount with Giovanni and wanted to prepare myself. I must have read for a long time, until I felt fresh breezes stirring the air. I got up to have a look at the stars that night like diamonds tossed across a moonless sky. As my eyes swept the horizon, I thought I saw something stir on the terrace. My imagination. Just one of those beach towels on Filomena's clothesline quivering in the breezes.

I hopped back into bed, turned off the lamp, leaving the shutters wide open, so that I could enjoy the cooling off. A whiff of my scented pillow and I was soon asleep.

Why I woke up at that instant is still beyond me. It must have been the stench of cigar smoke I thought I smelled.

A shadow-like man was leaning over my bed. He was very short. He wore a black stocking over his face. He stood over me, a dagger poised to plunge into my heart. He couldn't see my open eyes.

I screamed. I screamed so loud he ran away.

I jumped out of bed. No one on the terrace. He must have escaped by leaping from one roof to another.

When I opened the door, the hallway was full of annoyed hotel guests.

"*Che succede?* Are you all right, signora?" one of them had the decency to ask.

I could barely get the words out. "A masked man . . . he had a dagger in his hand—he was standing over me about to . . ."

"What a terrible nightmare!" a German guest said.

"I guarantee you it was no nightmare," I snapped back. I'd thought about calling my cousins and Caterina but I didn't have the heart to wake them in the middle of the night.

Stefano, the night clerk arrived. I told him what had happened. "You must call the police right away," I pleaded.

"Signora—are you sure you weren't dreaming? In all the years I've been the night clerk, nothing like this has ever happened in this hotel or in the rest of our little town. It would be a terrible thing for us for tourism in Puglia, if we were to notify the police! I hate to think of what the Rome newspapers would make of it! What might it do to our livelihoods?"

By then Filomena had arrived on the scene. She put her arm around me. "Don't worry, I'll stay with the signora tonight. No one will harm you with me around." She made the evil eye sign by folding the second and third fingers back and extending the index finger and the little finger like Satan's horns.

"I still want you to call the police. Not one of you has even bothered to look outside to see if there are any traces."

Stefano, followed by everyone else, pushed into my room and onto the terrace.

One of the beach towels had fallen to the ground. "This was hanging on the line when I went outside earlier this evening," I said, picking up the towel and waving it triumphantly.

"Signora, I often find a towel or two on the terrace floor in the morning." said Filomena. "Can't you hear that wind blowing in?"

Then I did something I hated myself for. I caved in. Weak, lily-livered Rose, I thought. You don't have the courage of your convictions. You don't deserve to be a mother!

Stefano ordered a cot and some sheets for Filomena.

For some strange reason, as I helped her make up the bed with crisp white sheets, I keep thinking of slick, black satin sheets I'd once seen in a shop window on Hollywood Boulevard. I remembered Brian's warning. *"Dr. Jung would have thought there might be a possibility of great danger to make the descent into the deep, dark pools of the unconscious all by one's self. Exploring the realm of the shadow can be a frightening experience, you know."*

Now it was time to go home. But I couldn't leave without seeing Monte Sant'Angelo—and Frederick II's Castel del Monte.

CHAPTER FIFTEEN

 FEW DAYS LATER I met Giovanni down at the *parcheggio*. As he revved up the Ferrari, he said, "Today we will go to the Foresta Umbra. From there we will head south to Monte Sant'Angelo. We can take the coastal road on the way back."

"It's hard to imagine a real forest so close by the sea."

"It's a real forest all right, with deer and wild boar and hedgehogs and owls.

Our tall oaks and the forest around our castle at Pirou—the hoot of scritch owls and the distant howl of wolves.

I saw the Knight Serlon's face in profile, the small red birthmark on his temple, the blond hairs on his tanned, sinewy arms guiding the wheel of a modern automobile. I wanted to reach out and stroke them. Instead, I folded my hands together tight, my fingernails digging into my knuckles.

Meadow grasses and scrub oak soon gave way to beech and Mediterranean oak, intensely green, in full leaf. Not a single car passed. We were in deep dense woods, seemingly many miles from the semi-arid seashore. Where was the Adriatic light?

"Would you please stop the car for a moment?" I asked.

He pulled to up to the roadside and we both got out. I looked up to the narrow blue ribbon of sky between tall trees and felt a pang of sadness. A déjà vu feeling. A finality I didn't understand.

"Snow falls here in winter, yet we never see snow in Vieste. Before the war they felled beeches for lumber—exported the wood to other parts of Europe—mostly for furniture. Now this forest is a nature and wildlife preserve. At last *i Pugliesi* are making an effort to preserve some of their natural patrimony."

He took a basket from the trunk. He poured water from a plastic bottle into a Styrofoam cup and offered me a Saran-wrapped sandwich.

"Italians are becoming as bad as Americans," I said, "using plastic for everything. Soon you'll have mountains of trash piling up outside your cities just like the ones we're faced with in the States. Matthew, my husband, is an engineer working on a project to convert inert materials into biodegradable matter."

Giovanni was intrigued with the idea. We discussed it as we ate our sandwiches.

After we finished there was a long silence. I tossed my bread crusts to the sparrows and larks, and dumped the litter into a trash bin.

"Would you like to take a little walk?"

"No, I don't think so, thank you." I didn't want to court disaster by allowing him to get romantic in the woods. As I brushed crumbs from my skirt, I said, "We should be heading on to Monte Sant'Angelo." I opened the car door, got inside, and strapped my seatbelt tight.

"Then if you'll excuse me a moment, I'll be right back."

I felt a flush creep over my face.

❧

The view became more and more spectacular as we climbed switchbacks high above the sea. Soon we could make out the medieval village of Monte Sant'Angelo, its flat white face peering over the ridge at its peak point.

"What do you remember from your research?" Giovanni asked.

I told him what I knew as simply as I could. "It was at this sanctuary that the Normans got the idea to conquer Southern Italy. When they went back to Normandy they recruited mercenaries—among them the sons of Tancred de Hauteville."

He turned his head from the wheel to look at me. "Long before the Normans arrived in Apulia, Monte Sant'Angelo was a sanctuary, a mystical place where the Great Goddess was worshipped. Later, with the establishment of Greek colonies, the mount became a dream oracle sanctuary. Most hilltop shrines were dedicated to Hermes—or Mercury, the messenger god. People came to solve their problems through dream incubation."

"How did they to do that?"

"The priestesses gave the supplicants a potion to drink or fumes to inhale, then they were covered with the skin of a black ram and left to sleep. When the person awoke, his dreams were interpreted as the voice of the gods. The pilgrims would leave small votive offerings of gold and silver, shaped as parts of the body they'd wished to heal."

"What happened after the conversion to Christianity?" I asked.

"Those high shrines were reconsecrated to Michael the Archangel—the angel who loves high places. Somewhere in my files I have a photograph of an engraved gemstone showing Saint Michael wearing Mercury's winged hat, with a caduceus in hand."

I remembered Brian's intaglio ring engraved with Hermes—or Mercury.

"In Revelations, when the war broke out in heaven, Michael and his angels waged war upon the dragon, or the serpent. I believe the serpent is a symbol for the old religion. The goddess who was worshipped here in the Mediterranean basin for thousands of years. The Magna Mater."

I laid my head back against the seat, closed my eyes and thought about what he had just told me. Strange that at that instant my mind flashed to Mr. Baryani's ruby, then to the rubedo at the top of Brian's Ripley Scroll, the stone he'd called "the heart" of the Great Goddess, Cybele.

We were starting to wind up the twisting road to the far side of the Mount.

"We'll come to a belvedere around the next turn," he said. "We can get out to look down at the panorama from the corniche road."

We stepped out into the bright sunshine. The breezes wafted rosemary and wild marjoram. The road was carved around terraced farms and olive groves. From the hilltop, we looked down to a cluster of white domed buildings perched on a cliff overlooking the sea.

"What are those white, Arabic-looking buildings?" I asked.

"A hotel—called *La Zagara*." He almost spat out the 'z.'

"Zagara." I tried to pronounce it the way he did.

"A word that has come down to us from the Arab occupation of Southern Italy and Sicily. It means, simply, the scent of orange or lemon blossoms. Orange groves used to be cultivated here—before the Gargano was opened to tourism."

"*La Zagara*," I repeated. "*La Zagara.*" *Their waxy blossoms giving forth a delicious scent as if it had wafted down from heaven.* I felt prickles on my arms.

"We'll stop for a drink on the way back, then take the coast road to Vieste."

As we ascended, Monte Sant'Angelo appeared to be a modern town, the lower, so called "new" town housed banks, mini-markets, condominium apartments, all the necessities of modern life.

We parked the car at the summit, some distance from Saint Michael's church. The old village was the tourist center, its narrow streets lined with souvenir and curio shops. Vendors hawked their wares along the way—garish painted plaster statues of St. Michael, tawdry scapulars and molded plastic rosary beads.

"Appalling, what's happened to Italian taste," Giovanni said bitterly as though he were reading my mind. "You'll see that most of this junk is made in Taiwan."

We approached the entrance just as a black-frocked priest was opening wide wrought iron gates to the sanctuary. The clock in the tower struck three, and we entered the Gothic courtyard.

Chiseled in stone above the portal I read:

TERRIBILIS EST LOCUS ISTE
HIC DOMUS DEI EST
ET PORTA COELIS

"This is a terrible place?" I began. "Or should it be—'this place is terrible?'"

Giovanni laughed. "Not *terrible* in the usual sense—Rosa, but impressive. Awesome. This is the house of God, His gateway to heaven."

Inside I smelled sweet rose attar. Nearby, in the souvenir shop, an old dwarfed woman was hunched over the glass counter spraying and polishing with Bel Profumo rose-scented foam cleanser.

I put a white scarf over my head and knotted it under my chin.

Giovanni held my arm as we made our descent down the eighty-six steps to the sanctuary.

"Not long ago these walls were massed with crutches and paintings and other ex votos for favors received. Then Rome ordered all the pagan paraphernalia stripped away."

A bare stone wall and an iron rail were all that remained.

At last we reached the mouth of the cave and the massive silver-inlaid bronze doors, etched with stiff, Byzantine figures.

"Rattle the handle, Rosa. An ancient tradition, my mother used to say."

The chapel had once been a cavern, the rock still visible all around us. "It's dry now," I said. "I remember . . ." I paused. "Wasn't a spring here once?"

"Yes. A few years ago the ceiling was plastic-coated and spread with netting. When I came here as a child my mother and I collected drops that fell from the ceiling. She'd put them into little crystal vials, then sent them off to all her friends in Rome and Naples." He sighed. "I remember how much colder it used to be, so deep in the earth's womb. Now all the mystery is gone."

Rows of pews were lined up on the cave's floor. Banks of votive candles impaled on iron spikes flickered. An ancient pulpit stood on one side, and a sixteenth-century stone statue of St. Michael wielding his mighty, serpent-slaying sword stood guard.

I approached the sacristan who sold Masses for the repose of the souls of the dead to ask if I might have one said for my father. When I had given him my father's name and made my donation, I knelt down in the pew beside Giovanni.

"Try to meditate, Rosa."

I was surprised that he didn't say "pray."

I closed my eyes and counted down only to the unfurled poppy.

Why had I come here? What within myself was I searching for? Was I trying to reconcile myself to death? Or had I come here to solve the mystery of Rosamonde's voice? But shouldn't I be praying for a child of my own? I wished I had some rosary beads to remind me how. I'd given my word to Matt that I'd decide by the time I returned—yet having a baby was the last thing on my mind these past few weeks. He was right. I didn't really want a child. Not mine, not his by surrogate, not even an adopted baby. Maybe I wanted Matthew all to myself for the rest of our lives. I breathed out an endless pent-up sigh and fell forward in the pew, head in my hands. Tears welled up at the admission I'd just made. At last, deep within the earth, I'd faced a part of my selfish, shadow self. I tried to pray. Caterina had said, "Make her hear you—make her hear you."

I began: *Hail Mary, full of Grace . . . Hail Mary, full of Grace blessed is the fruit of thy womb . . . .* I felt something moist and slippery creep around my bare heel. Turning my head to look behind me, I saw a snake. It undulated its way slowly along the sanctuary floor. I watched as it slowly coiled around itself.

I was paralyzed.

In a flash the snake straightened itself and darted through a crevice in the rocks.

A fat snake slithered out and curled into a circle around my feet. I do not move nor have I fear of the serpent, for this cavern was its home long before St. Michael came to claim it.

"Go ahead, Rose. Scream! Scream!" I want to scream out to the Knight Serlon. "The snake still lives in this cavern. I have just seen it!"

But I didn't scream. I fell forward onto the pew, buried my head in my arms and cried.

Giovanni put his arm around my shoulders, drawing me to his side. He reached for a handkerchief and gave it to me.

"This place has always had an effect on people of sensitivity. God knows how many ancient memories get stirred up here. Let's be off." He took my hand and led me up the steps, neither of us saying a word.

My bones had turned to ice. I was still shivering as we walked into the warm sunshine. Giovanni put his arm around me as I took a breath of herb-scented air.

"Feeling better now? You seemed so far away in your thoughts."

"Sorry. It's a . . . a habit I have."

"If you feel up to it there's a shop nearby. I'd like to look in."

"Of course. I'll come along."

We walked under the park's shady plane trees, down a narrow cobbled street to the antique shop. Through the plate glass window the stock seemed unpromising, mostly turn-of-the-century, rustic wood furniture.

He pushed the doorbell.

"*Buon giorno*, Filippo. Anything new?" Giovanni greeted the shop owner as he opened the door.

"Yes, *architetto*. Have a look at those Gnathian pots."

Giovanni only glanced at them. "Anything else?"

Filippo pointed to the vitrine in the corner. On one shelf was a collection of coins. One caught my attention. It was silvery-gold and concave. Exactly like one I saw at Spink.

The dealer unlocked the vitrine and handed the coin to me.

I turned it over in my palm. I was right. "This is an electrum—coined in the reign of the Emperor Manuel Comnenus," I said.

"You're exactly right—an electrum—silver and gold alloyed with mercury." Giovanni examined the coin. "In very good condition."

"Every once in a while one of these turns up," the dealer said. "I guess they were hoarded for centuries. When people remodel their houses or replant their orchards, they discover what their ancestors buried under olive trees or behind walls. Now they all go around with fancy metal detectors!"

While I was considering the electrum's market value, wondering if I should buy it, Giovanni's eyes were scanning the case. "Let's have a look at this other one," he said, pointing to a gold coin.

" I just got these coins a few days ago." He took it out. "This gold coin is Roman—one of the Caesars."

"You think so?" Giovanni said.

"Positive. Here, you can see for yourself. I haven't researched it yet but I'm certain."

Giovanni took the coins to the window and examined them in natural light.

I unzipped my purse, found my jeweler's loupe and handed it to Giovanni.

"Where did you find these coins?" he asked the dealer.

"In Manfredonia—I bought them at the Saturday market. From one of those itinerant Moroccans."

I recalled that Manfredonia was a nearby seaport town at the foot of the Gargano.

"Really? When?" Giovanni asked.

"On the 28th of April. I remember because it was my mother's birthday and I'd gone into Manfredonia to visit her."

"I'll take them," Giovanni said without a trace of emotion in his voice.

"Don't you want to know the price?" the dealer asked

"I know how much they're worth."

Giovanni had done exactly what I'd done when I bought his gold earrings. Bought them without bargaining.

"Then you must know that I want 500,000 for the two."

Giovanni nodded, pulled a fat roll of lire from his pocket and cinched the deal.

❦

"Let's go to the Angel's Bar for a drink," he said as we were leaving the shop. "I could use one."

"Signor Filippo didn't know what hit him when you bought those coins so fast."

"Didn't you recognize the gold coin?"

"To me it looked Roman. Classic period—just as he said."

"It wasn't Roman at all. It was an Augustales, the coin Frederick II designed, casting himself as a Roman emperor. Filippo doesn't know anything about coins. He's a local woodcarver who decided to open a shop to sell bric-a-brac and old commodes."

"I've only read about the Augustales. I've never seen one."

"Now you have."

"Please let me have a look at it again. I'd like to hold it in my hand."

"Let's wait until we sit down over a drink. We'll look at it together. It's not just finding the coin that I'm happy about—now I may have a clue to the robbery of the map. There were coins like these in the bronze box we found in Andria. This could be one of them."

❧

From the grapevine-covered terrace of the bar we looked out. The late afternoon sun had burnished the sea like a polished silver tray.

Giovanni signaled the waiter. "A grappa for me. For the signora a San Pellegrino. And please bring an *ostia ripiena* as well."

He reached into his breast pocket and took out the coin.

"Here, now you can have a good look."

Again, I felt around in my purse for my loupe.

"I've read about this coin. I've even tried to look it up in *Coins of the World*, but I couldn't find a mention or a photograph."

"They're very rare. This one is worn, but you can still make out the CESAR:AUG. IMP.ROM. That's where Filippo went wrong. Frederick went back to models of classical coinage. A step backward—but a huge step forward from early medieval iconography, which was still so Byzantine."

"What will you do with it?"

"Take it to the laboratory we've set up in Andria. After it's photographed, it goes to Bari. Would you like to make the drive with me? We'd have to stay overnight. Maybe your cousins wouldn't approve."

"They might not, but I feel that it would be such an experience to see your lab."

The waiter returned with our order. "*Ecco, signor, signora, l'ostia ripiena,*" he said with a wave of his hand. The oval sweet sat atop a white linen napkin on a silver platter. The "stuffed host" was a sandwich of two very thin white wafers stuck together with a brittle of whole toasted almonds and caramelized honey.

"The people of the Mount say it's bad luck to cut one with a knife." Giovanni wrapped his napkin around the confection and broke it with his hands. He handed half to me.

He sensed my hesitation. "But you must try it. It's part of the lore of the Mount. They've probably been making this sweet for centuries."

We were offered his castle as a halfway resting place. When we arrive we are served trays of a delicious sweet made from honey and almonds spread between pastries as thin as the Holy Wafer.

As we enjoy these sweet and sticky biscuits, a Knight gallops down to meet us on his white stallion and gives us greetings. "I am Serlon—cousin thrice removed of your aunt, Lady de Haute-ville," he tells me. "I was born in Apulia but have never set foot in Normandy."

I accepted the "host" and nibbled what tasted like a fragile communion wafer. I took another bite. Delicate yet crunchy. The most delicious biscuit I'd ever eaten—so delicious that I ate my half in an instant. I felt a reviving blood-rush, perhaps the effect of so much sugar all at once.

Giovanni broke the long silence. "Sometimes you seem in a world all your own. Even so, I am very happy to be in your company. I feel as though I have known you for a long time."

"You have," I said.

I saw the puzzled look in his eyes. He finished his *ostia ripiena* without another word.

After he'd paid the bill, we drove down the winding road of Monte Gargano back to the coastal road toward Vieste, then past a white stucco portal.

"La Zagara" was written across the top. Beyond was a grove of lemon and orange trees. I mused out loud, "I wonder what the hotel is like inside."

"Very comfortable. Divans and cushions, that sort of thing. Very arabesque. Would you like to have a look?" His eyes met mine.

"I'm expecting a phone call from my husband—from Tokyo. Can we save it for another time?"

"Whatever you say."

We were quiet. The silence was disturbing. He turned on his radio and we listened to San Remo festival music all the way back to Vieste, barely saying a word to one another.

When I returned to the Vesta, the clerk gave me a message from Matt. I'd missed him again! Maybe the difference in time between Italy and Tokyo was making it difficult to communicate. Or maybe it was time to admit to myself how little thought I'd given my husband these past few weeks.

❧

"*Architetto* Di Serlo drove me to Monte Sant'Angelo today," I told Filomena when she came to my room to turn down the bed cover.

She glanced up at me with curious, murky eyes. Watch out, they said.

"What's the matter, Filomena?" I asked. "Why are you giving me the eye. Please don't keep on with that sly business!"

"No, Signora Rosa. Listen to me, please. Who knows where he gets all his things to sell? People say the Mafia sent him here to do business for them. They even say he pays the farmers to bring him things they find in the fields when they plow, and that he has uncovered an entire sunken city near here, like Atlantis—but that story is just rumor, I'm sure. I am only telling you what I have heard. That's all." Again she made the sign of the horns against the evil eye.

I laughed. "I'll be fine, Filomena. Don't worry."

"I'm not worrying, but I'm sure your cousins are. They are keeping their eyes on you. I heard the *direttore* talking to Signora Marta. They must realize that you have been avoiding them, Signora Rosa. They must sense something is going on with you—and the architect. She laughed. "*Se ne mess' a corte.* They've caught on," she said in dialect.

"What do you mean, 'they've caught on?' We share a common interest in the Altavilla. Nothing else!"

She raised an eyebrow. "Maybe you should pay a visit to *La Voce*—maybe you can learn something from her."

"The Voice?"

"You mean no one's bothered to tell you about her yet?" I saw the sly look in her eyes. Her smirky little smile. I didn't understand what she was getting at.

"She lives down past the Duomo. If you walk by her house you can look up and see her sitting in her upstairs window, morning, noon and night. She hardly ever leaves her home. Always sitting in that window—just staring out at the passers by."

"Why is she called 'The Voice'? " I asked, feeling shivers traveling down the back of my arms.

"Why don't you ask Signora Marta?" She gave me another of her crooked smiles and a wink. "I'm surprised she hasn't told you about her. Tell her to take you to visit *La Voce*."

 The days pass, summer gives way to rains of autumn. The fruit of the olive is ready for gathering, nuts in their husks turn brown, and I begin to feel my burden. I say "burden" because I know that at its birth my child will be taken from me. I cannot think of it in any other way. My breasts will be bound and my child given over to a wet-nurse. I try not to think of that.

Joanna looks swollen of womb beneath her flowing robes, as though she, too, will bear a child. I pass my time with Caid, never leaving the fortress. The Knight Serlon attends to the gathering of olives on his property so I no longer have his visits to look forward to.

Sometimes I yearn for his arms around me, his lips pressed to mine—but he has kept his vow never to touch me in a lover's way. Once Queen Joanna receives my child, at least I shall have the Knight Serlon's love for solace. I am thankful for that.

I wonder what my child will be like, if he will be healthy and strong enough to stand in royal succession. Yet in my heart I know he will never sit on William's throne. The whole scheme seems too easy, too perfect.

On the night we get the news, the sky is dark. The sun retreats from the sky at an early hour; the clear blue sea turns to steel-gray capped with white. A cool wind blows—not like the sirocco, hot and dry, but damp and cold, the ill wind from the north.

The King's messenger rides in on his Arab steed.

He falls at Joanna's feet—quaking in fear as he delivers his hateful message.

King William is dead of a high fever. He died on the feast day of Saint Odo.

Queen Joanna must return to Palermo.

She weeps. The ruse is over. After all this—after she had planned this devious birth of William's successor. She must now return without a child. Joanna orders me to stay in Vieste with Caid Gregory as my protector. Before she leaves me standing there in tears, she vows that the child will be raised as royal blood. But I fear for my child and sense that it will never happen. Instead, I might be tossed into the Tiraz for the rest of my life. I know there will be strife between Constance and her illegitimate half-brother, Tancred, who was so angered by William's concession of his throne to his Aunt Constance. And I've heard many tales of her husband's brutality to her. What might Henry Hohenstaufen do to harm a child of William's and thus secure Constance's Sicilian kingdom as his own?

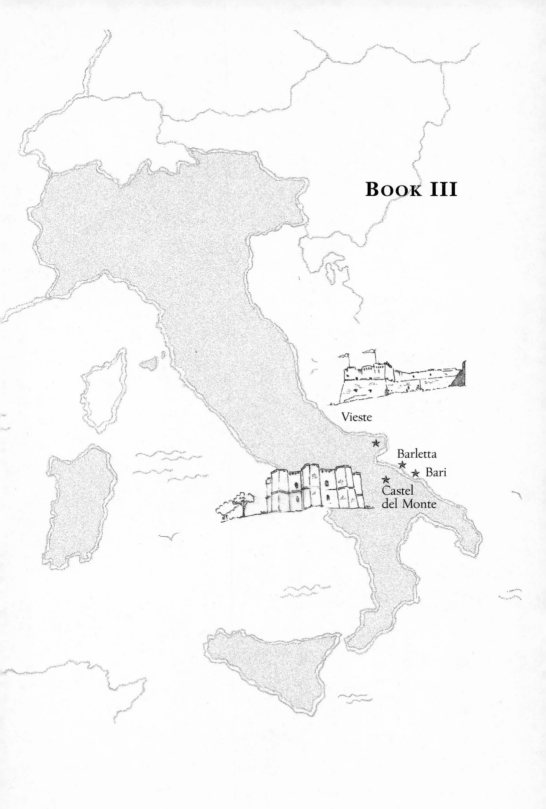

BOOK III

Vieste

Barletta

Bari

Castel
del Monte

CHAPTER SIXTEEN

A FEW DAYS LATER no sun came through the shutter slats. For once, a dark, gloomy day in Vieste. Black storm clouds hovered on the horizon. The air was cool and still. No swallows swooped in and out of chimney pots.

It was time for me to start pressing Don Gesualdo about my research at the Duomo. But how could I in this desolate mood?

The King's messenger rides in on his Arab steed.
  King William is dead of a high fever. He died on the feast day of Saint Odo.

I hadn't seen Giovanni since the day we drove to Monte Sant' Angelo. I sat on the edge of the bed and considered crawling back between the sheets. Instead, I reached for my journal and threw it hard against the wall.

I heard a knock on the unlocked door. It opened.

"Rosa—I'm so sorry—I didn't think you'd still be in bed!"

Marta. I hadn't seen her in a few days.

"*Andiamo*—we're going shopping, Rosa. I'm taking you to my friend's boutique. She has the best *costumi da bagno*. Toss out that ugly black bathing suit of yours! You're supposed to be my glamorous American cousin." She reached in her purse and pulled out a page from *Gente*. "Now, this is more like what you should be wearing, Rosa, with your figure."

"All right," I said. I was too depressed to enjoy shopping, but my instincts told me to listen to Marta. I knew I shouldn't have been hurt by Giovanni's silence, but I felt rejected, nonetheless.

"I'll get dressed right away. But not too skimpy, please. I think I'm too plump for a bikini."

"That's ridiculous!" she said. "Come on—we'll take the car, it's too far to walk."

As Marta drove, she pointed out the best fruit shop in town, the best profumeria, the best grocer. We parked the car in front of La Sirenuse, its window filled with bikinis in polka dots and tropical flowers, leopard spots and tiger stripes. Marta introduced me as her *cugina americana* who needed a two-piece bathing suit.

I chose two to try on. A nautical navy blue two-piece with white dots, a cotton suit in a bright Tahitian print, a bit more daring but with a sarong to cover it.

The salesgirl pulled a gold lamé number from a drawer.

I raised an eyebrow and shook my head. "May I try one in black?" I asked.

"No," Marta said as the saleswoman whisked the gold suit away. "No black. All those German women go on the beach topless and my American cousin wants black, like the old ladies of Vieste!"

I took the suits into the dressing room. I let my breasts fall into the wired bra cups. The top fit comfortably, the underwire pushing my breasts up, forming a valley between. I tugged and twisted the bottom half. Embarrassed, I stepped out from behind the curtain.

"*Stupenda*," Marta said. "What beautiful skin you have. What makes you think you're fat? What madness! You should see the spare tire I have around my waist. And stretch marks. *Gesù*, do I have stretch marks! Now let's see the other one. Try it on."

I obeyed. I was like a child with Marta, although there was hardly any age difference between us. I pulled off the bathing suit and looked at myself in the three-way mirror. I could see myself clearly in the rear view. My behind was not as high as it used to be. But what struck me suddenly was my back. It was as straight and lean as a sixteen-year-old's. The best part of me. I tugged on the bottom of the flowered suit.

"How beautiful you look. *La sirena del mare.*"

Those were Giovanni's words when he crowned me with seaweed.

❧

After I'd paid for the bikinis, Marta asked me where I'd like to go for lunch, or if there was anything special I wanted to do that afternoon.

"Well, yes, there is something," I said. "A few days ago Filomena, the housekeeper at the hotel, told me about a woman who lives close by—someone possessed of a 'voice,' whatever that means. Do you think we can pay her a visit? Filomena said you'd know where to take me."

Marta gave me an odd look. "Filomena was the one who told you about her? I'm surprised it wasn't Giovanni."

"Filomena said the woman gazes out from her window all day long—sometimes all night, as well, and that she hardly ever leaves her house . . ." I stopped, realizing that I just described my aunt.

"Caterina is *La Voce?*" I asked. I heard the incredulous tone in my own voice.

"She didn't want you to know about it," Marta said gently. "Caterina worried that her niece, a modern American business woman from California, might think her a crazy old lady."

And to think that I'd worried that my family would think me a crazy American!

"Can we put off our sightseeing until another day? I must go to see Caterina right away. I have to talk to her. Alone."

She drove me straight to the *parcheggio*; I left my shopping bag at the Vesta, and walked up toward the Duomo and *La Voce*.

From the street, I looked up to her window. Caterina sat gazing out. A few moments passed before she noticed me. I saw her step back from the window, and heard footsteps on the steep stone staircase. I waited for the door to open.

She was wearing a black dress. A very old black dress, so old that it looked rusty. Today her fluffy white hair was pinned back in a knot and she wore no makeup. She looked much older.

"Rosa, what a surprise! I was just sitting at my window when I saw you down . . ."

I put my arms around her, kissed her on both cheeks. She smelled of clove-scented carnations.

When we entered the darkened salone, she said, "It's almost one o'clock. You must be hungry. Shall we go to the kitchen? I will prepare some lunch for you."

"I'm not hungry. I'd rather talk."

She pulled open the shutters. "Please sit down. Tell me what you've been doing this past week. We haven't seen enough of you since the Festa." She motioned to the sheet-covered chair.

"Zia, I don't know how—where to begin . . . ." I heard my voice crack. "Filomena—the maid at the hotel—told me . . . about a woman who had, what she called 'the voice.' " I tried to read the expression on my aunt's face.

She nodded. "Yes, go on."

"She told me that I should ask Marta to take me to her." I felt my eyes brimming. "So here I am, Caterina. I've come to ask you about your voice." I stammered out angrily, "Why did you try to keep it from me? Why didn't you tell me about it earlier?"

I saw her eyes eyelids flicker as she tried to hold back tears. I got up from the armchair, knelt at the foot of her chair, and laid my head upon her lap.

She stroked my hair. "Please don't cry, dearest Rosa. There's nothing to cry about. You see, I thought you might think it strange to have such an eccentric aunt. That you might even have been embarrassed by me. But I also knew that if this voice were something pertaining to your life, in due time you would find out about me on your own."

"I've been hearing a voice in my head—a woman's voice. Since last November. I've been transcribing her words into a notebook. When I first heard her speak, I thought I might be going mad."

Caterina shook her head and sighed. "Let me tell you all I know." She wiped the beads of damp from her forehead with her apron. "When the voice first came to me, I was bewildered. But then, when I told my mother about it, she knew exactly what it was. Her mother had told her that this was a gift handed down from one generation of women to another to an eldest daughter. Since I had no children, perhaps the voice has come down to you, my brother's daughter. Nonna Rosina, your great, great grandmother, once told my mother that this gift has been handed down from the priestesses of Vesta, the ancient goddess, guardian of the sacred fires. My mother encouraged me to listen to the voice. To heed it. Though it may not seem a blessing, it is. The voice does not always express itself the same way. Mine is the voice of clairvoyance. Sometimes I sense things before they happen. Or I know how things will turn out. People are frightened by this inborn power. That is why I have removed myself from the world. How painful it is for me to be among people when I feel impending misery or illness . . . or death."

"Don't you foresee happy events as well?" I asked.

She smiled. "I was sure that if you had been given the voice, you would someday bear a child of your very own, so that your gift could be handed down to future generations of women. If you heeded it. I suspected on that very first night, from the questions you asked about the Altavilla, that you had a link to the past.

"Be secure with your gift, however, whenever it comes to you. Trust your dreams, trust your voice. Follow it."

"I'm here today *because* I followed it," I said.

I told her Rosamonde's story. Tears trickled from gray-violet eyes, still so young in her old face. She took my hands in hers. "Rosa, my dearest niece, you've taken such a long time to visit us. I have been waiting all these years, hoping to hear what you've told me today. Now, at last, I will be able to rest, knowing that you have found your voice, our voice."

"Caterina—I have something else to tell you. About Matthew and me. I don't want to shock you—but in America couples who can't conceive sometimes go to fertility clinics to find a surrogate mother to conceive for them by using the husband's sperm. Matthew wants us to do that. They can even plant yet another woman's fertilized egg in the surrogate womb, so that the surrogate doesn't bear her own biological child. At least this way the child would be half ours. And if I decide against a surrogate, then we'll begin adoption proceedings. Or else . . ." I held my breath waiting to hear Caterina's reaction of shock and indignation.

I wasn't prepared for her response.

"First of all—you must have tried the *in vitro* method," she said.

"Four times—but it didn't take. The doctors told us that the chances are slim that my ova will ever conceive *in vitro*. I'm surprised that you know about all this."

"Our Italian doctors are very advanced in fertility problems. The newspapers are filled with stories about this sort of thing. In a recent *Gente* I read about an Italian woman in her fifties who bore a child for her young daughter who was sterile. What miracles they perform these days! But before you resort to a surrogate, are you absolutely sure that Matthew isn't sterile?"

"He's had all the tests that prove that he's not. It's me, Zia. I know it's me and I don't know why because the doctors tell me everything is in order. They just can't understand what's going on inside."

"Have you ever had a lover?"

"I'm still deeply in love with Matthew."

"I guess things must be different in the States."

"What do you mean?"

"Maybe you should try to get pregnant with another man."

Now I was shocked. "In a way, isn't that as bad as finding a surrogate?" I stammered out.

"You would still be the biological mother for the child springs from your womb. Remember that we come from a culture that was a matriarchy for thousands of years."

"Maybe it would be simpler to adopt a child."

"Whatever way you choose— these decisions must be made between you *and* Matthew. And then as I told you before—you must make the Madonna hear you. You see, Rosa, I didn't heed the advice I just gave you."

There was no way I could either; I embraced Caterina and turned to leave.

Then, I saw Caterina ceremoniously remove the sheet from the chair she had been saving for me all these years.

❧

After the visit with Caterina, I felt in turn drained then exhilarated. Back in my room again, I tossed the plastic shopping bag stamped *"La Sirenuse"* onto the bed. Marta had been so insistent that I buy the bathing suits. Why had I listened to her? I had thrown money away.

As I put them in the drawer, I noticed a metallic sliver between the tissues. Folded between the suits I found the gold lamé bikini. Put in the bag by mistake? An envelope dropped to the floor. The card read, "A gift for Rosa, my favorite cousin, with a big hug from Marta."

At least try it on, I thought. When I slipped on the stretch silk, it fit like a second skin. But where would I ever wear a gold bikini? I took it off and shoved it back in the drawer. Marta was getting silly in her middle age.

Filomena had closed the shutters for siesta, blocking the view over the terrace and down to the sea. I was too worn out to write.

"Trust the voice," Caterina's voice echoed. I pulled back the bedcover and lay naked upon the sheets, thinking confusedly of Giovanni. And of the Knight Serlon. The two were becoming one.

The room was hot. A fly buzzed overhead. Motor boats hummed in the distance. I pushed my face into the pillow. This thinking was getting me into trouble, I remember telling myself as I fell asleep.

❧

I, Rose, float on my back in dark, warm water. I turn and swim to Giovanni's private grotto, gathering silvery mussels from the shoals. Giovanni calls out from his cavern. "Come, Rosa, come spend the day with me. We will dance together on my beach where the sand is ground pearls."

I answer him, "I have never danced, Giovanni. I cannot dance." At that I turn over my naked body and hoist myself into his boat. "Can't you see, I am a melusina," I laugh, twisting my green enameled tails together modestly.

When I woke up it was almost five o'clock. The sun was still strong. I would go down to the beach to write in my journal. I pulled the old one-piece off the peg, stepped into it and slipped on a beach robe.

Downstairs, in the lounge, a symposium was in full force: a noisy group of Apulian vintners discussing wine marketing, while their wives chattered away on the beach.

I settled down under an umbrella and took the notebook from my beach-bag. Before long, a little girl about three years old came by to peek over my shoulder, curious as to what I was writing.

"What's your name?" I asked.

"Annunziata," she said. "What are you doing?"

I turned my notebook so she could see that I was writing. She was plainly disappointed when the book didn't produce any drawings, so I turned to a blank page and, remembering my dream, quickly sketched a mermaid. I tore out the sheet and gave it to her.

She seemed pleased. "Now make a picture of me, please signora."

"If you promise you'll sit still," I said.

She was a sweet, angelic looking child with turned-up green

eyes, red hair and a scattering of freckles across her nose and cheeks. I drew her complete with freckles, pointing to my own. I signed it, "To Annunziata from Rosa—her friend from California."

She ran off to show the picture to her mother who gave it a quick glance, saluting me with a polite smile and a wave. She handed Annunziata a pail and shovel and motioned her to sit down on the narrow sand strip.

The child's mother began to talk heatedly with her friends. They were plainly arguing, while the child sat on the beach blissfully scooping, patting, dumping.

I lost myself in my journal. When I looked up, Annunziata was no longer playing on the sand, although her mother and friends were still intent on their conversation.

I felt my heart begin to pound against my tightened chest.

No—it couldn't be. I looked out to the water. No! No! I stifled my scream.

I ran to the water's edge and saw her hand break surface. The water was so clear I could see her little body, falling face down to the bottom.

I tossed away reality. Plunging into the water, kicking my way toward her, questions, answers rushed through my head in a torrent. My life unfolded before me. Through a blur of tangled black seaweed, I saw the chalk-white Quahog shells at the bottom of Narragansett Bay. I saw the little girl lying on the sand, golden light gleaming around her head like a halo waiting to be plucked. Separateness no longer existed. Annunziata and I became one. With strength I never knew I had, I grabbed her hair and yanked her to the surface. I remember in my rapture that the light above seemed dazzling, the warm air embracing, as I swam the short distance to shore.

The women were standing on the beach screaming hysterically.

I laid the child on the sand, and pushed the women away. They screamed at me. I screamed back at them. "*Lasciami stare!* Let me do this! I know how."

The child's face was bloodless white. I shook her body as I had been taught. No response. I felt her pulse. Although her heart was faint it was still beating. I bent over and began the motions that I learned in the CPR course.

I kneaded her chest trying to force out water that had filled the airways of her lungs. I tilted back her head, pinched her nostrils with one hand and pushed open her blue lips with the other. I put my open mouth on hers and breathed in the first of two breaths. I watched her chest to see if it would rise and fall.

I counted to five—out loud this time—and blew in another breath. I breathed in again.

Her chest heaved, a bit of spittle dribbled from the side of her mouth. Her eyelids fluttered. I shook her again. Out came more spittle, then a great heave of salt water, then vomit.

Annunziata opened her eyes wide and looked up at me.

"I think she'll be all right now," I said. "Let's wrap her with some towels."

The frantic mother hugged Annunziata in one breath, then shook, shouted, scolded her in the next. By now everyone was down on the beach hovering over the child and giving advice.

I slipped away from the crowd and climbed the spiral staircase. I have never known such a feeling of relief as I felt at that moment. Although my room was still hot, I felt chilled. I stood under the warm shower reflecting on the risk I'd taken when I'd jumped in to save the child. I knew that if I hadn't done so, I could never have lived another day of my life without regret. And sadness. But supposing I hadn't succeeded? My stomach flipped at the thought. I told myself that I would never look back and say "what if" again. I would follow my instincts and my instincts would be right.

In my elation I had the sudden urge to call Matthew to tell him what I'd done—to share my joy with him. I stepped out of the shower, wrapped myself in a towel, and placed a call to Osaka. No luck.

"Mr. Kirkland just went to Tokyo for two days," I was told.

⁂

That evening at Marta's, I learned that the whole town had heard about the American Rosa saving a child. My family was full of praise for me. Renzo said that Caterina had once told him how her brother Tommaso, my father, had saved a boy from drowning down off the cliffs by the Convent of San Francesco. "Like father like daughter," they said.

⁂

Three mornings later I was awakened by a deafening thunder-clap. I yanked open the shutters and looked out. Lightning zig-zagged across an obsidian sky, flickering eerie, jagged light on the water, illuminating the Pizzomunno. The rock could have been a tall, pale goddess emerging from the sea. I shivered at the sight. My mind flashed back, my body feeling the delicious tremor I'd felt in the grotto when Giovanni had brushed against my thigh. I picked up the phone and rang his number without thinking. The sound of his voice, gruff with sleep, comforted me.

"Does your offer to drive me to Castel del Monte still stand?" I said. "I hadn't heard from you, and . . ."

"I would have told you if I'd changed my mind. I've been very absorbed in my work—things have happened since I saw you last." He sounded hostile.

Silence on my end of the phone.

His tone softened. "Can you be ready to leave by eight o'clock? I have some business in Andria, but we can visit Castel del Monte first. Make sure you pack your bathing suit."

Of course I never mentioned the new bikini from Marta.

"We'll stop at Zagara Beach for a swim on the way back. I'll meet you down at the *parcheggio*."

By the time I was ready, the storm had passed. Dawn was a coral sky, the sun rising from the amethyst-streaked horizon. I smelled the fresh, mineral after-storm air. A rainbow stretched its arc across the sea. Gulls soared and wheeled, silver-winged, above tile roofs. On the beach below, the beach boy unfurled the orange and green striped umbrellas.

I thought about eating some black cherries from the giant fruit basket sent by Annunziata's grateful parents, but I was too excited about seeing Castel del Monte.

I got into an oversized pink cotton shirt, slipped my feet into sandals, and skipped down three flights of steps for an espresso on the terrace. I had come to a decision. At Castel del Monte I would tell Giovanni about Rosamonde. I could not keep her from him any longer.

CHAPTER SEVENTEEN

GIOVANNI was anxious to show me Castel del Monte before it closed for lunch. But before setting off, we stopped by Lanciani's pied-à-terre in new Vieste. I preferred to wait in the car.

Giovanni took his time. When at last he got behind the wheel he reeked of cigar smoke—the same stench that woke me up that night.

"What took you so long?" I asked.

"I'm sorry, Rosa—just business," he said. "I wanted to show Lanciani the coins, to discuss where they might have come from."

"Did you smoke a cigar—or did Lanciani?"

"No on both counts. Lanciani had just returned from a visit to your aunt Caterina. I did smell cigars, though, when I walked in. Guido always smokes when he plays cards."

It ran through my mind that Lanciani was much taller than the black masked man who stood over my bed, dagger in hand.

"Why would Lanciani go to see Caterina?"

"To seek her advice. Guido relies on her a lot."

"What kind of questions do you think he asks my aunt?"

"Who knows what people ask psychics?"

I was annoyed, mostly because Giovanni had never mentioned my aunt's clairvoyance to me. Now I imagined this patronizing professor taking advantage of her precious gift.

He must have sensed my irritation. "I know how you feel about Guido, Rosa, but I've known him for years. Helga insisted that we have a quick coffee while we discussed the coins. Don't worry. We'll still reach Castel del Monte before noon."

"Who's Helga?"

"She's his wife. She's German. They met in Lecce when he was working on his thesis."

"Oh?"

"We'll visit Andria on the way back," he said. "I promise to show you exactly where the restorers found the chest."

"I can hardly wait to see it."

"For a while the church was off limits to tourists. Curiosity seekers turned up in droves. Now it's all been put back in order. You won't be able to tell where we dug it up."

"Why don't you let me guess?"

Riding side by side, my left to his right, I could not keep my eyes from the red birthmark. I quelled an impulse to put my fingers to it and touch them to my lips.

"I'm surprised to hear how much you already know about Frederick," Giovanni said. "I have my own theories about him as well, about his public birth at Jesi."

"Tell me about your theories."

"I don't believe that Frederick's father was Henry of Hohenstaufen."

"How did you ever arrive at that?"

"I'm certainly not the first person in the world to have this opinion. But there's never been any historical proof. Only rumors."

"What do *you* believe, Giovanni?"

"Let us begin with Constance. She never wanted Frederick to become Holy Roman Emperor, she only wanted him to rule as king of Sicily—her Altavilla kingdom. And then she'd named her son Constantine, after herself. It wasn't until after she died that he was called Frederick."

I am silent. Constance and Godfrey of Viterbo in the cloister of Monreale. They seem to have eyes only for each other. He leans forward to kiss her lips. They do not know I have shared their private moment.

Sensing my distraction he took his eyes from the road to look at me. The car swerved. Horns blared.

"That was a Mercedes we almost hit." I tightened my seatbelt.

"They come here in droves—the Germans," he said. "To them Federico was a Hohenstaufen, a German, but here in Italy he is *Puer Apuliae*, son of Costanza d'Altavilla." He reached in his pocket for a cigarette. "Find a match in the glove compartment, will you?"

I struck the match for him. He turned to me, his eyes burning mine, as I touched the flame to the tip of his cigarette. This was the second time he'd reached for a cigarette when we talked about the Altavilla.

We were quiet for a while as he smoked. I remembered his gallant toast to me, "*Puella Apuliae*," then the hostility I'd felt from Lanciani.

As last I had a glimpse of Castel del Monte in the distance, like a golden crown rising above sloping vineyards and almond groves. As we drove closer, the giant octagon loomed up from a hill dense with pines. Octagonal towers projected from each of the castle's eight angles, repeating the octagon eight more times.

We wound up and around the wooded road to the castle's single entrance, its dentillated pediment, bold and classical.

"That portal could have been designed for the Gonzagas, or the Estes," Giovanni said. "A return to the taste of the Antique by a medieval emperor two hundred years before the Renaissance. Inside it's like being in a mathematical formula, an exercise in octagons. You'll see."

I remember the castle seeming so majestic, so purposeful against the cloudless periwinkle blue sky that I compared it to the Parthenon atop the Acropolis.

The castellan announced, "Go on in right away or you'll be out of luck. It's almost eleven-thirty. We close at noon for three hours."

Giovanni displayed his pass as we walked through the single exterior portal.

"We are now in Room One of the eight rooms on the ground floor," he said. "Can you find any traces of rare marbles?"

I ran my hand over hardstone veneer facing the rough Apulian limestone. "Porphyry," I said. "The color of dried blood."

"And the color of porpora," he added. "I often wonder how many local altars must have been made from these marbles. Can you imagine what the rooms must have looked like?"

I didn't tell him that my imagination was way ahead of his.

"Let's go outside. You'll see that the inner courtyard forms an octagon, as well."

In the warm, bright sunshine of the courtyard, he pointed out the equestrian bas relief in a lunette above the portal.

"And in the courtyard's center was yet another octagon, a shallow, octagonal marble pool with a fountain, dug up and removed in the nineteenth century."

I stood in the center of the Octagon and loaded my camera. "Why don't you let me take a picture of you by the portal?"

He stood stiffly as I moved back to get a long shot.

"Don't look so serious. This isn't for the *Soprintendenza*, you know."

He smiled his broadest.

I clicked the red button and looked up. A dense cloud climbed across the sky like a falcon in flight, darkening the sun and casting a shadow over the courtyard.

I felt my knees buckle as the courtyard began to turn, slowly, as though I were the hub of a wheel. It gained momentum and began to spin. I reached for Giovanni. The camera dropped from my hand to the ground.

He lunged forward to catch me. My lips brushed his face. "Rosa! Are you all right?" He held me close. I felt faint. "What did you have to eat this morning?"

"Just a cappuccino."

"Is that all? No wonder. Let's walk down to the Hosteria and have some lunch. The food is good here."

"Please don't worry." I said. "It was just a dizzy spell. Low blood sugar, probably. Let's have a look at the other rooms before lunch."

"Are you sure? Here, take my arm."

We climbed the narrow staircase to a room above. Sunlight shone through the quatrefoil rose window. He led me up the steps to Frederick's so-called stone "throne" and had me sit facing the room, my back to the window and the view over the Murge.

"I am convinced that Frederick was deeply involved in planning this place," he said. "He must have filled these rooms with Greek and Roman sculpture, just as he did in his castles in Foggia, Lucera and Canosa. He would have climbed these stairs, sat in this very niche—exactly where you're sitting now, a rose window above your head. He must have known you would come here one day."

I laughed. "Shall we sit and imagine what this room must have been like in his time?"

"You must describe it for me, then."

I had a good look around the room, closed my eyes and saw how it must have been. "The walls are draped with hangings of heavy purple silk from the Tiraz, a design of double-headed eagles woven with silver threads."

I paused.

He smiled. "Keep going."

"The floors are covered with crimson carpets from Antioch, the throne where I sit lined with sables, tribute from a Tartar prince. In the center of the room, a big brass brazier smolders with olive pits and sweet bergamot drifts in the air." I took a deep breath.

"Divans heaped with cushions embroidered with peacock feathers and seed pearls—chests of tortoiseshell and mother of pearl from Damascus filled with cinnamon, pepper, myrrh, musk, ambergris. Carved ivory boxes from Palermo store the Emperor's precious stones and intaglios and cameos."

I took another deep breath. "Against that wall is an intarsia olivewood table where Frederick sits, writing his book on falconry. In one corner of the room stands a marble statue of the Venus Pudica, and in the other corner a statue of Apollo."

He applauded. "*Bravissima!* And you say it is *I* who romanticizes! I'm sorry that I haven't yet found you that small bit of Tiraz silk. I'm sure we'll come across a little *ricordo* one of these days."

That first day in the shop I'd remembered thinking that his promise was charming and silly, one that he would soon forget.

"Come on, we've just enough time to see the Falconers' tower, and the mews where the Saracen guards kept watch over the Emperor's birds. In Frederick's Treatise on Falconry, he writes that the birds were fed with bits of prosciutto and ricotta."

I laughed. "Food habits haven't changed much in Italy, have they?"

We climbed the narrow, twisting stone staircase to the falconers' mews. "Look out there," I said. "Do you see those two dark birds darting and swooping above the pine branches? Hear the sounds they make?"

"They must surely be descendants of Frederick's birds," he replied.

An alarm sounded for all visitors to clear the building.

"Let's walk down to the Hosteria. You ought to have some food in your stomach."

The little inn at the base of the pine grove was crowded. We were shown to a pleasant table covered by a bright blue and white checked cloth anchored down by a basket of warm bread. We studied the surprisingly elaborate menu.

The waiter suggested *cinghiale alla cacciatore*, wild boar from the surrounding forest, a German favorite that didn't appeal to either of us. We chose Apulian pasta instead.

I glanced around the room assessing the crowd. "It's filled with Germans. I think we may be the only Italian-speaking people here today. Do you think it's because they consider Frederick one of their heroes?"

"Germans come here by the busload. You should see this place on weekends. For the Germans, tourism is the new colonialism. *Ich bin nie auslander*, which means 'I'm not a foreigner anywhere.' They make themselves at home in Apulia. Including the beautiful girls." He nodded over his shoulder.

I looked past him to a tall, long-haired blonde wearing short shorts and a clinging T-shirt that outlined her large nipples.

The waiter brought our *orecchiette* with wild broccoli. We began to eat with gusto. By then I was starving.

"What would you think of this, Rosa? Instead of going on to Andria and Barletta later on this afternoon, why don't we spend the night here and see the place by moonlight? It's a waxing crescent moon tonight, a perfect time to see Castel del Monte—like seeing the Taj Mahal at sunrise."

"Sounds . . . perfect." The word "romantic" almost slipped out. I was glad I caught myself. "Do you think it's possible to book two rooms in this busy season?"

"Certainly," he said. "I'll have to make some calls to Milano and Bari after lunch. I have an appointment that I'll have to cancel, but it will be worth it."

He excused himself and went to the front desk, returning a few minutes later with my key.

❧

I folded back the heavy white spread.

If the Knight Serlon comes to me, I, Rosamonde, will fling my arms around him and pull him against my body.

I laid my head back on the hard bolster pillow. Time passed. A firm knock on the door. The young waiter. I was disappointed.

"Architetto di Serlo had not wanted to disturb you," he explained. "He thought you might be resting." The waiter handed me an envelope. I tipped him and closed the door. The note was in English: "Rosa, I have gone to look at a project not far from here in Andria. I wanted you to have a rest. I'll see you later."

He had abandoned me at Castel del Monte. I had a sickening vision of him in bed with the lissome blonde German. I imagined her legs wrapped around his bronzed back. What were all these roiling, jealous feelings? At least he should have invited me to go to Andria, to show me where the box had been discovered.

By then, I didn't feel like writing. Instead I left my room and trudged up the steep and winding drive, past Styrofoam cups and cigarette papers. I wished Matt could see this mess! I kicked the wrappers out of my path and stomped back to the Hosteria. I would wait for Giovanni on the terrace.

After I'd settled down to read an old copy of *Epoca*, I heard a familiar voice. That voice with the curious lilt. Brian Lambeth was standing at the reception desk, speaking fluent Italian.

"Room fifteen. May I have the key? I can find the room on my own. Thank you."

I buried my face in the magazine. Had he tracked me down in Castel del Monte? How had he learned that I was there? Did he intend to surprise me? I fled to my room, went into the bathroom for a glass of water.

I looked into the mirror.

Rosamonde's face is as white as the cotton shift she wears. The blood spots over her heart are still bright and fresh. She takes a deep breath and swallows the water, her hand trembling as she holds the glass to her lips.

She locks and bolts the door, and falls on the bed to await his return.

It is almost six o'clock when she hears a gentle tap on the door.

❧

"Who is it?" I asked angrily.

"*Giovanni. Apri la porta!*"

I hesitated a moment before opening the door. He took me in his arms, his eyes searching my face.

I pulled away. "Brian Lambeth is here."

"I knew he'd be turning up soon. When I rang Bari after lunch, the Soprintendenza's office told me he was on his way to Andria, so I drove there to fetch him. But I just missed him—he was on his way to Castel del Monte by taxi. I stayed on in Andria to inspect the project with someone from the British Embassy in Rome."

"Why didn't you let me drive to Andria with you? You knew how much I wanted to see the church where the chest was discovered." I tried not to sound sorry for myself.

"It was business, and it was important. I thought it better for you to have a rest. You looked pale after that episode this morning. Besides, why are you so upset that Brian is here?" He narrowed his eyes. "Is there something going on between you two?"

"I'm upset because I don't want to get involved with him. Especially here. It's a long story, and I'm not going to tell you about it now."

"Was he your lover, Rosa?"

I was taken aback by so bold, so impudent a question. I looked straight into his serious eyes. "He was not."

"Don't worry, I'll dine with him alone. We'll be on our way first thing in the morning—at dawn, if you wish."

"That's not necessary. It's just that I was content to be here with you. Besides, I had something important to tell you. And Brian confuses me. He can be charming and I do like him. Sometimes."

"Then why not tonight?"

"You win. Go ahead. Tell him I'm here with you. Why shouldn't three friends enjoy an evening together?"

He smiled and left, satisfied that rationality had returned.

A sharp double rap on the door a few minutes later.

"I've told Brian you are here, with me as your guide. He assumed you are my lover. I did not disillusion him." His voice was cool.

"Perhaps you won't have to," I heard myself say. I walked into his arms.

He touches Rosamonde's mouth with his fingers, then his tongue, then moves his lips to the base of her throat, up to her ear until she feels unsteady—her legs giving way under her.

His voice is tender as he holds her close. "We will wait, for La Zagara. Tonight we'll have only a glimpse of the moon."

Then I stepped away from his arms. "No, Giovanni." I pressed my back against the door to support my weak legs. "I'm sorry I let that happen."

"Rosa, Rosa, what are you trying to do to me?"

"Forgive me. It was my fault. I don't know how she . . . whatever possessed me."

"You'd better get ready for dinner," he snapped. "Brian is waiting for us."

I stood silent for a few moments, confused, unable to separate myself from Rosamonde.

❧

When we met for dinner on the terrace. Brian threw his arms around me and gave me a big kiss. "We've got to drink to this." He called the waiter, ordered some prosecco, and asked us to raise our glasses in a toast to "the coming together of fans of Frederick, Stupor Mundi. It's amazing how Hermes, the trickster, comes among us, wing-footed, to make us see the connectedness of our lives." He smiled. "And now, my dear Rose, you're beginning to learn what synchronicity is all about."

"I drink to Fortuna," I raised my glass and clinked it against Brian's. Then against Giovanni's, who flashed me a yielding, conciliatory look as our eyes met.

Brian said, "Yes, dear friends, we've been brought together by Fortuna—and by the threads of common interests. Let's drink to the past glories of the Hautevilles." With a nod to Giovanni, "Your Altavilla—and to the three of us."

Giovanni touched his glass.

Brian went on, "Even under more ordinary circumstances, it seems natural that we might have met here at Castel del Monte in June, a typical time for pilgrimage in Italy.

"You see, Giovanni, I never told Rose why I was going to Bari. I never discussed the theft of the ivory box and the map with her. I was sworn to secrecy by Scotland Yard."

I heard the sincerity in Brian's voice. I believed him.

"But now there's no question in my mind that we must tell Rose about the discovery and what it means. Whether you know it or not, Rose, you're a part of all this. Maybe you can even help us recover the map."

"I can't imagine how I could be of help . . ."

Giovanni was serious. "Let me tell you how it all began. We were repairing the *Cosmati* work in the thirteenth-century pavement at the church in Andria when my men hit the bronze chest under the floor. Within the chest was an oak box. Inside that box we found an object wrapped in linen and a mummified tortoise . . ."

"A tortoise? Why?" I asked.

"Probably put there to consume the oxygen within. To leave it air-free, thus preserving the contents of the box. We know that the Etruscans always left a live animal in their tombs for that purpose."

Brian must have been reading the puzzled look on my face. "Save your questions for later, Rose. Let Giovanni go on with his story."

"Can you imagine our excitement when we unwrapped the linen and found a large ivory casket? Inside were some letters and a strange chart or map—written on parchment, also wrapped in linen, and pouches of coins wrapped in brocades, cendals—the silk shredded but the colors still vivid. Peacock blues, magenta, parrot greens. That day when you asked me about fabric from the Tiraz, you have no idea how astonished I was."

Brian spoke up. "By a stroke of luck, we have still have those letters in the lab. One bears the cipher of Constance de Hauteville. Unfortunately, the ivory box, the curious map, as well as the rest of the coins are still missing. Giovanni and his team were on their way to the lab in Bari when they were held at gunpoint."

My eyes fixed on Giovanni's face while my world spun and reeled and shook—this time the earthquake was in my head. I tried to grasp the meaning of everything he just told me. How could it have happened this way? These were the people of Rosamonde's world—and Brian and Giovanni were as involved with them in reality as I was in my dreams.

"How many men were there?"

"Four. All masked."

I tried to keep from sounding as angry as I felt. "Why didn't you tell me all this when you learned about my interests in the Altavilla and Frederick II?"

"Forgive us, Rose, for not telling you sooner," Brian said. "We had to respect the Yard—and Interpol as well. I thought it was extraordinary that you'd come to Oxford with these interests. Again, I chalked it up to the synchronicity you were activating by recording your dreams—going deeper and deeper into your unconscious. Besides, when I was with you I had other things on my mind."

"If only you had . . ."

"Let me speak," Giovanni said. "After I examined the letters and the map in the lab at Foggia, I realized that I had to reach Brian at All Souls. I knew he was an expert on reading deteriorated medieval manuscripts."

"I hadn't seen or heard from Giovanni in years, since our school days in Rome. I'd always looked up to him and so I was delighted that we'd have a chance to work together.

"We hear from the International Police that the Germans want that map, that it will be privately auctioned to the highest bidder. You know what they paid for the missal of Henry the Lion when it sold a few years ago—millions of deutschmarks. It was a national treasure for them. This map may also lead to historical revelation for the Italians, not to mention a national treasure. We've got to find it. Those two coins Giovanni bought at Monte Sant'Angelo may be a clue. They were apparently from the hoard."

I bit my lip, tasting my own blood.

"Despite their condition it was obvious that the letters were written in Latin—except for one that, curiously enough, was written in Norman French—the letter that was sealed with Costanza d'Altavilla's cipher. I'll attempt to translate that one first."

"They were written on both sides of the vellum," Giovanni said, "a very resistant material, even under adverse conditions. However, fluctuations in temperature within the metal chest caused parts of the vellum to partially decay."

"Vellum sweats," Brian explained, "and with all those changes over the centuries it relaxes and reverts to its old form—to its state before tanning. It becomes gelatinous and transparent, rendering the writing on both sides almost indecipherable. That's why we've lined up a team of experts, conservators from the British Museum, the Morgan Library. The Huntington Library sent advice and state-of-the-art electronic scanning equipment."

"What's Costanza's letter about?" I was amazed that my voice sounded at all normal.

"I have a good idea, but I'm going to wait for the rest of the equipment before I go out on a limb. All I can tell you now is that it's possibly in the hand of Constance de Hauteville. And not in such bad state as one might expect, given its age and the climatic conditions."

"As for the stolen map," Giovanni said, "we may never learn its secret."

Brian said, "Luckily Giovanni had taken some preliminary photographs of it. I had a good look at them. I was able to make out a few symbols."

"What kind?" I asked.

"What appears to be an octagon. Adam and Eve in the center. A pair of lions before a portal. And a red stone. They're rather like those alchemy symbols on the Ripley Chart. Remember, Rose?"

"Yes. But I still don't understand why they didn't take the letters, too."

"Because Giovanni had the good sense to hide them in a separate place—in the boot of the car—beneath a spare tire. The thieves found only the ivory box holding the coins and the map hidden under the back seat."

"When do you think you'll complete the translation?"

"In a few weeks. Conservation will have a go at it first. Now that Schools are over, I'm free to stay on here until I've finished."

"I almost forgot." Giovanni handed me a book, *Sicilian-Norman Treasures*. "A present I found for you in Andria." He flipped through to a marked page. "The stolen ivory box is similar to this one. Only larger."

I studied the plate of the Siculo-Norman ivory coffer from the Victoria and Albert, then leafed through the other color photographs. I stopped to admire a cap-like crown, with a carved ruby centered over the forehead, gold triangles dangling from each ear.

Tonight Queen Constance wears the royal crown, a cap embroidered with thick gold threads, a huge carved ruby set over her brow. Tiers of golden triangles hang to her shoulders.

I read the caption. "It says here that this crown, which is in the museum in Palermo, belonged to Frederick's first wife. I say it belonged to Costanza d'Altavilla, his mother."

Giovanni was startled. "How did you know that the origin has recently been disputed! Now some historians would agree with you."

"I know it was Costanza's crown."

"How can you possibly know? " Brian asked. "You told me you've never been to Palermo!"

"I know," I smiled at Giovanni, "because the blood remembers."

Giovanni grinned and put his arm around me. "Come on—let's go in to dinner. Brian has to return to Andria early tomorrow morning, and I have an appointment at the *questura* in Bari in the afternoon. The police may have some leads about an art theft ring. They've had a few anonymous calls. Will you come along with me—to bring us luck?"

I nodded and kept my silence, afraid that if I opened my mouth all the wrong things would tumble out. I could feel Rosamonde, quivering within.

That night I didn't write a word. Over and over again the astounding synchronicities leapt through my mind like a fire raging through my head. Toward morning I fell asleep.

 Tonight, my dead mother—to whom I pray—comes to me in a dream. A vision in white, she tells me I should trust the kindly Knight, that he will help me take flight into the Dark Forest.

I send Caid Gregory for Serlon. There is no need to beseech the Knight. He repeats his fealty to me, and to my unborn child. He will defect from the royal guard and will lead us to a hidden cave in the Dark Forest where he hunts wild boar and deer, where royal guards can never find us.

We three follow the pathway by the sea from Vieste, past olive groves and almond trees, past ruins of an ancient city. Then we turn westward from the sea into the forest thick with beech and ash and oak, where there is no path, at last finding a hermit's cave where we can hide until my child is born. I am weary and sore of bone. I have already felt the dropping within my womb.

There we make comfort for ourselves, at night taking shelter in the cavern. The Knight kisses me tenderly, as a brother would, but he does not touch me although I know he loves me. He cares for me with loving kindness. He vows that when my child is born we will journey to the Molise where Serlon's uncle, Count Robert, will protect us on his lands.

At night we watch the full moon take command of the sky. We lie in each other's arms, the Knight's sword between our bodies. Now I confess to him how long I have lived in terror of birthing—and now, without a mother or some good wife to help me through my labors, I fear for my life and for my child's life. What would happen to my baby if I should die delivering? If I should die, I beg the Knight that my child be given to my father to rear when he returns home from war in Thessalonica.

Serlon kisses away my fears. "You must not worry, Rosa-monde. I will protect your child until your father returns—and should he never return, I will raise it as if it were my own. I vow to you." With the tip of his sword he makes a small cut in his arm. Blood oozes from the wound. He pierces my finger with a thorn and presses out a drop of bright fresh blood. Three drops of our mingled blood trickle on my white shift. Just where my heart beats.

We make our pact. If we are separated in this lifetime, we swear that we will come together in another.

CHAPTER EIGHTEEN

THE NEXT MORNING, right after breakfast, Brian took a cab back to the lab in Bari, while Giovanni and I drove to Barletta. He was anxious to show me the bronze Colossus. We would drive on to Andria afterwards.

We stood at the immense feet of the "colossus" of Barletta, the giant statue of Marcian, a late Byzantine emperor. His right hand, raised high, grasped a crucifix.

"The colossus was part of the loot brought back from the sack of Constantinople in 1203, along with the bronze horses of San Marco," Giovanni said, "but the ship carrying him sank in this harbor. He was cast up on the beach and remained there two hundred years until they hoisted him next to this Norman cathedral."

I thought the statue stiff-limbed and graceless.

"The hand you see is a replacement. The original arm was melted down. The Dominican friars of Siponto used it for their church bell. We do know that. I suspected there might be another correlation. It appears to be the same combination of metal used to make the bronze chest we discovered in Andria. Most likely the chest was made around the middle of the thirteenth century, during the time of Frederick II."

"How can you tell?" I asked.

"From the designs of the fabric in the box, and by carbon testing. We'll probably never learn why or exactly when, but it's definitely the same mixture."

He looked at his watch. "Come on, you must be hungry. We can talk about it over lunch."

Giovanni was courteous but distant; I sensed that he was still smarting from what he perceived as my rejection. I hadn't referred to last night's incident. Nor had he.

From a trattoria in Trani we had a good view of the Norman cathedral, built right on the edge of the sea, its backdrop only the luminous sky melting into the Adriatic. While we ate our lunch, he pointed out its simple facade, monumental bronze doors, elegant tower.

Rosamonde is so close—I have to keep myself from merging with her.

Emma, my father's wife, is buried nearby . . .

Giovanni startled me. "I have to make a phone call to Bari," he said abruptly. "To confirm my appointment. Please excuse me for a few minutes."

When he returned to the table he said tersely, "We have to leave soon. The police had another anonymous phone call. A possible lead. I now have a seven o'clock appointment at the *questura*. He looked at his watch. "I know you want to visit the church where we made the discovery. We're not too far from Andria. Let's go!"

❦

We could have been on the outskirts of any other Italian city. Badly designed blocks of apartment buildings and shops with nothing to distinguish them, no visible connection to the great architectural heritage of the country.

"Patience, patience, Rosa," Giovanni said when I complained about the town's haphazard ugliness, its soiled pastel colors.

"I'd imagined it as a serene little jewel—Andria of the faithful, Frederick called it, his favorite town."

"You romanticize far too much." He sighed. "But I admit I have the same problem—always trying to strip away the *porcheria* almost burying these historical sites."

He parked as close to the church as he could. "You'll be happier when we can walk into old Andria, the very heart of the city."

❦

Since the church was locked, we found the sacristy door behind and rang the bell. A wizened, black-dressed housekeeper opened the door and peered out.

"*Signor architteto*, Monsignore isn't here today. He's gone to Lecce. I'll have to let you in."

I stroked one of the toothless stone lions guarding the front portal of the Norman church, as the housekeeper turned the key. Afternoon sunlight streamed through the high pointed arched windows, brightening the floor that was inset with colored *pietre dure*—agates, lapis, marbles, and porphyry in various geometric shapes.

"Now—I want you to show me the exact spot where you feel we dug up the chest. Let's see how intuitive you are," Giovanni said.

I was piqued by his challenge. "Let me try by the side aisle first." I took a step forward. I stopped, took another step and stopped again. Before long, I'd arrived at the main altar. Nothing yet. I turned, genuflected—surprising myself—and began to walk slowly up the nave.

My steps were as small, as measured as a bride's walking up the aisle. My heart began to rap against my chest wall. I stopped and looked down at my feet. I was standing on a tile—an octagonal tile. I felt as if my joints were frozen, unable to bend. I felt tingling, as though fine pins and needles were jabbing into the soles of my feet. I was a magnet held in place by a subterranean force. My body knew before my mind.

I stood there fixed to the spot. I heard faint, distant sounds in my ears. Ancient echoes singing in harmony—sweet voices unconnected to the present. I tried again to lift my foot. It wouldn't move.

Giovanni applauded. "Incredible! You've found the exact spot. The chest was discovered under this very octagon. How could you have possibly known that? This is more than intuition!"

I laughed nervously. "It's as though I were some sort of human geomancer. I'm not sure that I like this."

As we stood there together, Giovanni describing more details of that day of discovery, Professor Lanciani appeared out of nowhere. Neither of us heard him walk in on his crepe-soled shoes.

"*Buona sera, signora, architetto,*" he said in a voice as smooth as olive oil.

"This is a surprise, *professore,*" Giovanni greeted him. "We were told you were in Lecce. Signora Kirkland just showed me the spot where the chest was discovered."

"To enhance her Altavilla research, I suppose?"

"Aren't most people fascinated by buried treasure?" I knew instantly that I'd said too much. No one had mentioned anything about "treasure." I wasn't even sure why I'd chosen the word.

"Signora, as far as we know, there was no real treasure. Just a map. An interesting, cryptic map with strange symbols that we shall never decipher because it's gone—most likely forever—as well as the coin hoard. Giovanni, fortunately, has found two of the coins in Monte Sant'Angelo. You've brought him luck, signora." I heard the mockery in his voice.

"What makes *you* so sure the map will never be found?" I asked.

"Intuition, I guess," he said sardonically. He must have been listening to our earlier conversation.

"Well, it's your intuition against mine," I said. "Speaking of intuition, haven't you been by to see my Aunt Caterina? Several times? Haven't you asked her about reading the map? Clues to buried treasure?" Caterina had never mentioned that Lanciani paid her a visit. It was only from Giovanni I'd learned this. I was trying to fake Lanciani out. I suspected him.

I saw his mouth twitch, his nostrils flare slightly. "Buried treasure? What do you imply, signora?"

"Imply?"

"Come on, Rosa. We should get on the road." Giovanni grasped my arm tight. "Let's go."

We left the professor standing in the apse of the church and drove off, both of us silent for a long while. I knew Giovanni was angry about my confrontation with his colleague. He had great respect for his intellect.

"I still can't stand that man. And I don't know why exactly," I said.

"Southern Italian men are like that sometimes. Arrogant." Giovanni explained. "They think they are a breed apart—some of the older ones, like Guido. Guido's almost eighty, you know."

"He certainly doesn't look it."

"He takes good care of himself."

"I'm sure his German wife takes good care of him."

"You don't forget anything, do you?"

"Not when it has to do with Germans in Apulia."

"This place teems with Germans. It's the second language here. So get used to it. Tell me, what is the real reason for your dislike of Lanciani?"

"Do you want it straight?"

"Yes," he said.

"I have more than a feeling he has something to do with the theft of the map," I said. "And the coins. Some of those coins found their way out of the chest. Stolen and sold. Just like the corner of Saint Anthony's cape. Remember?"

"That's a strong accusation. How could we ever prove such a thing?"

"Just keep an eye on him—and so will I. I know he's suspicious of me. I felt that from the day I met him. The fact that I was in England first may have given him the idea that I might have been sent here by Scotland Yard or Interpol. And my passion for the Altavilla probably worried him."

He laughed, shaking his head incredulously. "Amazing. You've got an entire scenario worked out in your head."

"I always do. Only this time it isn't just my imagination. I know Lanciani is uncomfortable around me. And his wife, what about her?"

"Helga is from a socially ambitious family from Munich. They were furious with her for marrying a provincial Italian academic with no money. I must admit that she keeps a distance from the Viestani."

"It all adds up. Maybe a collector wanted the map. I've heard about those luxurious carpeted Swiss bank vaults furnished with antiques, where rich thieves secretly enjoy their stolen treasures."

"You may be right. But at least we'll soon learn the contents of the letter the thieves didn't steal."

"I can hardly wait."

"Let's be on our way. It's almost four o'clock. The traffic gets heavy in late afternoon. But first I must stop for *benzina* or else we'll never reach Bari."

❧

The meeting at the *questura*, the police station in Bari, started promptly at seven o'clock. I settled down in a comfortable sofa to read the few dog-eared copies of *Capital* and *Oggi*. I must have fallen sound asleep until I felt Giovanni's hand on my shoulder. I looked up to find him standing over me. I rubbed my eyes and yawned, unsure of where I was for a moment.

"We should be on our way," he said. "It's past eleven o'clock and there might be a storm coming. There are no stars and a strong wind is blowing from the north."

He pulled out a cigarette and tapped it against the back of his hand as though he were furious with it.

"How did your meeting go?"

"You were dead right. The police suspect Lanciani. It seems he's part of a ring. A German ring. After we saw him in Andria, he must have driven straight on to Rome. Interpol called in to say he flew to Zurich with his wife. I should have listened to you. Most likely the map is already hidden away in some obsessed collector's vault."

I didn't say a word. Giovanni was sullen, hardly speaking as we walked through the narrow streets to the dark alley where he had parked his car.

The road from Bari to Vieste was only a three-hour drive, but it seemed endless. I could hardly wait to get back to the Hotel Vesta to write in my journal.

At last we passed the old Basilica of Santa Maria di Siponto, barely visible in its pine grove. We passed the saline distilleries near Margherita di Savoia, a blight on the coastal landscape, huge metal vats gleaming like a cluster of silver warts in the moonlight. At last, the high cliffs of the Gargano promontory loomed in the distance and soon we began the tortuous ascent to Vieste. No ship lights flickered in the sea.

As we climbed higher, the engine of the old Ferrari choked and sputtered. We came to a halt.

"Strange," Giovanni said, "the motor sounds as though it's thirsty. How could that be? I just filled the tank in Trani." He checked the gas gauge. Empty.

"*Managgia la miseria!* Someone must have siphoned off the petrol. Right around the corner from the police station! *Che ti possano uccidere!*"

I had never heard him curse.

"I've got two liters in the boot, not enough to get us back to Vieste."

He pulled to the side of the road and poured the gasoline into the tank. As he revved the engine, I could see his jaw muscle moving nervously.

"If we're lucky we can make it as far as Baia delle Zagere. But you needn't worry, Rosa, I'll ask for two rooms," he said, not bothering to disguise his sarcasm.

He drove five or six snaking, grinding miles then turned into a narrow paved road. Beyond an avenue of squat palms the white cupolas of the Hotel Zagara thrust themselves like huge breasts into the dark dome of the sky.

Giovanni went straight to the reception while I waited behind in the lobby. We were then shown to a little villa with two separate doors. Under the entrance spotlight, the loggia was draped with bougainvillea, like swags of red-purple silk. White moths flitted about in the spotlight.

Giovanni opened the door and handed me the key.

"It's been a long day, and you've shown me so much. Thanks for everything."

"It was my pleasure," he said, speaking in the same formal tone he'd used when we'd first met. "Goodnight, Rosa."

I hardly looked at the room. All I could see was a bed. A big, comfortable looking bed, its covers already turned down, inviting me to crawl in. I lay down still dressed and looked at the ceiling. She appeared immediately.

 I am without strength in these last days, and then my body begins to cramp. For two days I have been lying here, my body twisted in the wretched agony of birthing I have always dreaded. At last I feel a dam burst within, then fluid pouring from me like a fountain onto the pallet of moss and leaves Caid Gregory has so lovingly made. I scream for the Knight and Caid. The pain possesses me—great waves of pain hammer me. Waves of agony closer and closer together until they leave no respite. The Knight leans to kiss my wet forehead and hold me down, prepared to cut the cord, as my child is born. The waves grow even stronger.

When I can no longer stand the pain, Caid gives me something hard to bite down upon. I see the Knight's face streaming tears and vow, in our double pain, that I will never forget him.

They hold up my son. I hear his first cry. I am happy, but tired, so tired.

I know if I close my eyes right now, I will not awake from darkness ever again.

I do not close my eyes. And for the last time I see the Apulian sky, a bright blue ribbon between tall, tall trees.

I woke with the feeling that an iron weight on my chest had been lifted. Booming claps of distant thunder seemed to confirm that I would never hear Rosamonde's voice again. It was as though the gods in the heavens above were applauding the last chapter in her life.

I pulled off my sweat-soaked clothes and found the bathroom. I grappled with a packet of bubble bath and squeezed its contents into steaming hot water. I wrapped my hair in a towel, stepped into the tub and lay back in the fragrant liquid. Hauteville: Altavilla. It came to me again. Rosamonde. Rosamonde, you have brought me here. I have come here because of you. Why do you push me to this man? My body floated in the water and my mind replayed the few weeks I had been away from home. The series of meaningful coincidences. And the choices I made. *In trutina mentis dubia.*

I remembered those lyrics from The Courts of Love. That high sweet, soprano voice.

In the wavering balance of my feelings
set against each other
lascivious love and modesty.
But I choose what I see
And submit my neck to the yoke
I yield to the sweet yoke.

And then, with no sense that time that has passed, Rosamonde steps out of the warm fluid and pats her body dry with the large towel. She slips on a hotel robe with a golden Z embroidered on its pocket, pulls the belt around her waist and ties it only once.

When she opens his door, Giovanni is standing there in his dressing gown. He goes into the shower but does not close the door. She can hear the shower beating down full force.

She unties her robe and glances down at her body. Rosamonde's.

She looks up to see the Knight Serlon standing before her. He holds her away from him to look at her, his body seems perfect. "*Ti voglio bene*," he whispers in her ear. Then, in English, he says, "I love you and I want you."

She feels him thrust himself against her stomach. He whispers that he will make love to her as long as she needs, till she can no longer stand it.

Serlon pulls her down on the bed, his hands sliding the heavy robe from her shoulders.

"How beautiful you are, *carissima*. So pale, like an ivory statue . . . like Galatea."

Rosamonde responds, "Breathe life into me."

"I will."

She pushes his robe back then, baring his tanned body, his muscles gleaming with beads of moisture.

He strokes her thighs.

She draws him closer, resting his head in the valley of her breasts, his lips brushing the tiny blue veins beneath her skin, his lips seeking their hard ruby tips while she breathes in the scent of his hair.

"Rosa, *amata, amata* . . ." His lips move down her ivory torso, never leaving her skin, his silken tongue marking a path to the shadowy delta and to the red berry hidden between.

She arches her body to offer it to him but he does not accept, his tongue moving instead to the inside of her thighs. *"Sapore di te, di te"*—until he is ready to spread her legs apart. And then he can see how eager she, Rosamonde, is to be loved, to be devoured, and as he presses his tongue against the berry, he feels the first tremors of her body.

She lies there listening to the vulnerable sound of his breathing, then rises from the bed and goes back to her room. She pulls the white chiffon scarf from her bag, and searches for the pieces of golden fabric, still folded in white tissue. She goes back to the bathroom and closes the door.

Standing naked before the full-length mirror, she looks at the woman reflected there. Rosamonde. She removes the wedding band and places the gold circlet in its small red felt envelope stamped with a rose.

From a leather pouch she takes a shaker of talcum powder, sprinkles it on a swansdown puff. She dusts her body with the fluff of feathers until her skin feels like velvet. Next she rouges her high cheekbones and the buds of her breasts, outlines her full lips with a brush and fills them in with pomegranate red. Her blue eyes she lines with black kohl, stroking the long lashes above and below with a small wand. Her eyes seem as star sapphires set in ebony. From the pouch come the hammered gold earrings. She lifts each crescent from a tortoiseshell box, seeks the tiny holes in her ears and threads the gold wires through. At the bottom of the pouch she finds a golden cuff, which she clasps on her right arm.

Next she takes a small pink razor and deliberately shaves

her private hair. Soon there is only a pale delta that she flicks with the swan's down puff, whitening it even more.

She slips her legs into the golden bikini, and as if in a gesture to which she'd long been accustomed, she flings the chiffon scarf over her shoulder, the purple meander border making an oblique line across her body. She takes from the chest a small bottle of bath oil scented with attar.

She sees Rosamonde's eyes gleaming in the mirror. She leaves the bathroom and returns to The Knight Serlon, now asleep on the *letto matrimoniale*.

He senses her presence and opens his eyes.

"*Che bellezza, amata*—you are ravishing this way! Come closer, let me look at you in your regalia. *Vieni* . . . You are ravishing."

"And I have come to ravish you," she replies. She kneels beside the bed and with her gold-cuffed arm folds back the linen sheet from his outstretched body. He is already aroused. "I will massage you with this," she says as she pours rose oil in her palm, rubbing it around with her fingertips to warm it. "Now you will smell of me."

With her ringless hands she spread the oil across his chest, fanning it out to his strong shoulders, caressing his muscles, sliding it down his taut stomach, gently brushing against his navel, then slowly moving down his body to the lightning rod, his power. Her hands rest there a moment.

"I know who you are," he breathes. "You are a goddess. You are Aphrodite."

She slips the scarf from her shoulders and, as it falls to the floor, he gives a small gasp of pleasure at the sight of her powdered body, her rouged nipples, the golden triangle between her legs.

Fully aware of her power over him, Rosamonde stands

there, glorious, to be worshipped. Then, with a quick and graceful movement, she pulls the golden fabric from between her legs.

He gasps, his power aching, shedding tiny pearls for her.

And there before him she kneels again, this time stroking the oil over his diamond hardness, firmly over and over, drawing him up and over himself into the heavens. Her auburn head falls upon him and she engulfs him with her pomegranate mouth, her tongue encircling the rim of his world, around and around and around.

"*Amata*," he urges her on, until he can speak no longer.

She feels the jagged bolts of lightning in the dark sky, the tremors of his microcosmos, as he surrenders his vitality to her.

The next morning as the sun came up over the Baia delle Zagare, I, Rose Orlando Kirkland, found myself lying in a bed beside Giovanni di Serlo. His body, so bronzed from the sun, contrasted with my body's paleness; his long lean legs still entwined with mine. I basked in his scent of almond oil and lemon leaves mingled with my faded rose attar. I felt no guilt, no remorse, no shame as I lay there in his arms, savoring this feeling of resolve, as though we four, Rose—Rosamonde—Giovanni—Serlon had merged body and soul.

"I feel as though I have come to life through you. Reborn," he said.

"Reborn? That reminds me of an image that often comes to mind."

As I began to tell him about the inn sign of The Rose Reborn and what it had meant to me all these years, I felt his muscles tense.

He drew me closer. "This may sound like a melodrama, or a line from the cinema . . ." he paused, "there have been other women—many women. People call me Don Giovanni behind my back, I know that. But when Brian told me about your passion—your obsession with the Altavilla, when I learned that your father was born in Vieste, that your name was Rosa Orlando Kirkland—all that intrigued me. That day when you walked into the shop I could hardly control my feelings. I wanted to take you into my arms. I knew you. I had been waiting for you, Rosa. But you didn't know me."

"I know now exactly who you were, and are, Giovanni."

He repeated the words of the riddle.

Quando si stacca dal muro l'eglantina
Quando lascia la sala scura la donnina
Per sempre restaurata sarà il lineaggio
Allora troverò la nostra sposa.

When the eglantine pulls from the wall
When the lady leaves the darkened hall
Our line is restored once and for all
And I will find our bride.

Rosamonde . . . . the eglantine clinging to the old stone wall at the castle.

"There's something about me you should know." I began to tell him of my voice, no longer afraid he'd think me crazy. I told him of Rosamonde, of Joanna, of Constance. Of the Knight Serlon. He listened, enthralled, as he held me close. When I had told my story, tears pooled in his eyes.

"Now I must recite to you the last part of our family's poem."

He spoke it fervently.

> *Quando l'ottavo lato tocca il nono lato*
> *Il mio vero amore scoprirà un segno*
> *Con viti intrecciate sulle colline d'argento*
> *Troverò la nostra Rosa.*

> *When the eighth side touches nine*
> *My truest love will find a sign*
> *On silvered hills where vines entwine*
> *There I will find our Rose.*

"Do you know what that means, *carissima*? That we have found our Rosa. For all these past generations we have searched. At last I have found her."

I tried to speak, but he found my mouth and wouldn't let me.

He made love to me again as though I were the very treasure he'd sought all his life.

We left La Zagara at nine o'clock. When we returned to Vieste, Giovanni dropped me off at the parcheggio and I made my way back to the Hotel Vesta on my own, faced with the reality of what I had done. The choice I'd made. "The sweet yoke" I'd accepted.

I checked the desk for any messages. "You do have one, signora. Signor Kirkland called from New York last night. He seemed very agitated."

"New York? May I have the message?"

It read, "Please call your husband at two o'clock, Italy time. He will be at the Kennedy Airport Hilton 1-800-445-8667."

I folded the message slip, put it in my pocket, and trudged up to my room. It was now only eleven o'clock. I sat down on the bed, kicked off my sandals, fell back on the pillows and tried to sleep, but my head was too quiet.

I heard Filomena and Gaetana chattering in dialect on the terrace below. They hadn't noticed my return.

"I wonder what *la Rosina* was up to last night. Her bed was still made up this morning." I heard them giggle.

"Maybe *architetto* Di Serlo had a lot to show her last night." Filomena chuckled. "It'll do her good."

I closed the doors to the terrace and sat down on the edge of the bed.

Reality began to sink in. What had I done? Why had I betrayed Matthew, the man I loved, my husband of fourteen years, by allowing Rosamonde to take over. How could I ever explain my infidelity?

I wiped the beads of sweat from my brow. The rich smell of garlic and onions frying in hot oil turned my stomach. There was nothing else I could do now. I would wait here until the dot of two o'clock. Then I would call Matthew in New York.

❧

When I dialed the number the phone rang once.

"Rose, darling! I'm glad you got my message. I was afraid they might not have given it to you."

I knew from his voice that something was wrong.

"The deal's falling apart. Ten years of hard work—down the drain. Finished. Just like that."

I heard false cheer disguising his despair.

"What went wrong?" I asked.

"Oh, God—a lot of things. Most of them seemed insurmountable. You're the only one I can trust to understand. I'm getting on the next plane to Paris. I've never felt so depressed in my life."

In the fourteen years we've been married, Matt had never once admitted being depressed.

"If you really feel the deal's falling apart, tell them you're not interested in doing the deal on their terms," I said. "Stick by your instincts."

"I've already made reservations in a little hotel on the Ile Saint-Louis. If you want, we can drive out to Normandy—and stay on until your birthday. I'd like you there as soon as possible after I arrive. How quickly can you leave?"

I heard myself saying without any deliberation. "It won't take much time to get packed."

Later on I remember hating myself for reacting not to Matthew's plight, but to the word *Normandy*.

"I'll book a couchette on the night train to Bologna. It leaves San Severo around ten o'clock. That way no one will have to drive me to Bari. From Bologna, there's a morning flight straight to Paris. Don't meet me. I'll get a taxi and come straight to the hotel."

We spoke for a while after that, until I sensed he felt better for the unburdening.

When he hung up, I sat on the bed to catch my bearings. I felt torn apart by this torrent of old feelings of love and respect I felt for Matthew, by these new feelings of merging, of completeness that I'd felt with Giovanni. By the certainty that I must now go on to Normandy. So, in the wavering balance, my instincts made my choice.

❧

Caterina was still there gazing out from her window. I heard feet younger than hers scurrying down the steps.

Marta opened the door. "Rosa—I've been calling you. They told me that you hadn't yet returned from Castel del Monte."

I felt the blood rushing to my face. "I just got back this morning and I have to leave Vieste tonight—to meet Matthew in Paris. Yesterday we drove on to Bari—Giovanni had an appointment with the *questura*. Someone had drained his car of *benzina* and we ran out around Mattinata. It was very late by then so there was nothing else that we could do . . . we had to spend the night there. It was too late . . ."

She put her arm around me. "*Calma, calma* Rosa, don't be so distraught. I was worried so I went to ask Caterina. I thought perhaps she might have some insight about you."

"What did she tell you, Marta?"

She fastened her eyes on mine. "She just smiled and told me not to worry—she knew that all was well with you—but she wouldn't tell me any more than that."

❧

I said goodbye to Caterina late that morning. "Please come to stay with us in California. If you're hesitant about coming alone I will come to fetch you myself and bring you back with me."

"No, Rosa, I will never leave Vieste. I am too old to travel half way around the world. It is enough that you have come here. What joy your visit has given me! Besides, my dear niece, I cannot be sad. I know that you'll soon be back to see us."

"For the Festa?"

"Oh—I have a feeling that you'll be back here much sooner than next spring." I caught the wisdom in her smile.

I hugged Caterina tight. "Knowing that it won't be very long makes saying goodbye easier, Zia."

I left Caterina sitting by her window and walked straight through the old town to Giovanni's shop.

❧

The carved wood palm tree still swayed over the Virgin in the shop window.

I pushed the buzzer and waited. No answer. I pressed again. In a few moments the door clicked open. I was relieved when I saw Giovanni in the shadows.

He was surprised to see me again so soon. "*Carissima*. I thought you might be taking a siesta. You hardly slept last night."

"Nor did you."

"But I don't feel tired. We were so lucky to have spent the night at La Zagara—in more ways than one. We owe our lives to love."

"What do you mean?"

"Last night, just past midnight, on orders from the Bari *questura*, the Gargano night patrols were checking out all suspicious cars. They found a car parked a few miles out on the Gargano corniche road—the road we took back to Vieste this morning. They arrested two notorious hired killers with guns under the front seat. I know they were the ones who siphoned off my petrol—leaving just enough for us to pass Mattinata. They were waiting to ambush my car and kill us. They underestimated the fuel that old Ferrari drinks up. If we hadn't stopped at La Zagara we might be dead by now."

I gasped and threw my arms around him I was so relieved. "What kind of characters were they? I have a reason for asking."

"Two brainless thugs from Reggio. One of them I'd heard of before. '*Giusepp' 'u puzz' di fum,*' they call him in dialect."

"Why the nickname 'smoke-stinker'?"

"Because he reeks of cheap cigars."

"How tall is he?"

"Just a little guy—but very strong."

"It was stale cigar smoke that woke me up about a week ago. I thought I saw a short man standing over me with a knife." My skin crawled.

"My god, Rose—and you never mentioned it to me?"

"Because everyone was so sure it was only a terrible nightmare they'd finally convinced me. I'm sure he was the man."

"Now you see how you must always trust your feelings? I should have picked up on your instincts about Lanciani sooner. It sickens me to think what if . . ."

"Stop thinking, 'what if,' " I said. "Be thankful that we're here, alive and safe."

He held me closer.

I pulled away gently. "I just went by Caterina's. To say good-bye."

Bewilderment in his eyes. "Goodbye? Why? What's wrong?"

I could hardly look him in the eye. "I came to tell you that I'm leaving Vieste. Tonight. Matthew called. I'll be in Paris with him tomorrow."

"It can't be! Why so soon?"

"Matthew needs me."

He held my head in his hands and smoothed back the hair from my temples, searching my eyes for an answer. Then he pulled me close and kissed me, his tongue pleading with mine.

I pulled back gently.

He studied my face, so many expressions crossing his as though a debate were going on inside him.

"Don't leave me yet. We've hardly begun. I won't let you go," he said.

"That's why I must leave. Before it's too late for both of us. I don't know how to tell you, Giovanni, I . . ." I tried to keep my voice from faltering. My stomach twisted tight.

At last he drew a long breath. "So soon, *tesoro.*" His voice caught. "I can't believe so soon. We never really had a chance, did we?"

I steeled myself. "It couldn't be any other way. For so many reasons. Your life's work, my life's work. We live in different worlds. I'm married. I do love my husband. He needs me now. " I felt tears trickling down my cheeks. "I'm sorry."

He put his arms around me and brushed away my tears with his lips. "You mustn't tell me that you're sorry. I should thank you, *tesoro*, for what you've given me. You've broken the curse. That old tradition that the men in our family never find the right woman is dispelled forever. All my life I've waited for you to love. I'd shut myself off from other women, distanced them—afraid that I, too, would make a mistake, like so many Di Serlo before me. My mind was closed, my heart was locked."

"And I thank you for Rosamonde . . . for setting her free. For setting me free."

He took my hand and put it to his lips. "Last night, I wished that tomorrow would never come—those few hours we had . . ."

I wiped my tears with the backs of my hands.

"Those few hours were lighted by the sun," he said finally. "Nothing in my life was ever as beautiful. Maybe it's better that you do leave me now—like the golden-chained mermaid who returns to spend a single night with her lover. But let us vow never to lose each other in this lifetime. Come back in the spring, *carissima*, in the season of *nespole*—for the Festa of Santa Maria di Merino. I will be here. Waiting."

I turned away so he wouldn't see my tears flowing unchecked. *Rosamonde, the Knight Serlon. After all these centuries only to part again.*

"I have something for you. I'll fetch it from the window. I saw you admiring it more than once."

He returned with the Flight into Egypt sculpture. "For you, Rosa, as a remembrance of your visit. I'll pack it and send it on to California. Think good thoughts of me whenever you look at it. Don't forget me. That's all I ask."

"Forget you, Giovanni? How could I?" My eyes met his in tender silence. How could I forget a crystal and turquoise sea, a falcon soaring high above a pine forest? Whenever sunlight makes olive branches gleam silver, whenever orange blossoms perfume the night, I would remember him.

"The blood remembers," he whispered. "You have never forgotten that, Rosa . . . Rosamonde."

I put my lips to his temple and kissed the spot of blood. Then, without looking at him again, I turned and left Giovanni standing in the shadows of his shop.

THE TOWER IN LUCERA

DAWN IS BREAKING in Lucera, and in the castle the Emperor still sleeps. A mosquito whines overhead, drawn to the fragrant unguent clasping the ruby to Frederick's forehead. The Magus puts down his quill. He does not dare clap his hands over the insect to kill it, lest he awaken the Emperor. He fans the air with his hand to drive it away.

Frederick's eyelids begin to twitch. His lips part as though to speak, his tongue moistening his lower lip. From time to time an arm flails out, his body jerks and starts. But he does not wake. Michael Scot sits gazing upon his sleeping master, a man whose mind thirsts to unravel the mysteries of the world—a savant far more brilliant than those sharp-witted scholars at the universities of Bologna, Salerno, or Naples. Frederick's mind probes the Great Questions, the secrets of nature, the habits of man, of birds, and animals.

Scot stands to stretch his weary limbs, to knead his gnarled, arthritic hands. His joints are sore, his fingers stiff from writing so long. This December night is cold, but milder than the windswept, forlorn cold of the Scottish highlands or the freezing damp of Oxford. He knows that the death he had predicted for himself will not be long in coming—but when? He sighs. The iron hat is so heavy. "To me it seems the helmet of the messenger god, Mercurius," the Emperor had teased him, "without the wings." How tired the hat makes him feel. How he wishes he had the courage to remove it. But the only time the hat ever leaves his head is during the Consecration of the Host.

He rummages in the chest, then takes the Empress Constance's letter from the ivory box hidden at the bottom. The Magus Umberto had entrusted him to deliver it to Frederick when the Emperor reaches his fortieth year. He will give the letter to him when he awakens.

Scot leans back in his chair and looks out to the sky. The moon has turned from crystal to a blood-red disc. He hears the *circ-circ* of falcons in their mews as they begin to sense light from approaching dawn.

He reaches out to touch his master's arm, then thinks better of it and pulls his hand away.

Although his sleep is restless, the Emperor Frederick's face is serene as if in death. But in that deathlike sleep it has become young, the burdens of forty years vanished.

Michael Scot keeps his gaze fixed on his master, aware of every motion, every flutter of his eyelids. The ruby gleams, reflecting fire in the flickering light.

The Emperor's eyelids twitch as he reaches the rim of consciousness and his sensuous mouth, hardened by power, begins to form silent words.

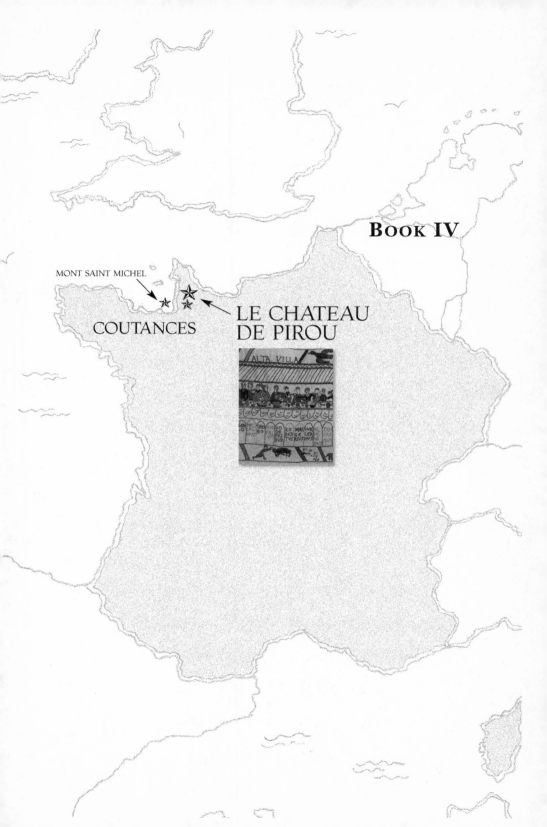

BOOK IV

MONT SAINT MICHEL

COUTANCES

LE CHATEAU
DE PIROU

CHAPTER NINETEEN

 HE CONCIERGE rang Matthew's room in the quaint little hotel on the Ile Saint-Louis.

"Madame Kirkland est arrivée."

"Tell her I'll be right down," I heard him say. I followed the porter to the elevator and waited with my arms wide for Matthew to step out.

We rode up the elevator, our bodies locked. I buried my face in the stiff, scratchy tweed of his shoulder and breathed in the shaving lotion he'd used all the years I'd known him, the scent of ferns and damp moss.

"This is the last time you go off by yourself," he said. "No more long trips—ever again—unless we go together." He kissed the top of my head. "I must have been crazy to let you leave me—too wound up in my own work to imagine what living without you would be like. Now I've got you back again."

I leaned back to look at him. He was even more handsome than he looked in that old photo I'd been carrying with me.

He opened the door to our room, turned over the door sign to *Ne Pas Déranger* and kissed me again.

On the bedside table was a bouquet of long stemmed red roses. Somehow their prim, tight-budded hothouse perfection bothered me. I buried my nose in the flowers. Hardly any fragrance. He took my hand and led me to the service table by the window. A silver bucket holding iced champagne sat on a starched white tablecloth. "To celebrate our reunion, Rose." He popped the cork, poured the wine and raised his glass.

"Here's to our trip! I've already walked down to Smith's and bought a Normandy guide for us to read."

We touched glasses. I took a sip, then quickly flipped through the guidebook.

"I went ahead and made some reservations. There's a charming old manoir hotel near the river—not far from Caen. We'll celebrate your birthday there."

I closed the book. "Please—before we talk about the trip you've planned, tell me how things went for you—from the beginning." I sat down on the bed. He sat close beside me, one arm holding me to his side.

"They finally discovered a problem in the final reduction-conversion phases of the waste refining process—the catalytic coils. I couldn't convince the bankers to give me a chance to create a substitute alloy. I'm sure the Japanese investors would have waited, but two of the American financers were unwilling to give it another try."

I had been right all along.

"They chickened out. It's as simple as that. I tried to convince them that time was of the essence, as much a race for the planet as for us, but their minds were made up. They couldn't see beyond the bottom line."

"They had no vision. I guess that's business. I'll never under-stand it."

"Darling, you're wrong. Business can embrace vision."

"Do you think you can pick up the pieces somehow, find some-one else to support you?"

"I'm going to try, but backers with creative minds are hard to find these days. I may have to rethink the entire project, restruc-ture it financially for a private offering. And I have to work on another alloy. But I'm not giving up. I need you, Rose. I was so depressed when I got on the plane to come here, but I feel better already—just being with you. I've missed you more than I thought I ever would."

I hugged him tight to me. "I love you. I want to tell you that over and over again." Then I was surprised when I heard myself blurt out, "But I'm not ready to make love to you. I can't—not yet." I felt his body stiffen, saw the troubled look cross his face as he set his jaw.

"Do you want to tell me about it now?" he said evenly.

I hadn't expected such a direct question. "Most of me says no, I shouldn't, but part of me says I must. There was a man."

"An Italian?"

"Yes—but I'm not going to tell you his name."

"What the hell difference does it make what he's called!"

"I imagined for a single night—that this man was someone else —that I was someone else, that we were somehow righting an ancient wrong."

He stood up and looked at me squarely. "Are you in love with him?" I could hear the strength of his restraint.

I looked straight into his eyes. "No. Although I care for him deeply, I knew I wasn't in love the morning after, when I heard your voice on the phone. It's you I love. And I always will."

Matthew's face was impassive. He turned his back to me and hit his palm with his fist.

He turned to me again. "Maybe it's better I leave. Right now!" he said brusquely, trying to mask the hurt in his voice. "I can get an early plane back to L.A. There's one at four o'clock."

I opened my carryall case and pulled out the journal. "Someday I'd like you to read what I've written in the notebook you gave me."

"Read? There's no need to read anything!" He yanked his clothes from the closet, hung them in a garment bag and tossed his shaving gear into a dopp kit.

"I'll try to get a plane back to California today. At least I'll have my hands full trying to put the deal back on track."

"Please don't leave, Matt." I tried to stop my voice from breaking as I threw my arms around him.

He pushed me away.

I sat on the edge of the bed and dazedly watched him gather up his belongings.

When he'd finished, he looked at me for a long, painful instant, his hand clasped around the doorknob. "Goodbye, Rose." He yanked off the *Please do not disturb* sign and tossed it at my feet. He watched as I picked it up, then slammed the door in my face.

Alone in Paris. I stayed in the room until late afternoon. The tears had come and gone. I couldn't write. I couldn't read. I couldn't think. The insipid, mock-garden scent of those perfect glasshouse roses was beginning to repulse me. I could keep on staring at the ceiling, or I could go out for fresh air and try to walk off the pain. I put on my raincoat and left the hotel.

As I crossed the Seine toward the Rue du Bac, Paris might as well have been Peoria or Patagonia. I didn't give a sideways glance at the antique shops along the Rue Jacob. I headed up the Rue de Rivoli, thinking I might find that old, familiar solace among books. In W.H. Smith, I leafed through the display of new British novels, but neither they nor cherished books could console me. I walked toward the Louvre and stood, forlorn, before the equestrian statue of Joan of Arc. "A lot of good voices do us," I said aloud.

Past the Louvre I walked, toward la Place de la Bastille, pushing against the crowds as Métro after Métro disgorged passengers into the fish-gray Paris twilight.

The city lights blinked on all at once, but I kept walking and hardly noticed. I found myself in the Marais, circling, recircling the square of la Place des Vosges, as if its sheltering arcades could protect me. Couples strolled by, hand in hand, scanning menus posted outside candlelit restaurants. How lucky they were to have each other, I thought.

I had lost Matthew. How could I ever learn to live without him, without his strength, his no-nonsense stability—the guidance I'd mistaken for control? What a cruel lesson Fortuna had taught me. Now that I was prepared to deal with what Matt called reality, I'd lost him. And he'd been right about my not wanting a child. I'd already admitted to myself that I hadn't wanted one—our own, his own, or anyone else's.

My feet were swollen, my heels domed with blisters. Midnight. A mist like sheer silver tulle fell over the city.

I hailed a cab—hoping, almost expecting, to find Matthew waiting for me in the room.

The bottle of champagne sat in a puddle of melted ice. I poured myself a glass. It tasted flat and sour. I took the bottle into the bathroom and poured the champagne down the drain, then took each stem of the flawless roses, pulled off their perfect petals one by one, and flushed them down the toilet. After that I felt better. Matthew *had* to understand. I would fly back to California and make him understand.

But first I had to drive to Normandy—to the Cotentin, to explore the land of the Hautevilles. On my own. I could not give up. I had begun this quest on my own and I would end it on my own. Rosamonde's voice was no longer with me; I had lost my husband because my own voice had blurted out too soon about my knight of love. Now I was more determined than ever to find out who she was and why she had intruded on my life.

"*Voilà, madame.*" The maid put the breakfast tray on the night-stand. "I hope you're feeling better today. *Le bureau* asked me if you intend to spend another night as booked. Monsieur paid the bill before he left. He asked the Reception to speak to you about your departure date."

"I had intended to leave today, but I don't feel at all well. I'll most likely leave tomorrow morning."

"Whenever you choose, Madame."

During the night I'd awakened doubled up with wracking, violent cramps and my period. I wasn't sure I wept from relief or sadness. Or both.

There was no way I could drive to Normandy today. I broke off a piece of roll. Cotton batting in my dry mouth. I sipped the bitter café au lait, all the while staring at the skeleton roses I'd crammed back into the crystal vase.

The next morning Hertz had a car waiting for me at Porte Maillot. I called ahead to confirm the room I knew Matthew had reserved at the manoir near Coutances.

I drove along the valley of the Seine, past apple orchards, past quaint villages of half-timbered houses and precise potagers until at last I reached the inn sign. The arrow pointed to an unpaved road cut through a marsh thick with reeds and cattails. The old hostelry of brown-pink herringbone brick and timbers was just the sort of place I had in mind. I parked the car and followed the arrow toward the reception, walking between wide borders of pink foxglove and antique roses. Butterflies fluttered over blue salvia edging the walk. The U-shaped manor had the haphazard look of countless expansions over the centuries, but the effect was still harmonious.

I spotted a stork guarding its nest in one of the manoir's many chimneys. I remembered that storks were a common sight in Northern Europe where they're considered to bring good luck.

Madame Gilbert, the innkeeper, greeted me as though I were an old friend and showed me to a cozy room with a view criss-crossed by lead-mullioned windows. The room was furnished in worm-eaten oak and polished walnut and smelled of beeswax and turpentine. A four-poster bed, canopied in crimson damask, centered the room, facing the marshes.

That night I couldn't eat dinner. I sat up in bed and read the Normandy guide Matthew had left behind. The one entry under Hauteville, the village of Hauteville-la-Guichard, was said to be the village of Tancred and his sons. I was disappointed that there were so few traces of the Hautevilles. Where in the Norman Cotentin could I possibly find a connection to Rosamonde? I fell asleep with her in mind.

✌

The next morning, when I was well on the road to Coutances, I realized I'd forgotten to pack Matt's Normandy guidebook. I wondered if it had fallen to the floor while I was reading in bed. Rather than drive all the way back, I decided to stop to buy another. It was false economy not to. After all, I hadn't come all this way for nothing. Luckily, I found another in a bookshop in the market square in Coutances. In the brasserie next door I ordered a giant cup of steaming café au lait and sat down to read. The new guide had a special Contentin section I was pleased to find. I looked up Hauteville, and was surprised that this book had two listings; I turned to the second entry under Lessay and read:

PIROU CASTLE. The castle is believed to have been owned by the Hauteville family, several members of which played an important role in establishing the Norman kingdom of Sicily.

Pass through a series of fortified gatehouses, into the bailey and the castle proper, a massive structure encircled by water. On display inside is a tapestry similar in style to the Bayeux tapestry, recounting the conquest of Southern Italy by the Contentin Normans. From the top of the square tower, on a clear day, are far-reaching views to Jersey.

Pirou Castle, classed as an historic monument, was discovered only recently, having been overgrown for centuries. Situated as it is away from the main roads, it is almost unknown to tourists, yet it is one of the most unusual strongholds to be found in Normandy. It is built on an island in a man-made pond, hollowed out in the schistous rock.

This castle *wasn't* listed in Matthew's guidebook. I remembered reading the article about a Seigneur de Pirou in the Anglo-Norman journal. Someone mentioned in *Le Roman de Rou*. This was just the sort of connection I'd been looking for. The Hauteville connection. Fortuna, I was convinced, had me leave the other guidebook behind.

Two o'clock, and the office of the Syndicat d'Initiative had just reopened. I was disappointed when the clerk told me that Pirou Castle was closed today but would be open tomorrow. This gave me the whole afternoon to spend at the cathedral, built with coin and treasure donated by the stalwart sons of Tancred de Haute-ville, who left Coutances to seek their fortunes in Calabria and Apulia.

I'd hoped that in that late afternoon stillness, Rosamonde's voice might come to me again. Under the soaring arches of the vast Norman nave I sat, waiting to hear her speak. I counted down to the unfurling poppy and breathed in the pale traces of last Sunday's myrrh and frankincense. But I didn't hear her voice—I heard Matthew's. "Goodbye, Rose."

❦

In the late afternoon I left Coutances and was back at the manor in less than an hour. When Madame Gilbert learned that I had-n't eaten lunch, she offered me tea and madeleines in the salon.

I sank into the shabby brown velvet sofa and bit into the shell-shaped teacake.

"Marcel Proust's recipe—given to me by my great-aunt," Madame said when I accepted another.

I told her my discovery of the Pirou tapestry in my Normandy guidebook. "Why is it that I've never read anything about the Pirou tapestry before?"

"Because it was embroidered only recently—within the past twenty years. By one woman. The project was the idea of the Norman poet Louis Beuve, and was created under the supervision of the Abbot of La Lucerne Abbey. The tapestry tells the story of our Viking-Norman ancestors in their conquest of Southern Italy and Sicily, embroidered just as it would have been in the early Middle Ages."

"What does it look like?"

"Like the Bayeux tapestry—embroidered in the same stitch, with wool yarn dyed in the ancient way. A few years ago we sent it to Oslo for the winter so the Norwegians could admire it and nurture pride in their Viking ancestry. We keep it here in the summer—when tourists begin to arrive. You're in luck, Madame Kirkland."

Eagerness must have been written all over my face.

"You won't be disappointed, I promise you. But it's not completely finished—the next section won't be ready for five years. I'll ring up the guardian to make sure he knows to expect you first thing in the morning."

❧

When I arrived at Pirou Castle, no one was there but a few British cyclists repairing a flat tire on the road outside the main entrance. The small barn had been turned into a ticket-souvenir office. "Would Madame like to buy a brochure?" The old custodian greeted me. "One should read the story of the tapestry as one follows it around the room."

I paid for the pamphlet and strolled through the oak grove toward the castle, its moat fed by a nearby pond where swans glided. Hazy morning sun dappled light between the ancient trees. Old roses and herbs bloomed in a garden where fat geese strutted.

I gazed at the surroundings. They seemed so familiar. Maybe my imagination was working overtime now that I'd finally come upon some Hauteville territory.

No. I was sure I'd been here before. I allowed myself to bask in the feeling. *Déjà vu* was a phrase coined for people like you, Rose, I told myself.

I sat down on the low fieldstone wall bordering the moat. Frogs croaked on the floating lily pads. A small, crude castle, just the right size for a petty Norman baron. I wondered if this had always been the castle's approach. After all, eight hundred years had gone by. Things change.

All at once I saw it as it was then. *Rosamonde's home. The eglantine growing on the stone wall.*

The old custodian broke my reverie. "Before the abbot came here, this place was overgrown with brambles and eglantine. For centuries shepherds took shelter here in winter. Until a few years ago the castle was completely hidden, like the castle of *La belle au bois dormant*. If you'll permit me, I'll show you where we've hung our tapestry."

He led me to a building made of old timbers and fieldstone where, displayed around the room was *La Telle du Conquest des Pouilles et de Sicile par les Fils de Tancrède de Hauteville*. From a distance, it looked like pictures I'd seen of the famous Bayeux tapestry. But instead of the Battle of Hastings in 1066 and the exploits of William the Conqueror and his Norman forces, this tapestry describes the prowess of the Vikings who came down the rivers of France in their drakaars, claiming the land, the women, then becoming farmers and Christians. It follows them on cloth to Apulia and Sicily, their other great conquests.

Guided by the legend in the brochure, I study the embroidered linen.

I see the ailing Norman Duke Robert carried on a palanquin,
on his way back from Jerusalem, signified by a palm tree like
one Rosamonde had struggled to stitch.

It shows his arrival at Monte Sant'Angelo where the Lombard Melus implores him to return with Norman troops to wrest away Calabria and Apulia from the Byzantine Greeks.

I move to the next scene.

The Seigneur de Pirou returns home from a pilgrimage to Mont Sant'Angelo and seeks shelter in a Hauteville castle where he is taken in by Tancred, the seigneur. Around the table sit all of Tancred's sons—William Iron-Arm, Drogo, Hugo, Blaise, Robert Guiscard, Roger. To Tancred's left, his wife, Fressenda.

And next to Fressenda, Serlon, the youngest son of Tancred de Hauteville.

I see that Tancred's youngest son, Serlon, is written "Serlo."

"I am Jean de Serlon—cousin thrice removed of your Aunt Lady de Hauteville."

I feel the sudden rush of breakthrough, the overwhelming discovery of truth.

Le Sang se souvient. The blood remembers.

I stand in wonder, cherishing the feeling.

At last I move on.

The pilgrim describes his journey in Apulia. He urges Tancred's sons to journey there to seek their fortunes.

I see the sons of Tancred riding forth from their father's castle just as I once imagined them before I set off on my own quest.

And here is the tethered bull like the one Joanna had embroidered, marking the very spot on which Monte Sant'-Angelo was founded.

Again and again I study the tapestry scene by scene. Before my eyes is the reason I was drawn to Normandy.

❧

Inside the rough stone rooms of the castle I found none of the refinement of Castel del Monte. The *cheminée* in the great hall reached floor to ceiling. Three coats-of-arms were chiseled in the limestone. One looked familiar, like one I'd seen in Vieste. The *stemma* of the Bishop Anselmo Orlando, three coins emblazoned on a shield. I'd packed the photo in my camera bag. I dashed to the car and back to compare the coat of arms in the snapshot to the one over the fireplace. The *stemma* in Vieste had a baroque cartouche around it, most likely added in the seventeenth century. Still, the shield shape was the same, and the three coins, torteaux—were in the exact same position. It occurred to me that Roland—Orlando *are*, after all, the same name!

My head reeled with this memory avalanche. *Rosamonde's castle. The Hauteville Castle at Pirou was Rosamonde's home.* I knew it was!

To catch my bearings, I stepped outside to sit on the low fieldstone wall edging the moat. Henbane springs from the crevices of the moat stones. And from the walls of the *Barbacano* in Vieste.

I closed my eyes.

I hear the horses' hoofbeats, the barking dogs.
At last my father is riding home from the war in Thessalonica.
I hear the shouts of the villeins, the drawbridge chains grinding,

scraping their channels, the thud of the drawbridge slamming the
earth. The shouts, the cheers of welcome. I run across the bridge to
embrace the man whose arms are outstretched to me.

"Earth to Rose. Earth calling Rose."

I heard Matt's voice and looked up to find him standing by me. I saw his face through blurry eyes.

He wrapped me in his arms. "The hotel told me you were here. I thought I'd surprise you." He kissed my lips. "Happy birthday."

I wiped my eyes with his handkerchief. "Thank you for coming back—it's the best birthday present I could ever have."

He held me tighter.

"I know now why I've been led to find this place. Can you understand? I've come home. Don't think I'm crazy—please!"

"It's all right, darling. Cry. Don't try to stop it."

I lay my head against his shoulder.

"I came back because I love you, Rose. I was hurt—wounded by what you told me. I had to get away to think it through, so I went to the local bar and sat there along with the old gents drinking their spiked coffee. I had a few myself. These past two days I've been roaming all over Paris on my own—but I just couldn't get on that plane. Now I think I understand why you did it."

"I love you, Matt. I always have and always will. Can you ever forgive me for what happened?"

"I've already forgiven you because the blame isn't all yours. I take part of it. I left you alone too much. I was always too preoccupied by my work. And I know I'd been pressing you too hard to make your decision. I began to understand why you had to try with another man. Time will take the pain away."

"I'm not pregnant."

"It would have been all right if you were." He held me close. "And I'll admit I didn't listen to your intuition. You were right about those executives. They tried to sabotage me and the project."

He took my hand and kissed it.

"You're still trembling. I'll find you some water."

The bright morning sun hid behind the clouds. A flock of wild geese honked overhead.

I sit with my father in the great hall. I hear the elder sing his song,
of who we were and how we came to be. The saga of the Hautevilles
of Normandy.
And on that night there was no moon to light the sky.
The darkness had been planned.
The fog rolled in from the deep green sea
Blanketing the land.

I had learned here at Pirou Castle who I was and how I'd come to be.

We stopped for sandwiches at a charcuterie in Lessay so we could have a picnic. What in all of France could taste better than a warm, crusty baguette spread with creamy Norman Camembert? We ate in the shadow of the cathedral towers, still stunned by the amazing morning at Pirou Castle.

Afterwards we strolled arm in arm through Old Coutances. While Matt was buying film, I crossed the street, curious to have a look at the window display of a shop called *L'Eglantine.*

Propped on a small easel was a page from someone else's sketchbook. A page of miniature watercolors, *capricci* of ancient temples, crumbling arches, fallen columns grown over with weeds. I read the signature. *"Comte de Millet, dessiné à Rome 1859."* The sort of thing I would have expected to find in England, a souvenir of some British peer's Grand Tour. I bought the page and gave it to Matt.

"To always remember our day at Pirou—and our reunion in Normandy."

He kissed me.

"And I want to tell you how grateful I am to you for not making me feel that I'm crazy. I've always felt so . . . flawed next to you."

He hugged me to his side. "I've always loved that wild, mysterious part of you—the part that's so unlike me. I know how cut and dried I can be sometimes. I'm not a poet, you know."

He kissed my fingers one by one.

"Matt—I have something else to tell you."

"What, darling?"

"I made up my mind today, here at Pirou. When we go home, we'll find a surrogate. I'm forty years old. It's time."

"You're sure, Rose?"

"I'm sure."

"You know what might happen, don't you?"

"What's that?"

"If we have a child, you may very well get pregnant."

I kissed him. "Sometimes that does happen. It's fine by me—we can make up for lost time. It wouldn't be such a bad idea to have our family all at once."

❧

Early that same evening the phone rang as I stood under the shower. I stepped out of the bathroom to hear Matthew's end of the conversation.

"Yes, I'd call that a real about-face. Incredible!" He grinned and threw a victory signal to me. "You do? What's the next step, then?"

I watched his face change as he listened. "I'm afraid that's impossible," he said. "I'm here with my wife. She's not ready to leave yet and I'm certainly not leaving her so that I can be back in the office tomorrow. Why don't you have the lawyers begin the paper work? I'll be back in California after the weekend. If you should need the patent documents, my secretary can give you my office copies. Whatever can't be done will have to wait until I get home. I'll be on the road for the next few days, so I'll call you. Don't try to phone me."

After he'd hung up, he turned to me. "We celebrate tonight, darling. The deal is back on—on the old terms. Walking out on them was exactly the right move. I have six months to replace the titanium. I'm in business."

I kissed his triumphant mouth, his tongue stopping my sentence.

"Shall we have champagne and dinner now? Or later? Or not at all?" he said.

"Certainly not now."

He led me toward the fourposter bed. I turned down the sheets still smelling of fresh Norman breezes. I opened my arms to him. We fell upon the bed together.

As his hands passed over my skin, I felt the old desire sweep over me, my body flooded with newfound feeling. As we pledged our love's renewal, I thought of Rosamonde in the Knight Serlon's arms, the sword placed between them. I remembered Rosamonde in Giovanni di Serlo's arms, completing their love after so many centuries had passed.

Now I was Rose, in the arms of the man I loved, giving myself to him, as I could never have before. I accepted Matthew without defense, gathering him into me again and again, as he scattered his seed throughout the enclosed garden of my being.

Rosamonde's soul, once so entangled with my own, was now unfurled. Freed. The golden chain was broken.

❧

After a dinner of shellfish, Dover sole, and Sancerre, we sipped the local calvados, apple velvet poured from a cobwebbed bottle the waiter produced from the cellar.

When we returned to our room, the bed had been turned down, my silk nightgown laid out. On the pillow bolster sat a small square package. I picked it up and shook it. Too light to be bonbons.

Matthew watched me with amusement. "Go ahead, open it. It's a birthday present from Uncle Raymond. Maybe you can design something around it. Only don't tell him." He laughed. "He might want you to leave this one alone."

I slipped off the ribbon and opened the maroon leather box. In the black velvet slot was a concave silvery-gold coin, bright, shiny, its impression as sharp as if it had just been cast. One side bore the replica of a Byzantine emperor in a dalmatic, an orb in his hand; the other, a chubby cheeked Christ. Constantinople—an electrum of Manuel Comnenus. Just like one of the coins Giovanni had bought in the antique shop in Monte Sant'Angelo.

"Where on earth did you find this coin?" I asked.

"It's a long story. It's from Uncle Raymond's personal collection. He even has the original ivory box it came in. It's in his safe in Montfort l'Amaury."

"Where did Uncle Raymond get it?"

"He rang me up while you were away and told me that one day soon he'd be dispersing his coin collection. He wants you to choose some when you have time. But this is one coin he didn't actually buy for himself."

"What do you mean?"

"It's been handed down in our family for generations."

"Why is he giving it to me?"

"Who else?"

"Matthew, this coin is an electrum. An electrum is a mixture of silver and gold fused together with mercury. This one was struck during the reign of the Byzantine Emperor Manuel Comnenus. I'm positive it's an electrum."

"That's exactly what Uncle Raymond told me. Manuel Comnenus—an electrum. I'll have to tell him you knew just what it was."

I sat down on the bed to steady myself. "Manuel Comnenus was the Byzantine Emperor during William Altavilla's reign in Sicily. Can't you see? There's a pattern here, an ancient link between my past and your past. All this is even stranger because I just came across a coin like this at Monte Sant'Angelo."

"Uncle Raymond said there must have been other coins in the same batch—but that's the only one left. He left for Katmandu last week so you'll have to wait until he returns to ask him questions about our family folklore."

I studied the coin. How did it fit into the puzzle?

I began to work on the scenario. Supposing that one of Matthew's ancestors and one of my ancestors . . .

Matthew laughed. He was reading my mind. "Hey—slow down—take it easy, darling. Wait until we take our next car trip. You'll have plenty of time to imagine another scenario." He put his arm around me. "I have something else for you, Rose. But this is a birthday present from *me*. Put out your hand and close your eyes—no peeking."

I extended my right hand, palm up.

"Take a deep breath—and don't open your eyes yet."

"Come on, Matt. The suspense is killing me."

And then I felt it—the smooth polished stone, its familiar oblique slant against my palm. I clenched my fist around it. My eyes were blurry when I opened them to look at what lay beating in my hand.

"Where did you ever find the ruby?" I asked.

I read the pleasure on his face, his triumph.

"Mr. Baryani hadn't sold it. I tracked him down in New Delhi. He was going to keep it for his personal collection, but I convinced him you should have it. Rose—I have to tell you, though, this isn't a ruby."

"What is it then?"

"Mr. Baryani told me it was a spinel, that it was certainly affordable and that . . . ."

"That I hadn't even bothered to ask the price!" I shook my head. "If I'd only looked at the stone with my loupe I would have known it wasn't a ruby. I went by color and cut. Then when I held it in my hand . . . the earth shook."

"Mr. Baryani told me that you were very moved by the stone, but since you didn't ask the price, he assumed you didn't want it."

"Because I knew a ruby that size would be beyond my means."

"He said the color was so good if he hadn't looked at it with his loupe, he would have made the same mistake."

"Spinels have always been confused with rubies," I said. "In the Middle Ages they were even *considered* rubies. The giant ruby in the Imperial Crown of England is really a spinel." I laughed. "I guess you could say that I made a 'medieval' mistake."

"With all your work problems, how did you manage to find this for me?" I began to cry. "I'm not sure I deserve this."

"I wanted you to have it. Something inside me told me you had to have it."

"Keep it for me until we get home?"

"I'll button it up in the inside breast pocket of my blazer."

We lay in bed in each other's arms for a long time talking about the synchronicity of the two electrums—of the mysterious "ruby." When I finally fell asleep, I slept more soundly than I'd slept in months. Dreamlessly. I didn't awaken completely, but I heard my restless husband climb out of bed. He reached for my journal and switched on the desk lamp, turning page after page to read what I'd written.

Of Rosamonde, Joanna, and Constance; of William Altavilla and Jean de Serlon.

When he'd finished, he climbed back into bed. I rolled against his body. He pulled me close, murmuring words of love, of forgiveness I only half heard.

I sank back into faraway sleep. When I awoke it was just daylight. The full moon still floated in the chalcedony blue morning sky. I saw something move near the chimney. The stork stood at its nest. Flapping its wings, it soared into the sky, across the moon, and into the reeded marshes.

I smiled at the cliché of the stork. I *knew*, the way Caterina *knew*, that the bird had come to bring us good luck. And a baby.

CHAPTER TWENTY

T WO DAYS LATER we were in Paris again. I called Brian in Bari.

"We've done it, Rose," he said. "The letter is translated. Prepare to be astonished by its contents."

"When do you make the announcement?" I asked.

"We'll be shooting a BBC documentary at Castel del Monte in a day or so. Why don't you and Matthew come for the big event? I'd like to see him after all these years."

"And he you, Brian. He has some business here in Paris—but I know he'll want me to be at the reading and I'm sure he'll join me as soon as he's finished. He's heard all about the letter and he's as excited as I am to know what it says."

This time I flew straight to Bari. At the airport I rented a car to drive to Vieste. As I drove north through miles and miles of vine-yards and olive groves, I remembered my old yearnings for this light, for the glow of silver olive branches turning toward the sun. I switched on my headlights and kept them beaming as I drove through tunnel after tunnel recently blasted from chalky Gargano cliffs. The road in time would make this limestone spur—this afterthought of a peninsula, the last untouched Italian paradise— accessible to mass tourism and ruin.

As I walked from the piazza to Old Vieste, vendors were setting up stalls for summer tourists. They were displaying *cose genuine*, honest wares made by local craftsmen: carved olive wood spoons, flasks of rich unfiltered olive oil, glazed terra cotta tiles painted with suns and moons and knights-at-arms from *Orlando Furioso*.

I walked straight to Giovanni's shop and rang the bell.

"Signora Kirkland," his assistant said. "*L'architetto* went to Bari today, to the laboratory, to meet *il professor* Lambeth who called to say that he had just finished translating the letter. He was so excited and wanted to talk to *l'architetto*. He'll be calling in tonight. I'll tell him to ring you at the Vesta."

I spent the rest of the evening visiting with Marta and with Zia Caterina, who had, after all, been expecting me. When I returned, I found a letter in Brian's familiar left-handed script.

Dearest Rose—Puella Apuliae
Welcome back! We plan the meeting at Castel del Monte tomorrow. We'd like you to be there for the reading of Empress Constance's letter. Giovanni has organized a camera crew. Please ring us in the morning, first thing. We'll be at Giovanni's shop—bright and early. Unfortunately, we haven't found the map yet. Nor has Lanciani been found. He most likely has the map with him or has disposed of it somewhere. The police found nothing in his apartments in Vieste or Otranto. Any ideas?

Brian

❧

The next morning the telephone shattered my dream. Although I was happy to hear Matthew's voice, for a fleeting moment I was uneasy about losing the dream and the feeling that I'd learned something important during the night.

"How did your meeting go yesterday?"

"Good news, darling—the deal's set. We go to work on the alloy on the first of July. We're going to experiment with *electrum* this time. Can you believe the coincidence? I'll tell you all about it when we're together."

"How fast can you get here?"

"I'm taking the three o'clock plane to Bari, and Avis has a car reserved. I should be there by evening."

"Good—you'll be just in time for the shooting. Brian is going to read the letter for a BBC documentary at Castel del Monte. They're sending cameramen, and the architect's restoration crew will be on hand to help set everything up. Lights, camera, action, all that stuff. We'll most likely arrive there by early evening and stay all night. Brian wants to get the morning sun rising over Castel del Monte."

"I've already found it on the Guide Michelin map—it's near Andria, not all that far from Bari. Don't worry! I don't intend to miss any of the fanfare."

How, I wondered, would I react to Giovanni in Matthew's presence, and how would Giovanni react to him, for that matter?

"I'm happy you're coming," I said. "I want to share this with you."

When we finished our talk, I stepped into the shower, luxuriating in the warmth streaming over my body. I doused my head with slippery Swiss green shampoo and scrubbed my scalp, thick foam sliding down my arms to the bracelet I'd forgotten to take off last night. I still missed its mate. As I breathed the fragrance of crushed pine needles, my dream surfaced through the steam.

I, Rose, was in the duomo standing before the stemma of Anselmo Orlando. I ran my fingers over the three coins in the stone shield. The Madonna di Merino kneeling upon her altar beckoned with her upheld hand. She was wearing my gold bracelet on her wrist. I slowly walked to her.

I darted from the shower, spinning like a naked dervish as I dried myself. I tugged on my clothes and rushed down the steps of the hotel and into the streets of old Vieste toward the duomo.

Mass was over. Three old ladies wearing black kerchiefs knotted under their chins stood talking on the steps. I pushed open the sagging oak door. The church was empty. Santa Maria di Merino looked out across her altar.

I knelt at the alabaster balustrade, before the phalanx of candles burning on their iron pricketts. I remember that I nervously snapped off some brittle wax drippings. Then I reached for a taper and touched it to a candle. Zia Caterina's voice rang through my ears. *"Make her hear you, Rosa—make her hear you."* I knew I had to ask just one favor of her. I gazed up at the Madonna. "Show me that my dreams, my voices are real," I said to her aloud. "That I'm not crazy. Please, that's what I ask of you."

I closed my eyes and breathed in, then out. Fingers together, five, four, three, two, one.

I begin my descent, step by step, until I arrive at the garden gate where the fountain splashes and crimson and white rose garlands loop the domed roseraie. I see my guide walking down the gravel path, hands outstretched to greet me.

I don't know how long I listened to the soundlessness of my own breathing before I opened my eyes.

Santa Maria di Merino is no longer a kneeling painted effigy. The ancient stone statue of the Daughter has come alive, a woman of flesh and blood. In one hand she holds a stalk of wheat, its ripened grains like amber beads. In the other hand a pomegranate, bursting garnet kernels. At the base of her throat lies Rosamonde's amulet hanging on the red cord.

The Daughter's robe turns palest blue; the long veil falls from her head and shoulders as Joanna's long wheat-gold hair ripples to her waist. "Forget Palermo," she says. "You must forget Palermo, Rosamonde."

And as she utters Rosamonde's name, so Joanna's face became Rosamonde's face—her eyes serene untormented. "You are freed of my spirit, Rose—I leave you in peace." She smiles and smoothes the auburn hair away from her face, the face that then becomes Constance's, with her fair hair caught up by a silver fillet, her pale green robe fading now to purest white.

Framed by the dazzling light of Fortuna's wheel, the Lady in White stands before me, her robe gleaming satin against a nimbus of golden stamens, quivering with pin-points of diamond *mêlée*. She steps from the great chalice of ruffled, silken white rose petals and extends her hands like pink quartz tipped with milky moonstones.

She points to the stemma on the wall. The three coins begin to spin, balls of gold and silver twirling, then flashing flame red, rivulets of molten mercury connecting them as three points in a triangle. Like the symbols on the stemma and on the coat of arms at Pirou. Like the symbols in the Ripley Chart.

She speaks. "Rose, you have learned that dreams and illusion, the world of your imagination, are the only true reality. Now you must go to the place where the past and future meet. You will know when you are there. You will have the sign. You will hear the beat."

I extend my hand without fear. The Lady's smooth fingers entwine with my own, the blood beating so hard in my veins that I feel I might explode, be multiplied, tossed into infinity—then divided, reduced to a single golden chain of being, becoming one with everything in the universe. I collapse to the floor.

Next I heard a voice ask, "Are you all right, signora?" Don Gesualdo was standing over me with a glass of water.

"I'll be fine. Thank you. Please don't make a fuss." I took a few sips, grateful that he was holding the glass.

"I am so sorry, Signora Rosa. After you came to see me, *il professor* Lanciani called. He told me that you were a troublemaker— to stay clear of you. I didn't know what to think. I didn't understand what he had against you, but I thought I'd better be a bit reticent about showing you our church records. He used to be a very powerful man here in Southern politics, powerful enough to transfer a little priest like me to some poor parish in Lucania." The sacristan rubbed his hands together. "Please accept my apologies. My church records are open to you."

"*Tante grazie*, Don Gesualdo," I said as he helped me to my feet. "I really don't need them any more."

❧

It was eight o'clock in the evening when we arrived at Castel del Monte. Vans and cars backed up to the portal. A catering truck was assembling a *tavola calda* for the crew.

Brian kissed me on both cheeks, then introduced me to the director, who said, "We've been waiting for you to turn up, Mrs. Kirkland. Professor Lambeth and I decided that it would be much more effective if a woman read the letter."

"So you're the chosen one, Rose." Brian said as he flashed me a conspirator's smile. "You are, after all, our Puella Apuliae. I didn't want to tell you about this earlier. I thought you might fret about it."

I hesitated. "A few months ago I might have been too timid to say yes," I said. "But I'd be honored to read it. Thank you, Brian."

"We brought along a stereo and a CD of your favorite *Carmina Burana* to use as background music for the filming. I thought that might please you."

They led me up the narrow winding staircase to Frederick's throne niche over the main portal. Giovanni was there helping the crew set up the equipment. He greeted me formally, by kissing my hand, but I knew by his eyes and his smile how happy he was to see me again.

"We've decided that the rose window facing Andria should be right above your head as you read the letter. Do you remember when I told you that Frederick must have known you would come here one day? Come, let me help you." He took my arm and led me up the steps to the seat in the niche.

When all the lamps and spots were adjusted, the room was flooded with light. Cameras began to roll. Brian and Giovanni in turn, began to narrate the story of the discovery of the letters and their historical importance. When they'd finished, Brian introduced me—Rose Orlando-Kirkland as part of their team. I looked out into the room hoping that Matthew had arrived. He stood far back, half hidden by the standing spotlights. In one fleeting glance I caught his pride, his love.

My eyes dropped to the page before me. I began to read:

Carissimus Federicus, filius meus—

As I lie here, my body weak and worn, the memories of my life, your birth are all that remain. I take pen in hand to record them.

It was my hope, in those last days of my life, that this letter and the ruby of the Altavilla reach as you neared your fortieth birthday. By then you will have proven to be a leader, beyond the flush of youth, the same age as I when I bore you in that market square of Jesi.

I never knew my father, the great King Roger. He died before I was born. While I was growing up in the Joharia, I had never thought about the succession of our line. My brother had become the King. His son, William, my nephew, was just one year older than I. We were as brother and sister. I knew William would someday be king.

No brilliant marriage was made for me, and so as a maiden lady with no prospects of a husband, I begged to live my life away from the pleasures of the court. I chose the convent of the Order of the Basilean at St. Salvatore, where I lived in prayer and meditation. I did not take Holy Orders. I never meant to.

When King William feared the Norman kingdom was at stake, he had me taken from the convent. If he had no heirs, he told me, I might some day succeed him on the throne. He had accepted Walter of the Mill's scheme to wed me to the brutish Henry, son of the German Emperor called "Barbarossa." Pope Alexander had also given the Emperor the title, "Holy Roman Emperor." Walter of the Mill had won. He had convinced King William that civil war would rend the country, should King William die without an heir. But then William swore to me that since Queen Joanna was still so young, they hoped to have their own heir to their throne.

And so, within a year, I left Palermo to marry Henry Hohenstaufen.

We were wed in Milan. The patriarch of Aquileia placed the iron crowns of Lombardy upon our heads. My husband was ten years younger than I, although he seemed much older. And, as I would soon learn, he was unspeakably cruel.

From time to time I would visit King William. I had much in common with him, for he venerated the Virgin as did I. The cathedral at Monreale he was building in honor of the Virgin took much of his time. And yet the wars against the Byzantines in Thessalonica weighed heavily upon him.

Henry was impatient. We had been married seven years and were still childless. He made me consult the famous doctors in Salerno. But still I produced no heir. Alas, when King William died, so quickly and in apparent good health, I was overcome with grief. I knew then that the end might be in store for me as well.

Soon after, my father-in-law drowned in a stream in Asia Minor and I then became the Empress of my despised husband.

Joanna departed from Palermo. Her brother, Richard Plantagenet, the Lion Heart, made plans to marry her to Count Raymond of Toulouse.

Young Tancred had seized the throne. At first I was held hostage, but then I was treated with respect and honor: I was released.

It was during those days in Palermo that I heard the rumors rife throughout the land. Rumors flew from every corner of the kingdom that William had had a child born to a woman from Normandy. A hermit in the Dark Forest of Apulia swore the child, a son, had lived. His mother had died delivering. Thus her child had every right to succeed his father, William.

One night, soon after, I had a dream. An abbess robed in white appeared before me and whispered wisdom in my ear, to counsel measures I should take. Upon awakening, I vowed to Our Lady, then and there, that if I should ever conceive, my child would be born without shade of doubt, in full view, in a market square.

Now as the end draws near, I remember as though it were yesterday how we journeyed through the Marches toward Jesi. On those long dark December days the winds howled from the north, and though I was bundled in furs, my hands and feet were numb with cold.

I had sent an advance guard to advise the Duke of Ancona that I would rest at his castle for the Vigil of the Feast of the Birth of our Saviour.

I can still remember the castle, hugging the rise in the horizon behind the leafless poplars. As we grew closer its rounded turret loomed like the Emperor's crown set against the dark sky. We were greeted by the plaintive sounds of the shepherds' bagpipes. On St. Stephen's Day I commanded my attendants to make haste and set up my tent in the market square of Jesi. There I would prove, before all who wished to witness, that this child I was to bear belonged to me, Constance de Hauteville. My child would be born to be King of Sicily, for I knew I had a son within. I had already chosen his name—Constantine, a name derived from my own. Soon you would be called Frederick after my husband Henry's father, but only I knew your real father's name.

When they carried me into that brilliant blue and silver tent, throngs gathered as word spread that I would birth before any matron who cared to witness. And there were many. I was frightened yet secure that I would produce a healthy son. A wizard in the court had told me so and a Thracian woman who had the power to divine the future. Their prophecies allayed my fears and gave me courage.

The seers had not misled me. "Long live Costanza and her son," they cried when they held you aloft for all to see. A celestial choir of angels sang above, and the earth quaked beneath us as I put you to my breast.

Three months passed before I was forced to return to Palermo to oversee my kingdom. For reasons of my own, I left you, still in swaddling clothes, in the care of the Duchess of Spoleto and her wet nurse. You would be in her charge until you became King of Sicily. I had no ambitions for you to take Henry's throne or to be Emperor of that crude country so unlike our civilized Sicily.

As we bore you in procession to the castle of the Duchess in Foligno, your swaddling clothes were stacked in a chest of gold-framed rock crystal. It would be three years before I would ever see you again.

You may wonder how came I, Constance de Hauteville, by this precious stone.

It was given to me by King William as he lay dying in Palermo, while Queen Joanna sojourned in her county of Vieste. William saw the end was near and feared civil strife within his kingdom, even though he had ceded his throne to me. And he was right.

He told me that the ruby came from the treasure of Prester John buried by my father, King Roger, in his garden at Favara. As a boy, William had heard the tales of Prester John and his fabled kingdom in the East and then, one day, began to believe that he was Prester John himself, the good and Christian king.

Flowering forth from his mind came this fantastic letter, which he read to entertain his court. He told his barons that Prester John's emissary had brought the letter to him but it was William himself who had written it while he waited for Pope Alexander to set sail for Venice.

My nephew William envisioned a kingdom far richer, far more wondrous than the Byzantine Empire of the Emperor Comnenus. He knew that this letter diminished the magnificence of Byzantium. And of Comnenus. He had never forgiven Manuel Comnenus for twice withdrawing Maria's hand in marriage.

So, my beloved son, this is how the ruby comes to you. Now you know the Altavilla secret. At forty years of age, it should make no difference to you whether or not you are a Hohenstaufen born, my beloved son. You will have proven yourself a leader of men—as "the future Saviour foretold by the prophets," so proclaimed Godfrey of Viterbo, my most entrusted friend, my teacher, my lover. Your father.

There were cheers and applause throughout the room. "Well done, Rose," I heard Brian shout. Matthew rushed up to embrace me. Body to body, I felt the ruby in his pocket pressing against his heart—and mine.

"Darling, may I have the stone?" I said.

He reached into his blazer and unbuttoned the pocket against his heart. Out came the velvet pouch.

I took the "ruby" from the pouch and held it in my open palm for Brian and Giovanni to see.

"Mr. Baryani was told that this stone came from Prester John's treasure."

"I remember having a good laugh over that one, Rose." Brian's face was dead serious now as he admired the lustrous gem, passing it on to Giovanni.

"Do you have shovels in the work truck?" I asked Giovanni.

"Of course—archaeological experts always have shovels."

"Can you give an order to dig?"

"How do you mean?"

"Dig—right here in the earth, in the courtyard. Do you have your measuring instruments? And your metal detector?"

"Always. They're in the truck."

"Come, I'll show you. We don't need the stolen map. Follow me." I moved through the rooms and into the courtyard.

"Can you have the boys set up the flood lights? We'll need all the light we can get while we dig—here in the center where the octagonal marble fountain used to be."

Now it was almost midnight, but with the lamps on full force it was daylight in the courtyard.

"How deep does your instrument register?" Matthew asked Giovanni when his men returned with the metal detector.

"To ten feet with the 'bloodhound' attachment," he said as he began to pass the detector over the earth.

We heard a low, constant drone, and as it moved closer to the center its sound began to increase in pitch and volume, whining to a high wail, an electronic "scream."

I saw the excitement in Giovanni's face. "What a roar! That has to be a fairly sizable piece of metal. Around seven feet deep."

He gave the signal to dig. "Who will begin? Matthew?"

"No. You had better start, Giovanni," Matthew ceded. I saw him look straight into Giovanni's eyes, a look of strength, of silent recognition and reconciliation.

Giovanni's shovel hit the earth and cut through the hard, packed crust. There was a rataplan of drums, the cadence of cymbals clashing. Everywhere music began to sound—a choir of voices singing Fortuna's hymn from the tops of the eight towers as we dug deeper and deeper into the ground, earth flying up, earth piling up, earth encircling us.

Trails of gold dust danced in the light beams. I saw a shooting star dart across the sky. The full moon glowed, a gray pearl in the heavens. A rim of quivering yellow light ran along the edges of the octagonal courtyard that began to turn slowly, slowly as I stood in its very center. I felt the ruby throbbing in my hand, its pulse becoming faster, louder, as I became the hub of Fortuna's octagonal wheel.

When we had shoveled almost seven feet of earth and pebbles. I began to have my doubts. "Please, Giovanni, let's keep going. Just a bit more," I pleaded.

At exactly eight feet the spade hit metal. Slowly they worked the heavy metal chest free.

"This thing must weigh about 100 kilos," Brian shouted as he and Matt lifted the strongbox from the earth in which it had lain for eight hundred years.

We all helped to scrape, brush, whisk the earth from the encrusted metal. Until Giovanni found the lid seam.

"Do you think it's made of a bell metal, like the one you found in Andria?" Brian asked.

Giovanni shook his head. "I'm certain that this one is made of lead."

A silence fell over the courtyard as Giovanni pried it open.

I squeezed Matt's hand tight.

The case was only half an inch thick on all sides. It had been made as protection for the gold-framed rock crystal coffer inside.

"What could it be?" I asked.

"When I first saw it I thought it might be a reliquary," Giovanni said. "But I'm sure it's a ritual presentation box—the kind used to hold an infant's swaddling clothes in royal baptismal ceremonies. Whoever buried it here was clever enough to know that lead, being fairly airtight, would protect the contents. And so would the rock crystal." He wiped the clouded surface.

It seemed forever as they dripped oil into the gilt hasp. Finally they pried it open. Inside, lying on what looked like layers of fine linen, was still another smaller crystal box.

Giovanni said, "Go ahead, Rosa—you lift the lid."

I held my breath and lifted. Inside the box was lined in crimson silver-shot silk.

Silk woven in the Tiraz.

On the silk sat a ruby, a ruby the same color, the same oblique cut as Mr. Baryani's "ruby."

I took my ruby and placed it against the ruby in the box. The two oblique cuts were a match. The stone formed a heart. Prester John's ruby. The ruby of the Altavilla. I held it tight and felt my blood racing as I became one with the heart of the octagon.

There were cheers and shouts.

Giovanni put up his hands to shush his team. "Wait . . . there's something else!"

I looked into the box. "A lock of hair—dark red hair!"

Reading my mind, Giovanni grinned and nodded. "Yes, Rosa, I'm sure the lab will test this for DNA."

Matthew threw his arms around me. Giovanni and Brian embraced the two of us. The pearl moon turned rock crystal, and weighed heavily in the sky with the rise of the sun. The chorus sang on around us as Fortuna's winds carried her melodies into the heavens.

THE TOWER IN LUCERA

THE CALL OF THE MUEZZIN floats on the dawn of Lucera. Frederick's eyelids flicker.

Michael Scot moves closer to the awakening Emperor—so close he can hear his heart, beating to the throb of the ruby on his forehead. He feels the Emperor's pulse become faster, stronger.

"Godfrey . . ." the Emperor murmurs. "So it was Godfrey of Viterbo . . ."

Scot puts down his quill pen and stands over Frederick. With the rod of Mercurius he touches the Emperor's shoulders once more.

"Awake, awake from distant lands," he says. "It is now morning, My Lord, and you must return from the past and future of your night. Today the court moves on to Andria."

Frederick opens his eyes. The whites are bright and clear, darkening the pupils to the green of his emerald ring.

"I beg leave to touch His Majesty's royal person," Scot says, removing the giant ruby from Frederick's forehead, wiping the wide, high brow with a linen cloth. He drops the gemstone into a beaker and pours in foaming liquid from an alembic.

The Emperor heaves a deep sigh and rises languidly from his pallet. He stretches his arms overhead, massages his sinewy calves and thighs with his strong hands.

"Magus, I have been far from Lucera this night," he says. "To a distant past in Normandy, where I saw my Viking forbears in their longboats and then far beyond to the future. Now I have an inkling of the world to come, both the wonder and the weirdness of it. I have seen the lack of respect for our cities, for our earth, our forests, and for our ancient shrines. People speak across space; we leave the earth behind in star chariots. Only my beloved Mons Garganus remains somewhat the same.

"I have learned, too, the answer to my question, the identity of Prester John—an Altavilla secret that I may later share with you." His green eyes twinkle. "But not yet, Michael Scot. As for my mother . . . and my father."

"Now His Imperial Majesty shall receive the letter from Queen Constance, the letter she entrusted to me with Prester John's ruby." Scot hands the letter to the Emperor.

"I need not break this seal," Frederick says. "I tell you now that I already know full well the message my mother writes to me. For I have heard and seen the letter read in my dream—by a Rose of my line who will, eight hundred years in the future, merge the blood of Altavilla with that of a Plantagenet, as William and Joanna could not do. That child will follow the vision of his father. He will try to cure the ailing earth."

The Magus heeds his master, all the while stroking his helmet.

"Eight is the magic number, Magus, mark eight hundred years hence. In The Year of Our Lord 1994, close to a new millennium. In that future time it will matter not a whit that I was not a Hohenstaufen born. At my birth I was hailed as a savior of the world by a man beloved by my mother—Godfrey of Viterbo. And why? Because I am a powerful dreamer."

"Godfrey . . . ," Michael Scot whispers. "It was *he* who entrusted this letter and gemstone to the Magus Umberto of Bologna."

"Tonight we have had many answers, Michael Scot, but there is one thing I must change in order to ensure that the future comes to pass as I have seen it in my dream."

"What is that, My Lord?"

"The ruby. When we reach Andria—there is a lapidary there, an aged Syrian from Damascus—I will have him cleave this stone in two, in an oblique cut. You shall have one half, for having had the wisdom to lead me from the past to the future. You may dispose of your half of the stone as you wish. I trust that Fortuna will bear it along to the rightful Rose."

Scot takes the ruby from the Emperor and holds it to the morning light, then clenches his fist around the stone. "I am indebted to you, My Lord, for such a generous gesture. I shall treasure this glorious ruby for the rest of my days."

"I will order my men to begin digging and quarrying stone at once," said the Emperor, "for my castle of octagons will be a monument to the Altavilla. Deep within the earth, my half of the ruby will beat as its very heart, and shall remain there until it is found by a Rose, when Fortuna has worked her course."

They hear the muffled sound of a velvet hammer hitting the bronze gong.

A young page enters bearing a salver of oranges, dried figs, goat cheese, and a brew of manna gathered from the Emperor's Apulian ash trees.

"Let us partake of this simple repast and be ready to join the procession in one hour. I shall bathe and shave and be ready to mount Dragon. Prepare yourself, Magus. Strip yourself of your astrologer's cloak—assume now the dress of scholarship."

He inverts the hourglass to mark the time.

"Since I neither bathe nor shave, I shall be ready even sooner," Michael Scot replies. "I have only to pack my few possessions in my trunk."

The Wizard exchanges his astrological cloak for the black academic robe of the scholar. He passes his hand over his iron hat again to make sure it is still in place.

Frederick drinks the manna brew from his golden cup. "There is one more thing on my mind, Michael Scot. That letter from Prester John needs rewriting. After all, it has been heard in that form for nigh on sixty years now in Norman French.

"Have your Hebrew scribe Andreas write a new letter in his own language. Have him address it to me. I will read it for the pleasure of my court. Instruct him to include fantastic animals—as far as possible from those of our earth that you describe in your translation of Aristotle's *De Animalibus*—beasts even more exotic than the specimens of my menagerie."

"I will have him begin to write as soon as we arrive in Andria, My Lord."

The Emperor smiles to himself. It will amuse him to continue the Altavilla story—carrying on the hoax his cousin William had begun.

The Magus moves to the window of the tower to view the procession of the court from Lucera to Andria, where the Christmas Court is gathering to celebrate the Emperor's fortieth birthday.

Crowds throng the city gates and line the roadside awaiting the spectacle. This is surely a day the Emperor's subjects will never forget. Scot himself never ceases to wonder at the panoply and splendor of the Imperial Court.

The advance guard, turbaned Saracens in flowing white robes and mounted on Arab steeds, brandish their lances to drive the Emperor's eager subjects back from the roadside.

The Emperor's menagerie, strange, exotic beasts from faraway lands, move at the fore of the cortege. First, led by an Indian mahout, comes the elephant, so tall he is barely able to pass through the arched portal. The animal swings his incredible snout sideways, frightening the children. Three Saracens sit atop the big gray beast in a howdah, trumpeting flourishes to announce the start of the parade.

The fleet of camels trots out, palanquins swaying on their backs, enclosing within drawn curtains the sloe-eyed dancers and houris of the Emperor's harem. Giant eunuchs in baggy trousers swagger alongside the camels, prodding them with long poles. Others wear sharpened scimitars by their sides, fiendish looks upon their faces.

When the Emperor's favorites have passed, the crowds

begin to cheer the strangest animal they have ever seen, the spotted giraffe—the only one in Christendom, so the Emperor boasts. The long-necked creature is so tall he, too, barely makes it through the portal.

Next come the Keepers of the Giant Cats. Black men with oiled bare chests lead lions, leopards, panthers and lynxes on chains. Hunting cheetahs follow, and then Egyptian cats on velvet-cushioned cruppers atop the horses of their Saracen trainers. Finally, a flock of ostriches, wings aflutter, pecking the earth; then peacocks and pelicans, parrots and nightingales, all squawking and singing in their cages.

The crowd hushes at the fierce-faced Saracen bowmen in chain mail and burnished pointed helmets, crossbows aimed straight out before them as they march.

Everyone claps and cheers for the reluctant snow-white bear from faraway northern climes, for the antics of the bawdy court dwarves, the jesters and tumblers.

Entrusted with the Emperor's precious birds, proud falconers in their striped hose stride by with falcons safely perched on yokes around their waists.

The Emperor lets his menagerie pass first. Then, as the dust settles, lackeys clear away the dung and spread the road with scented earth to mask the stench of camel piss.

Pages and courtiers arrayed in embroidered tunics and crimson and saffron-colored mantles strut and preen as they wait to take their places in the parade. Women with small children are drawn behind them in litters and wagons; others ride sidesaddle on piebald horses.

Now the time has come for the Wizard, Michael Scot, impressive in his academic robes, to descend from the tower to find his station among the ranks of scholars, other wizards and astrologers in their tall, pointed hats. He passes his hand over his helmet as is his habit.

The wagons are being loaded, the last of the entourage. Muleteers swear and curse at the animals and at each other as they strap the heavy chests to the sumpter mules and donkeys bearing the Emperor's treasure: his books, documents of his chancery, records of his notaries—Michael Scot's own iron-bound box—all these would arrive last of all to Andria. And in a special silk padded carriage guarded on each side by Apulian knights is carried the Emperor's most precious treasure, the gold banded rock crystal case holding the swaddling clothes in which he had been wrapped when he was born in the market square at Jesi.

Trumpet fanfares sound from all the battlements and ramparts of the city. The Emperor's double-eagle Imperial standard, carried aloft by a knight riding a white Arabian steed, alerts the throng that the Emperor will soon be approaching.

The Emperor mounts Dragon and calls out to Michael Scot from the high-stepping stallion: "You will follow just behind me, Michael Scot, before all the other scholars—and before my poets. You will have the place of honor on this day's march to Andria. And from this day hereafter, for the rest of your life."

Scot looks up at his master, Frederick, Wonder of the World. The Emperor is dressed in his favorite hunting green, his hair glinting copper-red in the morning sun. A carved ivory horn hangs from a heavy gold chain around his neck, a peregrine falcon is held aloft on his gloved wrist. Dragon neighs and paws the earth with his hooves.

"It is a great honor you do me, My Lord. I will continue to serve you faithfully for however long I shall live," Scot replies.

The stallion rears, shaking his trappings. Frederick strokes Dragon's sleek black mane and rides away, his reins held high, his wide shoulders erect as he moves with majesty through the gates of Lucera, the jess of the falcon clenched tight in his right fist. So that his subjects might catch a glimpse of him full-face, Frederick slowly turns his head from side to side.

The crowds shout excitedly, applauding as the Emperor passes. "*Vivat—vivat Stupor Mundi!*" All of their lives they will remember this day. The story of Frederick's pageantry will be told over and over again for countless generations, until it becomes a vision to be glimpsed only in the dreams of their descendants.

Soon the procession passes far beyond the city walls, well on its way to Andria. Now comes the moment for the Emperor to test his new bird. He releases the jess of the falcon and shouts out a command in Arabic, "*Se'er fels'ma al gazahal.* Fly, my beauty!"

The bird springs as a Saracen arrow into the air, bells ajingle, wings beating as it soars, arching, darting, circling against the lapis lazuli sky, its unseeled eyes searching for prey.

Michael Scot's eyesight has dimmed with age, and the falcon soon disappears from his view. But he sees the bird's tail pennon as it floats to the ground, reaching the earth before his feet. Holding his metal hat secure with one hand, he stoops with effort to pick it up from the road. He blows the dust from the feather and tucks it in the folds of his Oxford robe. He will fashion it as a new quill. To record another story. On another night.

With my golden pen, the Horseman's pen,
I wrote in big bold letters.

FINIS

I capped my pen and closed my journal.
Rose Orlando Kirkland
December 26, 1994

ACKNOWLEDGMENTS

My grateful thanks go to all those who have helped me in countless ways over the time it took to write *The Blood Remembers*. However, I would like to single out the following:

The late Alan D. Williams, editor extraordinaire, who led me to new insights.

Professor Jenijoy La Belle, dear friend, always ready to read a sentence or a draft.

Professor Kenneth J. Atchity for his enduring enthusiasm and counsel.

Dr. Claire Douglas, who taught me about journeys and all they imply.

Barbara Plumb for having had enough confidence in this novel to submit the first draft.

Professor Eleanor Searle, scholar of The Norman Conquests, who helped me to enroll as a Reader at The Huntington Library.
continued overleaf

My grateful thanks to:

Professors Elizabeth and Daniel Donno, our next-door neighbors, Professors John Steadman, Robert Essick, all Readers at The Huntington Library in San Marino, for sharing their lunch breaks with me.

Beth Farrell, Hazel Cox, and Lois Pendleton, of Elton-Wolf, who so sensitively supervised the production of *The Blood Remembers*.

My cousins in Vieste, Rome, Florence and Bergamo, who shared family history and folklore with me.

My husband and children Francesca, Sara, Dennis, for their always-loving support and encouragement.

★ OXFORD

MONT SAINT MICHEL

COUTANCES

LE CHATEAU
DE PIROU

Vieste

★ Barletta
★ ★ Bari
Castel
del Monte